"I haven't been able to stop thinking about you," Garrison said huskily.

Heat flooded Imani's cheeks, spread through her belly. "Garrison," she murmured in protest, glancing around self-consciously for eavesdroppers.

He didn't seem to care. "I'd be lying if I said I didn't enjoy our encounter yesterday."

Imani hesitated, bit her bottom lip guiltily. "Did you?"

Garrison's gaze followed the innocently provocative gesture, and he felt desire stir to life in his groin. He wanted to kiss her. Wanted her with an intensity that was becoming less foreign to him the longer he knew her.

The flicker of awareness in her dark eyes told him she had read the hunger in his gaze. Read it, and felt the same. "What I feel for you, Garrison," she said quietly, "is so wrong. So completely wrong."

"Keep telling yourself that," he said, his voice low and soft. "Maybe you'll eventually start to believe it's true."

She closed her eyes on a wave of helpless frustration. He traced his thumb lightly across her cheekbone, trailing a fiery path to her lips, which parted almost instinctively for his touch.

"Look at me," he gently commanded.

Her eyes fluttered open to meet the intensity of his piercing gaze.

"I won't take you anywhere you don't want to go," he whispered.

BOOK YOUR PLACE ON OUR WEBSITE AND MAKE THE ARABESQUE ROMANCE CONNECTION!

We've created a customized website just for our very special Arabesque readers, where you can get the inside scoop on everything that's going on with Arabesque romance novels.

When you come online, you'll have the exciting opportunity to:

- View covers of upcoming books

- Learn about our future publishing schedule (listed by publication month and author)

- Find out when your favorite authors will be visiting a city near you

- Search for and order backlist books

- Check out author bios and background information

- Send e-mail to your favorite authors

- Join us in weekly chats with authors, readers and other guests

- Get writing guidelines

- AND MUCH MORE!

Visit our website at
http://www.arabesquebooks.com

With Every Breath

Maureen
Smith

BET Publications, LLC
http://www.bet.com
http://www.arabesquebooks.com

ARABESQUE BOOKS are published by

BET Publications, LLC
c/o BET BOOKS
One BET Plaza
1900 W Place NE
Washington, DC 20018-1211

All Kensington Titles, Imprints, and Distributed Lines are available at special quantity discounts for bulk purchases for sales promotions, premiums, fund-raising, and educational or institutional use. Special book excerpts or customized printings can also be created to fit specific needs. For details, write or phone the office of the Kensington special sales manager: Kensington Publishing Corp., 850 Third Avenue, New York, NY 10022, attn: Special Sales Department, Phone: 1-800-221-2647.

First Printing: November 2004
10 9 8 7 6 5 4 3 2 1

Printed in the United States of America

To my beloved husband, Lorrent
Thank you for being my "real" superhero

Acknowledgments

To my husband and soul mate Lorrent Smith. How can I begin to thank you for everything you've meant to me over the years? If not for you and the sacrifices you've made, none of this would be possible. Thank you for your eternal love and support, and for allowing me to be myself. You are, quite simply, the wind beneath my wings.

To my parents, Dr. Anthony and Cecilia Morah, for the precious gift of life and your unconditional love and support.

To Chibs, Sylvia, and Julie, the best big sisters anyone could ever wish for. Stay strong and beautiful.

To Maravia and Jared, for allowing Mommy to write and pursue her dreams—even if it meant that I sometimes couldn't play with you or refill your juice cups fast enough. You are both very important to me, and I thank God for blessing me with such precious gifts!

To my extended family members and in-laws, thank you for reading my work and providing your enthusiastic feedback. Each and every one of you is special to me.

To my best friend Gequeta Valentine, for your unwavering faith and support.

To my agent Sha-Shana Crichton, for believing in my work and helping me strive toward literary excellence.

To the FBI Supervisory Special Agent who asked to remain anonymous. Thank you for taking time out of your busy schedule to answer my million questions about the FBI and to provide extensive details about how abduction cases are investigated.

To my wonderful author friends—Virginia "Ginny" Albert, Nathasha Brooks-Harris, R. Barri Flowers, and Tracee Garner—a million heartfelt thanks for your friendship and support!

To the many wonderful men and women at Heartland Health of Hyattsville, for giving me my first bulk order for *Ghosts of Fire* and for coming back again and again to buy more copies!

To everyone who supported me as a self-published author, thank you so much for helping me make a lifetime dream come true. You will never be forgotten.

Chapter 1

University of Maryland, College Park, Sunday evening

The shuttle was late.

Althea Pritchard jammed her hands into the pockets of her jeans, then rocked back and forth on her heels. At least it wasn't cold. That would have made the delay that much worse. She glanced over her shoulder, trying to quell the uneasy sensation of being watched. The campus, which normally bustled with the activity of students walking to and from classes, was unusually deserted. Even for a Sunday night.

She looked down the street again, expecting to see the twin headlights of the red and white UM shuttle bus, her favorite wisecracking driver behind the wheel. But the street was empty. And dark. She frowned, glancing up at the street lamp, with its intermittent flickering. Probably a short circuit. She silently willed the light to remain on, afraid to be plunged into complete darkness.

A faint breeze stirred the surrounding trees, the rustle of fall leaves making an oddly eerie sound. She shivered, told herself she was being spooked for nothing. Nonetheless, she wished she had accepted a ride from her professor. Althea had decided to go back to her dormitory to grab an overnight bag in case she wound up spending the night at her boyfriend's apartment. She wanted to kick herself for not thinking of the idea earlier. She could have saved herself a lot of time and aggravation.

A movement to her left caught her eye, and she glanced around to see a dark sedan creeping slowly down the street. She sucked her teeth in disappointment, her frustration mounting. What was taking that darned shuttle so long?

By the time the car rolled to a stop at the curb, it was too late for her to run.

Imani Maxwell wakened with a start and bolted upright.

Her cotton nightshirt was drenched, plastered to her body like a second skin. She blinked in the still darkness, her heart beating rapidly in her chest. The clock on her nightstand glared at her.

Twelve thirty-four.

She shivered, easing back against the pillow unsteadily. No matter how many times she had the dream, she still awakened the same. Depleted, haunted, struggling to shake the remnants of horror the images left behind.

Trembling, she slipped from the bed and padded barefoot across the chilled hardwood floor to the adjoining bathroom. Flipping on the light switch, she winced against the sudden glare and ducked her head to splash cold water over her face.

Lifting her head to blot her cheeks with a towel, she peered at her reflection in the mirror and frowned at her bloodshot eyes. She wondered, perhaps for the millionth time, when her sleep would not be plagued by the dream.

Something cold and wet nudged her bare thigh, and Imani looked down into a pair of somber, dark eyes. "What're you staring at?" she groused, giving her face one last dab and tossing the towel into the wicker hamper. "You know the routine, Shiloh. I'm having another bad night."

Panting lightly, the golden retriever watched her, unperturbed by her grumpiness.

The phone rang suddenly, piercing the stillness of the night.

Imani jumped, then craned her neck around the bathroom door to stare into the darkened bedroom at the phone on her cherrywood nightstand. *Who on earth could be calling at this late hour?* she wondered, swallowing instinctive panic. She knew all too well that late-night phone calls never bore good news.

Shiloh released a short bark, his tail wagging excitedly as he bounded toward the nightstand. Imani followed on his heels, picking up the phone on the final ring before voice mail intercepted. "Hello?"

"Professor Maxwell?" ventured a low, tremulous voice. "This is Malik Toomer."

Cold unease slithered down Imani's spine at the sound of her student's voice. "Malik? Is something wrong?"

"I don't know . . . Is Althea there, by any chance?"

"No." Imani frowned, pressing the receiver closer to her ear. "We finished our meeting hours ago. Why?"

There was a heavy pause, deepening the foreboding in Imani's chest. "She never came over like she was supposed to," Malik continued unsteadily, "and no one's seen her around."

Comprehension slowly dawned. And still Imani resisted. "What are you saying, Malik?"

"I-I think something's wrong . . . I think something's happened to her."

Baltimore, Maryland, Tuesday morning

"FBI! Freeze, drop your weapon!"

Although the streets of Baltimore were still slick from last night's downpour, Garrison Wade's steps were swift and sure, his movements mirroring the agility of a panther as he

propelled his body over a barbed wire fence and landed on
both feet, barely missing a beat as he continued the chase.
Twenty paces behind him, Special Agent Edward Balducci
followed in pursuit, leaving a trail of muffled curses in his
wake.

Relentless, Garrison cut across a narrow side street and
followed his prey down a dark, fog-drenched alley littered
with hypodermic needles, empty liquor bottles, and other
discarded trash. Anger and impatience surged through him
like an electrical voltage, mingling with the adrenaline and
blood rushing through his veins as he closed the distance.
He ducked behind a Dumpster just as his quarry fired another shot at him. The shot came so close that Garrison
could smell the smoking lead as it just missed his shoulder
by a fraction of an inch, making him grateful that his partner
had fallen far behind, out of harm's way.

The ensuing silence told him that John Doe had stopped
running, likely taking cover in an abandoned store doorway
further down the alley. Garrison listened keenly for a moment, his nine-millimeter Glock drawn and safety thumbed
in preparation. The beginning rays of dawn arced across the
fall sky, a slice of lavender peeking from the orange horizon.
Soon the city would be awake, with morning commuters
bustling to work and school, oblivious to the volatile situation unfolding in their own backyards. He couldn't risk the
lives of innocent bystanders again.

Garrison heard a faint sound and slowly emerged from
behind the Dumpster just in time to see his prey make another dash down the alley. With controlled precision, keeping his eyes trained on his target, Garrison raised his Glock,
aimed, and fired once. John Doe went down hard, clutching
his ruptured knee with a surprised howl. He lay on the
ground, writhing like a wounded animal. As Garrison hurried toward him, John Doe's bloodied fingers reached out,
groping along the concrete for his fallen weapon. With light-
ning speed, Garrison cocked his gun and squeezed the trig-

ger. John Doe screamed in outrage as the bullet tore through his palm, sending his weapon flying.

Garrison was upon him in a heartbeat. He forced the man's arms behind his back, turned him over onto his stomach, and planted a knee firmly in his back. "You have the right to remain silent," Garrison began.

Balducci approached, panting briskly as he glared at the man pinned to the ground beneath his partner. "You crazy son of a—"

"Not now, Eddie," Garrison muttered. He fastened handcuffs onto the perpetrator and hauled him unceremoniously to his feet.

Eddie bent over for a moment, bracing his hands on his knees as he labored to catch his breath. "Christ," he panted, "you would think I still smoked."

Garrison raised a sardonic eyebrow as he half dragged their suspect toward the black federal-issue Crown Victoria that had just screeched to a halt at the alley's entrance. Two plainclothes federal agents spilled from the car and strode briskly toward them.

"I want my lawyer," groaned the wounded John Doe as Garrison handed him over to the waiting federal agents. "He busted my kneecap! I'll never walk right again!"

Eddie laughed scornfully. "For where you're going," he called after him, "that was only going to be a matter of time!" Shaking his head after the prisoner in disgust, he turned to Garrison and pointed matter-of-factly to his forehead. "You're bleeding, by the way."

Garrison reached up, grimacing when his fingers touched the sticky wetness that confirmed the rupture of stitches only two weeks old. The wound had come as a result of an early morning raid on an East Baltimore crack house. The perpetrator was a reputed drug dealer directly responsible for the shooting deaths of several local teenagers. He hadn't gone down without a fight.

Garrison hated hospitals. The idea of having to return to

one to have his forehead restitched irritated him beyond reason.

"He didn't finish reading my Miranda rights!" John Doe complained to the grim-faced FBI agents who lowered him into the backseat of the Crown Victoria. "That's against the law. My rights have been violated. I demand justice!"

Garrison sauntered over to him. Heeding his murderous scowl, the two agents glanced away as Garrison seized the hobbled man by the lapels of his shirt and spoke in a low, scathing tone into his startled face. "Don't talk to me about rights. Not after the way you tortured those innocent children. You want justice? How about we go for a little walk, just you and me, and we'll talk about justice, you sick piece of sh—"

"You can't threaten me!" wailed John Doe, but with less bravado than before. The corner of his bloody mouth trembled as he eyed Garrison warily. "I know my rights. I know a threat when I hear one, and that was definitely a threat."

Garrison's dark eyes narrowed for only a fraction of a second before his fist connected with John Doe's sallow cheek, snapping his head hard to the left. John Doe cried out in protest, slumping weakly against Garrison.

With a lethal smirk, Garrison pulled the man's face to his. "You have the right to remain silent. Anything you say can and will be used against you in a court of law. You have the right to consult with an attorney before being questioned. If you cannot afford an attorney, one will be appointed to represent you. Do you understand these rights as they have been read to you?"

Not long after the infamous John Doe was taken into custody, a horde of reporters descended upon the FBI field office headquarters in Baltimore in anticipation of the scheduled press conference. News vans with antennas lined the curb, and helicopters bearing the emblems of local media stations swarmed overhead. The oppressive glare of camera lights shone on the heavily made up faces of reporters as they provided minute-by-minute updates to their respective stations. Their competing voices created a cacophony of chatter that could be classified only as noise pollution.

At precisely eight forty-five A.M., Garrison and Eddie emerged from the FBI building with senior members of the task force and Baltimore Chief of Police Darrell Morrison to answer questions about the arrest of the serial child rapist who had plagued the Baltimore area for well over a month. The case had commanded the attention of a national audience.

For the press conference, Garrison and Eddie had traded in jeans and sweatshirts, their surveillance attire of the night before, for business suits. They stood beside their boss, FBI Special Agent in Charge Timothy Street, as he fielded questions from hungry reporters from behind a hastily erected podium. Tim Street was known to intimidate anyone who opposed him, often with just one look from piercing aquamarine eyes that softened only when he spoke of his wife and four children. He was still trim and athletic at the age of forty-six, with sandy brown hair that was beginning to recede from a broad forehead that seemed perpetually furrowed.

Agent Street chose and answered the reporters' questions with clipped precision, providing only the most pertinent details. He described how John Beaufort, aka John Doe, had been apprehended by federal agents acting on a tip from an anonymous caller.

"The agents conducted overnight surveillance of the property," Street explained in the same terse tones he used when reprimanding his subordinates. "When the subject arrived home at five A.M. this morning, the agents closed in for the arrest. Period."

A reporter from NBC Channel 4 shouted from the back,

"Agent Street, can you tell us more about the Baltimore Division's Violent Crimes and Major Offenders program and its involvement in the investigation and capture of John Beaufort?"

"First of all, the VCMO Squad is responsible for investigating a wide range of criminal activity that includes kidnapping, extortion, and major thefts from interstate shipments and interstate transportation of stolen property. Additional violations investigated by this squad are carjackings and bank and armored vehicle robberies. The main programs that fall under VCMO are the Bank Robbery Program, the Safe Streets Program, the Fugitive Program, and Operation Innocent Images, which is a large-scale investigation of child pornography and pedophilic activity on the Internet that was initiated by the Baltimore Division.

"To answer your question directly, the Maryland Joint Violent Crime Fugitive Task Force—or the Force as it's commonly called—was largely instrumental in John Beaufort's capture and arrest. The mission of the Force is to identify fugitive felons in the greater Baltimore area who have been charged with the most serious violent criminal offenses, and to conduct investigations to apprehend those individuals. Examples of the criminal offenses committed by the Force's target fugitives include murder, armed robbery, assault, rape and other sex offenses, child abuse, home invasion robberies, and carjacking."

"What has been the task force's success ratio?"

"Since its inception in September 1992, over two thousand arrests have been made by the task force members in and around Baltimore City. The task force is comprised of five FBI special agents, two Baltimore City detectives, one Baltimore County detective, two Maryland state troopers, one detective from the Baltimore City Housing Authority, and one Baltimore City sheriff's deputy. Two of the FBI special agents representing the Baltimore field office are to my right—Special Agents Garrison Wade and Edward Balducci."

This was the opening the press had been waiting for.

They surged forward eagerly, firing questions at the two silent men. Eddie stepped to the microphone first and provided additional information about the Force. With his dark good looks and casual air of disregard, the camera would love him—even as he skillfully deflected the more probing inquiries.

"Special Agent Wade," a pack of reporters shouted in jumbled unison, "sources tell us that *you* made the actual arrest this morning. Can you tell us whether or not the suspect resisted capture?"

Garrison knew they were seeking their sensational angle, the juicy details that would be rehashed ad nauseum on evening broadcasts and in print publications everywhere. "The suspect was taken into custody without incident," he said neutrally.

"So you *didn't* receive that cut in the course of apprehending Beaufort?"

Garrison lifted a hand slowly to the freshly sutured wound above his eyebrow, stitches he had grudgingly consented to receiving only after Eddie harangued him, personally escorting him to Sinai Hospital.

The corners of Garrison's mouth twitched now, faintly mocking as he regarded the smug reporter. "Sadly enough, Mr. Berger," he drawled, "I obtained this little battle scar during an encounter with an overly ambitious reporter not unlike yourself."

The crowd reacted with laughter and skeptical guffaws as Daniel Berger ducked his head, grinning sheepishly.

"Special Agent Wade," another voice piped up, "given your successful track record of capturing violent perpetrators, and now your arrest of John Beaufort, many are once again calling you a hero. Do you see yourself as such?"

Garrison frowned. "With all due respect, ma'am," he said quietly, "I think we as a society apply the term too loosely. I think everyone here would agree that the real heroes in this case are the young victims who must overcome the physical and emotional scars of what was done to them, who were

brave enough to come forward with their stories so that we in law enforcement could do our jobs."

In the somber silence that followed, Garrison stepped away from the podium. Tim Street took his place.

"In closing, I would like to thank the various members of the law enforcement community who lent their resources to us throughout this investigation," Street said. "Baltimore Chief of Police Morrison and his staff were invaluable to our task force. We'd also like to thank the public, particularly the citizens of Baltimore, for keeping abreast of this case and phoning in their tips to the hotline. Your patience and vigilance helped get a dangerous predator off our streets." He paused. "Now if you ladies and gentlemen would excuse us, we need time to regroup so that we may prepare ourselves to assist with the prosecutorial phase of this case."

Heedless to the remaining questions thrown at him, Tim Street pivoted on his heel and marched back toward the building. He paused to murmur to Garrison, "You and Balducci head home and get some rest. I want your prosecutorial report by the end of the week."

Inside Eddie's black GMC Jimmy a few minutes later, Eddie threw a teasing glance at Garrison. "Think Beaufort's gonna squeal about the right hook you gave him?"

Garrison slid on a pair of mirrored aviator sunglasses against the blinding October sunshine. He quietly worked a stick of peppermint gum around his mouth. "He's lucky that's *all* I did," he muttered ominously. "God knows, I wanted to do more."

Eddie snorted, his expression grim. "You and me both. If you hadn't done it, *I* woulda." He shook his head, his thick black hair gleaming in the morning sunlight. The piercing hazel eyes he now watched Garrison with were a startling contrast to his deep olive complexion, as disarming as the dimple that flashed in his cheek.

Although the good looks that had rendered him a favorite with the ladies often drew jokes from his colleagues,

Edward Balducci was, without question, one of the Bureau's best special agents. Sharp, tough as nails, with a mind for the kind of investigative casework required of them.

Six years ago, he and Garrison met as new agent trainees at the FBI Academy in Quantico. Over the grueling sixteen weeks in which trainees had to endure the rigors of academics, firearms, physical training, and defensive tactics required for graduation, both men excelled, distinguishing themselves above their classmates. Back then, before the FBI made diversity recruitment a priority, Garrison found himself the only minority in the group. Fresh out of law school with a chip on his shoulder the size of Plymouth Rock, he knew he had to work twice as hard as his peers to prove himself. Edward Balducci was a brash young Army reservist from Brooklyn. What began as a bitter rivalry between the two men gradually evolved into one of grudging respect and mutual admiration. By the time they stood beside each other at graduation to accept the Oath of Office, they were practically inseparable.

Trying to rouse himself from the reminder of the atrocities John Beaufort had committed against his innocent victims, Garrison reached over, raising the volume on the truck's stereo.

"That was 'Sweetest Taboo' by the songbird of soul herself, Sade," 105.9's Jay Lang announced in his textured baritone. "As many of you have already heard, the FBI has made an arrest in the serial child rapist case. The menace known to federal investigators as John Doe was taken into custody early this morning.

"And now in late-breaking news, police in College Park are reporting the disappearance of a University of Maryland student. According to police sources, the missing girl is the eighteen-year-old niece of Prince George's County Executive Louis Pritchard."

Garrison and Eddie exchanged somber looks as the radio announcer continued. "The county executive is expected to

issue a statement later this afternoon. We'll keep you posted
as more details become available. In the meantime, let's all
keep County Executive Pritchard and his family in our
prayers."

As the station segued to a commercial break, Eddie said,
"I guess we know what our next case is gonna be."

Garrison's grim expression was answer enough.

Imani Maxwell's students weren't interested in participating in a discussion about the latest novel she had assigned
for their Introduction to African-American Literature
course. Their attention was focused on their missing classmate, her absence punctuated by the empty chair she usually
occupied.

Halfway through the hour, Imani abandoned the notes
she'd prepared for class and indulged their need to commis-
erate, to speculate, to share their own thoughts about Althea
Pritchard.

Even in this group of streetwise, enlightened Generation
Xers, no one wanted to believe that any serious harm had
come to Althea. To accept the unthinkable, the possibility
that someone with violent intentions had abducted their
classmate, forced them to acknowledge their own suscepti-
bility to crime, even death. The female students expressed
their fears about walking across campus alone at night, and
Imani suggested making it a practice to travel in pairs or
groups.

"What if someone was watching her when she was with
you, Professor Maxwell?" asked one student, her dark eyes
widened almost to the point of melodrama. "Does that scare
you at all?"

Imani pursed her lips in thought for a moment, wondering how much of her own personal demons would be exposed in her answer. "That possibility does give me chills,
yes. But I can't become afraid to leave my house every day,

Yvette. I have to exercise caution as much as possible, and hope that the police are doing their best to keep the community safe."

"Are you afraid for Althea?" another student asked bluntly.

Imani folded her arms across her chest, with a shapely hip propped against the lectern at the front of the small classroom. She remembered the way her heart had plummeted when she received Malik Toomer's phone call just three nights ago, heard the ominous words that still haunted her every waking thought. *"I think something's happened to her. . . ."*

She lifted her head and met the girl's expectant gaze. "Yes," she answered honestly, the single word escaping on a husky half whisper. "Yes, I am afraid for Althea, Denise. Let's all keep Althea and her family in our prayers."

Restless murmurs filled the room. "I'm gonna do even better than that," Denise announced, her delicate jaw set with determination. "I'm going down to the student union right after class to sign up for those self-defense classes they're offering. And if y'all were smart, you'd do the same. Right, Professor?"

"It certainly wouldn't hurt," Imani agreed, glancing down at her slim gold wristwatch and giving a tiny start. It was nearly three-thirty. Time had gotten away from her. If she didn't hurry, she'd be late for her four o'clock appointment with the police.

"All right, class," she called over the noise of mingled voices and scraping chairs, "be sure to finish reading the remainder of the chapters and come prepared for discussion on Friday."

The students grunted in compliance as they shuffled from the room, still murmuring about Althea. Imani sympathized with them, lamented that their tenuous grip on innocence had been shattered by the disappearance of one of their own. She hated the idea that their college experience would be forever marred by Althea Pritchard's abduction.

But even more disturbing were the images that replayed in her mind, mental pictures that depicted one of her own students—alone, terrified, at the complete mercy of a madman.

A shudder swept through her as she gathered her belongings and headed for the door. *Lord,* she offered up a silent petition, *please bring Althea home safely.*

Chapter 2

Palmer Park, Maryland, Wednesday afternoon

"Gentlemen. Hope you haven't been waiting long."

The key players in the Althea Pritchard kidnapping investigation were already assembled by the time Garrison arrived at the Palmer Park police headquarters for the preliminary inquiry. For the FBI to initiate an official investigation, they needed to obtain specific facts indicating that a violation of federal law within the FBI's jurisdiction might have occurred. After evaluating the evidence and circumstances pertaining to her disappearance, Garrison, acting as liaison, would determine if an investigation was warranted.

Police Chief Wayne Taggert sat around a conference table in a nondescript room with three other men. A rotund, fiftyish man, he lumbered to his feet as Garrison entered. "Agent Wade," he greeted him, extending a beefy palm as he rounded the table. His pinstriped tie was crumpled like an accordion over his protruding belly, and he used his other hand to smooth it down.

Garrison accepted the police chief's handshake with a short nod. "Chief Taggert. Pleased to meet you."

"The pleasure's all mine, Agent Wade. Your special agent in charge speaks highly of you. We're all looking forward to having your expertise on this case."

The introductions were quickly dispensed. The room's other occupants consisted of the county sheriff, a stocky Hispanic man with a ruddy pockmarked complexion resembling the actor Edward James Olmos. There were two Prince George's County detectives, one tall and dark-skinned with the athletic build of a former professional basketball player. Detective Aaron Moses, who had a solid reputation that spanned several years and several high-profile cases. The other detective, Cole Porter, was medium height and burly, with soft black hair and baby-smooth skin.

The three men regarded Garrison with cool, assessing looks as they mumbled greetings and exchanged handshakes. Garrison pretended not to notice as he lowered himself into a proffered seat. In his line of work, he had grown used to the varying reactions his arrival on the scene always evoked. Some hailed his presence like weary soldiers awaiting a relief battalion, while others perceived him as a threat, an unwelcome intrusion. The local authorities were protective and liked to handle their investigations with little or no outside interference, although it was true that federal and local authorities had, in recent years, begun working more cooperatively.

But the fact that County Executive Louis Pritchard had gone over their heads to contact the FBI director for assistance undoubtedly rankled with these locals, burned in their guts like sour whiskey. According to Street, Garrison first came to the county executive's attention two years ago when Garrison successfully ensured the arrest of a fugitive in a high-profile case involving a reputed child abductor, whose modus operandi included mutilating and sexually assaulting the victims before dumping their bodies into the Chesapeake Bay. The perpetrator had evaded the authorities for five years, until Garrison joined the task force and pushed for the reopening of the investigation. The fugitive's capture and prosecution made national headlines for a whole year, and with it came the kind of media spotlight Garrison generally disliked. Add to that the recent arrest of John Beaufort, and he wasn't overly surprised when he received the summons from the top. Within seventy-two hours following the disappearance of Althea Pritchard, Garrison had been briefed on the case and summarily dispatched to Palmer Park.

County Executive Louis Pritchard had friends in high places, and nothing else mattered. Period. And while Garrison sympathized with the wounded pride of the local law enforcement officials, the bottom line never changed. What mattered was solving the case, not seeing who had the most testosterone.

"Let's get down to business, gentlemen," Chief Taggert pronounced, lowering himself gratefully into the chair he'd vacated upon Garrison's arrival. Although the room was air-conditioned, a fine sheen of sweat misted the chief's balding head, the pale skin gleaming bright red. He reached for a carafe on the table, the artificial wood-grain surface stained by years of coffee mug rings and cigarette ashes. "Would you like some coffee, Agent Wade?"

"No, thanks. Water's fine."

Taggert poured two glasses of ice water from a pitcher. "I assume you've already been briefed on the specifics of the case, Agent Wade," he began as Garrison accepted the glass.

"For the most part," Garrison concurred.

"Here's the case file," the chief continued, sliding a folder across the table. "Detective Moses is the primary in the investigation, so you'll be working closely with him. Sheriff Garcia is here to offer the additional assistance of his office. With no current leads, we need all the manpower we can get."

Garrison perused the police report with a practiced eye. "No eyewitnesses?"

Taggert shook his head, lips pursed. "Althea left R.J. Bentley's on Route 1 with her professor around seven P.M., said she was heading to her boyfriend's—Malik Toomer. He lives in a Leonardtown dorm where she hung out a lot. It's across the street from campus. When she never showed, he got worried and started calling around to her friends."

"What time was this?"

"Around eleven-thirty," Detective Cole Porter chimed in as the chief paused to gulp down water. "No one had seen her. That's when he called the professor."

"Toomer's been brought in for questioning?" Garrison asked.

Porter nodded. "His alibi checks out. He had some fraternity brothers over until eleven. They verified for him."

"Was anyone drinking that night?"

"No."

"So he claims," Detective Moses broke his silence to add in a surly drawl.

Garrison lifted his head from the report to meet the detective's dark gaze. "You think he's lying?"

Moses crossed his arms, took his sweet time replying. "Don't know, Agent Wade. Guess that'll be our job to find out, won't it?"

Sheriff Garcia snickered.

Garrison's expression was imperturbable as he calmly regarded the detective.

"If we can prove that alcohol was a factor," Taggert hastily intervened, "then it's a possibility that Toomer could have left the dorm undetected at any time during the evening."

Garrison's gaze sharpened on the police chief. "Is Toomer a suspect?"

"Not exactly, not for now," Taggert hedged. "But we're leaving the door open for any possibilities. The county executive's anxious for leads. The community's in a state of shock. If the CE's niece can be kidnapped, it can happen to anyone. That scares people, Wade."

Garrison nodded, mentally translating what was left unspoken. Wayne Taggert and his department were under tremendous public pressure to find a suspect as soon as possible.

He'd seen it countless times before and was no longer surprised when desperation turned into something worse, something uglier, and the lives of innocent people were ruined.

"Any priors on Toomer?" Garrison asked, thumbing through the file.

Cole Porter shook his head. "He's an honor student at the university, admitted on a basketball scholarship. They say he's bound for the pros."

"What about Althea's friends? Does anyone have reason to suspect Toomer's involvement in her disappearance?"

"We've only spoken to her best friend at this point, Elizabeth Torres," Taggert answered. "She said Althea and Malik were practically inseparable. But the night before she disappeared, they had a big argument. Althea wouldn't tell her what it was about."

Garrison nodded, absorbing the information and filing it away for future reference. "I wanted to bring Professor Maxwell in for additional questioning. Will she be coming this afternoon?"

"She'll be here at four," Taggert assured him.

Detective Moses curled his lips in what resembled a snarl. "My partner and I questioned Ms. Maxwell pretty thoroughly, Agent Wade. I doubt there's anything more she can tell us that would prove useful to our investigation. If anything, we need to be hauling Toomer's skinny black behind back in here."

"We'll bring him in, too," Chief Taggert decided. "It's worth a shot if we can uncover any new piece of information. Althea Pritchard has been missing almost seventy-two hours," he added grimly, passing a hand over his doughy face. "We all know what the statistics are on these cases. We're running out of time."

Porter rose from the table. "I'll get on the horn now, see if we can get Toomer down here again."

"You've got the tap and tracer on Pritchard's home phone?" Garrison verified with Taggert.

The chief nodded. "Done. And I've got some men doing surveillance."

"We'll need to get our hands on her computer, check old e-mail messages for anything."

"Not a problem. We'll pick it up tomorrow."

"Let me head back to the station," Sheriff Garcia announced, standing and starting for the door. "I've got my men following up on a few calls. Probably just cranks, though."

"Anything's better than nothing," Taggert said wearily. "And we need to get more men out there canvassing the neighborhood, talking to shop owners. Someone must have seen *something.*"

"When's the press conference?" Garrison asked.

"Tomorrow morning. Pritchard wanted to wait until he'd had a chance to meet with you before facing the media vultures. We issued a brief statement that the investigation is ongoing, left it at that."

Garrison nodded, watching as Detective Porter and the sheriff left the room. "I'm meeting with him at six. You sitting in on that?"

"I'll be there," Taggert grumbled, sounding as if he'd much rather not. He reached into his shirt pocket, extracted a roll of antacids and thumbed one off, then offered Garrison the pack. When Garrison declined, the police chief struggled to his feet again. "Well, I'd better head back to my office. Lot of calls to make, fires to put out."

Garrison nodded distractedly, busy making notations on his notepad. A moment after the police chief's departure, Porter returned, followed by a newcomer. When he announced her name, Garrison glanced up from his notes.

And stared.

Although it had been ten years since he graduated from college, he still remembered what professors were supposed to look like—staid, uptight, sporting tweed blazers and worn-out loafers. None of the above applied to the young woman who followed Detective Porter into the conference room. With her black hair worn in a neat, curly Afro that looked incredibly soft to the touch, Imani Maxwell could easily have stepped from the set of one of those blaxploitation films made popular in the seventies, although hers was a far more subtle look. Denim bell-bottom jeans molded long, impossibly sleek legs. Beneath the belted russet leather jacket she removed, she wore a flowing peasant blouse that flared at her slender brown wrists, which were encircled by simple bands of gold. The soft Afro dramatically accentuated high cheekbones, a slim nose, and a delicate chin that hinted at a stubborn streak.

Upon her arrival, both Garrison and Detective Moses rose to their feet to greet her, but it was Garrison who spoke first. "Ms. Maxwell?" he verified, unable to mask the surprise in his voice.

Those exotically slanted dark eyes narrowed on his face. "That's right," she confirmed, and Garrison half expected her to roll her beautiful neck and add, "jive sucka."

He cleared his throat, attempting to recover his professionalism. "Special Agent Garrison Wade," he introduced himself, offering a handshake.

She hesitated before accepting his proffered hand. Something like awareness passed between them when their skin made contact. Those gypsy eyes flew to his face for a startled moment before she withdrew her hand and said coolly, "Nice to meet you."

"We appreciate your taking the time to meet with us." Garrison stepped back, gesturing to the chair across from his own with a hand not as steady as he'd have liked. Every nerve ending in his body was thrumming with a raw, inexplicable energy. "Please, have a seat."

Imani complied, crossing her legs as she sat down with an almost feline grace. She pretended not to notice the way Detective Moses's hawkish gaze followed the gesture and settled on the shapely curve of her thighs. He'd rubbed her the wrong way the first time he'd questioned her, the day after Althea's disappearance. Imani had half hoped he wouldn't be present that afternoon.

"Would you care for something to drink?" the detective with the baby face asked her politely, taking the seat beside her.

"No, thank you. I'm fine."

Aaron Moses didn't take a seat, but stood at the head of the conference table, draping his hands across the back of a chair as he watched her closely. "Ms. Maxwell—I'm sorry," he interrupted himself, with that same hint of a mocking smile, "would you prefer to be called 'professor'?"

"It doesn't matter," Imani answered, too distracted by the other man to notice the detective's condescending tone. Tall, at least six-four, with broad shoulders and a wide chest that tapered down to a trim, athletic waist and long, lean legs, he was an incredible specimen of male beauty, even with that tiny, angry cut zigzagging across his left eyebrow. Dark brown skin, rich as warm mahogany, with ruthlessly hard cheekbones and a square jaw. Not to mention those penetrating black-as-midnight eyes that could land an unsuspecting woman in a world of trouble.

He sat across from her, strong, capable hands folded on the table. He had shed his dark suit jacket, and his broadcloth shirt was rolled back to lean forearms with a sprinkling of black hair. With little or no effort, he exuded more raw masculinity than Detectives Porter and Moses put together.

"Ms. Maxwell, how long have you known Althea Pritchard?" Agent Bedroom Eyes asked in an equally potent voice—a deep, commanding caress.

"A little over a year," Imani answered, irritated by her body's uncharacteristic response to this complete stranger. "She was in my freshman writing course, which I used to teach before Introduction to African-American Literature."

"Althea's enrolled in that course this semester, is that right?"

"Yes."

"On the night of her disappearance, you report that she was with you until seven."

Imani nodded. "We were meeting about a program the

African-American Studies Department is sponsoring in the spring. For the recruitment of minority students. Althea's the student panelist."

"Is it customary for you to spend so much time outside the classroom with your students, Professor?" Aaron Moses sneered.

Imani looked at the detective, and Garrison almost braced himself when he saw the flash of indignation in her dark eyes, the spitfire defiance. "Are you familiar with the student demographics at the university, Detective Moses?" she asked coldly.

"Can't say that I am."

"The minority students are outnumbered by a ratio of three to one. Some are there on scholarships, but most are admitted by the skin of their teeth and are totally dependent on financial aid and state-funded grants. They come in at a considerable disadvantage, looking for mentors to help guide them through a challenging college experience. If you're waiting for me to apologize for reaching out to my students, Detective Moses, I'm afraid you've got a long wait. My conduct has never extended beyond the boundaries of professional propriety; therefore I have nothing to be ashamed of."

The smirk on the detective's face disappeared. He crossed his arms and stared at the carpeted floor like a sullen child. Resisting the urge to grin, Detective Porter became engrossed with the condensation lining his glass of water.

Garrison calmly continued, "No one has reason to doubt your ethics, Ms. Maxwell. Your reputation as an outstanding educator and mentor precedes you. I'm told that even the county executive is impressed with you. His niece always spoke highly of you."

"Althea is a remarkable individual," Imani said, a bit sadly.

"Did she have a lot of friends at the university?" Garrison asked, touched by the melancholy in her voice.

"Not a lot, no. Althea was well liked by her peers, but she chose her friends very carefully. Selectively."

"Did she feel that people treated her differently because she's the county executive's niece?"

"Sometimes. But it's a large campus. Many people didn't know who Althea was unless she told them."

"Did she have any enemies that she might have told you about?"

"Not that I recall. And certainly not someone who might have disliked her enough to—to *kidnap* her," Imani struggled with the word, fighting a shudder.

"What about Malik Toomer?" Garrison prodded. "Do you think he could be involved in Althea's disappearance?"

"Not for a minute. Malik and Althea were very close; he would never hurt her." Even as Imani spoke, she saw Detective Moses exchange dubious glances with Cole Porter. She looked askance at Garrison, incredulous. "Don't tell me Malik is a suspect?"

"We're exploring all possibilities," Garrison answered neutrally. "Her best friend says Althea and Malik argued the night before she disappeared."

"Malik Toomer had nothing to do with Althea's disappearance," Imani insisted emphatically. "He worshipped the ground that girl walked on—argument or not."

"With all due respect, *Professor,*" Moses interjected dryly, "unless you have a degree in law enforcement, let those of us with experience handle the investigation as we see fit. That is, if you're as eager to help as you claim to be."

Imani's eyes narrowed to dangerous slits.

Before she could respond to the barb—and he had no doubt that she would—Garrison interjected, "We're doing everything we can to find Althea, Ms. Maxwell. Believe me," he added, with a pointed look at Detective Moses, "no one's going to be charged with anything without hard, concrete evidence."

Moses straightened against the wall, his expression tightening. Cole Porter cleared his throat. "We'd better wrap this up soon if we're going to make it to Pritchard's house by six," he reminded Garrison.

Garrison nodded, consulting the file before him. "Just one more question, Ms. Maxwell. Did Althea ever confide in you about anything particularly personal—past or present—that could have potential bearing on her disappearance?"

Imani hesitated, searching her memory. Finally she shook her head. "No . . . nothing that comes to mind."

Garrison studied her a moment longer before nodding briskly. He glided to his feet and started around the table, shrugging into his suit jacket. "Thank you for your time, Ms. Maxwell."

She nodded, rising, with her own jacket draped over her arm. "I'm eager to help any way I can."

"We appreciate that," he said, and meant it.

Moses and Porter hung back as Garrison escorted Imani from the conference room and down the near-empty corridor. "You're parked out front?" he asked.

"Yes," she answered, slipping on her jacket and fastening the belt around her slim waist. A lock of curly hair fell onto her gently rounded forehead and landed just above her right eye, giving her a sexy, tousled look. She had the most glorious brown skin Garrison had ever seen. Flawless, as creamy as milk chocolate, with rich undertones of sienna. And then there were those lips. Full, sensuous lips that could bring a man indescribable pleasure. He felt a stab in his lower abdomen that felt suspiciously like lust. Totally inappropriate.

"We'll be in touch if anything else develops," Garrison informed her.

"Please do."

"And if you think of anything," he added, reaching into his breast pocket and extracting a business card, "don't hesitate to contact me. Day or night."

Imani nodded, accepting the card from his hand and forcibly ignoring the frissons of heat that shimmered through her body at the brief contact. She slid the card into her purse after a cursory glance and affected a brisk, businesslike tone. "Have a good evening, Agent Wade."

He inclined his head. "Same to you, Ms. Maxwell."

She turned and started away, her high-heeled leather boots clicking smartly against the precinct's tiled floor as she stretched the distance between them. Garrison watched her, trying not to admire the undulating rhythm of her hips as she walked. He found himself willing her to glance back at him, to give him some sign that he hadn't imagined the chemistry between them. He was almost relieved when she didn't.

Appearing beside him, Detective Moses whistled softly in appreciation. "College professors didn't look that good back in my day," he drawled. "If they had, maybe I wouldn't have dropped out."

Ignoring the remark, Garrison turned toward the detective. "You're not going to have a problem working with me, are you, Detective Moses?" he asked, deceptively soft.

The detective's smile faded. He regarded Garrison with narrowed eyes, coolly assessing. "No problem at all, Agent Wade."

"Glad to hear it." Without another word, Garrison turned and started back toward the police chief's office.

Chapter 3

County Executive Louis Pritchard and his wife lived in a wealthy suburb of Prince George's County, Maryland. Their home was located in a gated community that featured sprawling three-story mansions resting upon acres and acres of manicured emerald lawns. Alone, at the top of the hill, sat the Pritchards' stone house—formidable, proud, solid, impressive. Courtesy of taxpayer dollars.

Garrison parked his black GMC Envoy at the curb, last in a row of several other cars, and made his way up the brick-paved steps leading to a wide, arched door. The doorbell seemed to reverberate throughout the entire house, announcing his presence like a trumpet blast. He half expected a uniformed butler to answer the summons, and was surprised when the door was opened by Barbara Pritchard. With her black hair swept off her neck in a neat chignon, the county executive's wife was effortlessly elegant in a cashmere sweater and tan slacks. Her cream-colored complexion was smooth and unlined, but beneath the expensive cosmetics she wore, her face was drawn with fatigue and worry.

"Hello. You must be Special Agent Wade," she greeted Garrison warmly, stepping aside to gesture him into a cavernous foyer with cathedral ceilings and a marble-tiled floor. "We've been expecting you. Everyone's in the living room."

Garrison followed her as she started down the foyer. She opened a door to their right and gestured him into a large room with a fire burning in a massive stone fireplace and a thick Aubusson rug spread across the glossy oak floor. Louis Pritchard's closest friends and advisors were already assembled, there to lend their support and offer words of solace to their grief-stricken comrade.

Chief Taggert, standing in a corner with Detectives Aaron Moses and Cole Porter, was the first to notice Garrison's arrival. He hurried across the room to greet him, his expression one of immense relief. "Wade. Thought you wouldn't make it, after all."

"I apologize for being late. I had to tie up some loose ends in Baltimore."

"Of course," spoke a third voice. "You're coming off one high-profile case only to jump right into another."

Louis Pritchard appeared behind the police chief. "Special Agent Wade," he greeted him, clasping Garrison's hand in a firm handshake as Chief Taggert retreated back to his corner. "Thanks so much for coming."

Garrison inclined his head politely. "No thanks necessary, Mr. Pritchard."

The county executive waved a dismissive hand. "Please, just call me Louis." In his early fifties, Louis Pritchard was tall and broad shouldered, the strands of gray woven liberally through his hair lending him a distinguished air. But, like his wife, stress had taken its toll, evidenced by the dark circles rimming his eyes and the deep creases etched around his mouth.

"I've heard so much about you," Pritchard confided. "When this thing happened—" He broke off as his voice hitched. When Barbara Pritchard stepped forward with a look of concern, he waved her away, forcing a strained smile. "I'm fine, Bobbi. As I was saying, Agent Wade, I've been following your career. When our Althea disappeared, you were the first person that came to my mind. I make no apologies for calling in favors to get you on this case," he added, almost defensively.

Garrison nodded, respecting the politician's candor. He swept a cursory glance around the room, meeting several watchful pairs of eyes. "Is there somewhere we could talk in private? I wanted to ask you a few routine questions."

"Of course," Pritchard quickly agreed. "We can use the study."

He led the way into a spacious office suite and closed the door behind them. The room was dominated by a massive mahogany desk and mahogany-paneled walls containing everything from legal tomes to political treatises. He offered Garrison one of the oxblood leather chairs across from the island of a desk before seating himself in the high-backed executive throne behind it.

Garrison's practiced gaze strayed to a wall that held an assortment of framed photographs, many of Pritchard posing with various dignitaries and politicians, including Nelson Mandela, Reverend Jesse Jackson, and former president Bill Clinton. Interspersed with these were photos chronicling Althea's life from infancy through high school. There were only a few photos of Louis and Barbara Pritchard, and even most of those were taken with Althea, their arms around her as they beamed proudly into the camera. It was obvious that she was the center of their universe, a universe that had been turned upside down in the wake of her disappearance. Their world was now held together by the barest thread of hope that she would be returned safe and sound.

"Forgive my manners, Agent Wade. Would you care for something to drink? Some coffee, club soda, or brandy perhaps?"

"No, thanks. I'm fine."

Pritchard chuckled. "What am I thinking, offering you alcohol? You're not supposed to drink on the job. Although," he added, assessing Garrison with those shrewd dark eyes, "my guess is you're not a drinker, anyway. Am I right, Agent Wade?"

Garrison knew Pritchard was taking his measure, trying to determine what he was made of. It was the oldest trick in the book, turning the tables on the interrogator. "I would say that's a fair assessment," he answered evenly.

Pritchard nodded, then leaned back in his chair. "Now, what was it you wanted to ask me, Agent Wade? As I already told the police, I was at a fund-raiser with Barbara the night of Althea's disappearance. Not that I'm considered a suspect, of course," he added with a strained half laugh.

"When was the last time you saw your niece?"

"Friday. Althea came home faithfully every weekend, no matter what was going on at school. The only reason we all agreed to her living on campus was because of her heavy workload—we didn't want her having to commute back and forth on top of everything else she was juggling. She's premed, wants to become a doctor so that she can cure the poor and sick. Barbara and I are very proud of her. But sometimes I wonder if we put too much pressure on her," he added with a mixture of sadness and guilt.

"What was her frame of mind on Friday?"

"Upbeat. She was telling us about a minority recruitment program she was working on. She'd just been selected as the student panelist, and she was rather excited about it. She had so many ideas she couldn't wait to share with Professor Maxwell. She told us they were meeting about it on Sunday, along with some other student participants." He chuckled with fond recollection. "She was trying to be so modest about being chosen, saying the others' essay submissions were probably just as good as hers. Althea's always been that way. No matter how many awards and accolades she receives, she's always gracious about it. We believe that's why the Lord has blessed her with so much. God knows she's been a blessing to *our* lives. I'm sorry," he whispered as moisture filled his eyes. His hand trembled as he reached for the eight-by-ten silver-framed photograph on his desk. He smiled down at the image for a moment before passing it to Garrison.

It was Althea's high school graduation picture. Her pretty brown face was lit up with a dimpled grin and a ready sparkle in her brown eyes. The yellow runner reserved for honors students was draped across her narrow shoulders over the royal blue graduation robe.

"Do you have children, Agent Wade?"

Garrison glanced up from the photograph. "No, sir."

"But I would imagine, in your line of work, that you don't need to be a parent to understand the absolute horror one experiences in losing a child."

Garrison nodded grimly as he handed back the photograph.

Pritchard gazed toward the window, his expression remote and reflective. "She never knew her father. He was just another junkie that my sister sold her body to in exchange for a hit. Did you know that Althea was born premature and crack addicted? The doctors didn't expect her to live beyond her first week and were fully prepared to have her buried beside her mother, my baby sister, who died a few hours after her delivery. But Althea proved them wrong, showed them that fighting spirit we all came to love. When she celebrated her first birthday, plump and healthy as she wanted to be, the entire hospital staff who'd treated her attended the party." A soft, reminiscent smile touched his mouth before bitterness hardened it. "I cannot accept that the Lord would give us this precious gift, our Althea, only to let her be taken from us this way."

Garrison started to remind Pritchard that Althea might still be alive, but he'd seen too much loss, consoled too many devastated families, to bring himself to offer any false hope—however well intentioned.

"What do you think of Althea's boyfriend?" he asked instead.

"Malik? I had my reservations at first. Althea has never

been into boys the way most teenage girls are, so I was surprised when she introduced us to an athlete, of all things. But he seems to have a decent head on his shoulders." Pritchard lifted his shoulders in a casual shrug, still gazing out at nightfall. "My guess is that he'll forget all about her once he goes into the pros, and Althea will move on to someone more suited to her professional interests. An aspiring doctor or lawyer, perhaps."

Garrison wondered how much of Pritchard's predictions were based on wishful thinking.

"Can you think of anyone who might want to harm your niece? A disgruntled associate or constituent perhaps—"

Pritchard swung his startled gaze from the window. "You mean like an enemy?"

Mildly amused by his scandalized tone, Garrison continued, "We see it all the time, unfortunately. People abduct the spouses and children of high-profile individuals for ransom, or to get their fifteen minutes of fame."

"This is hardly a Patty Hearst situation," Pritchard said dryly. "I'm no wealthy publishing tycoon, Agent Wade, not by a long shot."

"True, but if the individual responsible for taking Althea knew she was the county executive's niece, we have to consider ransom as a motive." When Pritchard remained resistant, Garrison added in a knowing drawl, "You've become quite a powerful force in this county. Surely you didn't get where you are without making a few enemies along the way."

Pritchard pursed his lips, shaking his head emphatically. "Not possible. I've always held myself to a strict code of ethics and moral integrity. Even when I ran for office, I never resorted to the mudslinging my opponents were so fond of, and I've *certainly* never indulged in shady business dealings that could come back to haunt me."

"Be that as it may," Garrison said evenly, "it may be worth our time to go through a listing of your campaign supporters and contributors, as well as any past and present business associates."

"Do you know how long—"

Garrison's expression was impenetrable. "If there's one thing you'll learn about me," he said, a hint of steel underlying his words, "it's that I believe in covering all my bases. Given the situation, I would think you'd want any investigator on this case to be as thorough as possible."

Pritchard faltered a moment, at a loss for words. And then, his face relaxing into a wide grin, he said, "You're a cool customer, aren't you? I had heard that about you, and now I see that it's true."

"I'll take that as a compliment," Garrison murmured.

"You should. At any rate," he flicked a glance at the gold Rolex on his wrist, "I'm afraid we'll have to wrap this up soon. Barbara and I are scheduled to meet with our pastor this evening." He leaned forward in the chair, folding his hands on the gleaming surface of the desk. "I want you to know that you have my full cooperation, Agent Wade. I want Althea's kidnapper captured and punished to the full extent of the law. Promise me that you'll do everything in your power to bring my niece back home where she belongs. Street says you're the best, and I firmly believe that."

Garrison's expression was deadpan. "I'll do my job, and I'll do it well. You have my word on that. Beyond that, I make no promises."

Pritchard hesitated a moment, then nodded briskly. "I'll have my secretary fax that list to you first thing in the morning, Agent Wade."

Garrison stood. "Thanks for your time. I'll be in touch."

For the second time that week, the street was cloaked in darkness by the time Imani pulled into her driveway.

She sighed and shook her head, staring up at the silent house that had only become her home within the last month.

With its long, sloping roof and wide, sheltering overhang, the New England bungalow-style home appeared to nestle into the earth. With pillars that broadened at the base, the porch was wide enough to feel like an outside room. The porch was just one of the features she'd fallen in love with at first sight that had hastened her to sign on the dotted line. The house's proximity to the university had sealed the deal for her.

"Now if they could just do something about these streetlights," she muttered under her breath. She made a mental note to lodge a complaint with the homeowners' association and, if necessary, the city council.

She reached across the passenger seat, grabbing her leather briefcase. She opened the door and stepped down from her burgundy Jeep. She didn't see the dark figure creep from the shadows until he was upon her.

Too late, she screamed as a gloved hand clamped over her mouth, muffling her cry for help.

Chapter 4

She struggled valiantly to escape, twisting her body and kicking out blindly. She was rewarded when the heel of her boot connected with bone and muscle, extracting a surprised grunt from her assailant.

Her short-lived satisfaction turned to shock when the muffled groan was followed by deep male laughter. "Imani! It's me, baby. Stop!"

She whirled around and stared into the familiar handsome face. *"David?"*

"Yeah, baby girl," he gasped.

She gaped up at him for another prolonged moment before anger mingled with intense relief replaced the shock, and she began pummeling his broad chest with her fists. "Are you crazy?" she shrieked. "You scared the mess out of me! What were you thinking, sneaking up on me like that?"

He laughed in protest, seizing her arms to ward off the onslaught. "I'm sorry. I didn't think—"

"Obviously!" Furious, she snatched her arms away and bent to retrieve her briefcase from the ground where it had fallen. Straightening, she dug her keys from her jacket pocket and stormed up the porch steps to the front door.

"Baby—" David started after her.

"Don't you 'baby' me, David Scott. You scared me half to death! I thought I was being attacked in my own front yard."

"I'm sorry—" David's next plea was met by the front door as Imani slammed it in his face. She was striding toward the kitchen, Shiloh on her heels, by the time he opened the door and caught up to her. Grabbing her arm and ignoring the dog's low warning growl, he turned her around to face him. "Come on, baby girl," he said coaxingly. "Don't be mad. It was a stupid, childish prank. If I had given it more thought, I wouldn't have done it."

Imani crossed her arms. "You know how on edge I've been since Althea's disappearance."

"I know. And I'm deeply sorry for scaring you. You know I'd never do anything to deliberately hurt you."

She stared up at him through a sweep of thick lashes, considering the sensitive brown eyes that crinkled at the corners when he smiled, the strong curve of his jaw, the wide, generous mouth framed by a trim moustache. A face as familiar to her as her own. They'd grown up together, chasing each other around the backyards of their Upper Marlboro homes until David turned thirteen and decided it wasn't cool to be seen playing with his best friend's kid sister. Three years her senior, he soon assumed the role of protector, coming to her rescue against her own brother, Irvin, who'd made it his life's mission to torment his younger sibling. Over the years, David and Imani's friendship remained platonic, if not distant, until he returned from law school—mature, sophisticated, with a head full of knowledge that appealed to her thirsty mind. The sexy goatee and new muscle-toned physique didn't hurt, either.

A reluctant smile tugged at her full lips now. "You're lucky you identified yourself when you did. You almost got the beat-down of your life out there."

"I know. I think I'm going to need shin replacement surgery." He chuckled. "Remind me never to sneak up on you again."

"Serves you right," she retorted, starting for the kitchen once again. It was a cozy room with modern appliances and gleaming hardwood floors, an island in the center and a wide double-sided refrigerator with a stainless steel front consuming much of the space.

David followed and stood in the arched entry, watching as she opened the pantry and removed a bag of Alpo. Shiloh wagged his tail excitedly as she knelt and shook the beef-flavored contents into his metal feeding dish. "There you go, boy," she crooned. "Get your eat on."

Ignoring her, Shiloh dove into his meal with his usual gusto. Shaking her head, Imani passed a hand over his silken fur. "Ingrate," she muttered under her breath.

Bemused, David shook his head at the pair. "You and that mutt. I still don't understand why you think you can handle a pet, with everything else you've got on your plate."

"First of all," Imani protested, brushing past him as she left the kitchen, "Shiloh is *not* a mutt. He's a purebred golden retriever. And second, I couldn't just let him go to the pound. Do you have *any* idea what those places are like?" She shuddered, propping her weight against the wall to remove her boots.

David grinned sarcastically. "Oh, that's right. I forgot I was talking to The Great Imani Maxwell, Associate Professor Extraordinaire and Savior of the World."

She glared at him. "Don't start with me," she warned, removing her jacket and hanging it in the hall closet. "You're still treading on thin ice from that little stunt you pulled."

David leaned against the wall, an indulgent smile on his caramel-toned face. "Maybe if you get scared enough, you'll consider moving in with me."

Imani groaned, rolling her dark eyes heavenward. "Not

that again. We've been over this a million times, David. I can't move in with you, you know that."

"Can't or won't?"

"Both." Exasperated, Imani padded over to the sofa in her stockinged feet and plopped down. She felt the onset of a migraine behind her eyelids, tiny pinpricks of pain that intensified with each blink.

David followed and stood before her so that she had to angle her head to look up at him, putting her at a disadvantage. "I still don't understand why you insist on renting out someone else's home when I have a perfectly nice penthouse big enough for both of us." Before she could answer, he hastened to add, "I know you don't want to commute from the District, baby, but we'll both have to make sacrifices eventually."

"David," Imani spoke quietly, resolutely, "my decision has nothing to do with the commute from Washington, D.C. Nor does it have anything to do with my old-fashioned values—although Mama raised me better than to shack up with some man, childhood friend or not," she added with a teasing grin.

When David didn't laugh, she sobered. "You know it's nothing personal, David. I just need my own space, that's all. Why is that so hard for you to accept? Besides," she hedged, "if memory serves me correctly, we broke up last year and are supposed to remain as such until we both decide otherwise."

David knelt before her with an imploring expression. "That's why I'm here, actually." He hesitated, watching her carefully. "I thought we could discuss getting back together."

Imani's eyes widened in surprise. "David—"

"Look, I know what we told each other about taking time to reassess our priorities, take a breather from each other. But that was only because we were both so busy, you with your Ph.D. studies and me trying to make junior partner at the firm. We were feeling burned out, that's all."

"I think you know there was a bit more to it than that," Imani murmured. Even before they had reached a mutual decision to break up one year ago, they had been slowly drifting apart. The first obvious sign of trouble had been their rapidly disintegrating love life, the routine excuses they passed back and forth on the rare occasions they did manage to see each other. Too tired, don't feel well, not enough hours in the day, maybe next time. But it wasn't just about the sex, or lack thereof. There had been other intangible things that made her wonder if, perhaps, they weren't the soul mates their close-knit families expected them to be.

"Have you met someone else?" David angrily demanded.

"Of course not."

"Then why are you so reluctant to pick up where we left off? Look, Flannery says it's only a matter of time before I make partner. Now that you've completed your dissertation and fellowship, I think it's time we started giving serious thought to our future. I'm ready to take our relationship further, Imani."

Guilt assaulted her. She reached for his hand, still encased in the brown leather that matched his expensive trench coat. "First of all," she said gently, "you know I could care less whether or not you make partner—they'd be fools not to reward you for all the hard work you put in for that firm. But I didn't get involved with you for your earning potential, David."

"Maybe, but it certainly never hurt my appeal." When she didn't laugh, he continued persuasively, "If I make partner, I'll be expected to attend all kinds of soirees and social functions, even more so than now."

Imani arched an eyebrow. "And you think having a devoted wife on your arm will bolster your image among the senior partners?" When he offered no denial, she shook her head in disbelief. "David, you know good and well I don't do the trophy wife thing."

"No one said anything about that," David argued, sounding mildly peeved. "If I wanted some trophy wife, I certainly wouldn't marry a headstrong sister sporting an Afro and harboring less-than-favorable opinions about greedy corporate attorneys." He smiled as he peeled off his gloves and shrugged out of his coat. "Will you at least reconsider my offer about moving in with me?"

She groaned and threw her head back against the sofa. "Absolutely not, my mind's made up. And I think it's best that we remain friends, David. It's less complicated this way."

But David would not be deterred. "So friends can't live together?"

"Not us. Besides," Imani said, lifting her head from the sofa and peering at her surroundings, "I like this house. Don't you?"

David shrugged, casting a dismissive look around. "Sure, if you like colonial."

She bristled. "As a matter of fact, I do."

The interior of the house was as charming as the exterior, the woodwork heavy and dark, ornately built up in layers. Beamed ceilings, oak wainscoting in the dining room, and the kitchen's built-in buffet added to the home's appeal. Warmth and ambience were created by yellow lanterns hanging from the ceiling, and the great room where they sat—Imani's personal favorite—featured a fireplace and hearth made of earthy bricks and rustic river stones. The fireplace was framed by symmetrical bookshelves, a camelback sofa that converted into a sleeper, and comfortable, mismatched chairs purchased on sale from Pier 1 Imports.

The small, simplistic layout emphasized a low, compact design—two stories with little space on the second floor, which suited Imani's needs just fine. Two bedrooms and a huge, newly renovated master bath were more than she required at this point in her life.

"I feel comfortable here," she said. At David's injured look, she hastened to add, "Not that I don't feel comfortable at your place. It's just that this house reminds me a bit of the cabin in West Virginia. You know . . ."

David nodded as melancholy settled over her expression like a veil. He knew all too well about the painful memories that still haunted her, plagued her dreams. Seeking to lighten her mood, he announced, "I'm starving, Cleopatra Jones. Have you had dinner yet?"

Imani shook her head absently, not even reacting to the nickname he'd given her when she swore off perms two years ago, much to his displeasure. "What's wrong with your straight hair?" he had demanded like a petulant child. "A woman's long hair is her crown of glory. Besides, there are other ways to celebrate your ethnicity. You don't have to boycott perms."

Although her curly natural eventually grew on him, Imani knew it was no coincidence that David began inviting her to fewer functions at the firm. She also knew that he would vigorously renew his pro-perm campaign if they ever got married.

David clapped his hands together. "Why don't we order some takeout? Chinese okay?"

She finally managed a wan smile. "Menu's in the kitchen, bottom left-hand drawer. Order whatever you want—it doesn't matter to me."

While David called the restaurant, she rose from the sofa and wandered over to the sheer-curtained window overlooking the front yard. She noticed David's sleek, dark green Mercedes-Benz parked at the curb and chuckled quietly to herself, wondering how she had missed hearing him pull up behind her earlier.

Night had wrapped itself around the house, an eerily ominous shroud. All was still and silent outside, not a soul in sight. Yet she hugged herself as a fine chill passed through her, raising the tiny hairs on the back of her neck.

"Food will be here in twenty minutes," David spoke behind her. "I settled on the usual. Hope you're in the mood for Szechuan chicken."

Imani nodded distractedly, peering into the darkness and

telling herself she was crazy for imagining movement in the shadows.

"Come sit down so I can tell you all about my crazy day." David's warmth surrounded her suddenly, the pressure of his hands upon her shoulders comforting in its familiarity as he steered her from the window.

They left an audience of one hidden in the shadows across the street.

The same local university where Imani had taught for the past five years was also her alma mater. She'd earned her undergraduate and master's degrees from the University of Maryland, College Park, and had just completed her dissertation for a Ph.D. in English Literature. She would receive her diploma at the graduation ceremony in December.

On Mondays, Wednesdays, and Fridays she taught Introduction to African-American Literature at two o'clock. The remaining days were reserved for the endless administrative tasks required of faculty members—reviewing the syllabus, rereading course materials, grading assignments, and keeping office hours for students seeking academic counseling.

That Thursday morning, she arrived early at her office in the English department's main building. The room was a narrow cubbyhole with a scarred wooden desk and two old chairs with coffee-stained seat cushions. Her leather jacket hung on a nail that substituted as a coat rack. The room's drabness was lessened by lush ferns and African violets, and photographs pinned to a bulletin board. In one photo, Imani had her arms draped around a group of beaming children from the youth center where she volunteered. Another showed her posing with her family at her college graduation, their joined arms raised in the air in a gesture of shared triumph. They were blissfully unaware that within a year, their tight circle would be ripped apart by unspeakable tragedy.

Imani was bent over a stack of papers when she heard the knock on her door.

She looked up and smiled at the tall, dark-skinned young man who stood hesitantly in the doorway. "Malik," she greeted him warmly. "Come on in."

Malik Toomer sauntered into the office and lowered his lithe frame into the chair opposite Imani's desk. He wore the red and black sweat suit of the university's basketball team over a gigantic pair of Nikes, and his bald head gleamed under the room's fluorescent lights. "Hope I'm not disturbing you, Professor," he mumbled apologetically, stretching his long legs forward.

She shook her head. "Just grading papers, nothing I can't take a break from." To demonstrate, she laid down her red pen.

"We missed you in class yesterday," she said quietly. "How are you holding up?"

Malik shrugged. "All right, I guess. Sorry about class. I just couldn't get myself going yesterday."

"Not easy getting out of bed these days, is it?"

He hesitated, then shook his head. "I can't stop thinking about her, Professor," he admitted, staring down at his folded hands. "I can't believe she's gone. It's unreal, you know?"

Imani's heart melted at the sheer misery on his face. "If it'll make you feel any better, I miss her, too."

Malik nodded. "I'm scared," he confessed, his voice thick with suppressed emotion. "I don't know what I'm gonna do if anything's happened to her."

"Try not to think the worst, Malik."

"I can't help it. What if they don't find her in time? And you can't tell me that ain't a possibility, Professor," he rushed on before she could open her mouth, "because you don't know that for sure. Nobody does, except whoever took her."

Imani pursed her lips for a moment, trying to think of the best way to reassure Malik without misleading or patronizing him. She'd hated it when people did that to her after her father's death. The conciliatory pats on the shoulder, the endless reassurances that everything would be all right, the lie that in no time at all she'd recover from the loss. The reality was that it had taken years to restore some semblance of normalcy to her life, and even to this day she wasn't whole, doubted she ever would be.

She decided to be straightforward with her student. "You're right, Malik," she murmured. "No one knows the outcome of this nightmare. I guess all we can do is hope for the best, and prepare for the worst. The rest is up to God."

Malik nodded slowly, thoughtfully. Imani marveled that beneath the dark good looks, trademark swagger, and the dynamic athletic prowess on the basketball court that had rendered Malik Toomer the most popular student on campus, deep down inside he was still just a boy. A scared, helpless boy.

He lifted those wide, brown eyes to her then. "The police want to talk to me again," he said nervously. "Do they think I did it?"

"I'm sure they haven't pinned you down as a suspect, Malik," she said carefully, "but you know they have to cover all their bases. It's standard procedure to question everyone who has a connection to the missing person. They called me, too."

Malik slumped forward, passing a hand wearily over his shiny bald head. "And now the FBI's involved," he muttered. "I saw the press conference on the news this morning. That brother ain't no joke."

"They say he's the best," Imani murmured, recalling the hint of steel in Garrison Wade's dark eyes as he assured the seven-thirty A.M. viewing audience that everything possible was being done to find Althea Pritchard, announcing that the Prince George's County police had the full cooperation of the FBI and asking viewers to come forward with any information they might have. "I think Althea deserves the best, don't you, Malik?"

"No question about it, Professor. Just so long as he don't come knocking on my door with no arrest warrant. I mean, just because me and Althea argued the night before doesn't mean I did something to her." His eyes were desperate, entreating her to believe him.

Imani said carefully, "I think the police and FBI are committed to conducting a full investigation before any arrests are made."

Malik looked unconvinced. "Would you go with me, Professor Maxwell? For questioning, I mean."

She hesitated, surprised by the request. "What about an attorney, Malik? And your mother? Shouldn't she be there with you?"

"I don't want her worrying about me. She's got enough on her hands with my younger brothers and sisters. She don't need to be at no police station with me."

"I'm sure she knows you're innocent—"

"That's all right, forget I asked. I don't mean to get you all caught up in this."

"I'm already caught up in it, Malik. Don't forget that Althea was one of my students. All I'm saying is that you would be better served having, at least, an attorney present, not your college professor. However, if you'd really like for me to go with you, I will. Just let me know when."

Malik brightened for the first time since his arrival. "Thanks, Professor. I appreciate it. And Coach says he knows a good lawyer if I need one. Maybe I'll take him up on that."

"You might want to consider it," Imani advised, recalling the tense exchange between Detective Moses and Agent Wade during the interview yesterday. Although Garrison Wade may have been committed to conducting a fair and thorough investigation, there was no telling what the detective had in mind.

"I guess I'd better get going," Malik said, unfolding his long body from the too-small chair and standing. "I haven't even cracked open a book to study for this sociology test I've got in an hour."

Imani stood, reaching for her jacket. "I'll walk out with you," she offered. "It's almost two, and all I've had today is a muffin."

Malik grinned. "You on a diet or something, Professor?"

"No, and you'd better not be implying I need to be," Imani quipped, shrugging into her jacket and starting for the door.

"No, ma'am."

Three years ago, the men's basketball team had celebrated their final season playing at the aging Cole Field House by winning the NCAA championship. Cole's heir apparent, Comcast Center, was located on the campus's North Field, adjacent to the intramural athletic fields. The new multimillion-dollar facility boasted a 17,000-seat arena, an academic support and career development center, a student activity center, and accommodation facilities for twenty-five different sports.

That evening, Garrison watched the players running through practice drills in the center of the gleaming hardwood floor while their head coach observed from the sidelines, barking instructions from a clipboard. Even from where he stood, planted half the distance to the court, Garrison could see why all the sports analysts were buzzing with anticipation over Malik Toomer. At six-six, weighing 210 pounds of solid power and muscle, Malik already had the build of an NBA shooting guard. A third of the way into last year's season, he had averaged twenty points per game. Points he scored almost effortlessly—or so it seemed to the news cameras that captured him gliding through the air. His body always appeared suspended in time before he angled down, draining the basket with one hand over his opponent's head.

As Garrison watched, Malik executed a series of jumpers from every angle of the court, sending the balls swishing through the hoop in fluid succession. He flashed a white grin as some of his teammates reacted in disbelief, guffawing and slapping him jovially on the back. As he turned to retrieve another basketball, his gaze lifted, meeting Garrison's, and the relaxed grin faded at once.

For a moment he looked ready to bolt in the opposite direction, and Garrison slowly unfolded his arms, primed for the unpredictable. But then Malik jogged off the court and joined his coach on the sidelines, and after a moment both turned and looked up in Garrison's direction. Malik bent his head, nodding at something his coach said before starting up the stands toward Garrison.

"Mr. Toomer," Garrison said coolly as he approached, "we've been trying to get in touch with you."

Malik halted two rows down, looking edgy as he stared at some point beyond Garrison's shoulder, not meeting his eyes. "I was out last night."

Garrison's eyebrow lifted. "Are dormitories still equipped with phones, or has it been that long since I was in college?"

"Yes, sir, they are," Malik mumbled. "I was gonna call Detective Moses back this morning."

Garrison flicked a pointed glance at his own wristwatch. "It's almost eight P.M."

"I know, but uh . . . I got busy."

Garrison was silent, his expression inscrutable as Malik shifted his weight from one foot to another, eyeing him warily. He looked like he'd jump out of his skin if Garrison made a sudden move.

Switching tacks, Garrison inclined his head toward the court below. "That's quite a jumper you've got," he said conversationally.

"Thanks." Somewhat mollified by the compliment, Malik regarded Garrison curiously, considering his height and athletic build. "You ever play basketball?"

"In high school. Of course," Garrison drawled, "I was nowhere near as good as you obviously are."

Malik ducked his head, but not before Garrison saw the trace of cockiness in his grin. The boy's cockiness amused Garrison.

He slanted his head to one side, his expression thoughtful. "A good-looking star athlete like yourself. Bet you could have any girl on campus you want. Come on, tell the truth," he cajoled, settling into the I-could-be-your-friend guise he'd perfected his first year in the Bureau, "you probably have all the honeys breaking down your door."

Malik grinned, a touch embarrassed as he admitted, "Yeah, something like that."

"Uh-huh, that's what I thought. And I bet Althea didn't take too kindly to that."

Malik's grin faltered. "Nah, not really. She always thought I liked all the attention."

Garrison's gaze sharpened, hawk-like. "Is that what the two of you argued about on Saturday night?"

Malik looked startled, as if wondering how he'd been maneuvered into this line of questioning, although he knew he should have expected it. "I don't wanna talk about it, Agent Wade," he mumbled unhappily.

Garrison waited a beat. "You wouldn't be hiding anything from me, would you, Malik?"

Malik lowered himself weakly onto the back of a seat, eyes downcast. "What we argued about . . . me and Althea . . . it's too personal."

"Do you understand what is meant by the term 'obstruction of justice'?"

Malik's gaze flew upward. "I'm not trying to hinder the investigation, Agent Wade. If I knew anything, and I mean *anything*, that might help you find Althea, I would tell you in a heartbeat, I swear. You gotta believe that."

"You ever hit Althea?"

"What?" Malik nearly choked on the word.

Garrison drew closer, no longer the easygoing confidant as he brought his face level with Malik's. "Restaurant manager says you and Althea came in one night, a while ago, and ended up in a heated argument before you left. Guy says he watched from the windows as you shoved Althea against your car." His tone turned dangerously soft. "So I'll ask you one more time: did you ever hit Althea?"

Malik licked his lips, shamefaced. "Once. But she hit me first! I was just trying to defend myself."

Garrison's dark gaze narrowed. Again he spoke in that low, controlled tone, "How much do you weigh, Malik?"

"Two ten."

Garrison said nothing, watching Malik so long that the younger man began fidgeting with his hands, looking everywhere but at his cross-examiner's face. The sweat beading his forehead had nothing to do with his exertions on the basketball court.

Garrison reached into his breast pocket. "In case you think of anything else you might want to tell me," he said coolly, passing Malik his card.

Surprised, Malik accepted the card and spoke without thinking, "Is that it? That's all you wanted to ask me?"

"For now." Slowly, deliberately, as if he had all the time in the world, Garrison slid a mint-flavored toothpick into the corner of his mouth. He shifted his gaze to the court below and inclined his head in a slight nod at the head coach who waited on the sidelines, pretending not to watch his star player being interrogated by the FBI.

Malik stood. "Look, Agent Wade, I know how these things work. I know the husband or boyfriend is always the first suspect when a woman disappears or gets knocked off. But I can tell you, that's not the case here. I didn't do anything to Althea." Garrison slipped one hand into his pants pocket, his expression impassive as Malik pled his case. "I'm gonna play in the NBA someday, maybe even next year.

I wouldn't mess up my future by hurting anybody, especially not the girl I love."

Garrison didn't respond. Instead, he turned and started up the stands, saying over his shoulder, "I'll be in touch."

"By the way," Malik called, frowning at his back, "who was the restaurant manager who saw me and Althea?"

Garrison glanced back long enough to reply, his expression one of blank innocence, "What restaurant manager?"

Chapter 5

"So you're absolutely sure you liked the cake with the French vanilla buttercream frosting? The three-tiered one with the pearl strands and edible roses?"

"Absolutely," Imani said, smiling across the linen-covered table at her companion. Truth be told, after the first hour of the consultation, the multitiered confections with blooming bouquets of hand-sculpted flowers and truffles had all started to look—and taste—alike.

She stared down at the meal she'd ordered, penne pasta covered with a rich, creamy alfredo sauce, and felt her stomach lurch in protest. God, had they *really* expected to enjoy dinner after sampling so many cakes that evening?

Obviously.

Across the table, Jada Jamison dug into her crawfish étouffée with her usual enthusiasm, her appetite suffering no loss. "That was my favorite one, too. Great minds think alike," she added with a grin.

They'd often been mistaken for sisters which, as first cousins, was close enough. They were both the same height at five-seven, sharing their mothers' pronounced cheekbones, slanted dark eyes, and full, stubborn lips. But where Imani's complexion evoked comparisons to rich milk chocolate, Jada was a shade lighter, a smooth terra-cotta. Were it not for the threats issued by the ratings-conscious producer at WJZ-TV Channel 13 where she was a popular news anchor, Jada would have duplicated her cousin's curly natural, replete with a clenched-fist Afro pick—the kind where the steel teeth broke off if your hair was too nappy—for good measure. But Neil Greenberg had warned Jada in no uncertain terms that their viewers might not take too kindly to an Afro-wearing anchorwoman—never mind that their Baltimore-area viewing audience was predominantly black. Afros were not politically correct anymore, he'd insisted, suggesting that a shoulder-length relaxed mane was more suitable. She'd chopped it off the very next day, and when she strolled into the station sporting a dramatic pixie cut, the length rising on the top no higher than a pinky finger, she swore they'd have to rush the apoplectic man to the nearest hospital.

Even now Imani chuckled at the memory, the wicked satisfaction in Jada's voice when she'd phoned Imani from her office before going on the air. "Girl, you-know-what has hit the fan for sure this time!"

Imani sipped her strawberry daiquiri. "Do you think Marcus will like the groom's cake we selected?"

Jada waved a dismissive hand, the diamond solitaire on her left hand glinting under the restaurant's low, recessed lights. "You know that man doesn't care. He probably doesn't even know that a groom can *get* his own cake."

"Prior to helping you plan this wedding," Imani murmured wryly, "I didn't know either."

Jada laughed. "I think he'll like it, though, the way it'll be shaped like a lightbulb to reflect his occupation. Girl, I thought that was such a neat idea." Jada's fiancé, Marcus Hooks, was an electrician. Prior to launching his own contracting business last year, he'd worked for Baltimore Gas and Electric. On a service call to Jada's downtown apartment, he'd shown up in uniform, navy blue coveralls and construction boots—and that was all she wrote. She fell in love with the ruggedly handsome utility worker on sight.

"Forget those pinstripe-wearing Wall Street types," was Jada's longtime mantra. "Give me a brother who knows how to work with his hands, who ain't afraid to get 'em a little dirty. Now *that's* what I'm talking about."

She hadn't cared one iota that all her girlfriends and coworkers thought she could do better than an electrician. Her flagrant disregard for others' opinions was just one of the many things that Imani adored about her cousin.

As inseparable as they were, everyone had been shocked when they decided to attend different universities. While Imani accepted a full academic scholarship from the University of Maryland, Jada remained steadfast in her childhood oath to graduate from a historically black institution. At Howard University, she majored and excelled in journalism, pledged Delta Sigma Theta sorority, and graduated summa cum laude.

Not that attending different universities could have kept the two of them apart. The close proximity of their schools only made it easier for them to continue living in each other's back pockets. They made full use of public transportation until Imani inherited her mother's old Volvo. Weekends together were spent cramming for exams, looking out for each other at campus parties, or taking spontaneous road trips to New York for Jamaican beef patties in Brooklyn and forays to the Guggenheim in Manhattan. Broadway performances were usually beyond their budget, a rare indulgence undertaken to celebrate an aced exam or assuage the heartache of a relationship gone sour.

"Something wrong with your pasta?" Jada inquired, watching her cousin push the noodles around her plate disinterestedly.

"No," Imani answered quickly before Jada could summon the waitress to complain about the meal. Even as a child, Jada had never been one to hold her tongue, demanding to see the manager before she was even old enough to foot the bill. Imani could not remember how many times she had left establishments ducking her head in embarrassment over her cousin's antics.

"I think I lost my appetite somewhere after the tenth piece of cake we sampled," she drawled.

Jada arched a perfectly sculpted eyebrow, courtesy of her favorite makeup artist at the MAC store at Pentagon City Mall. "What did you think I meant when I told you we were going to a *cake tasting*?" she asked pointedly.

"I didn't think you meant I had to fast weeks beforehand in order to have some semblance of an appetite afterward."

"Girl, please. Any excuse for you not to eat. Don't think I haven't noticed the way you've been going lately, snacking here and there, not getting enough sleep."

Imani dropped her fork onto the plate, abandoning all pretenses of eating. "You've been talking to my mother again," she said, frustration edging her voice.

"So what? The woman's worried sick about you, and with good reason." Her expression softened with concern. "Mani, you know you can't keep blaming yourself for Althea Pritchard's disappearance. And don't even try telling me you're not," she added when Imani opened her mouth to protest, "because I know you."

Imani averted her gaze, becoming absorbed in a study of an elderly couple seated three tables away. Their hands were clasped across the table as they smiled into each other's eyes. Imani wondered idly if they were married and what it must feel like to be in love with the same person for so long. Her parents had been robbed of the opportunity to grow old together.

When she spoke at last, her voice was low. "I keep wondering if things might have been different if we'd had the meeting somewhere else, like on campus or something. Or if I'd adamantly insisted on driving her back to her dorm instead of letting her take the shuttle alone—"

Jada sat forward in her chair. "Stop right there. Don't say another word."

"Jada—"

"No, I'm not going to sit here and let you blame yourself for what happened to Althea. You know very well it wasn't your fault."

"I know, but—"

Jada shook her head emphatically. "But nothing. You've held meetings with your students before, and nothing ever happened. Besides, no one knows where exactly Althea disappeared. She could have been on campus, for all you know. And as for taking her home, she refused your offer because she wasn't going straight back to the dorm. What else could you do?"

Imani lifted her shoulders in a defeated shrug. "I don't know. I just feel so helpless . . . so useless."

Jada gazed at her, recognizing the familiar guilt in her best friend's eyes. "Don't do this to yourself, Imani," she murmured gently. "Don't go down that road again."

Imani felt her throat tightening and reached for her glass of water. The water felt like sandpaper going down her constricted throat.

"I know it's hard to sit around waiting for something to happen," Jada continued in the same soothing tone, "but you don't have much of a choice. Let the police and FBI do their jobs."

"The way they did before." The minute Imani heard the bitter words leave her mouth, she wanted to snatch them back. They were futile, as pointless as all the time and energy she'd wasted on anger and blame.

She forced an apologetic smile. "I'm sorry, girl, I don't mean to be such a drag. Especially since our outings together are numbered."

"What's that supposed to mean?"

Imani laughed. "Oh, you know you and Marcus will hardly come up for air once you're married."

Jada grinned. "You've got a point there. That man's gotta make up for all these months he's been neglecting me, trying to establish his business." She wriggled her eyebrows suggestively. "You know I'm looking forward to having him all to myself on our honeymoon."

"I don't doubt that," Imani murmured dryly.

"Speaking of marriage," Jada said, signaling the waitress for the check, "what's up with you and David?"

"Nothing. Why?"

"My point exactly. I thought we'd be planning a double wedding by now."

Imani shrugged dispassionately. "I don't think I'm ready for all that right now. Marriage, as you well know, is a serious commitment."

Jada sent her a knowing look. "Um-hmm."

"What? What's that supposed to mean?"

"You know what your problem is, don't you? You don't love him."

"That's ridiculous," Imani protested vehemently. "I *do* love David. How can you even say something like that?"

Jada watched her, deadpan. "You love him, yes. But you're not *in* love with him. There's a big difference."

"I don't know what you're talking about. I've known David practically all my life—"

"Which is what makes him such a safe choice. Familiarity breeds comfort."

"I thought familiarity bred contempt," Imani countered sarcastically.

"Not in your case. Tell me something," Jada said, eyes narrowed shrewdly on Imani's face, "do you honestly think that you and David are ever going to get back together?"

Imani shrugged a dismissive shoulder. "It's possible. We've always been very close. And we still enjoy each other's company." At Jada's skeptical look, she added defensively, "We're taking things one day at a time, that's all."

"Listen to yourself. Does any of that sound right to you? You and David have been together for years, and then all of a sudden you break up, leaving the door open for a future reconciliation. You date occasionally, no sex and no strings attached, yet you feel obligated to keep him around instead of being honest with yourself and admitting that David is not the right one for you. As a result, you have convinced yourself that it is a mortal sin to even *look* at another man, much less date one." She paused before continuing gently. "I know why you're doing this to yourself, Imani. It's because your father handpicked David for you, and in some way you feel that you would be betraying his memory by not marrying David."

Imani glanced quickly around the restaurant in search of eavesdroppers and to avoid her cousin's stare. Jada's words were hitting too close to home, inflicting unwelcome feelings of guilt. "I don't want to discuss this right now."

"Look," Jada said at her cousin's lethal tone, "don't shoot *me*. I'm just the messenger."

"Well," Imani said through gritted teeth, "I don't recall signing for the delivery."

They said their good-nights in the large parking lot outside the restaurant, kissing each other's cheeks. Their parting was unaffected by the heated words exchanged over dinner. Both women knew that it would take a lot more than a mild disagreement to threaten their rock-solid friendship. Blood's thicker than water, Jada would always remind her. Imani smiled at that as she waved at her cousin's passing champagne-colored Camry.

There was a slip of granite-colored paper wedged between Imani's windshield wipers. The edges fluttered in the chilly night breeze like a ghostly summons. She thought nothing of it as she reached out, dislodging the paper and preparing to discard it along with the countless other unsolicited flyers she received—offers for discounted carpet cleaning, auto detailing, advertisements for local hair salons. She unfolded the paper, read it—and froze.

Printed on the paper was a strange cryptic note, almost chilling in its brevity.

THE PLAYERS HAVE BEEN SELECTED.
LET THE GAMES BEGIN . . .

Shaken, Imani swung her frantic gaze around the half-empty parking lot. The elderly couple she'd observed earlier was walking in the opposite direction, their hands still joined. As their footsteps receded, an eerie silence descended upon the darkened lot.

Without wasting another second, Imani hurried back to the safety of the restaurant, her cell phone already in hand.

Garrison Wade arrived within minutes of her call.

From inside the restaurant's waiting area, Imani watched as he veered to the curb and climbed out, his long-legged strides carrying him forward with purpose. Although the temperature had dropped to fifty degrees that evening, he wore no coat over his dark suit, showing a reckless disregard for the elements.

Imani stepped outside to meet him. "Thanks for coming. That was fast."

"I was nearby in College Park," he answered, and those fathomless black eyes settled upon her face. "Are you all right?"

She nodded jerkily, oddly touched by his concern, although she knew it was strictly professional in nature. Her hand trembled as she passed him the note.

Garrison accepted the paper and read it—quickly first, then again slowly, his blood growing colder with each typed word. He lifted his sharpened gaze to her face. "You said you found this on your windshield?"

She nodded, fighting a tremor that had nothing to do with the cold. "What do you think it means?"

"I don't know." His expression was grim as he carefully folded the paper and slid it inside a plastic bag he'd extracted from his breast pocket. "We'll see if we can lift some prints, although it's highly unlikely. Whoever left this probably wore gloves."

"Why do you think the note was left for *me*?"

Dark, assessing eyes met hers. He looked like he was trying to decide whether or not to be honest with her. She shivered inside her peanut butter wool coat, her imploring gaze never leaving his.

Finally he said, "I'm going inside to talk to the hostess for a minute, see if anyone saw anything. Why don't you wait inside my truck? It's warm in there."

"But—"

"I won't be long." With a gentle but firm hand on her arm, he ushered her into the waiting truck before she could utter another protest, locking the doors behind her. The leather interior was immaculate. His clean scent lingered in the air, soap and the subtle spice of expensive cologne. Polo, she decided, then berated herself for taking note of such a trivial thing at a time like this.

He returned after a few minutes, climbing into the truck. He turned halfway in his seat to face her, his expression still grim. "No one saw anything unusual. It was a long shot, anyway. How long had you been parked here?"

"Since about four. We were going to have dinner first—"

"We?"

"My cousin and I. We were going to a cake tasting in Baltimore, and the appointment time got changed at the last minute, so I just left my Jeep here and rode with her."

"So that means your Jeep was parked here at least four hours." More than enough time for anyone to plant the note and slip away undetected. But when? Had she been followed to the restaurant? Or had she been tracked from Baltimore? His mind clicked with all the possibilities, but no matter how he looked at it, each outcome suggested premeditation. As much as he'd have liked to dismiss the note as a stupid prank, every gut instinct warned him it wasn't. The eerie message rang like a bell of doom in his head: *The players have been selected. Let the games begin . . .*

Players. For some reason, Imani Maxwell had been chosen to participate. But in what kind of game?

Imani was watching his face carefully, noting the imperceptible tightening of his square jaw. "There's something you're not telling me."

He didn't answer, a habit that was beginning to wear on her already frayed nerves. Finally he said, "I called Detective Moses, told him to get some men down here to search the area. I've also requested an ERT."

"ERT?"

"Evidence Response Team." His eyes lifted to the rearview mirror, which afforded him a view of the dense, dark woods flanking the restaurant. He added softly, almost to himself, "There may be something we're missing here."

Something or someone. Imani shuddered at the unspeakable thought, drawing Garrison Wade's gaze back to her. "Where are you parked?" he asked. "I'll follow you home."

Ordinarily, she would have protested, put up a fight. But the reality that someone with a sinister agenda may have followed her there that evening struck undeniable fear in her heart. She didn't even object when Garrison took her keys from her numb fingers and climbed behind the wheel of her Jeep. He started the engine for her after a careful inspection of the interior.

"Nothing's been tampered with," he assured her. "Get in and I'll follow you."

When they reached Imani's house, she invited Garrison inside for a cup of coffee. She told herself that her solicitude had more to do with good manners than the fact that she was suddenly leery of her own shadow and didn't want to be alone.

"Hope you're not afraid of dogs," she said over her shoulder as she unlocked the front door, "because I have one."

"I'll consider myself forewarned," Garrison drawled with wry humor.

"He's a sweetheart once you get to know him," she continued, flicking on a switch. Warm, yellow light, soft as butter, flooded the foyer. As if on cue, Shiloh trotted from the kitchen. "Hey, boy," she greeted him, hoping to put him at ease in the presence of their visitor. "It usually takes him a while to warm to stran—" She broke off in midsentence as, to her utter amazement, Shiloh went straight to Garrison. Garrison knelt down, and the golden retriever wagged his tail blissfully as Garrison scratched behind his ear.

Imani's mouth hung open. "He likes you," she said, half accusingly.

Garrison looked up at her with an easy smile, flashing strong white teeth and a dip in his right cheek that hinted at an incredibly appealing dimple. And for the first time, she noticed that he had long black lashes, the kind that any woman would kill for. *Oh, Lord.*

"What's his name?"

"Huh? Oh. Shiloh."

"That's a good name," he crooned to the dog, who promptly rolled onto his back and offered his belly for scratching. Garrison chuckled, and it was an unexpectedly sexy sound. Imani's heart skipped several beats.

To distract herself, she crossed to the thermostat and adjusted the heat settings. "It took him forever to get used to me," she complained. "You're here all of—what?—ten seconds and he's putty in your hands." Not to mention the fact that the dog could barely tolerate David.

Garrison rose to his full height, suddenly dominating the tiny space with the sheer width and breadth of his wide shoulders. "When I was a kid, my mother wouldn't let us get a dog. She said she had enough hounds to clean up after, between me and my brothers."

Imani shrugged out of her coat, her curiosity piqued. "How many brothers do you have?"

"Two."

"*Three* boys?" Imani shook her head sympathetically. "That poor woman."

Garrison chuckled. "That's what she used to say." He stepped aside as she approached to hang her coat in the closet. She wore a form-fitting buttoned dress that belted at the waist, accentuating her graceful curves. The earthy brown material blended beautifully with her skin tone, and in the warm light he saw that she wore a soft shade of raisin on her lips. The glossy sheen made her pouty lips look moist and inviting. He was jarred by a sudden jolt of hunger in his lower belly.

She turned, at that moment, and their gazes collided. The moment stretched into two.

Garrison stepped back, willing the coiled tension from his body. His attraction to Imani Maxwell was a lousy inconvenience. He was here to help solve an abduction, nothing else.

Imani looked equally unsettled. "Let me start that coffee," she muttered, carefully sidestepping him to head toward the kitchen. She waved in the general vicinity of the living room, adding over her shoulder, "Make yourself comfortable, Agent Wade." He knew it was no accident that she inserted his title, firmly establishing distance between them. He'd do well to remember that himself.

Bemused, he moved toward the brick fireplace. On the mantel were several wood-framed photographs. Garrison studied images of Imani with people he presumed to be her parents, an attractive older couple with laughing dark eyes and warm smiles. Next to that photograph was a brown-skinned brother with a serious expression, a trim goatee framing a no-nonsense mouth. Another photo revealed a pretty woman whom Imani bore a striking resemblance to, and it was with some surprise that Garrison recognized the anchorwoman from Channel 13.

He picked up the photograph and turned as his hostess reentered the room. "Are you two related?" he asked.

Imani nodded. "Cousins. Our mothers are twins."

"No wonder. You look so much alike." He returned the frame to its place, nodded at the unsmiling man. "Your brother?"

Again she nodded, and Garrison was irritated to feel relief. For some reason, he hadn't wanted to imagine a boyfriend or lover holding such a place of honor next to her family members.

He should have known, right then and there, that he was in trouble.

"His name's Irvin. We all call him Vin because that's the only part of his name I could manage when I was a baby."

Garrison smiled. "Does he live in the area?"

"D.C. He's an auditor for the Department of Housing and Urban Development."

"Ah, an accountant. That explains it." At her quizzical look, he nodded toward the photo, explaining, "He seems pretty serious."

Imani bit her lip to keep from grinning because that was the only way Irvin Maxwell, Jr. could be described. Serious as a walking heart attack, they'd always teased him. And Garrison Wade had discerned this.

"Coffee's almost ready. We can have it in the kitchen."

As Garrison followed her, he forced himself not to notice the shapely expanse of her calves that weren't covered by the brown leather boots she wore. The spiky heels made a staccato rhythm on the gleaming hardwood floor.

"This is a nice place you have," he commented, sitting at the small oak table and watching steam rise from the coffeemaker. "How long have you been living here?"

"About a month. I'm renting, actually. The owner's a colleague of mine, and he gave me a really great deal." Imani reached up, removing two ceramic mugs from the cabinet above the stove. The fabric of her dress stretched snug across her hips with the movement. Garrison cleared his throat, averting his gaze.

"How do you take yours?"

"Strong. Black."

Not unlike yourself. The thought rose suddenly, unbidden, making Imani blush like a schoolgirl. She scooped cream and sugar into her coffee, probably too much in her haste, then carried the mugs over to the table.

"Thanks," Garrison said, accepting his from her hand, careful not to let their skin touch. She made good coffee, he decided after a sip. Not like the watered-down muck Eddie offered him every morning at the office.

Imani took the chair across from him. "Should I be worried for my safety?" she broached the subject foremost in their minds—or at least it would have been, were it not for these crazy undercurrents passing between them.

Garrison lifted his dark gaze to hers. "I don't want to alarm you," he said quietly.

"Someone left a threatening note on my windshield. I think it's a bit late for that."

"We don't know that it wasn't a prank."

Her eyes narrowed suspiciously. "You don't believe that any more than I do." When he didn't answer right away, her hands tightened reflexively around her coffee mug. Frustration brought her forward in her seat. "I'm not a child, Agent Wade. I deserve to know if my life is in danger."

His expression was impenetrable as he answered evenly, "There is a possibility, yes." Garrison was confused by his own evasive response. He'd leveled with Louis Pritchard about the harsh reality of the situation. Why did he feel the need to protect this woman from the truth?

Imani felt the air escape from her lungs, soft and shaky. It wasn't the answer she'd hoped to hear. Her fault. She shouldn't have asked if she couldn't handle it.

"I can't believe this is happening," she murmured, lifting the coffee to her lips with a trembling hand. "First Althea's disappearance, now this . . . It's all so surreal."

Garrison watched her quietly, anger tightening in his gut. Anger at some unnamed threat, a faceless enemy that held them hostage to the unknown. He said in a low voice, "I'm going to do everything in my power to find whoever's behind this. I promise you that."

She looked at him, saw the steel resolve in his eyes, and knew he meant what he said. She didn't believe in heroes anymore, had stopped looking for Superman long ago. But for some reason, Garrison Wade made her feel safe, and it had little to do with the weapon she knew from past experience was strapped to a shoulder holster beneath his suit jacket. Just as instinctively, she knew it was dangerous to trust so easily, so foolishly.

Shiloh padded into the kitchen just then and claimed his favorite corner of the room. As they watched, the golden retriever settled down on the floor, burrowed into his front paws, and drifted off to sleep.

Garrison finished his coffee and stood. "I'd better head back to Laurel, see if Detective Moses and his men have made any progress. Thanks for the coffee."

Imani rose from the table with him. "Thank you for following me home."

"Not a problem. I'll send an agent out here to do some surveillance." He paused. "Are all your windows locked?"

"Yes." She managed a weary smile of appreciation for his concern. "I'll walk you out."

As they neared the front door, the doorbell rang, pealing through the silence of the house. They exchanged glances, Garrison's thick eyebrow raised questioningly. "Are you expecting anyone tonight?"

"No." She moved toward the door and called out, "Who is it?"

"It's me, baby. Open up, it's cold out here."

Relief and something she couldn't identify—guilt maybe?—surged through her as she unlocked the door. "Hey," she greeted David warmly. "What're you doing here? I thought you'd be working late tonight."

He lifted the leather briefcase in his hand. "Brought it home with me." He bent, planting an unexpected kiss on her mouth. His lips were soft and cool. Familiar.

He shouldered past her into the house. "Hope you don't mind. I just wanted to see—" He broke off, noticing Garrison for the first time. He stiffened in surprise. "I'm sorry. I didn't realize you had company."

Imani stepped forward quickly, performing the introductions. "David, this is Special Agent Garrison Wade. Agent Wade, this is David Scott."

The two men shook hands, coolly assessing one another. David looked askance at Imani. "Did something happen?"

Her glance shot to Garrison, who remained silent, observing. "It's a long story," she answered.

David frowned. "Well, I'll be here all night," he said, the implication clear. Imani didn't know whether it was for her benefit or Garrison Wade's.

Garrison moved to the door, opening it. "I'll send that car out."

Imani swallowed, her hand pressed to her cheek. Her skin felt flushed, and she didn't know why. "Thanks again. Good night."

He nodded shortly, closing the door behind him. David whirled on her. "Are you going to tell me what's going on?" he demanded.

"Someone left a note on my truck this evening," she explained, helping him out of his cashmere overcoat.

"What do you mean, a 'note'? What did it say?"

"I don't want you to worry—"

"Imani," David warned sharply.

She stood with his heavy coat draped over her arm and, in a resigned tone, recited the chilling message she knew would haunt her for a lifetime.

David jerked at her words, concern filling his eyes. "What's that supposed to mean?"

"I don't know, David. I'm afraid it has something to do with Althea's disappearance."

"What's he going to do about it? What was his name again, Agent—"

"Wade," she supplied, hanging up David's coat. "He's sending an agent out here to watch the house for a while. And the police are searching the area behind the restaurant, just in case."

"I knew I did the right thing by coming over tonight. It's like I just knew something didn't *feel* right, and I couldn't get here fast enough." He slid his arms around her waist, burying his face in the curve of her neck. "God, I don't know what I'd do if anything ever happened to you," he said with a ragged breath. "You've been in my life for so long. You're a part of me now, Imani."

"I know," she murmured, allowing herself to bask in his fragrant warmth. But as she closed her eyes, it wasn't David's scent she was remembering.

It was after eleven-thirty by the time Garrison returned to his downtown Baltimore apartment. A search of the woods behind the Laurel restaurant had turned up no clues, much as he'd suspected.

"This nutcase is playing with us," Detective Moses had growled in disgust after reading the cryptic note. "He's sending us on a wild goose chase while he sits back and laughs at us."

Garrison didn't have to guess the identity of the "he" Aaron Moses referred to. Like a rabid pit bull, the detective had seized Malik Toomer as their prime suspect and wouldn't let go. He was one step away from slapping the cuffs on the kid and throwing away the keys. Although Garrison hadn't ruled Toomer out as a suspect, he also understood that they didn't have time to go on witch hunts. With abduction cases, time was something they never had enough of.

The media had converged upon the restaurant by the time he returned. News vans lined the curb and helicopters swarmed overhead to film footage of the police trudging through the dark woods. Garrison had instructed Moses and the others not to provide any details to the press, but that didn't stem the flow of speculation.

"Agent Wade, does this search have any connection to the Pritchard kidnapping investigation?" the reporters shouted at him from behind the yellow police tape. "Can you confirm reports that a note was left on the windshield of an unidentified restaurant patron this evening?"

"No comment," Garrison said flatly, bypassing their microphones and the oppressive glare of their cameras. The last thing he wanted was a herd of reporters camping out at Imani Maxwell's home, disrupting her privacy and harassing her as she tried to go about her business.

He'd missed dinner altogether, but what Garrison craved more than nourishment was a long, hot shower. Ignoring the blinking message light on his phone, he stripped out of his clothes and headed for the apartment's only bathroom.

As the hot water pelted his torso and sluiced down his body, he reviewed the day's events in his mind, turning over facts and theories. Hypotheses churned in his brain like mathematical equations.

Shutting off the water a few minutes later, he toweled himself dry and put on a pair of black sweat shorts. Dialing a number to retrieve his voice mail messages, he listened to a series of calls pertaining to cases that had been reassigned since he had been placed on special assignment. Special Agent Collins, who'd taken over one of his murder cases, wanted his advice on pursuing a particular lead. Cradling the phone to his ear, Garrison scribbled a reminder to himself to return the calls tomorrow.

Desiree Williams's voice, sultry with sleep, greeted him last. "Hey, there. I was on duty this evening. I got home a little while ago and woke up thinking about you, wondering how things were going. I didn't want to call your cell phone in case you were in the middle of some top-secret federal negotiation or something." Her chuckle filled the air, low and soft.

Garrison walked barefoot to the kitchen as her voice continued in his ear. "Anyway, I just wanted to make sure you haven't ruptured those stitches again, Mr. Tough Guy. Lorna told me you came in the other day, surly as ever. Anyway, call me when you get in. Any time, it doesn't matter. I'll be here."

Garrison deleted the message and set the cordless phone

down on the counter. He closed his eyes briefly, as if to shut out the memory of the fateful night he had sought refuge in Desiree Williams's arms. A night on which his life had been irrevocably changed.

He pulled open the Sub-Zero refrigerator—probably the most expensive thing he owned—and grabbed a bottled water, draining it in ten seconds flat. A man of simple tastes, Garrison had made an exception in purchasing the costly refrigerator because he had to have his beverages ice cold, so cold you got a brain freeze if you drank too fast.

Next he reached for a cherry Popsicle, discarding the wrapper along with the empty water bottle. Desiree had once told him that he had an oral fixation. She discerned this by the way he kept his mouth constantly busy—be it chewing gum, a toothpick or lollipop, it didn't matter the vice.

Garrison had chuckled at the idea. "Is that an official diagnosis, Dr. Williams?"

"Yep. After a long-term observation of the patient, that is my medical opinion." She sent him a wicked look from beneath her lashes. "But I'm not complaining. That must be what makes you such an amazing kisser, all that exercise your tongue gets."

Garrison grimaced at the memory, regretting the impulsive decision that had complicated an otherwise platonic relationship between friends—for friends was all he and Desiree Williams could ever be, even if he'd wanted otherwise. Smart, beautiful, a well-respected emergency room physician at Sinai Hospital in Baltimore, they'd met through his mother, whose own doctor's office was located at the hospital. Although Desiree had expressed an immediate interest in him, Garrison had not reciprocated her feelings, much to his matchmaking mother's chagrin. As attractive and successful as Desiree Williams was, Garrison knew he could never offer her more than friendship. Which only compounded his guilt over the way he had crossed the line on that devastating night four years ago. The fact that it had happened only once did not lessen his sense of responsibility or the remorse he felt each time he gently rebuffed Desiree's advances.

As Garrison chewed on the bare Popsicle stick, he realized that Desiree had been right, at least, about his oral fixation. It reminded him of his mother's insistence that he'd been born hot-blooded.

"Could never keep a blanket on you, even when you were a baby," she'd clucked in exasperation during one of his recent visits. He had arrived with no coat on. "You'd kick the blanket right off the minute it touched your skin. That's why you hate wearing coats now. You never wondered? Hot-blooded, that's what you are, boy."

And all this time Garrison had attributed his coat aversion to the nature of his profession, the need to be able to reach for his weapon on the turn of a dime without the hindrance of extra layers of clothing.

Tossing away the Popsicle stick, Garrison left the kitchen and headed back down the hall to his bedroom. He climbed into the king-sized bed, sliding beneath the crisp sheets. But once his head hit the pillow, he felt wide awake and restless.

He sat up and swung his long legs over the side of the bed, his mind on alert mode. He knew it had nothing to do with the coffee he'd shared with Imani Maxwell earlier. At the thought of her, his pulse skipped. She fascinated him as no other woman ever had. There was an unmistakable chemistry between them, the electric kind that scorched nerve endings and promised indescribable pleasure. Their attraction was a powder keg waiting to be detonated.

To distract himself from such dangerous musings, Garrison stood and crossed the large, sparsely furnished room to his dresser. Grabbing a notepad and pen, he settled in the leather chair by the window overlooking downtown Baltimore. The city lights twinkled below him, illuminating the night sky. With the silvery moonlight as his guide, he sketched out a diagram with Althea Pritchard's name at the center and lines pointing outward. At the top of each line, he wrote the names of people directly connected to the missing girl. Louis and Barbara Pritchard, Malik Toomer, Imani Maxwell, Althea's best friend, Elizabeth Torres. From these subjects, he scribbled names associated with each individual. Louis Pritchard had political rivals and disenfranchised constituents who had not voted him into office. Malik Toomer had frat brothers and teammates, Elizabeth Torres had her own circle of friends—not all of whom had appreciated her friendship with the county executive's overachieving niece.

And then there was Professor Imani Maxwell.

Garrison paused, tapping the pen against the notepad. Now that the perpetrator had made the first move by drafting Imani into the so-called game, the waters were more murky than ever. Had the note been planted on her truck as a diversion? Was it simply, as Detective Moses insisted, to send them on a wild goose chase?

Garrison stared at Imani's name again. He knew very little about her. What possible reason could someone have for singling her out alongside Althea Pritchard? Did the kidnapper believe she'd witnessed something incriminating? Or was her inclusion in the "game" to satisfy a personal vendetta? A disgruntled former student, perhaps?

The questions and scenarios swirled in his head at warp speed. Beside Imani's name, he listed *students, colleagues,* and *David Scott.*

It wasn't much, Garrison knew, but it was a start. The key to Althea Pritchard's whereabouts was out there somewhere. Now it had become a race against time . . . and the whim of an unknown predator.

Chapter 6

She awakened to a dull throb in her head, the metallic taste of blood in her mouth.

Her tongue felt thick and heavy, swollen to twice its normal size. Her ribs felt bruised, like she had been hit by a steamroller. She tried to open her eyes before remembering the coarse band of cloth knotted around her head, blindfolding her.

She didn't know how many hours or days had passed since she'd been brought to this place. Her prison, she'd come to call it.

The air was damp and stale, with traces of a cloying odor she couldn't immediately identify. The space felt hollow, echoing every now and then with sounds from above. Disturbing sounds. Once she thought she heard a scream filled with unimaginable terror, but when it was followed by dead silence, she told herself she'd only imagined it. And then she realized the scream had been ripped from her own throat as she surfaced from a nightmare.

Only to discover that the nightmare had only just begun.

She was lying sideways on a hard wooden platform. When she raised her knees, they collided with a cold cement wall. Her arms and legs were bound, a strip of duct tape plastered across her mouth. It occurred to her, belatedly, that the tape was new. Meant to silence her screams.

And that's when the hot fear coursed through her veins.

She heard the heavy fall of footsteps on stairs. Her heart pounded with each menacing step that drew her captor closer. She heard the abrasive scratch of a match striking, heard the soft hiss of a flame growing near. She squinted against the blindfold, struggling to make out a shadow or silhouette—something, anything.

Her next and last scream was swallowed, savagely shoved back down her throat.

Chapter 7

It was always with myriad emotions that Imani returned to her childhood home in Upper Marlboro. That Friday evening was no exception.

For several minutes after she pulled into the circular driveway behind her mother's Buick, she sat contemplating the red brick façade of the three-story Georgian colonial. The entrance was decorated with columns stretching nearly to the gabled roof. The large magnolia tree she and Vin had climbed as children stood proud and erect, its yellow-brown fall leaves creating a blanket on the manicured lawn, now maintained by the neighbor's fifteen-year-old son, who used the extra cash flow to purchase the latest designer clothing.

They'd moved into the house when Imani was eight, and she still remembered the shining excitement in her father's eyes when he brought them to see their new home for the first time. She still remembered the way her mother had gasped and clapped a trembling hand to her mouth. She had exclaimed that the house was too much and they could never afford it. Imani and Vin had already spilled from the family station wagon and had begun racing around the front yard that was twice the size of their old one.

Imani sighed aloud. There was no denying that the house held precious memories for her, some that brought tears of pure joy, or nostalgic recollections of a first date or a new driver's license. But it was the more recent memories, the ones cloaked in heavy sorrow, that kept her away more often than she dared admit.

The house was dark and silent when she entered. She made her way to a Victorian lamp resting upon the cherry-wood console, turning it on and bathing the spacious foyer in soft light. Cathedral ceilings stretched upward from golden pine floors. Custom crown moldings created an elegant finish.

"Mom?" Imani called out. Her voice sounded hollow in the stillness of the house. An unnamed fear wound its way into her heart and quickened her steps as she passed the empty living room and made her way to the spacious gourmet kitchen in the rear.

"Mom?" she called again when she was greeted by an empty kitchen. She spun on her heel and retraced her steps to the foyer, hurrying up the winding staircase. Her father's handsome face smiled down at her from a portrait hung on the maple sugar walls. His dark, intuitive eyes seemed to follow her progress at every turn. After his death, Vivienne Maxwell had enlarged every photograph she could find, filling nearly every available space with his cherished image.

At the end of the wide corridor on the second floor, the door to Imani's parents' bedroom was closed. Soft light slipped from beneath the door, but there was no sound. Imani knocked once, lightly at first, then harder, with growing insistence. There was no response.

She turned the brass doorknob and entered the master suite. "Mom?"

"Imani? In here, baby."

Imani released a breath she hadn't realized she was holding. In the adjoining bathroom, Vivienne Maxwell was immersed in the marble whirlpool tub, her brown body covered in foamy suds from her neck to the tips of her polished toes.

Her full lips spread in a smile, albeit a tired one, at the sight of her daughter. "Hey, baby. I didn't hear you come in."

Imani folded her arms, leaning on the doorjamb and willing her heart to stop racing. She'd overreacted. Again. It wouldn't be the last time. "I thought you were sleeping."

"I was, but your aunt called and woke me up. She wanted me to see some color Jada was wearing on the news. Said she's thinking about wearing the same color to the wedding."

Imani, who had caught a glimpse of the newscast before leaving her house that evening, wrinkled her nose. "Aunt Vanessa can't wear burgundy. She's the mother of the bride. She's supposed to wear cream or something like that. At least that's what all the etiquette books say."

Vivienne heaved a sigh that was part exasperation, part affection. "Don't get me started. You know your aunt marches to the beat of her own drum, always has."

"Like mother, like daughter," both women chimed in unison, then laughed.

"So how was your day? You look tired," Imani remarked, noting the deep shadows under her mother's eyes. She knew chronic insomnia had put them there.

"We implemented a new payroll system today. There were a lot of kinks that had to be worked out. I swear," Vivienne muttered, frowning up at the skylight above the tub, "sometimes I wonder why I don't just walk away from it all. I'm too old for the workplace of tomorrow."

"No, you're not, and the reason you don't walk away is because you love what you do." And because Imani could imagine how much worse off her mother would be without her job as human resources director at the Arlington-based accounting firm where she'd spent her entire career. Lack of employment would surely hasten her descent into severe depression, a path she'd been steadily following for the last six years.

"I *used* to love it," Vivienne corrected her daughter. "Now it all seems so tedious, so unrewarding. Hand me my towel, will you, baby? I'm turning into a raisin in here."

Imani obliged and stepped out of the bathroom to give her mother privacy. Vivienne emerged a minute later, lavender scented and wearing sherry-colored silk pajamas. Her relaxed graying hair, medium length when styled, was wrapped tightly around her head in preparation for the satin bonnet she would don before going to bed.

"How's David?" she asked, sorting clothes to be dry cleaned. Silk blouses and scarves, designer suits that hung a little too loosely on her shrinking frame.

Imani sat on the four-poster Queen Anne bed, idly tracing a pattern in the satin duvet with her finger. She hadn't told her mother about their breakup. "He's fine, working hard. Said he expects to make junior partner soon."

"That's good. If ever there was a man who deserved a promotion, it would have to be David." A poignant smile touched her lips. "Your father always said he had a good work ethic. He said David would have no problems providing for any woman he married."

"I remember," Imani murmured. It was no secret that Irvin Maxwell, Sr. had held David in the highest regard and had hoped to see him become an official member of the family someday. That Imani and David would eventually tie the knot was a foregone conclusion in everyone's minds. Except hers.

Finished with her task, Vivienne joined her daughter on the bed. Her dark eyes were soft with concern. "How are *you* doing? I know it's been a difficult week for you."

"I'm all right." Imani considered, then promptly decided against telling her mother about the threatening note she'd received the day before. Worrying about her child's safety was the last thing Vivienne Maxwell needed. As if she hadn't suffered enough.

"I heard they're having a prayer service for Althea this evening. Are you going?"

Imani nodded. "I wanted to see you first though."

Vivienne smiled, visibly touched. "Have you eaten?" she asked, a gentle hand on Imani's back. "I was just about to have dinner, if you'd like to join me."

The corners of Imani's mouth lifted in a smile. "Thought you'd never ask."

That evening, First Baptist Ministry on Church Street in Upper Marlboro was filled to capacity for the prayer service. People came from all walks of life, from nearly every corner of the community. Men and women with their children in tow. Politicians, loyal constituents, local business owners, Althea's classmates and friends—they filed into the candlelit sanctuary with somber faces and hushed voices. They came to offer support to the devastated county executive and his wife, to lift their voices in prayer and songs of hope. To petition God for a miracle.

Garrison Wade and Detective Cole Porter were standing outside the stucco church building with stained-glass windows when Imani arrived, steering her Jeep into a narrow space in the packed parking lot. Her heartbeat quickened as she climbed out and started toward them, her hands tucked into the pockets of her wool coat. Dried leaves crunched underneath her feet, and a brisk wind pressed against her suddenly flushed face.

At her approach, Garrison murmured something to the detective, and with a short smile and wave at Imani, Cole Porter disappeared through the high arched door.

"Hello." Imani mumbled a polite greeting to Garrison Wade, intending to follow the detective into the building.

"I was hoping to catch you before you went in," Garrison said.

She stopped, turning to face him and thinking how ridiculous it was to be so fearful of this man and the power he wielded so effortlessly over her. She looked up at him expectantly.

"We're setting up a command post at the old Moose Lodge in College Park," he informed her.

"A command post? You mean to organize search efforts?"

"Something like that. It's not routine Bureau procedure to

establish command centers when there haven't been any ransom demands, but that note you received comes close enough. Anyway, Chief Taggert and his men are stretched pretty thin and could use all the help they can get. I've already been in touch with the phone company to set up hotlines for the tips we receive from the public, and a local business is donating copy and fax machines for the flyers. I'd like you to help organize the volunteers, work the phones, supervise operations, whatever's needed. In your spare time, of course. Are you interested?"

Imani didn't hesitate. "Definitely." She welcomed the opportunity to help with the search efforts. If nothing else, she hoped that passing her time in such a purposeful way would prove to be the distraction she so desperately needed. She hated sitting around on her hands, waiting to receive bad news about Althea.

Garrison nodded briskly in satisfaction. "I'll let Taggert know. And I'll have someone make an announcement tonight after the prayer service."

"Thanks for thinking of me," Imani said sincerely.

He shrugged. "I know how much you want to help with the investigation." Their gazes locked and held for a prolonged moment. Again that tingling awareness passed between them.

"You look cold. Let's go inside," Garrison suggested, his hand resting lightly at the small of her back as he guided her toward the door. Imani tried hard not to shiver at the contact.

During the service, Reverend Otis Milsap exhorted the congregation to be vigilant in prayer and steadfast in their faith. "Yea, though I walk through the valley of the shadow of death," he quoted Scripture, "I will fear no evil, for Thou art with me. Your rod and Your staff, O Lord, they comfort me."

Following his brief sermon, the mass choir sang a few selections. By the time they completed a stirring rendition of "Precious Lord, Take My Hand," nearly every hand was lifted to the domed ceiling in praise, and people's hearts and minds were filled with hope and encouragement.

When Louis Pritchard stepped to the podium to speak, a

hushed silence fell over the sanctuary. In a voice tinged with sadness and the quiet dignity that had won him such favor in the community, he shared with the audience how much his niece loved life and enjoyed helping others, how she dreamed of becoming a doctor and providing aid to those in impoverished countries. By the time he finished, there wasn't a dry eye in the house, and everyone was eager to do their part to help bring Althea home.

Imani was heartened by the swarm of citizens who approached her about volunteering. Their genuine concern and willingness to lend their time and support in the search efforts were more than gratifying. They went a long way toward renewing her faith in humanity.

As she stood in the rear of the sanctuary, answering questions about the volunteer center, she was approached by a caramel-skinned woman in a black Chanel maternity dress and low heels. With luxuriant ebony hair framing a gently rounded face that glowed with health and contentment, the sister was a sight to behold.

"Hi, Imani," the woman greeted her in a surprisingly pleasant voice—soft and husky, with just a hint of a southern drawl. "Agent Wade told me to see you about the delivery of some fax and copy machines. I'm Rachel Hunter."

"Oh, yes, hi." Imani smiled, shaking the woman's hand gratefully. "I can't tell you enough how much we appreciate the contribution."

Rachel waved a dismissive hand. "It's the least I can do," she said easily. "Agent Wade provided me with one of Althea's photographs, which I'll use for the flyers. The flyers will include all of the pertinent information—Althea's vital statistics, date of disappearance, contact information."

Imani nodded. "So you're the owner of Calloway by Design?" she asked, citing the prominent graphic design firm located in the city's business district.

"That's right. I'm supposed to be on maternity leave, but sitting home doing nothing has been driving me up the wall."

Imani grinned. "When are you due?"

"End of the month officially, but the doctor says it could be any day now. I've already dilated one centimeter." A poignant smile touched her lips as she stroked her protruding belly. "Nick and I are both hoping for a girl this time, but what's most important is a healthy baby." Her tone softened as she glanced around the room and added, "I think this experience has taught us all how fragile and precious human life is."

"You're right about that," Imani agreed quietly.

They stood for a moment, watching as Louis and Barbara Pritchard were embraced by well-wishers. The county executive brushed back tears as he spoke to his supporters, comforted by their soothing, heartfelt words.

"I know what it's like to lose someone you love," Rachel Hunter said softly, "and I wouldn't wish that upon *anyone.*"

"Neither would I," Imani murmured, thinking of her father and the desolate shell her mother had become in the aftermath of his death.

When Rachel turned back to her, both women's eyes shone with mutual understanding, an unspoken connection. "I wanted to check with you on a good time for delivering the equipment," Rachel continued. "Agent Wade says he and the police will be there at six tomorrow morning, but I know they'll be busy setting up and attending to other things."

"I plan to be there pretty early myself. Is seven-thirty a good time for you?"

Rachel nodded. "I'll make sure the truck is prompt. I'd like to be there to help pass out flyers, but my overprotective husband won't go for it."

"You got that right," concurred the man in question, appearing suddenly at her side.

Imani recognized Nicholas Hunter's good-looking face from television. The high-profile cases he'd prosecuted and won over the years had earned him legendary status in the community, which ultimately had led to his election as state's attorney when Louis Pritchard vacated the office to run for county executive. Hunter's overwhelming popularity with county residents had secured him a landslide victory over his opponent and colleague, the deputy state's attorney.

After Nicholas and Imani exchanged introductions, he turned to his wife. "I know your heart's in the right place, baby, but you're supposed to be on bed rest," he gently reminded her.

Rachel made a face. "Maternity leave," she corrected him. "Bed rest makes it sound so dire, like I'm in serious danger or something."

"You're splitting hairs," Nicholas said, but the adulation in his gaze lessened the disapproval in his deep, resonant voice. Rachel's answering grin was mischievous.

"Don't worry, I won't let her anywhere near the place," Imani reassured Nicholas Hunter.

He flashed her a disarming smile. "Thanks, I'd appreciate that."

"Congratulations on the pending arrival," Imani said to them. "Decided on any names yet?"

"Robert if it's another boy," Rachel answered proudly. "He'll be named after his grandfather."

"And Juanita Simone if it's a girl," Nicholas said.

"After my mother," Rachel added, with a tender look up at her husband. He curved an arm around her expanded waistline and smiled into her eyes as if they were the only two in the room.

As the couple departed a few minutes later, Rachel managed to press her business card into Imani's hand and whisper conspiratorially, "Call and let me know if there's anything else you need. I mean it."

Imani nodded and grinned, already deciding that Rachel Hunter was a sister to have in her corner. Beautiful and big hearted, with her own successful business at that.

Her thoughts were quickly diverted by the sight of Malik Toomer hurrying in her direction. Concerned by the haunted look on his face, she called out, "Malik? Are you all right?"

Without sparing her a glance, he rushed past her and disappeared through the sanctuary doors. She frowned after him, wondering what had spooked him so badly. When she turned her head and met Garrison Wade's speculative gaze, she knew he was thinking the same thing.

By ten o'clock the following day, the command post was bustling with activity. The first two groups of volunteers had been dispatched with flyers to distribute all over the community: to be papered across storefront windows, placed on bulletin boards, stapled to light poles, tucked under windshield wipers, passed along to people on the street. The hotline telephones had been set up, spaced apart on a long bank of conference tables. All four phones were already staffed and busy. Copy and fax machines sat along the opposite wall. At another table, volunteers were stacking up the flyers that had been delivered that morning and running off additional copies as needed. Envelopes, staplers, stamps, and boxes of rubber bands littered every available surface.

Members of the press filed into the room periodically, taping footage of the volunteer efforts and interviewing anyone who seemed willing.

Surveying the chaotic harmony that filled the volunteer center, Imani felt a deep sense of pride wash over her. *Who says black folks don't know how to come together for a common purpose?*

Down the hall, away from the noise of the volunteer station, the police had designated another room a makeshift War Room, where members of the task force gathered to compare notes and collaborate on investigation strategies. Maps of Prince George's County and the state of Maryland covered the bulletin board, red pins poked into them marking search territories. A chart taped to the long wall recorded a timeline of the investigation, from Althea's last sighting to the restaurant parking lot where the note had been found on Imani's Jeep.

Around the donated conference table sat Garrison, Chief

Taggert, Detectives Moses and Porter, Sheriff Garcia and the
deputy sheriff, Special Agent Eddie Balducci from the
Baltimore field office who'd been sent to assist Garrison, a
county prosecutor, and an aide to the county executive who
had been cleared to sit in on the meeting to report back to his
boss on the status of the investigation. As the men sat around
the table chugging inordinate amounts of black coffee and
throwing theories around, tempers were wearing thin. They
had no suspects, no witnesses, no viable leads whatsoever.

And time was running out.

It was in this state that Imani found them when she came
to report that a representative from the National Center for
Missing and Exploited Children was on the line, asking to
speak with Garrison.

Wearing a black scowl, he stood and started from the room.
Instead of a suit and tie, today he wore a black turtleneck over
a pair of khaki trousers and Timberland boots that gave him a
rugged, dangerously masculine appeal. As he drew nearer,
Imani forced herself not to stare at the way the fabric stretched
across the hard, planed muscles of his wide chest.

Otherwise she'd be no better than that loathsome
Detective Moses, who hadn't stopped leering at her since her
arrival at the command post that morning.

"How's everything going?" she asked, following Garrison
from the room. She had to walk fast to keep up with his brisk
long-legged strides down the hall.

In a far corner of the volunteer center, a phone had been
specifically designated for incoming calls for members of
the task force. Garrison scooped up the receiver and spoke
to the representative from the National Center for Missing
and Exploited Children. His posture was rigid, thrumming
with impatience. Imani realized how frustrated he must be
feeling at the moment. Even without having firsthand knowledge, she knew the investigation wasn't going well. Althea
had been missing for nearly seven days now, and so far the
police had no leads and no suspects. The countdown had
begun, and time was their enemy.

Getting off the phone, Garrison walked over to her. "Hey," he said quietly, greeting her for the first time that day.

"Everything okay?" Imani asked.

"Yeah, they just needed some information to include in their national database. And they offered to send a representative down to help. That's the *last* thing we need in there, another helping hand," he grumbled, his expression grim. "There's too much politicking going on as it is."

Imani grimaced, comprehending his meaning. "Too many roosters in the pen, huh?"

"Exactly." Garrison shook his head, the corners of his mouth twitching. And it struck him how easily he fell into a confiding mode with this woman, venting his frustrations as if he'd known her all his life instead of a mere few days.

Imani smiled. "Well, you know how to put 'em in their place," she said, the feistiness of their first encounter surfacing. "Remind them who's in charge."

Garrison chuckled, and was surprised to feel some of the morning's tension ebb from his body. "Maybe you'd better come with me, to back me up. I bet you're no joke in the classroom."

"Yeah, you know I got my students in check," she quipped, surprised by her playfulness.

Garrison smiled a little. "Listen, I didn't mean to be rude a few minutes ago when you came to get me."

Imani waved off the apology. "Don't worry about it, Garrison. I know you have a lot on your shoulders right now. I didn't take it personally." Too late, she realized that she had called him by his first name. The flicker of his dark eyes suggested he'd taken notice, too. Stricken, she hastened to amend, "What I meant is—"

"It's okay," he said huskily. "I was going to suggest that we drop the formal addresses, anyway. Considering that we'll be working so closely together."

"Right. Of course." She glanced away self-consciously, watching as some of the volunteers distributed lunch cartons. A local diner had donated soup and sandwiches and hot chocolate, its contribution to the volunteer efforts.

"So may I?"

Her gaze snapped back to his face. "May you what?"

"Call you Imani." Her name rolled off his tongue beautifully. Heat stung her cheeks. Stupid girl, silly girl.

She affected an air of nonchalance. "Sure. Absolutely."

"Good." He watched her from his superior vantage point, his intense gaze searching her face. "How are you, anyway?"

She shrugged, folding her arms across her chest in an almost protective gesture. "I'm okay. Under the circumstances." She thought of her sleepless night with thoughts of Althea and her own father racing through her mind.

She glanced around the bustling room to divert his attention. "Everyone's doing a really great job here," she said sincerely.

"No question," Garrison agreed, sweeping an appreciative look around.

One table of volunteers was spending their time stamping reward information on flyers. Another table addressed and stuffed envelopes, and yet another sorted the packets by zip code and bagged them for delivery to the post office. The flyers would be sent to law enforcement agencies, civic organizations, businesses, and schools across the country.

"The one bright spot in all this is seeing the community pull together," Garrison said. He didn't voice aloud his very next thought, that no matter how hard they worked or how much they all willed her safe return, they were all at the mercy of Althea's kidnapper. It was that cut and dry.

Frustration simmered in his gut. "Well, I'd better get back in there." Truth be told, he didn't want to sit around talking. He wanted to hit the pavement, pursue leads, and follow them to the ends of the earth, if need be. Hunting fugitives, that's what he did best. But these types of cases were always different. He had to follow protocol, and this meant collaborating with the local authorities, appeasing their need to be involved and consulted every step of the way. And the county executive's personal connection to the victim meant he had to tread with extra caution.

But Garrison's razor-thin patience was quickly evaporating, and if something didn't break soon, he knew he'd have to shake things up a bit—and risk his own neck in the process.

He touched Imani's arm briefly as he made a move to leave. "Thanks again for all your help here. It means a lot to me."

"*Althea* means a lot to me," Imani said softly. "And you don't have to thank me."

He nodded, already heading back down the hall. "I'll talk to you later." Imani watched him go, telling herself that the odd tingling in her arm had nothing whatsoever to do with his fleeting touch.

Liar.

"What's the story with Taggert?" Eddie demanded.

"Meaning?"

"Meaning that he seems a little too eager to curry favor with Louis Pritchard."

Garrison was sifting through pages of printouts, data generated from the list Louis Pritchard's secretary had faxed to him yesterday, one day later than promised.

He didn't miss a beat as he answered, "Porter says Taggert is indebted to Pritchard for saving his job. Seems there was a scandal a few years ago, corruption in the ranks, and the public called for Taggert's resignation. Pritchard came to his defense, said the chief had no way of knowing that one of his detectives was a loose cannon. And since the menace was killed in a fire, there was no point in destroying more lives."

"Very altruistic of Pritchard," Eddie said dryly. "Smells an awful lot like *quid pro quo* to me."

"Why, Edward," Garrison drawled with mock severity, "how very cynical of you. You wouldn't be suggesting that the county executive expected favors from the chief of police in return for his magnanimous gesture, would you? Tsk, tsk."

Eddie grinned. "Shame on me." He glanced out the passenger window at the darkened house on Adelphi Road. The command center had long since been vacated by the task force members and volunteers, and now sat as empty as Imani Maxwell's cozy bungalow. The temperature had dropped, producing a chilly October wind.

"So what're we still doing here? It feels like we're on a stakeout."

"And I know how much you love those," Garrison murmured. Eddie had spent their last surveillance assignment bitterly complaining about everything from the cold to having to urinate every five minutes.

"Like a needle in a haystack," Eddie commented, glancing across at his partner paging through the voluminous printouts he'd provided for him earlier. Eddie had run checks on everyone from Pritchard's list, even cross-referenced data through the FBI's Criminal Justice Information Services Division. If any of Pritchard's associates had so much as a parking ticket, had even *thought* about committing a crime, the FBI knew about it. Big Brother in all its omniscient glory.

"Tell me again why we're watching an empty house?"

"We're watching for suspicious activity," Garrison corrected, still not looking up from his paperwork. "In case our poet decides to leave another masterpiece."

"Ah, that's right. And here I thought we were waiting for the professor to get back from her hot date."

The look Garrison sent him would have sent Goliath scurrying for cover. Eddie only laughed. "Come on, Wade. Tell me she doesn't remind you of a reincarnated Foxy Brown with an Afro. She's got that whole sexy Pam-Grier-meets-Beyoncé-Knowles-in-Austin-Powers thing working for her. Did I ever tell you that Pam Grier used to have a starring role in my dreams, by the way?"

"I'm sure I could have done without that piece of information," Garrison drawled, resuming his search. Or at least attempting to.

"How old is she, by the way?"

"Who? Pam Grier or Beyoncé Knowles?"

"Your professor."

"Twenty-nine. And she's not mine."

"Too bad. She sure is a sweet number."

Garrison's mouth twitched. "You're Italian, Eddie. You're not supposed to like black women—didn't you see *Jungle Fever*?"

Eddie grinned, taking the barb in stride. "I won't tell if you won't." He leaned forward, opening Garrison's glove compartment and thumbing through part of his CD collection, knowing the rest took up considerable wall space in Garrison's apartment. Coltrane, Commodores, Earth Wind & Fire, Bob Marley, Marvin Gaye. The contemporary variety consisted of such artists as Brian McKnight and Anita Baker. And Sade, who helped him unwind at the end of each day, crooning about sweetest taboos and no ordinary loves.

"If you're looking for Sinatra," Garrison said dryly, "you're outta luck."

"Very funny." Eddie settled on the Commodores, popped the disc into the player and selected "Nightshift" because the title seemed apropos. The twitch of Garrison's mouth let him know he'd read his mind. As usual.

Eddie reclined in the scooped leather seat, stretching out his long denim-covered legs.

Eddie was from a family large enough to populate Brooklyn, where they had lived since emigrating from their native Italy. In addition to a bevy of cousins, aunts, and uncles, Eddie had three sisters and two brothers. Both Eddie's father and grandfather, the latter, the irascible patriarch of the Balducci flock, were retired NYPD. That Eddie would follow them into law enforcement was a foregone conclusion, although no one expected him to go a step further and become a fed. Venting their displeasure, they eventually rallied around him and turned his "defection" into fodder for lively debates around the dinner table, as was Balducci custom.

They'd welcomed Garrison into their fold with an ease

that initially surprised him, embracing him as one of their own. Eddie's grandfather, lovingly known to everyone as Pops Balducci, swore that Garrison must have been born Italian in another life. As a result, Garrison had enjoyed many enormous meals at the Balducci home, defending the Bureau and warding off the women's incessant matchmaking attempts right alongside Eddie. While Garrison lived in New York, the Balduccis became his family away from family. When he and Eddie accepted assignment transfers to the Baltimore field office, the family protested for weeks. Eddie's mother and sisters wailed and wrung their hands as if someone had just died. They finally took some consolation in the fact that the two men would remain together and could continue looking out for each other.

"So listen," Eddie said now, "I was thinking about cooking for Annabella one night this week. Maybe you could bring Desiree with you."

"Thanks, but I'll have to pass."

"Come on, Wade. You need to take a breather from this case, and one night off won't make or break the investigation. What's the matter? You don't wanna lead Desiree on by inviting her? That's cool, I can understand that. I think it's respectable the way you've refrained from sleeping with her again all these years. I don't know how you do it, man, but I respect it." He paused. "What?"

Garrison was frowning, but it had nothing to do with Eddie's rambling. "Interesting," he muttered, half to himself. "Torres. Carlos Torres. Ran against Louis Pritchard in the county executive race three years ago."

"And?"

"He took the loss pretty hard. Retired completely from politics after that. Died in a boating accident last summer. Apparently there was some fundraising scandal that cost him the election, and I'll give you three guesses as to whose political camp uncovered the discrepancies."

Eddie's lips spread in a slow grin. "Mr. Quid Pro Quo

himself. Louis Pritchard. Wait a minute." He frowned. "Torres. Isn't Althea's best friend named Elizabeth Torres?"

"One and the same. 'Carlos Torres is survived by his wife, Emilia, and two children, Joaquin and Elizabeth,'" Garrison read from the printout.

Eddie's frown deepened. "Coincidence?"

Garrison folded the paper slowly. "That's what I intend to find out."

Chapter 8

"Professor Maxwell?"

Imani was grading quizzes before class on Monday afternoon. She glanced up from the tidy pile of papers on her desk and smiled at the dark-haired young woman who stood almost hesitantly in her office doorway.

"Is this a bad time?"

"Not at all. Come on in, Elizabeth." Imani rounded her desk and lifted a stack of papers from the chair, then waved her visitor into it. Resettling into her own chair once again, she asked, "How are you doing, Elizabeth?"

Elizabeth Torres's expression clouded as she sat down and crossed her long legs. "Oh, as well as can be expected. You know, with Althea missing and all . . ." She trailed off, tears filling her dark eyes.

Imani opened her desk drawer, retrieving a box of Kleenex and passing it to the girl. She waited in respectful silence as Elizabeth dabbed at her eyes.

"I'm sorry," she mumbled self-consciously. "I just can't believe that she's gone."

"No need to apologize," Imani gently reassured her. "I

understand how difficult this week has been for you, losing your roommate and best friend."

Elizabeth sniffled and gulped wordlessly. Although she was enrolled in another African-American Literature course, Imani had always treated her as one of her own students. A smart, popular freshman business major, Elizabeth Torres commanded the respect and admiration of her peers.

And it didn't hurt that she had the exotic looks of a Latina supermodel.

"What can I do for you, Elizabeth?"

"Well," she began with difficulty, balling the Kleenex in her hand into a damp wad, "I wanted to talk to you about the minority recruitment program."

"Okay." Imani smiled, prompted her to continue.

"Well, I know this may be awkward, under the circumstances, but I wanted to ask you about serving as a student panelist. In case . . . um, well, in case Althea isn't able to." Her gaze shifted, settled on a point beyond Imani's shoulder.

"I see." Imani nodded slowly. "Well, I certainly appreciate your coming to talk to me, Elizabeth. As you know, the student panelist was selected by a committee of department faculty members. We'll be meeting at the end of this week to decide on a course of action and review the other entries, if necessary." She paused, noticing the barely perceptible tightening around Elizabeth's naturally pouty lips. "I believe we already have your submission, is that right?"

Elizabeth nodded, a bit impatiently. "Can you give me an idea of how close my essay was? I mean in terms of being selected the first time around?"

Imani pursed her lips for a moment. "To be honest with you, Elizabeth, I really don't remember. There were so many submissions, and of course so much has happened since then . . ." Her words trailed off, with pointed emphasis.

"Oh, I understand. I feel so bad about what's happened to Althea, and I honestly didn't know what you would think about me coming here like this—"

Imani waved away her concern. "Don't worry about that. I know how much you'd like to participate in the program, and I think you'd make an excellent panelist."

Elizabeth beamed, and was extraordinarily stunning. "I'd really appreciate the opportunity to work with you, Professor Maxwell. I always hear such good things about your classes, and it makes me kick myself for registering for the wrong time. Not that there's anything wrong with Professor Brown's course," she hastened to add at Imani's mildly embarrassed look. "It's just that I wish I were in yours."

"That's very kind of you, Elizabeth. At any rate, I'll let you know when the committee has reached a decision on selecting another student panelist."

Elizabeth looked crestfallen. "All right, thanks," she mumbled dispiritedly.

"Was there anything else?" Imani patiently inquired.

Elizabeth glanced toward the door for a moment. "Well, I was just wondering . . . that is, I wanted to know if you might be able to, um, put in a good word for me. With the committee, I mean."

Imani leaned back in her chair, her eyebrow arched. "I don't have a problem recommending you as a strong candidate, Elizabeth, but the ultimate decision is up to the entire committee. I can't promise you anything. I'm sure you understand that."

"Of course. I just thought . . . well, since you were able to pull a few strings for Althea." Dropping all pretenses, she met Imani's confused look unflinchingly. Almost as a challenge. "Or was that just a special favor to Althea?"

Imani sat forward slowly, deliberately. "What are you suggesting?"

There was no mistaking the threat in Elizabeth's dark eyes now. "I think you know," she said coolly.

Imani's eyes narrowed. She felt her temper flare, felt the rising indignation that would, under vastly different circumstances, make her roll her neck and read sister-girl the riot act. But she had to remind herself that she was an adult dealing with a spoiled seventeen-year-old accustomed to getting her way.

"Tell you what, Elizabeth," Imani said, understated menace in every inflection. "I'm going to pretend that we never had this conversation. I'm sure you didn't intend to imply that I exhibited favoritism in selecting Althea's essay for the program. You know, as well as anyone, that your best friend is more than qualified to serve as a student panelist."

"I know, Professor Maxwell," Elizabeth said, suddenly contrite. "I'm sorry if I've offended you. I didn't mean to, I just wanted to know if there was anything you could do for me."

"Elizabeth, if you had any confidence in yourself, you wouldn't think you needed special favors," Imani said quietly. "You're not always going to get everything you want. Life is full of disappointments. The sooner you accept that, the easier it becomes to roll with the punches."

Something remote flickered in the girl's eyes. "Believe me, Professor," she said with a trace of bitterness, "I know *all* about life's disappointments. I certainly don't need a lecture from you about it."

Imani was silent, regarding the young woman another moment, wondering what had triggered the sudden animosity. Reaching for the sheaf of papers she'd been grading, she said coolly, dismissively, "If there's nothing else, Elizabeth, I'd like to get back to my work."

Elizabeth stood, her shoulders rigid beneath the leather trench she wore. "Thanks for your time, Professor Maxwell." At the door, she turned and looked back at Imani, her gaze hostile. "I guess this means I'd better forget about serving on the panel."

Imani didn't look up from her paperwork. "All submissions will be reviewed by the committee. Including yours. Have a good afternoon."

She thought she heard Elizabeth whisper, "We'll see about that," but when she lifted her head, the doorway was empty.

* * *

Garrison was en route to College Park when his cell phone rang. He picked it up, then gave a clipped, "Wade."

"We got him," Detective Moses spoke without preamble.

"Got who?"

"Toomer. An unidentified woman called the command post this morning to report seeing our little hoop star on the night of Pritchard's disappearance. *Not* in his room like he claimed to be," Moses added with almost sinister glee. Garrison could just imagine the detective salivating at the prospect of getting Malik Toomer alone in a very dark, very tight corner.

"We're on our way to see him now," Moses announced firmly, as if to override any objection Garrison may have posed.

"I'll be there in five." Garrison disconnected, his expression grim. Since Friday night's prayer service, he'd wondered what—or whom—had sent Malik Toomer fleeing from the church like a demon was hot on his heels.

Now it appeared he was about to find out.

Malik's guilty expression spoke volumes.

He sat in a straight-backed chair in his empty dormitory suite, his furtive glance darting between the three men who stood over him, closing in on him, it seemed.

"Y'all still think I had something to do with Althea's disappearance," he said, his voice rising with a nervous tremor. "And I'm telling you that I didn't."

"Then explain why you lied to us about your whereabouts that night," Moses sneered. "And I suggest you start talking fast, boy."

Malik's fearful gaze shot to Garrison, who stood with his shoulder propped against the wall, his arms folded in a relaxed pose. He nodded subtly for Malik to answer the detective.

"I was in my room—"

Moses shoved his face into Malik's, snarled, "Try again, Toomer. Our eyewitness saw you on campus around six-thirty. Says she stopped you and asked for your autograph because she knew you'd be worth millions one day. Don't believe me? She's got the piece of paper with your signature *and* date to show for it." He smirked cruelly. "Ironic, isn't it? Dimed out by an adoring fan."

Malik licked his dry lips. "I only left for an hour. Ask my frat brothers, they'll tell you."

Garrison raised a dubious eyebrow. "The same ones who already told us you never left that night?" He shook his head, a mild rebuke. "You ever heard of obstruction of justice, Malik? Carries a mighty hefty prison sentence."

Malik's eyes watered. Hunching over, burying his face in his hands, he began sobbing uncontrollably. "I-I went to see someone," he choked out. "I knew Althea was coming over, but I wanted to straighten something out first."

Moses exchanged triumphant glances with the silent Cole Porter. Garrison stepped forward, his steely gaze signaling the two detectives to take a step back, give the boy some breathing room. Porter complied at once while Moses did so grudgingly, rigid with defiance.

"Who did you go see, Malik?" Garrison asked quietly.

Malik lifted his tortured gaze to Garrison's face. "Elizabeth."

Garrison felt, rather than saw, Moses and Porter trade knowing looks. Garrison's own expression remained neutral, inscrutable. He waited a beat before stating the obvious. Flatly, with no inflection. "You and Elizabeth were sleeping together."

Malik bobbed his head, shamefaced. "She came to me one night about a month ago. Althea and I had just had an argument. I-I knew it was wrong but—" His voice caught, and he coughed wetly into his hand.

Moses smiled narrowly. "You couldn't resist that fine piece of tail."

"It wasn't like that," Malik wailed. "She was being so nice, so understanding. Said she knew how much it hurt me to fight with Althea. And then she started talking some other mumbo-jumbo, told me I-I deserved better and . . . I was weak," he confessed in a low voice, as if eavesdroppers awaited on the other side of the door. "I fell for it, man. Hook, line, and sinker."

"What did you go to straighten out with her that night?" Garrison asked.

Malik gulped. "I wanted to tell her it was over, do it in person so she could look straight into my eyes and see I wasn't playing." He scrubbed a trembling hand over his bald head, closed his eyes briefly in exhaustion.

"Don't tell me," Moses goaded ruthlessly. "You got over there, took one look at her fine behind, and couldn't go through with it."

Malik shook his head. "She wasn't there. And no one had seen her for hours. Guess she called me from somewhere else."

Garrison slowly unfolded his arms. "She called you?"

"Yeah. Making all these threats—"

Garrison's gaze sharpened. "What kind of threats?"

A fresh wave of guilt washed over Malik's expression. He averted his eyes, becoming evasive once again. "Nothing really important—"

"Malik."

Reluctantly he looked up, meeting the unrelenting command in Garrison's eyes. "She said she was gonna tell everyone about us," he mumbled unhappily, "including Althea. Said she'd even go to the police, and I'd get in trouble because she's underage." His gaze turned pleading, swinging desperately between Garrison and Detective Moses. "Am I gonna get locked up for statutory rape?"

When the two men exchanged brief looks, Malik insisted, "I didn't rape her. She wanted it just as much as I did, if not more. *She* seduced *me*!"

"Calm down," Garrison said, a firm hand on the boy's shoulder. "You're not going to be charged with statutory rape. The legal age of consent in Maryland is sixteen, not eighteen. And I'm betting Elizabeth knows that. Where did you go after you left her dorm?"

"Straight back here, I swear. I didn't want to miss Althea." He shuddered, slumped weakly against the back of the chair. Tears rolled from the corners of his closed eyes, marking a wet path in his dark skin. "God, I never meant to hurt her," he groaned, agonized. "I'm so sorry, Althea. So sorry."

Moses looked like he wasn't buying Malik's anguish, or was trying hard not to. He glanced over at Garrison, one eyebrow raised expectantly. *Well, what's our next move?* his expression asked.

Garrison's narrowed gaze was fixed on Malik, assessing, scrutinizing. A suspicion that had taken root in his mind on Saturday night began to grow, spreading its thorny thistles. "Did you hear from Elizabeth again that night?"

"I called her to ask if she'd seen Althea." Malik paused.

"And?"

"She still wasn't there."

Although Imani knew there had been no merit to Elizabeth Torres's claims, she couldn't dismiss the encounter as easily as she would have liked. Hours later, it still troubled her to think that any student could believe her capable of showing favoritism when she'd always endeavored to treat all her students equally. Perhaps she'd failed. And if Elizabeth felt this way, how many others did?

She was so deep in thought that the ringing of her phone nearly went unnoticed. She finally picked it up, answering distractedly, "Imani Maxwell."

"Hey, there." The warmth of David's voice was a welcome diversion. "I almost hung up. Thought you might have already left for the day."

Imani consulted her wristwatch, saw that it was approaching five o'clock. "In a few minutes. Where are you?"

"Still at the office," David hedged. "Listen, I hate to do this to you, baby girl. But I'm going to have to bail on the play tonight."

"Oh no. Why?"

"Flannery's annual dinner party is tonight. I had forgotten all about it until Suzanne reminded me."

Imani bit her lip. "Well . . . do you want me to go with you?"

David chuckled. "You know you'd rather wrestle an alligator," he teased, and Imani smiled because it was true. She detested the pretentious faculty events she herself was often forced to attend. All those plastic smiles, inane conversations meant to perpetuate one's own intellectual superiority.

"I wish I could just blow it off," David said, "but you know how important it is for me to show my face at these functions if I want to make partner. Besides, you have to attend the play. Rebecca would be crushed if you weren't there."

"You're right," Imani agreed, thinking of her former student who had gone to all the trouble of tracking Imani down to send her two complimentary tickets to her debut theatrical performance.

"I'll make it up to you, Imani. I promise."

"Don't worry about it," she said mildly. Although this would make the second time in two days that David had stood her up. He'd called on Saturday night to cancel their dinner date, citing the onset of a stomach virus. Already at the Georgetown restaurant where they were supposed to meet, she'd left and spent the entire evening alone in a darkened movie theater, hugging a greasy tub of buttered popcorn and praying against acne in the morning.

"Look, I have some loose ends to tie up before leaving, so I'd better go. You'll tell me how the play goes?"

"Of course. Have a good time."

David gave a derisive snort. "As if." A woman's voice spoke in the background and David's answer was muffled as he covered the phone with his hand. He returned a moment later, a smile in his voice. "I'll call you tomorrow."

"Okay." Imani hung up, lamenting how she hadn't planned to spend another solitary evening in a theater. Oh, well. David was a successful, upwardly mobile corporate attorney. Canceled dates were par for the course. And besides, she reminded herself, they weren't technically a couple again.

"Evening."

Imani started violently at the deep voice, the phone receiver clattering noisily into the cradle. Her widened eyes flew to Garrison Wade standing in the doorway. "You scared me half to death!"

That sensuous mouth twitched. "My apologies."

Her gaze narrowed on his face as she wondered how much of her conversation he'd overheard. It was bad enough she'd made a point of telling him she had a date on Saturday night, had stayed out most of the evening just so that he wouldn't know she had been stood up.

And now to be in the same position.

She tried to inject coolness into her tone, tried to reestablish the safe distance between them that seemed to corrode with each encounter. "How long have you been standing there?"

"Not long," he murmured, watching her carefully.

His sudden presence filled her tiny office, making it smaller than she had ever remembered. He was dressed in a slate-colored suit with the jacket unbuttoned, the silk tie tugged loose, the stark white broadcloth shirt contrasting magnificently with his deep mahogany coloring. He was so ruggedly handsome, oozing such pure unadulterated masculinity, that she had to avert her gaze.

"What're you doing here? On campus, I mean?" she asked unsteadily.

"Looking for someone." He didn't elaborate, and she didn't pry. He slid his hands into his pants pockets. "I hope you don't mind that I dropped by?"

She shook her head, trying to regain her composure. "I was just finishing up in here," she said, straightening the papers on her desk. "Would you like to sit down?" she asked, with a vague wave at the cushioned chair across from her. Her heart was racing painfully, choking the breath from her.

What was *wrong* with her?

Garrison declined the chair, his eyes sweeping briefly around the room, noting the photographs tacked to a bulletin board. He wandered over for a closer examination. More family photos, another displaying Imani with a group of beaming children in identical red T-shirts. A camp or volunteer group, he surmised.

There were no frills in her office, he noted with a practiced eye, observing the worn oak desk with its seventeen-inch Pentium monitor, the solitary chair opposite the desk, the metal file cabinet. Apart from the snapshots, the only personal effects were plants beside a tiny window, their cloying fragrance mingling with her own unique sweet nectar. Her scent had already been branded on his senses, perhaps permanently.

He turned then, finding her wary gaze fixed on him before her eyes slid away.

"Have dinner with me, Imani," he said, and it was a gentle command more than a request.

Her eyes flew back to his face. "Dinner?" she echoed, dumbfounded. A fleeting image of them gazing into each other's eyes across a candlelit table in some darkened restaurant made her blush furiously like an awkward schoolgirl.

He seemed amused by her predicament. "You do eat, don't you?"

"Of course. It's not that. It's just that I have other plans."

"I see. Well, maybe another time." He paused, then started for the door.

A sudden, crazy idea struck her and she acted upon it—impulsively, foolishly—before she had a chance to think twice. Contradicting the reminder she had just issued herself about keeping her distance. "Do you like plays?"

He turned, the corner of his mouth tilted ruefully. "I think so. It's been a long time since I attended one."

"Well, I'm going to see one tonight. At Center Stage Theater. You're welcome to come if you'd like," she said, trying to sound offhand. Stupid girl, silly girl. Hadn't her father always taught her not to play with matches or she'd get burned?

Garrison couldn't deny an overwhelming desire to spend time alone with Imani Maxwell, couldn't deny that she'd been on his mind since he first met her.

Less than a week ago. An eternity, it seemed.

"Sounds good," he said at length.

Imani released the breath she hadn't realized she was holding. Inaudibly, praying he wouldn't detect it. Two of her colleagues walked slowly past the door, peering into her office with undisguised curiosity. Imani smiled at the white women, knowing they would be parked in her doorway first thing in the morning brimming with questions about her mysterious visitor.

She rose to her feet. "I just need to go home first and change, and then we can be on our way."

Garrison checked voice mail messages and made phone calls while Imani dressed upstairs. After much deliberation, standing in the middle of her walk-in closet for longer than it should have taken, she finally settled on a steel-gray sleeveless wool bodice dress cut close to the body, accentuated with a woven leather cord at the waist and worn with matching spiky-heeled leather boots. The finished effect made her look effortlessly chic and elegant at once, which seemed perfect for an evening performance at the theater.

When Garrison took one look at her, she knew she had subconsciously selected the outfit for him and him alone. He drank in her appearance thirstily, his dark gaze raking over her form in one hot, sweeping caress that left her tingly and breathless.

He murmured something into the cell phone cradled to his ear before hanging up, sliding the compact instrument back inside his breast pocket.

"You look good," he said huskily.

"Thank you. Ready?" she asked, feigning detachment as she slipped into a trendy ecru trench.

"Absolutely," Garrison said, a hint of promise in that single word.

She grabbed the bouquet of yellow roses she'd bought for Rebecca Pearson on her way home. "I'll just follow you to the theater," she said over her shoulder as she locked the front door. She made the suggestion casually, nonchalantly, as if she weren't terrified at the prospect of spending time alone in the car with him. Even the thirty-minute ride to Baltimore would be far too long. "It makes no sense for you to have to come all the way back here to drop me off afterward."

"It's no problem."

"No, really, I can drive myself—"

"Imani." The quiet authority in his voice stopped her cold in her tracks. She turned and, nodding mutely, followed him to his truck, docile as a lamb. He held the door open for her, assisted her inside before skimming the fender and sliding in behind the wheel.

"Put your lap belt on," he ordered as the automatic shoulder strap slid across her with the start of the engine. She obeyed without a second thought.

They left College Park and headed onto I-95 North in complete silence. Imani sat as close to the door as possible, unwilling or unable to relax around this dangerously virile man with his piercing bedroom eyes. *Then why did you invite him to the play?* an inner voice demanded. *You're playing with fire.*

When at last they spoke, it was at the same time. Garrison chuckled, low and soft. "You go first."

"No, no, that's okay. You go." She had forgotten what she wanted to say anyway.

He sent her a long look. "I think it's no secret that I find you very attractive," he said huskily.

His words, so unexpected, sent a melting warmth rushing through her. "I-I don't know what to say," she stammered.

"You don't have to say anything. I just wanted to put it out there, get it out of the way. To break the ice a little. And maybe," he drawled, slanting her an amused look, "to get you to stop gripping the door handle so hard, like you're going to roll out any moment."

She laughed self-consciously and relaxed her stranglehold, feeling incredibly foolish and transparent. "Are you always this direct, Garrison Wade?"

"Generally." He maneuvered through evening traffic with skilled ease. Something soft and bluesy by John Coltrane floated from the CD player.

"So where are you from originally?" she asked conversationally.

"Baltimore. Born and raised." At her inquisitive look, he elaborated. "When I graduated from the Academy, I was assigned to New York for two years before requesting to be transferred to the Baltimore field office. Wanted to be close to home to keep an eye on my mom."

Imani nodded, thinking of Vivienne Maxwell's long-held belief that how a man treated his mother was a reliable indicator of how he'd treat his wife. Not that it made a difference to her in this instance. "Tell me more about your brothers. Two, right?"

He nodded. "Reginald, the oldest, has his own dental practice in Philadelphia. Damien's finishing school here, getting his bachelor's degree in journalism."

"So you're the middle child." She slid him a teasing smile. "Is it true, that old saying? That the 'middle child is never wild.' "

He chuckled softly. "Guess that's something you'll have to find out," he drawled.

Heat stung her face at the hidden implication. She turned her head, gazing out the darkened window. Fall was in full bloom, a brilliant splash of reds, oranges, yellows, and golds in the thick brush of trees flanking the road.

Garrison glanced over at her. "So tell me more about yourself."

She threw him a wry look. "I'm sure you can access any information you want from your federal database. Isn't that right, Special Agent Wade?"

He didn't rise to the bait. "Everything I want to know about you, Imani Maxwell," he said quietly, "can't be limited to the files in a mere computer database. Trust me on that."

She shivered, told herself it had nothing to do with his silky words. "What do you want to know?"

Garrison shrugged, switching lanes to cut in front of a crawling minivan. "How long have you been with David Scott?" His tone was casual, masking the fact that the question had been burning a hole through him for days. Try as he might to deny it, the thought of Imani Maxwell with another man, being held and caressed, sickened him, made him want to put his fist through a wall. Feelings he knew were completely irrational, but there just the same.

When she hesitated, he glanced at her sideways. "I'm sorry, was that too personal?"

"Not at all." *Of course it was.* "I had to think about it for a minute. We've known each other practically all our lives." She saw no point in telling him that she and David were not currently in a relationship. No point in inviting the ravenous wolf to your straw house, was there?

Garrison nodded, his expression betraying nothing.

As they approached North Calvert Street, he offered to drop her off in front of the theater while he found parking.

She shook her head. "I'll walk with you," she said. "I don't mind."

They parked in the crowded lot across the street and joined the flow of other theatergoers wearing everything from denim jeans to mink coats, although it clearly wasn't cold enough for furs on this unseasonably warm evening.

Rebecca Pearson had secured terrific seats for them in the

AP Center Orchestra section, just four rows from center stage. She had landed the minor role of Rena in August Wilson's critically-acclaimed play "Jitney." Rebecca was to play the sweet, practical girlfriend of the impetuous, hardheaded Youngblood. The play was set in the urban decay of 1977 Pittsburgh, and the jitney service provided the framework for an intricate mesh of personalities, relationships, and issues that was at times humorous, at other times downright edgy.

Although Imani had always enjoyed the black play-wright's work, she found it hard, if not impossible, to con-centrate on anything beyond Garrison Wade's nearness in the darkened theater. His clean-scented warmth surrounded her, tantalized her senses. His long muscular legs were stretched out before him, but the proximity of the next row of seats occasionally caused him to adjust his position. When his knee accidentally brushed hers, Imani stiffened as liquid heat erupted in her belly and trailed a searing path through her entire body. Their eyes met in the shadowy dark-ness, both murmuring quick apologies, but the next time it happened, Imani shamefully willed his warm leg to remain in place against hers. And it did.

His low, deep laughter was as potent to her as she imag-ined the gentle stroke of his big hand would be. And the thought was so shocking, so vividly erotic, that her cheeks flamed with guilt.

Garrison chose that exact moment to glance at her pro-file. "Something wrong?" he inquired, his voice a low mur-mur near her ear. His breath was cool, minty sweet.

She shook her head wordlessly, staring straight ahead.

By the time the play wound to a close, she felt as unset-tled and flustered as a jack-in-the-box. Even more frustrat-ing, perhaps, was the fact that Garrison, in contrast, seemed completely unruffled.

"I enjoyed that," he remarked as they rose from their seats. "How about you?"

"Absolutely. Definitely." *You've got serious issues, Imani Maxwell.*

"Garrison, I *thought* that was you."

They looked up in unison as a gorgeous light-skinned woman wafted toward them. Her chestnut hair was long, flowing past sleek shoulders draped with a cashmere shawl.

Garrison's smile was quick, full of unaffected warmth. "Hey, you," he drawled. "Following me or something?"

"Or something." The woman laughed, leaning into him for a kiss that landed too close to his mouth. She drew back slowly, an elegant hand curving around his cheek as she smiled into his eyes. "Since when did you start allowing yourself leisure time, Garrison Wade?"

He smiled again, briefly, before turning to Imani at his side. "Desiree, I'd like you to meet Imani Maxwell. Imani, this is Desiree Williams."

The woman's relaxed smile faltered, her eyes clouding with resentment as she shook Imani's hand. "A pleasure," she murmured.

Politely, Imani said, "Nice to meet you," wondering at the strange knot in her stomach. "If you'll both excuse me, I want to catch Rebecca before she leaves."

Garrison inclined his head, and she started up the aisle, sensing the woman's assessing gaze on her back.

Rebecca was exhilarated, bursting with excitement over her debut performance. "I'm so glad you could make it, Professor Maxwell. So did you *really* think I did well, or are you just saying that to spare my feelings?"

Imani smiled indulgently. "I think you know better than that. You did a wonderful job. I'm very proud of you."

"Oh, thank you, thank you." Still in costume, Rebecca threw her arms around Imani's neck. Imani laughed and hugged her back.

"I was so nervous," Rebecca confessed, drawing away on a girlish giggle.

"No one could tell." *Least of all me,* added a guilty voice. "Oh, and these are for you. Congratulations."

"Thank you *so* much," Rebecca gushed, accepting the

bouquet of yellow roses. Her amber eyes misted with tears. "I wish my family could have made it from Seattle."

"Well, I'm sure they're immensely proud of you, just the same. I think you've got Broadway in your future, girl."

Rebecca's eyes lit up. "Oh, I hope so! That would be so amazing." Her sparkling gaze drifted fleetingly beyond Imani's shoulder. Her face, heavy with stage makeup, broke into a mischievous grin. "By the way," she whispered dramatically, "who's that gorgeous man you were sitting with? He is fine with a capital *F,* Professor Maxwell."

Imani didn't look over her shoulder, didn't want to be greeted with the sight of Garrison huddled familiarly with the beautiful Desiree Williams. "He's just an acquaintance," she answered lamely. Knowing, deep down inside, that he was quickly becoming so much more than that.

She and Rebecca chatted easily for a few minutes, playing catch-up before the girl was whisked away by fellow cast members who wanted to introduce her to their friends and families.

Imani turned, colliding with the solid wall of Garrison's chest. His arms came up to steady her as she lifted her eyes, embarrassed, to mumble an apology. "I didn't see—"

His mouth curved in wry amusement, dismissing her apology. "It's not like you have eyes in the back of your head."

She backed up a step, needing the distance. "Has your friend left?" she asked, trying to sound casual.

"I think so." His dark eyes bored into hers. "Are you all right?"

She blinked innocently. "Fine. Why?"

"You just seem a bit tense."

"Probably just tired. You ready to go?"

"Ready when you are."

In the truck a few minutes later, Garrison glanced at her. "Hungry?"

She looked startled. "What?"

"You want to get something to eat? I know it's after ten, but these places stay open pretty late."

The image of a candlelit dinner returned to her and she shook her head hard, like a recalcitrant child refusing to eat her brussels sprouts. "I am kind of hungry, though," she admitted sheepishly. "Starving, actually. But I don't want anything fancy," she hastened to add. "Something quick, maybe even a little greasy."

Garrison grinned, paying the parking attendant and swinging the truck onto the busy street. "I know just the place."

He took her downtown to a sports bar and grill that was more of a hovel, neat but impossibly tiny inside. MULLIGAN'S announced the neon sign beneath the green awning. The proprietor, a rotund Irishman with ruddy red cheeks, greeted Garrison boisterously by name, clapped a welcoming hand upon his shoulder. "Good to see you again, lad. The usual?"

"You know it. The same for the lady."

Their host nodded approvingly, calling orders to an unseen cook in the kitchen before turning back to them. "Where's your right arm tonight?"

"God only knows," Garrison grunted, and was rewarded with uproarious laughter and another jovial pat on the shoulder.

"He's a character, this one," Cappy Mulligan spoke to Imani following the introductions, his heavy Irish brogue filled with warm regard. "Known him since he was this high," he said, his fleshy arm outstretched to knee level. "Used to come in here and sit at this very same counter, skinny legs dangling over the stool. Watching what everyone else was doing. A lawman even then."

Imani smiled, touched by this poignant glimpse into a Garrison Wade she didn't know. His mildly embarrassed expression was endearing.

Their meals arrived in no time at all. "Let's eat outside," Garrison suggested. "It's a nice night."

"Might as well enjoy some of this warm weather while you still can, eh?" intoned their gracious host with a knowing wink at Garrison. Imani pretended not to notice.

They crossed the street to the Inner Harbor, walked along the red-brick pier eating succulent crab cake sandwiches and sipping frothy root beers.

Imani slanted Garrison a disbelieving look. "How'd you know that root beer is my favorite soft drink?"

"Is it?" Garrison smiled, shrugged. "I took a chance. It's my favorite, too."

"Imagine that." She grinned and bit into her sandwich. "How is it?"

"Mmmm." She closed her eyes on a languorous sigh. "I think it's the best crab cake sandwich I've ever had."

"That good, huh?"

"You didn't notice that I haven't come up for air yet?"

He chuckled. "Glad you like it." He could always appreciate a woman with a healthy appetite. Come to think of it, he was finding a lot to appreciate about the woman beside him. More than he cared to admit.

It was an exceptionally warm evening, the moon a glowing silver disk against the clear black sky. A warm breeze danced off the murky water beneath, carrying the ocean's salty mist and the crisp scent of fall leaves. Even at that late hour, the pier was not deserted. Students taking study breaks milled about aimlessly and couples strolled hand in hand boarding water taxis for moonlit tours down the Chesapeake.

They finished their meals and discarded the empty containers into a trash receptacle. "Tell me something," Imani began as they fell in step beside each other once again, walking so close that the sides of their legs brushed, "what would a kid be doing hanging out in what is, essentially, an Irish pub?"

Garrison grinned. "I knew that was coming. Actually, my father used to take me there. Back in its heyday, Mulligan's was a popular hangout for cops."

She looked at him in mild surprise. It was the first time he had ever mentioned his father. Not that they'd had that many conversations to date. "Your father was a cop?"

Garrison nodded, a hint of pride in his voice as he replied, "Baltimore's finest."

Imani hesitated. "Is he retired, then?"

Something like melancholy descended upon his features. He said evenly, "You could say that." Sensing pain beneath the surface of his veiled response, she didn't probe. She knew all too well about loss, about trying to move beyond it through the quicksand of grief. And not for the first time, she felt that inner stirring, felt herself inexorably drawn to this man who was, for all intents and purposes, a stranger to her.

Ruthlessly banishing such dangerous thoughts, she continued. "So I guess law enforcement has always been in your blood."

"In a roundabout way, yes."

"How's that?"

"When I left home for college, I had every intention of returning a civil rights lawyer." He told her about his summer internships on Capitol Hill with the Supreme Court and NAACP Legal Defense and Education Fund, and working as a racial justice fellow with the ACLU during his third year of law school. He had even spent a month in South Africa at the personal invitation of Nelson Mandela, conducting research on the inner workings of the African National Congress for an article that was published in the *Columbia Law Review* and garnered national recognition. He shared all of this in a voice devoid of emotion or conceit.

"That's quite a résumé," remarked a suitably impressed Imani.

Garrison shrugged dismissively. "I can be very motivated when I want something. I wanted to secure my future law career."

"So what happened?"

His expression grew remote. "Somewhere along the way, my game plan changed. I still wanted to help people, but from a different angle." Even after joining the Bureau, his plans had once again been altered, the decision spurred by a single defining moment that would haunt his memory for a lifetime.

He turned his head, meeting the speculative curiosity in

Imani's dark gaze. He smiled. "So what about you? Has teaching always been in your blood?"

"Definitely." She chuckled. "Although there was a time I seriously entertained the idea of joining the Peace Corps."

"Really?"

She nodded. "During my junior year in college, I participated in a study abroad program where I lived in London for a year." A smile touched her lips as she described her host family, a generous middle-aged white couple with three active children who had embraced her as one of their own. To this day, she still got teary-eyed whenever she received a letter or e-mail from the Winthrops. "That experience whet my appetite for other opportunities to broaden my horizons. The summer after graduation, before I started my master's program, I accompanied a missionary group to Ethiopia to aid in the relief efforts of famine-ravaged villages."

Garrison listened with rapt attention as she described the experience of digging ditches for water to bring to crops that would feed the people. His admiration grew as she told him that no matter how physically punishing the labor had been beneath the scorching African sun, the reward had been the knowledge that she was helping others, improving the quality of their lives. The villagers were overwhelmed with gratitude; one particular young mother whom Imani had bonded with reminded her that her name meant *faith* in Swahili, which was what she and the missionaries had brought to the villagers. Faith.

Imani was so moved by the experience that she seriously contemplated staying there.

"What changed your mind?" asked Garrison, secretly grateful.

"What or *who,* you mean," Imani countered with a sardonic grin. "My father told me that although my intentions were noble, he knew God had other plans for my life. He encouraged me to follow the education path I had started upon. Told me I was needed to impact fertile young minds in my own homeland."

"Wise man." Garrison's mouth twitched. "And I'm sure his counsel had nothing to do with the fact that he didn't want his little girl living halfway across the world from him."

"Of course not," Imani concurred, tongue in cheek. She and Garrison exchanged teasing grins.

"Well, it seems that father *does* know best," Garrison observed. "You have an amazing rapport with your students."

Her smile softened. "Think so?"

"Judging from your interaction with Rebecca Pearson tonight, it's pretty obvious. They adore you." When her smile deepened, he added intuitively, "And something tells me it isn't one-sided."

Imani lifted her shoulders in a self-conscious shrug. "I enjoy what I do," she said simply. She thought fleetingly of Elizabeth Torres, the pure venom in her eyes as she hurled her outrageous accusation. Imani's tone turned rueful, contemplative. "Someone once told me that educators are essentially egomaniacs at heart. We actually believe we can make a difference in our students' lives, shape their minds in a positive way. Mighty presumptuous of us, wouldn't you say?"

"Not at all," Garrison said quietly, touched by her transparency. "I think the word that comes to mind is 'noble.' I know it can be a thankless job at times, but you remain dedicated to it. I think you're amazing."

Imani's steps slowed. Garrison stopped, turning to her. They had nearly covered the distance of the pier, passing the Inner Harbor's restaurants and specialty shops without noticing, so absorbed in their conversation, in each other.

Imani's face was illuminated by a towering lamppost, her expression serene. "You don't know how much I needed to hear that today," she whispered. "Today more than ever."

Garrison gazed down at her, felt his heart swell inexplicably. "I meant every word," he said huskily.

"I know," Imani murmured, "and that's why it meant so much."

The air between them changed, crackling with the now-familiar electricity. Garrison took a slow step forward, bringing their bodies together. He felt her breath quicken, watched her sooty lashes flutter as her eyes drifted closed. His heart pounded, blood pumping hard through his veins.

"You are so beautiful," he uttered, his fingers gently tracing the high curve of her cheek, the lush ripeness of her lips.

Imani wanted this so much, had been aching for his forbidden touch so long. Against her will, against her better judgment. What was this intoxicating power he held over her?

When his warm lips finally covered hers, she ceased to think of anything else. It felt so right, so perfect. Like coming home, like finding your soul. A dizzying heat swept through her body. From head to toe she craved whatever he had to offer, taking and giving back as their mouths meshed and parted hungrily, almost desperately. She moved higher in his arms to match herself more equally to his height, kissing him like her very survival depended upon it.

A low, guttural moan tore from his throat as he scooped an arm around her waist, pulling her hard against him until her feet nearly left the ground. He coaxed her lips apart with his tongue, plundered the sweetness of her mouth when she opened eagerly to him. She kissed him with an urgency that stole his breath away, threatened to knock him right off his feet. Their tongues mated, moving in perfect harmony like they had been created for this sole purpose, expressly made for each other.

"This is wrong," Imani whispered on a shuddered plea, trying to summon David's image. "It's so wrong."

Garrison's hand cupped the nape of her neck, his fingers brushing down to the delicate base of her throat. Imani drowned in the slow, drugging nectar of his kiss and trembled as he whispered her name across her cheekbone. She wrapped her arms around his neck, clung to him for dear life.

I love you.

Her eyes flew open. Had she actually uttered those words to him? It was impossible. She hardly knew him!

Shaken to the core, she broke the kiss and retreated backward in silence. She watched his eyes open slowly to reveal the burning need there.

For a prolonged moment neither of them spoke, facing each other with the moonlight between them, the distant cry of a seagull. Garrison's eyes were glittering onyx, filled with an inner tumult she understood only too well.

"I think you'd better take me home now," she whispered, her throat painfully constricted.

He hesitated, then inclined his head in the barest hint of a nod. "As you wish."

They rode back in complete silence.

When they arrived at her house, Garrison climbed out of the truck and walked her to the front door, always the gentleman.

"For what it's worth," Imani said softly, "I had a really good time. Thank you for coming."

"No thanks necessary. I enjoyed it." He tipped his head, coolly polite. "Good night."

"Good night, Garrison." Safely inside the house, she rested her forehead against the door and smoothed an absent hand over Shiloh's silken head. He regarded her solemnly, as if he could feel her pain, could empathize with her dilemma.

Imani groaned. "You don't know the half of it, Shiloh."

Her steps were heavy as she climbed the stairs and walked down the hall to her room. As she slowly undressed and slipped into a nightshirt, she thought of all the reasons why Garrison Wade was wrong for her. The first, and most obvious, was her past relationship with David. Try as she might to deny it, Jada had been right about her. Imani *did* feel a certain obligation to fulfill her father's desire to see her and David happily married. Although Imani was not exactly beating down the doors to the chapel, somewhere in the back of her mind was a vague acceptance of the fact that she would, in all likelihood, eventually become David's wife.

There were other reasons why Garrison Wade was completely wrong for her. These reasons were less definable, perhaps less logical, but just as compelling.

Padding across the room to her walk-in closet, Imani reached up and pulled a shoebox from its careful hiding place in the back of the shelf. Lowering herself to the floor, she sat cross-legged and opened it, sifting through old newspaper clippings, the obituary notice she'd long since committed to memory. She found what she was looking for at the bottom and lifted it out slowly, almost reverently.

Her father's darkly handsome image greeted her, sober eyes filled with that uncanny wisdom, the eyes of a man who had seen one too many atrocities and lived to tell about it. Until the fateful night his number was called. Gunned down in the line of duty.

FBI Supervisory Special Agent Irvin Maxwell, beloved husband and father, service martyr.

Imani ran trembling fingers over the laminated identification card, felt the telltale tears burn the backs of her eyelids. She heard his resonant voice, as clear as if he now sat beside her in the stillness of her room. "Marry someone with a safe occupation, Buttercup," he'd warned her just two nights before he died, the twinkle in his eyes belied by the somber tone. It was as if he knew his end awaited him around the corner. "A doctor, lawyer, even a shoe salesman, doesn't matter. Just as long as their job description doesn't include the use of firearms. You promise me that?"

She'd giggled, rolled her eyes heavenward. "I promise, Daddy."

Imani smiled at the memory as a tear rolled, unchecked, down her cheek. "I miss you, Daddy," she whispered brokenly. "Wish *you'd* been a shoe salesman."

Chapter 9

Garrison awakened in a seriously foul mood.

He'd tossed and turned most of the night, catching only one hour of shut-eye around dawn. In his line of work, sleepless nights were nothing out of the ordinary and often came with the territory.

It was the reason behind this particular sleepless night, however, that unnerved him.

He took a quick shower and dressed, pulling a charcoal suit from the arsenal of dark suits he owned. All of them were professionally pressed and lined the large closet with military precision. He shrugged into a starched broadcloth shirt from another endless collection, fastened the cuffs and left it untucked as he grabbed his weapon and leather holster.

He wasn't in top form this morning. He felt it in his bones, in the tautness of his muscles, and was powerless to do anything about it. For the first time ever, he'd allowed himself to want a woman, really want her, and he couldn't have her. It left him frustrated and on edge, full of self-deprecation for his own weakness.

He made phone calls while his coffee brewed. He called

Moses first to see if the detective had had any success reaching Elizabeth Torres. He hung up, irate, when all he got was Moses' voice mail announcing it was his day off. Next he called housing at the University of Maryland, wanting to learn how Elizabeth Torres and Althea Pritchard came to be roommates.

He phoned the office to confirm with the forensic technician that no prints could be lifted from the note, before asking to be transferred to his supervisor. He gave a brief status update of the kidnapping investigation before disconnecting, just as the coffee percolated.

He perused the *Baltimore Sun* while he drank, not really absorbing anything, just turning pages mechanically. Going through the motions as he'd done all morning. When he found himself critiquing the coffee, thinking Imani Maxwell's tasted better, he swore under his breath in disgust. He dumped the rest down the drain, grabbed his suit jacket and Glock, and left the apartment. A moment later he returned, grabbing a cherry Popsicle from the freezer.

The Popsicle was history by the time he stepped off the elevator to the covered parking lot. He slid on his mirrored shades as he pulled his truck onto the street. He was hit by bright sunlight slanting through the windshield, warming the leather exterior. Trane was still playing softly from last night and Garrison ejected the CD, not needing any reminders. Wanting something that would drive out all dangerous thoughts, any stupid regrets, he listened to old Dr. Dre tunes, letting the hard bass wash over him, through him, obliterating everything else.

He wasn't surprised to find himself pulling up to his childhood home in East Baltimore fifteen minutes later. He needed familiarity, some normalcy, if just for a few minutes.

"What's up, G-man," a loud voice greeted him, using the nickname Garrison had earned long before he joined the FBI.

Garrison's mouth curved in a slow grin at the sight of his old running buddy approaching. Gone was the gangly prankster from his youth, replaced by a burly six-footer sporting dreadlocks and a cocky swagger. Now a Pro Bowl middle linebacker for the Baltimore Ravens, Nate Jones had never forgotten his roots, returning to the old neighborhood every chance he got to check on his family, see if there were any newcomers to the block, "playaz to put correct."

"What's up, Nate," Garrison said. The two men exchanged the combination handshake and hug that had been perfected by black men, mutual affection still evident although little body contact was made.

Nate's grin widened as he drew back, giving Garrison an approving once-over. "Still smooth as ever," he remarked. "And you all cut like I don't know what. Arms feel like steel, man. Super Agent, that's who you are."

Garrison chuckled, sliding off the sunglasses. "How you been, man? Congratulations on Sunday's game, by the way."

"Thanks, you know it's all good. To make it even better, Nakia and I just found out we're gonna be parents."

Garrison grinned. "Get outta here. Congratulations, man. That's good stuff, really good."

Nate's thick chest was practically puffed out with pride. "Thanks, man. I appreciate that. We were talking about naming you the godfather, in fact. What do you say? Think you can fit a baby into your busy schedule, G-man?"

Garrison was touched, and it showed in his answering smile. "You know it would be an honor," he said quietly, sincerely. He was proud of his friend for building a life with his high school sweetheart despite the pressures of being a professional athlete, the temptations thrust upon him by fame's spotlight.

He'd called Garrison from his hotel room, sweating bullets after being drafted by the Washington Redskins, the first team he'd signed with before being traded to the Ravens. "G-man, you wouldn't believe all the hotties up in here. Honeys *foine* as all get out, man. What am I gonna do?" he begged for counsel, near panic.

Garrison, cramming for the law school entrance exam,

was barely lucid as he mumbled a reminder to his friend about how special Nakia was, not worth losing over some gift-wrapped groupie. When he stood as best man at the couple's wedding two years later, the radiant bride's eyes shone with gratitude as she smiled at him, then mouthed a silent thank-you.

Nate laughed now, clapping a meaty hand on Garrison's shoulder. "Man, you everywhere! On the news, on *America's Most Wanted.* Saw the episode on Saturday night, told everyone that you were my boy from around the way. Man, you're more famous than me."

Garrison grinned, shook his head in denial as he started up the steps to the brick row house. "Hey, who's the one with the Super Bowl ring?"

Nate laughed, waved him off even as the gold ring in question glinted in the morning sunshine. "Tell your mama I said hello."

"Will do. And tell Nakia I said congratulations."

Using his old key, Garrison let himself into his mother's modest but tastefully furnished house. The living room walls and ceiling were spackled. A gilt-framed oil painting of a baptism was suspended above an artificial fireplace, and the contemporary furniture consisted of a cream vinyl sofa and matching love seat. He found his younger brother seated on the sofa. Bent over a textbook perched on his left knee, Damien Wade bounced a whimpering toddler on the other. His desperate pleas for her cooperation went unheeded.

They both looked up at Garrison's entrance, their strikingly similar faces mirroring surprise and relief. "Uncle Garrison!" the curly-haired child cried, holding out chubby arms and wriggling her fingers insistently.

"Hey, sunshine." Garrison crossed the room, scooped her into his arms. She lifted her cherubic face eagerly to his, her lips already puckered for a kiss. He planted one on her, loudly, with an exaggerated smacking noise, drawing hysterical giggles from her.

"What's up, little man?" he greeted his brother, although

twenty-six-year-old Damien Wade was only four inches shorter than him, hardly little. "Where's Ma?"

"She had a doctor's appointment. Said she'd be back as soon as possible." Damien glanced at his watch, looking harried.

Garrison nodded at the textbook. "What're you studying?"

"Psych. Got a midterm exam in an hour, and Angelique hasn't shown up yet. I've been blowing up her cell phone, but she isn't answering. I think she's trying to avoid me," he added, his lips twisted in an annoyed grimace.

No stranger to his brother's ongoing baby's mama drama, Garrison sat down on the sofa, drawing India (named after her mother's favorite solo artist, India Arie) into his lap. Comforted by his presence, she became absorbed in the television, her round, dark eyes dancing with the reflection of the *Powerpuff Girls.*

"Why don't you go on ahead," Garrison suggested. "I'll stay here with India until Ma gets back."

Damien looked hopeful. "Are you sure, man? I mean, I don't wanna inconvenience you or anything."

"It's no problem. I'll just chill with my niece for a bit," he said, digging his fingers playfully into her ribs. She squealed in delight, squirming in his arms.

Damien closed the textbook, quickly gathered his belongings. He was beside himself with relief and gratitude. "Thanks, Garrison. I really owe you one. I hate to bother you like this, knowing how busy you are."

"Relax, Damien. It's really no big deal. I wouldn't offer if I couldn't do it."

Damien grinned, flashing dimples. "Yes, you would," he countered, knowing from experience that his older brother would do anything for him.

It was Garrison who crashed his pity party after Damien got Angelique pregnant. Garrison had threatened Damien with bodily harm if he didn't pick himself up and get his black behind back in school. "Be a man and handle your business," Garrison had scolded him, a lethal challenge in his dark eyes that reminded Damien of the butt whippings Garrison used to deliver in place of their absent father. It wasn't their eldest brother Reggie whom Damien had grown up fearing, but Garrison.

"Get out of here before you're late for the exam," Garrison ordered, and Damien hustled to the front door like he'd done as a child whenever Garrison issued a command.

Grinning, he called over his shoulder, "Thanks again, man. Be good, India. Daddy'll see you later, okay?"

She gave a distracted wave as he left, nestling into the curve of her uncle's arm once again. Garrison stroked the shiny black curls atop her head, inhaled the sweet scent of Johnson's baby oil clinging to the bronzed skin inherited from her mixed mother. Part black, part second generation Cherokee, and part trouble, as Rosemary Wade was fond of saying.

The Powerpuff Girls were battling some one-eyed green glob of a monster on television. Garrison smiled absently before his mind began to wander. He leaned his head back against the sofa, closed his eyes briefly. Images flashed across his brain like movie reels in fast forward. The stammering cashier behind the counter. The hooded figure with the semiautomatic, twitchy eyes shifting nervously to the door and back again to the cashier. *Hurry up, man. Hurry up.* Garrison arriving, unsuspecting, pulling to a dead stop as the nose of the gun swung and aimed straight at his heart. *Walk right back out that door and pretend you never saw anything.* Garrison's cold refusal, even as he caught a glimpse of a little girl huddled fearfully against her mother. In a heartbeat she was a hostage, viciously seized by the menace with the gun. The tense standoff, neither man backing down, locked in a deadly battle of wills. Then a sudden flurry of activity behind Garrison, an accomplice waiting in a car. Shrill screams and the blast of gunfire. And then the blood, pools of it smearing the dirty linoleum floor. The gunman lay prone, his trigger finger still jerking spasmodically

over the discharged weapon he clutched in his death grip.
The young mother also lay wounded, grabbing her leg and
wailing for someone to help her baby. Garrison crawling on
all fours to the tiny crumpled form, holding her in his arms.
The gaping wound in her fragile little chest. The eyes fluttering open, blood vessels burst around the pupils from the
blunt force trauma. *Please, Mister, don't leave me. Please . . .*

"Uncle Garrison, you're squeezing me too hard. Stop."
The tiny body in his arms was real and very much alive, the
pleas for release plaintive and irritated. Garrison opened his
eyes and realized he'd drifted off to sleep and relived the
nightmare once again.

He relaxed his hold on India, still shaken by the memory.
"I'm sorry, baby girl. I didn't mean to hurt you." He kissed
the top of her head and smoothed a trembling hand over the
springy curls. He set her off his lap, stood on legs that felt
like rubber. "You want some juice?"

She gazed up at him before bobbing her head vigorously.
"And some cookies." She held up pudgy fingers. "Three."

Rosemary Wade opened the front door just as Garrison
returned from the kitchen with India's spoils. "Hey,
stranger." Rosemary's gently rounded brown face lit up at
the sight of her son, and she crossed the room quickly to
greet him with a warm hug and kiss. "I was almost afraid to
believe that was your truck parked outside."

Garrison flashed a somewhat wobbly grin. "Believe it.
How are you doing, Ma?"

"Can't complain, now that you're here." She kissed her
granddaughter absently and slid a coaster under her plastic
cup before turning back to Garrison. "Come on into the
kitchen, baby, I'll fix you some breakfast."

Garrison glanced at his wristwatch. "Maybe next time,
Ma. I gotta run."

"So soon? But I just got here. Stay for another minute. I
promise I won't keep you any longer."

Knowing better, Garrison followed her into the immaculate sunny kitchen with its buttercream walls and shiny new appliances, a Mother's Day makeover gift from her sons. Petite and slightly stocky, her silvered hair attractively stylish in short cropped layers, Rosemary Wade ran her household with the same iron fist she'd used in the classroom before retiring three years ago. She was respectfully known as Mama Wade by all the neighborhood children.

Casually she said, "Desiree told me she saw you at the theater last night. With another woman."

Garrison smiled, unperturbed as he propped a shoulder in the arched doorway. "Did she also tell you that she was there with another man?" he inquired mildly.

"She said it was a colleague, purely platonic. She told me that up front, didn't want you getting the wrong idea."

"I didn't," Garrison countered, stepping forward to retrieve his mother's blood pressure pills from the cabinet for her as she reached on tiptoe, straining. He shook his head at her with an indulgent smile. "Why do you keep these things so high where you can't reach them?"

She made a face, wrinkling her pretty nose. "Because I have three giants for sons who can always get them down for me. Don't change the subject," she chided, pouring herself a tall glass of water to swallow her medication with.

"I'm not." He shrugged. "Desiree can date—or not date—whomever she chooses."

"Don't say that, baby. You know how she'd feel if she heard you talk like that, like you don't care. Don't you have any feelings for her at all?" Rosemary's expressive dark eyes twinkled hopefully.

Garrison chuckled. "We've been over this a million times, Ma," he said patiently. "You know my answer isn't going to change."

"All right, all right." Her deep sigh was resigned. She sent him a probing look, her smile knowing. "So who was this woman you were with last night? Must be someone special to make you spend a whole evening at the theater."

"I wouldn't say that," Garrison said evenly, neutrally. He consulted his watch once again and straightened from the door. "I really have to go, Ma."

"Well, at least take a muffin with you. I know all you've had this morning is coffee." She approached with a banana nut muffin nestled in a napkin. She held it to him and he opened his mouth obligingly, biting into the fluffy warmth.

"Good," he mumbled around a mouthful, and she nodded in satisfaction.

"Baked a whole batch first thing this morning," she proudly announced, feeding him the rest as if he were still her little boy. "Here, take another one for the road."

He accepted the offering, knowing he had no other choice. And the muffins *were* good, melt-in-your-mouth good. He finished the next one in two bites, washed it down with the glass of pineapple juice his mother thrust in his face. "Thanks, Ma. Call you later." He leaned down, kissed her smooth, ageless cheek before heading out of the kitchen. He made a left turn and went down the narrow corridor to Damien's bedroom. Just as he'd expected, the room was cluttered. Books were piled haphazardly on the study desk, papers and clothes littered the floor, and the bed was unmade. Shaking his head, Garrison reached into his wallet and peeled off ten twenties, sliding the money under his brother's pillow—the only place he could safely guarantee it would be found amid the chaos.

In the living room, he deposited another kiss on India's upturned forehead, ruffled her hair affectionately and whispered conspiratorially, "Take care of Grandma."

She nodded solemnly and smiled. "Love you, Uncle Garrison."

"Likewise, sunshine." He winked at her as he went out the front door.

Imani had underestimated Elizabeth Torres.

She realized this the minute she received the late-afternoon summons to the African-American Studies director's office.

To say that Dr. Anthony Yusef was an asset to the university's faculty was a gross understatement. With a Ph.D. in both history and public policy, he was published in every professional journal of these disciplines, was fluent in several languages, including Arabic and Swahili, had aided in the relief efforts of war-torn African countries during a stint with the Peace Corps, had marched alongside Dr. Martin Luther King, Jr. during the turbulent civil rights era, and was known to travel in the same sociopolitical circles as Nelson Mandela and Colin Powell.

He was, without question, one of the most accomplished men Imani had ever had the privilege of working with. When he invited her to contribute a literary essay to the anthology the department was publishing in the spring, she nearly fell out of her chair. When he enthusiastically endorsed her proposal for the minority recruitment program, she stopped just short of doing cartwheels all the way out of the building.

That afternoon, however, she had a sinking sensation in the hollow of her stomach as she faced the venerable professor across the width of his massive cherrywood desk. His hair was salt and pepper, adding distinction to his aristocratic features. Strong broad nose, astute brown eyes flecked with gray, firm no-nonsense mouth.

"Good afternoon, Professor Maxwell. Or should I say Doctor Maxwell," he corrected himself with an engaging smile. "I understand you've recently completed your dissertation. Congratulations."

Imani nodded stiffly. "Thank you. Professor Maxwell is fine." She didn't get hung up on titles the way many of her colleagues did.

"Please, have a seat." She complied and he leaned forward in his chair, folding his hands atop the gleaming surface of the desk. "I'll get right to the point. It has come to my attention that a student has questioned your objectivity in the selection of the student panelist for the minority recruitment program. Is this correct?"

Imani's chin lifted a defiant notch. "Yes, it is."

"Well, let me just say right off the bat that I don't believe it for one second. I consider myself an excellent judge of character, Professor Maxwell, and I don't think you're capable of the breach in integrity you're being charged with. Having said that, however," and Imani's heart dropped like a plummeting elevator in a skyscraper, "the call is not solely mine to make."

"She came to see you," Imani spoke low, more statement than question.

"Miss Torres? Yes, she did. Yesterday afternoon." He cleared his throat, looking, for the first time, slightly uncomfortable. "She was very adamant in her claims that you exhibited favoritism in selecting Althea Pritchard, and in using your authority as committee chair to influence the others' votes."

"She's lying," Imani stated flatly.

Anthony Yusef's expression turned grim. "Be that as it may, unfortunately, she has threatened to go to the university president, as well as the media, with her accusations. And as I'm sure you realize, Professor Maxwell, with all the news vans already crawling all over the campus from Althea Pritchard's disappearance, we don't need the additional media glare, especially not of this negative nature. If it were any other time, I would recommend taking this matter before the honor council. But we really can't afford the delay, with the program scheduled for spring. We've got grants and corporate sponsors to consider."

Imani felt lightheaded, disconnected, like she was having an out-of-body experience. "What, exactly, are you proposing?" she asked faintly.

He hesitated. "I think it's best that you excuse yourself from the committee."

The ground tilted beneath her. "But . . . the minority recruitment program was *my* idea," she reminded him, hoping she didn't sound like a sulking child arguing over a toy. *It's mine. Give it back!*

"I realize that, Professor Maxwell. And believe me, I can appreciate how difficult this must be for you. You're more than welcome to contribute in an advisory capacity, but I think your continued presence on the committee is just going to cause more harm than good at this point." He paused before adding gently, almost coaxingly, "You do understand, I'm sure."

Her eyes narrowed on his face. "I understand your position, yes," she answered tactfully, boldness gathering momentum with each word, "but with all due respect, sir, I think you're making a mistake. We're giving Elizabeth Torres exactly what she wants, at the expense of everyone else. What kind of message does this send to other students whose essays aren't accepted? That if you cry foul and make threats, you'll get your way?"

Yusef regarded her silently, his expression one of surprise mingled with a touch of admiration. He pursed his lips, straightened the blotter on his desk while she waited, heart fluttering wildly in her throat like a captive bird. Finally he said slowly, deliberately, "I know you want what's best for the students, Professor Maxwell. So I'm confident that you'll do whatever is necessary to make this program go off without a hitch."

She met his gaze directly, read the unmistakable implication there. She trembled inside with suppressed fury, a choking sense of betrayal. She forced herself to remain calm, mustered every ounce of dignity she could summon. "Will that be all, Dr. Yusef?"

He nodded, watching her almost guardedly as she stood, poised and erect, and stepped quietly from his office.

He watched her emerge from McKeldin Library trailed by a small entourage of her friends. Girls who probably counted themselves fortunate to know her, let alone befriend her, be seen in her company. She was a queen holding court, and they followed her like loyal subjects, docile puppies begging for scraps at the table of her affection.

Garrison sat on a bench on the Mall, a wide expanse of manicured lawn that marked the center of the large campus and was flanked by several stately buildings. He appeared to be a casual observer enjoying the warm fall afternoon with his newspaper and a cherry lollipop tucked into the corner of his mouth. As she drew nearer, he lowered the *Diamondback* campus newspaper he'd been pretending to read and slowly stood.

"Miss Torres." She turned her head, surprise flickering across her face, followed swiftly by pleasure. "A moment of your time, please."

Her friends stared at him, then at her, their expressions a mixture of curiosity and envy. The look Elizabeth shot them was smug, almost triumphant. As if she'd just been singled out from an audience of screaming concertgoers to join the rock idol onstage.

"I'll catch you guys later." She dismissed them haughtily. As they shuffled away whispering among themselves, Elizabeth started toward him, hips swaying, sultry dark eyes fixed on his inscrutable gaze behind the mirrored shades he wore. Her legs were impossibly long beneath the denim micro-miniskirt she wore, a femme fatale disguised as a seventeen-year-old college freshman. She was, undoubtedly, accustomed to men salivating after her, undressing her with their lascivious stares. The poor saps on campus, most still wet behind the ears, had ceased to be a challenge for her. She thought she was ready for the big time.

Garrison's mouth twitched as he slowly removed his sunglasses, gestured her toward the bench he'd just vacated. She sat down and crossed one leg over the other, deliberately, provocatively, exposing a good amount of thigh. The girl had been watching too much Sharon Stone in *Basic Instinct*.

Garrison took a seat beside her, maintaining adequate distance without really seeming to. Something told him that

Elizabeth Torres could sniff out male weakness, real or imagined, like a vulture homing in for the kill.

"I'd like to ask you a few questions about Althea Pritchard," he began.

She swung her lustrous mane of hair over one shoulder in a maneuver meant to be seductive. "I was wondering when you might show up, Agent Wade," she said coyly. "I've been waiting for you."

He arched an amused eyebrow. "Is that so?"

"Umm-hmm. It's not every day one gets to be interrogated by such a good-looking FBI agent. I always thought that stuff only happened in the movies. But here you are," she drawled, raking a slow, appreciative gaze over him, "tall, dark, and one hundred percent dangerous." She laughed, a low, throaty chuckle, at her own ingenuity. "So what took you so long to find me?"

Garrison didn't answer right away, contemplating the slim remnants of his cherry lollipop before sliding it back into his mouth. Out of the corner of his eye, he saw Elizabeth watching his lips, almost mesmerized. It amused, then saddened him. She was too young to be so sexually conscious. He thought fleetingly of his three-year-old niece, so sweet and angelic, and felt his gut tighten on a wave of protectiveness. How long had it been since Elizabeth Torres had known such innocence? And who or what had stolen it from her?

With an impatient flick of his wrist, Garrison tossed the lollipop stick in the trash bin beside her. She jumped at his sudden movement, then smiled to cover it. "What did you want to ask me about, Agent Wade?" she asked, purring his name.

"Why don't you start by telling me where you were on the night Althea disappeared?"

"I already told—" His expression stopped her cold. She tried again, nervously. "All right, I was with someone. Someone I wasn't really supposed to be with. That's why I told the police I was in my room all night."

"Who?"

"What?"

"Who were you with?"

"I'd really rather not—" Again his hardened expression made her come clean. "His name is Brian. Brian Ritter. He's a senior engineering major."

"Why weren't you supposed to be with him?"

Elizabeth pushed an errant strand of dark hair behind one ear. "Because he has a girlfriend," she answered, feigning guilt.

But Garrison knew better. "You'll understand, of course, if I corroborate your story with Mr. Ritter."

Something akin to panic filled her eyes, but it was gone so quickly Garrison may have imagined it. Only he knew he hadn't.

He leaned close. "Lie to me once, and you might be forgiven," he said, lethal promise in every inflection. "But two strikes and you're out."

Her eyes wide, Elizabeth stared at him with a mixture of fear and fascination.

"Are we understood?" he prompted, dangerously soft.

She nodded wordlessly, pulling her bottom lip between her teeth.

Garrison drew back, and in a blink was conversational. "So, do you make it a practice of sleeping with your friends' boyfriends, too?" At her surprised look, he elaborated, "Come now, you didn't think we wouldn't find out about you and Malik Toomer?"

Elizabeth shrugged dispassionately. "I don't care. Malik is a spineless coward."

"I'm sure you were betting on that when you paid your late-night call. You knew he'd be putty in your hands, yours for the taking."

Elizabeth smirked, heady with power. "Aren't they all? Haven't met a man yet I couldn't tame, Agent Wade." Her gaze, meant to be alluring, locked onto his mouth as she whispered, "Not one."

Not missing the implication, Garrison drawled, "Guess there's a first time for everything."

She frowned at the unexpected response.

He continued casually, "Bet you have guys doing stuff for you all the time. Dinner, movies, buying you clothes and jewelry . . ."

She smiled. "Of course."

"What about kidnapping?"

Her smugness faltered. "What?"

"You heard me, Elizabeth. You ever push up on a fella, maybe hint that you wanted someone taken off your hands? Come on, you can tell me."

"There's nothing to tell," she hissed, affronted. "I would *never* do such a thing. If you're implying that I had something to do with Althea's abduction—"

Garrison remained impassive. "No implication. I'm asking you directly."

Elizabeth gaped at him, then shook her head. "Man, you people must really be desperate if *I'm* the only suspect you can come up with. How weak."

"Not necessarily. Someone who seduces her best friend's boyfriend might be capable of anything. And then there's that whole thing with your father," he added, almost as an afterthought.

Elizabeth froze, staring at him with shock and anger. "What about my father?" she whispered harshly.

Garrison watched her carefully. "It must have been difficult for you when he lost the election to Louis Pritchard. And the scandal, having people whisper about him behind your back. The endless speculation: did he really try to buy the election? And then to lose him so suddenly, so tragically. My deepest condolences," he added, disingenuously.

He could feel Elizabeth trembling, struggling to rein in her emotions. He'd struck a raw, festering nerve. "My father has no place in this conversation," she said stiffly.

"Maybe you're right." Garrison nodded in concession, staring off into the distance. "Still, I must commend you for being big enough to put all that aside to befriend Althea once you arrived at the university. In fact, I understand you went out of your way to room with her. Something about a friend of yours in housing switching your room assignment at the last minute."

Elizabeth was rigid with anger now. "That doesn't prove anything."

"Probably not. Anyway," Garrison shrugged nonchalantly, "I admire you for not holding it against her that she's the county executive's niece. Have you ever been to their house, by the way? It's nice. I imagine that's where you and your family would have been living now, had things worked out differently. Tough break, kiddo."

Elizabeth was groping for her Coach backpack on the ground beside her. "I don't have to sit here and take this," she muttered furiously.

Garrison reached out, staying her with a gentle hand upon her arm. "Don't be mad, Elizabeth. I don't mean to offend—you know I'm just doing my job." The smile he offered was conciliatory, completely guileless.

She paused, eyeing his hand upon hers, the flattering contrast of their skin tones. But it was his smile that won her back. A trace of her former coquettishness returned. She resettled into the wooden bench, crossing one leg over the other once again.

Garrison's smile changed, became a sharp, almost predatory smile she never even detected. "I just have one more question for you, and then I'll let you go."

Her look was demure. "No rush. Ask away."

"When was the last time you saw or spoke with your brother, Joaquin?"

She shrugged. "I don't know. A while, I guess. He moved away after our father died, didn't leave a forwarding address. Doesn't really keep in touch with us anymore."

Garrison nodded once, slowly. "Thanks for your time, Miss Torres."

"No problem." She draped a slender arm across the back of the bench, her smile enticing as she leaned into him. "Are you absolutely sure you don't want anything else, Agent Wade? My dorm's on the other side of campus, but I guarantee I could make it worth your while. And," she added, twirling a strand of hair around her finger, "I won't tell anyone if you don't."

Garrison looked at her. She returned his steady gaze, blatant invitation in hers. When he leaned a little closer, her breath hitched audibly, her eyes darkened with anticipation. He murmured silkily, "I'm sorry, there must be some misunderstanding. You're not really my type."

Surprised, her mouth tightened with haughty disdain. "And what type would I be?"

"Spoiled brat."

Her face turned crimson with humiliation. Before she could recover from the insult, he patted the top of her head lightly, stood, and slid on his sunglasses. She angled her head and stared up at him hopefully, half expecting him to change his mind.

He didn't.

Sauntering away, he tossed over his shoulder, "Run along now and do your homework, Little Lizzie. You know a mind is a terrible thing to waste."

"That little hussy!"

Jada was beyond righteous indignation. She was spitting mad, wearing a hole through Imani's Berber carpeting as she paced back and forth in her lavender Ferragamo pumps, an enraged lioness coming to the rescue of her defenseless cub. At any minute, Imani half expected her cousin to kick off those shoes and smear Vaseline all over her face the way she had done as a child in preparation for a fight.

As if reading her mind, Jada ranted, "You're doing better than me, Mani, 'cause if it had been *me* girlfriend lied on, I would have marched straight to that little hooker's dorm and beat her behind right in front of all her little friends. Don't think I ain't tempted to do it now!"

"Jada, stop it," Imani ordered, half laughing. She could just picture her cousin, crisp and polished in her lavender Donna Karan suit, face professionally made up, knocking on some college freshman's door and dragging her outside like a madwoman.

She shook her head ruefully. "If your viewers could see you now."

"I could care less." Jada stopped pacing long enough to glare at Imani. "You're not nearly as upset as you should be."

Reclining on the sofa, Imani shrugged, her chin propped in the curve of her palm. "I feel a whole lot better now that you're here," she admitted. Jada had called as Imani was driving home from campus and, detecting the distress in her cousin's subdued voice, had rushed right over, was in her car barely minutes after the evening news broadcast went off the air.

Jada sat down beside her, brushed a stray curl off Imani's forehead, more to comfort than out of necessity. "Sweetie, I'm glad you feel better," she said, her tone gentle once again, "but I still think you should do something about this. You can't let that heifer get away with this."

Imani smiled, absently, because Jada had called Elizabeth Torres every derogatory name in the book—in less than ten minutes. "She's just a child, Jada."

Jada snorted derisively. "That *child* is trying to ruin your career."

Imani threw her hands up in the air. "Well, what am I supposed to do? Dr. Yusef was pretty clear about wanting me to step down from the committee. He's worried about Elizabeth making good on her threats to go to the media."

"Let her go to the media." Jada was on her feet again, pacing angrily. "I'll do a counter story on *her,* dig up some dirt on Little Miss Daddy's Girl. 'Go to the media,'" she mimicked, rolling her neck on another wave of indignation. "I got something for her, all right. Spoiled brat."

Imani rubbed the bridge of her nose tiredly. "Jada, you will *not* use your television station to satisfy a personal vendetta. I wouldn't let you even if it came to that."

"Well, what about David? He's an attorney. Tell him to do something, write the university a threatening letter or something. Nothing changes minds faster than the threat of legal action."

Imani shook her head, defeat a bitter taste in her mouth. "Yusef was right about one thing. He said I wouldn't want to jeopardize the recruitment program, and he was right. I don't." She shrugged with a nonchalance she was far from feeling. "It's not about me, anyway. It's about the students, about giving more minorities an opportunity to attend college."

Jada scowled. "How very noble of you."

Imani closed her eyes on a fresh stab of pain that had nothing to do with her removal from the committee. *Noble.* Hadn't Garrison Wade called her that very same thing just last night? A lifetime ago, it seemed.

"I'm worried about you, Imani." Jada joined her on the sofa once again, her concerned expression mirroring her words. "All the fight's gone out of you. Where's the woman who worked her butt off to earn her Ph.D. in less time than anyone credited you for? Where's the woman who forced her way through adversity and discrimination to establish herself as a legitimate faculty member at a predominantly white institution? Where's the nonconformist who swore off perms as a statement to her colleagues that she was embracing and celebrating her uniqueness? Are you going to let those idiots get to you now, when you've come this far?"

Imani rose abruptly and wandered to the window. "I hear what you're saying, Jada, believe me I do. But sometimes I get tired of fighting. The past six years alone have been one big fight, day after day, just trying to keep my head afloat after losing Daddy, worrying constantly about Mama." Her voice caught, the words drying up on her lips.

The weight of everything hit her at once. Althea's disappearance, the very real possibility that her own life was at risk, her taboo feelings for Garrison Wade, and then today's stunning development. She suddenly felt very tired, heavy and incredibly oppressed. She dropped her chin a moment, allowed her forehead to rest against the cool windowpane as she willed away the traitorous tears. *You have to be strong for your mother, Imani,* the well-meaning mourners had whispered to her at the gravesite, their hands finding and grasping her numb fingers. *She needs you now more than ever. So does your brother. Look at him. He idolized his father. Oh, you did, too, but it's different for a son. You understand.*

Jada approached, wrapped her arm around her cousin's waist. "I didn't mean to come on so strong," she said, gruff and tender at once. "You know how overprotective I am where you're concerned."

Imani managed a strangled sound that could have been a laugh. "It's okay. Besides, maybe you're right about me not being a fighter anymore." She gazed unseeingly out the window, added in a remote voice, "Sometimes it's just easier to go with the flow. Go with what's expected."

Like marrying David.

Jada's hand stilled its soothing circular motions against Imani's back. "Occasionally, maybe. But just as long as you don't stop fighting altogether." Her tone grew sage, a subtle warning. "Because once you stop fighting, Imani, you stop living. Remember that."

Garrison was on his way home from the command post when his cell phone trilled in the silence of the truck.

He picked it up slowly, his sixth sense already on alert mode. "Wade."

He listened a moment, heard the hollow disembodied voice

that could only be produced by a voice scrambler. The kind that obscured the natural pitch of the voice. Disguised race and gender.

Masked the identity of a predator.

When he replaced the receiver a moment later, his expression was grim. He made a hard U-turn and headed back in the direction he'd just come from.

Chapter 10

The backpack sat propped against the trash receptacle in front of the 7-Eleven in College Park. Exactly where the phantom caller had said it would be. An ordinary red canvas backpack, the kind toted around by hundreds of other students at the university.

Except that this particular one belonged to Althea Pritchard.

Garrison swung into the first available parking space, a handicapped slot, and climbed from the truck. A student wearing a Terrapins baseball cap backwards was approaching the backpack, his expression curious.

Garrison descended upon him, flashed his identification. "FBI. Step away from the bag," he ordered brusquely.

The boy retreated backward, held up his hands in surrender. "No problem, man," he spoke fast, anxiously. "I wasn't gonna take it or anything. I just wanted to check what was inside."

Garrison pocketed his credentials, his gaze narrowing on the boy's pale face. "Did you see who left this?"

"Yeah, some guy just dropped it off."

"What'd he look like?" Garrison demanded.

"Kinda tall, had on a black Terps hat like mine, black sweatshirt—"

"Which way?"

The boy looked confused. "What?"

"Which way did he go?" Garrison bit out impatiently.

He pointed beyond Garrison's shoulder with a quivering finger. "That way, down the street. He just took off."

"Stay away from the backpack," Garrison commanded, his steely expression leaving no room for negotiation.

The boy gulped, bobbed his head in compliance. "I'll keep an eye on it," he called after Garrison's retreating form, "make sure no one else touches it."

Garrison moved swiftly through the busy parking lot, swore under his breath that their adversary had chosen such a public venue to play his psychotic game. Because he was convinced, now more than ever, that this was exactly what it was: a game. And the only guaranteed rule was that there were no rules.

He saw the shadowy figure ahead, loping easily down the darkened street of fraternity row houses. Garrison proceeded stealthily, waited until an approximate distance of twenty paces separated them before shouting, "FBI! Freeze!"

The figure turned, glancing over his shoulder in surprise and nearly losing his balance. He stumbled, clumsily regained his footing and began running faster. But the delay cost him precious time, and Garrison, already closing in fast, was upon him in a heartbeat. He hauled him to the ground, planting a knee in his back. The black cap fell off, a shock of wavy red hair spilling out. He was just a kid, a student in all likelihood.

His panting was hard, panicked. "I didn't do anything, man! I swear!" he cried, his cheek pressed to the concrete.

"Where did you get it?" Garrison demanded.

"The backpack? I don't know, man. I got a call this afternoon, this guy told me I could make some quick cash for dropping off a package—"

Garrison's gaze was razor-sharp. "How do you know it was a guy?"

The boy hesitated, trying to crane his neck to get a better look at Garrison. "I-I don't. Whoever it was had a weird voice, like they were in a tin box or something. I thought it was one of my frat brothers playing a joke on me. This person told me to look outside my window and when I did, the backpack was just sitting there on the lawn. He told me to drop it off at the 7-Eleven, seven-thirty sharp. But I was running a little late and—" He broke off, gasped for breath. "I swear, man, I don't know what's in that bag or who it belongs to. I was just trying to make a little extra cash."

"How much?"

"Two hundred. Said he was gonna pay me two hundred bucks after I dropped it off, as long as I didn't screw it up. Guess I won't be seeing that dough," he concluded disconsolately with a short, strangled laugh.

Garrison lifted his head, scanned up and down the darkened street. Rock music blared from inside one of the fraternity houses. Someone shouted a profanity that was followed by raucous male laughter. There wasn't a soul in sight.

He pulled the boy to his feet, not releasing him entirely. "What's your name, kid?"

"Brian. Brian Ritter."

The name gave Garrison a mild jolt. His eyes narrowed in shrewd speculation. "You know Elizabeth Torres?" he demanded.

Brian's face reddened. "Um, yeah." A guilty, sheepish smile appeared. "Who doesn't?"

A dark green Ford Taurus rolled to a stop beside them. Detective Cole Porter leaned out the window. "Got here as fast as I could. Moses is on his way with more backup." He scrutinized Brian Ritter before his gaze returned to Garrison. "Need some help?"

"Take his statement, keep him with you until I'm done." Garrison lowered Brian Ritter into the backseat of the detective's unmarked vehicle, slammed the door, and strode purposefully back to the 7-Eleven. As promised, the skinny kid wearing the baseball cap stood guarding the book bag, his posture erect as a centurion. A few curious onlookers had already gathered, parting as Garrison approached and ordered them to keep their distance.

He dropped to a crouch before the backpack. It was partially unzipped, and even before he reached inside to gingerly extract the note he knew was there, the reaction began. The tightening of nerves, the electrical surge of adrenaline, honed instincts strained to a fine pitch. A premonition of doom sat heavy on his chest.

Using the very tips of his fingers, he unfolded the paper and read its contents. As with the first note, the text was in standard typeface, generated from a laser printer and printed on the same granite paper. Nothing out of the ordinary, nothing incriminating. Just the start of an old saying. Eerily ominous, haunting in its significance.

WHAT A TANGLED WEB WE WEAVE . . .

"What does it mean?" Aaron Moses demanded twenty minutes later, irate because his evening off had been interrupted by what, in his mind, was the stupid prank of a twisted kid with too much time on his hands.

"It's part of an old saying," Sheriff Garcia attempted to explain to the surly detective, whose face bore a day's growth of dark stubble. He'd been camped out before the television watching Monday Night Football highlights on ESPN when Porter called. "You know. It ends, when first we practice—"

"I know how it ends," Moses snapped. "I'm not an idiot. What I want to know is, *what* does it mean? *Who's* practicing to deceive *what?*" And he swept his ill-tempered glare around the parking lot, at the growing crowd of spectators that had assembled to watch the unfolding drama. They congregated behind the yellow police tape cordoning off the entire parking lot, buzzing with excitement and speculation.

Local residents and retailers, students abandoning their studies in favor of the ongoing saga surrounding their missing peer. News crews had appeared, drawn to the developing story like bloodhounds following the scent of a fresh kill.

Garrison glanced up from conferring with the leader of the Evidence Response Team that had arrived on the scene shortly after Detective Moses. They were combing the surrounding area in search of evidence to be used for forensic analysis, although Garrison knew it would be like searching for a needle in a haystack. He knew that their phantom menace had selected the bustling, heavily trafficked Route 1 corridor for the deliberate purpose of covering his tracks. Like a puppet master, he wanted to control the pace of the game, drop clues at his own insidious whim, and dictate their movements. String them along for the thrill of the chase.

He scanned the faces in the crowd, knowing that their predator could very well be in the midst, posing as an innocent bystander. Taking sadistic pleasure in his own handiwork.

Fury tightened in Garrison's gut. Hot, boiling rage fueled by a gripping sense of frustration and powerlessness overtook him. He detested the idea of being toyed with, having no control over the outcome. It was like playing Russian roulette. And unlike his comrades, Garrison felt particularly vulnerable, edgy. Their predator had thrown down the gauntlet at *his* feet, had issued a challenge and then, like a frolicking child, had slipped away undetected. *Catch me if you can.* That kind of maneuver not only reeked of arrogance, but of cold, calculated premeditation. *Let the games begin . . .*

Althea's backpack containing the latest note was being carted away by the evidence technicians. When the police removed Althea's computer hard drive from her dorm room on Thursday, they had assumed that her missing personal effects, specifically her purse and backpack, were with her when she disappeared. The reappearance of her backpack effectively put to rest any lingering doubts that she had, indeed, been abducted. The accompanying note sealed the nail in the coffin.

Chief Taggert was being interviewed by the press, briefing the public on this latest development without giving away details that could compromise the investigation. When they had finished with him, their voracious gazes turned in Garrison's direction. Like a herd of charging bulls, they started toward him, microphones extended, questions shouted to be overheard above the rest. Like a classroom of first graders with hands jutted anxiously in the air, vying for the teacher's attention.

"Special Agent Wade, would you like to comment further on the status of the investigation?"

He shook his head once, a terse refusal, before turning on his heel and walking away. College Park police officers and sheriff's deputies served as a barricade between him and the swarm of buzzards.

Cole Porter fell in step beside him. "I told Mr. Ritter to be on hand this evening in case we need to speak with him again."

Garrison nodded shortly, his temper worn dangerously thin. His cell phone rang and he snatched it up, barked without thinking, "Speak."

There was a moment of startled silence. And then a sweetly familiar voice, tentative and soft. "Garrison? This is Imani."

He relaxed a fraction, closed his eyes briefly. "What can I do for you?" he asked evenly.

"I just saw the news, about the recovery of Althea's backpack?"

His deadpan silence prompted her to continue. "Something isn't right, Garrison."

The tension returned, tightening his muscles. "What do you mean?"

"I mean," Imani sounded both puzzled and concerned, "Althea didn't have her backpack with her on Sunday night. At least not at the meeting."

"Are you sure?" Garrison demanded.

"Positive. She was kicking herself because she'd forgotten it in her room, and she had to borrow notebook paper from one of the other students. She felt really bad about it, too. Said it made her look unprepared, and I assured her it was no big deal." She paused, a thread of something akin to dread in her next question. "Where did you find her backpack?"

"I didn't find it," Garrison said flatly, his mind already racing. "It was brought to me, so to speak."

He could almost see Imani's frown, her pretty lips pursed. "I don't understand."

"That makes two of us. Look, thanks for the tip. I'll be in touch."

He disconnected, a solitary muscle in his jaw clenched. Cole Porter took one look at the lethal intent in his dark eyes and asked automatically, "Where to?"

"LaPlata dorm. Seems we need to pay our friend Miss Torres another visit."

Elizabeth greeted him with a smile of undisguised pleasure.

"Agent Wade, I was hoping you would change—" The smile died on her lips at the sight of Cole Porter standing behind him. "Oh, you brought a visitor," she said flatly.

"This isn't a social call, Miss Torres," Garrison said coolly, his deadly expression fixed upon her face as he sauntered into the room uninvited. She backed up as he approached, stalking her step for step. Her cheeks were flushed from being outdoors, her hair windblown.

He raised an eyebrow. "A bit late to be out and about, isn't it?"

"What are you talking about? I've been here all night."

Garrison shook his head slowly, his expression one of mild disappointment. "What did we discuss earlier, Miss Torres?" he asked, his voice dangerously soft again. "Do you remember what I told you about lying to me?"

She smoothed a trembling hand over her hair. "So I stepped out for a minute. There's no law against that, is there?"

"Depends. Where did you go?"

"To see a friend." She shrugged, plopped down on her bed. "He wasn't there."

"This friend wouldn't happen to be Brian Ritter, would it?"

"No." She had to angle her head to look up at him as he towered over her. A slow smile crawled across her face. "That was a one-time thing. Would you care to have a seat?"

Garrison ignored the invitation. "Are you aware that Althea Pritchard's backpack was found on Route 1 tonight?"

Her dark eyes flickered, shifted from his momentarily. "Really? No, I didn't know that." She paused, allowed concern to enter her voice. "What does that mean?"

"You tell me."

"Tell you what?"

"Where was Althea's backpack on Thursday when the police came to take her computer?"

"It wasn't here."

"Think harder," Garrison said, a low command.

Elizabeth's confused gaze darted to Detective Porter's. "You were here. Did you see it?" He said nothing, watching her silently. She looked back at Garrison, incredulous. "What are you saying? You think *I* had the backpack?"

"Miss Torres, my patience is wearing extremely thin. It's been brought to my attention that Althea didn't have her backpack on Sunday night when she disappeared, that she left it here. So," he said with increasing menace, "that leaves only two possibilities. Either you or someone you know had the backpack. Or one of the police officers confiscated it during their search and failed to mention it to anyone. Now why, Miss Torres, would they do something like that?"

"I don't know," Elizabeth huffed. "Ask *him*."

Garrison flicked a glance over his shoulder at Cole Porter, who shook his head adamantly from side to side. "It wasn't here, Agent Wade. I even checked for it myself."

Garrison's inscrutable gaze returned to Elizabeth. "Who else has been in this room?"

"I don't remember. My friends are in and out of here all day. If you don't believe me, just ask the girls down the hall." Her tone turned mocking. "It's a *dormitory*, Agent Wade. No one stays in their own room all the time."

Garrison regarded her in silence for a moment. Taped to the wall behind her was a heart-shaped photograph of her and Althea Pritchard, smiling and hugging. EL AND AL, FRIENDS FOREVER, the pink lettering across the top proclaimed.

"What line of work was your father in before he ran for political office, Miss Torres?" Garrison inquired, already knowing the answer.

She hesitated. "Electronics. He ran his own company."

He nodded once, slowly. "Thank you for your time." Without another word, he turned on his heel and started from the room. Cole Porter met the apprehension in Elizabeth's gaze, smiled narrowly before following Garrison out.

She waited until the door had closed behind them. Only then did she allow the smile to break through. A slow, cunning smile.

Garrison left College Park and headed onto the beltway toward Upper Marlboro. Although he figured Louis and Barbara Pritchard had already seen the evening broadcast, he thought he owed it to them to deliver the news himself. Just as he knew it would be his duty to tell them if—and when—Althea was found.

Dead or alive.

On that grim note, Garrison picked up his cell phone and punched numbers. Eddie answered on the first ring, not at all surprised to hear from his partner at such a late hour.

"What took you so long?" he drawled. "I was expecting your call hours ago."

"I got distracted. Any progress on locating Torres's long-lost brother?"

"Still on it. Last known address was somewhere in Richmond, Virginia. I've got a special agent down there checking into it now."

Garrison nodded briskly. "What about Althea's e-mail messages? Any red flags yet?"

"Negative. The usual girly stuff. Notes to friends about cute guys, tough classes, boring professors—*your* foxy professor not included, of course. Althea had nothing but glowing praise for the beloved Professor Maxwell."

"What about Web sites she visited?" Garrison asked impatiently, not wanting to think about Imani Maxwell any more than he already had.

"Nothing out of the ordinary. She did visit some chat rooms, though. We're looking into it some more. And we're running a list of sex offenders through the system to see what comes up."

Garrison glanced in the rearview mirror, noting a dark sedan that was following a little too closely. "While you're at it," he said, "run a background check on Detectives Aaron Moses and Cole Porter. I want to make sure Chief Taggert doesn't have any more rotten apples in the bunch."

Eddie chuckled dryly. "Naturally. So what do you make of it?"

Garrison didn't have to ask what his partner meant. The personal phone numbers of FBI personnel were unlisted, classified information. Whoever had called him that evening had somehow obtained access to his cell phone number, which suggested Garrison already knew the individual. Or the person had used other means. And to what end?

"I'll let you know when I decide," he answered neutrally.

"Well, will that be all?" Eddie drolly inquired. "Because if it's all the same to you, I have a very nice warm body waiting for me in bed."

Garrison chuckled, thinking of the cold, empty bed awaiting him at home and suppressing an uncharacteristic pang of envy. "Give Annabella my regards."

"I'll do even better," Eddie promised with a wolfish grin.

Garrison shook his head ruefully as he disconnected. Not for the first time, he wished he could be more like Eddie Balducci, whose carefree nature had never interfered with his effectiveness as a special agent. Although their work was challenging, it was possible to have a life outside of the Bureau. Garrison knew special agents who, barring any unforeseen developments in their cases, punched the clock at six P.M. and went home. To loving wives with open arms, to children who awaited them with tales of schoolyard antics. Garrison knew that putting in overtime on the job was far easier than returning to the stark loneliness of an empty apartment.

The reason behind his self-imposed isolation was rooted in his secret. The deep dark secret that after six years in the Bureau, he still hadn't mastered the art of suppressing the nightmares, the visions of countless innocent people who had met with violent ends. Children whose lives were cut brutally short, snatched away before their time. Occupational hazards, he and his comrades were told, as they got shuffled to the next case. Whenever Garrison found himself questioning if he was in the right line of work, he remembered the satisfaction, the pure exhilaration that went with apprehending violent criminals and ensuring justice for the victims' families.

And he knew he could never walk away.

But on rare occasions, driving alone at night on a mostly deserted highway, he wondered if there would ever be room in his life for something more. Something permanent.

Banishing these gloomy thoughts from his mind, Garrison

threw another glance in the rearview mirror. The dark sedan had switched lanes and was now several car lengths behind him. A false alarm, nothing more.

At least not this time.

Chapter 11

Imani was deep in thought as she left her office the following afternoon. She hadn't slept well, thinking about Althea's recovered backpack and all the implications that had. Who could have removed the backpack from her dorm room? And, more to the point, why?

She was so distracted with these questions that she didn't hear one of her colleagues calling her name until he was upon her.

"You're not old enough to be losing your hearing," panted Julian Jerome, falling in step beside her, "so you must have been ignoring me on purpose."

Imani gave him an absent smile. "You know that isn't true. I didn't hear you, that's all."

"Good, because you know how fragile my ego is. I couldn't handle being ignored by a beautiful woman."

She chuckled. "God forbid."

Julian Jerome was the most popular instructor in the African-American Studies department, and one only had to look at him to understand why. With wavy black hair and green eyes that betrayed his biracial heritage, he looked more suited for Hollywood than a college classroom. His lectures were layered with enough charm to make the female students clamor for seats near the front, and it was no wonder that his courses had the longest waiting lists every semester.

At thirty-five, he'd already authored seven books on African-American history and was working on his latest. He had future aspirations of becoming president of the university, a major accomplishment among those in higher education, particularly when it came to black faculty members, who were still greatly outnumbered at almost any large university. But if anyone could break through those racial barriers, Julian Jerome could.

He flashed Imani one of those gleaming white smiles that made his female students swoon. "Are you in training for a marathon or something?"

"No. I'm just ready to go home, that's all. It's been a long day."

"Guess that means dinner with me is out of the question," he lamented, affecting a look of genuine disappointment.

Imani laughed. "As if *you* ever have to worry about eating alone. Besides," she added mildly, "you're supposed to be recovering from a divorce. How are you, by the way?"

He shrugged. "Taking it one day at a time. Sylvia and I were together for ten years. You don't just get over something like that overnight."

"I can imagine," Imani murmured sympathetically.

"So how are you enjoying the house?"

"It's wonderful. I love it."

"Glad to hear it. Sylvia and I had a lot of happy times in that house, believe it or not. It's good to know that someone else will be able to create their own special memories there."

"Thank you. And thanks, once again, for renting it out to me."

He grinned, sliding his hands into the pockets of his khaki trousers. "Well, I just figured if you're half as good a tenant as you are a professor, then I should have no problems. Listen," he said, abruptly switching gears, "we need to get together to discuss the recruitment program. I have—"

Something in her pained expression halted him. "What's wrong?"

"I guess you haven't heard. I'm stepping down from the committee."

Julian stopped in midstride. "What? Why would you do that?"

"I'd really rather not say," Imani hedged. "I'm drafting a memo to distribute to all the committee members. You'll have to elect a new chairperson."

"I see." Julian pursed his lips, deep in thought. Imani wondered if he was already envisioning himself in the coveted position, then promptly berated herself for such a nasty thought. Julian Jerome had shown her nothing but kindness in the years she had known him. It was unfair to think he would derive some personal satisfaction in capitalizing on her removal from the committee.

"I know how much the program meant to you," he said, his expression somber. "It was *your* brainchild, for God's sake. Are you sure you have to do this?"

A lump tightened in Imani's throat. She ignored it. "Positive. Anyway," she added breezily, waving off his concern, "maybe it's for the best. God knows I have enough on my plate as it is."

But the words hung between them, hollow and ringing with untruth.

The smile Julian sent her was gentle, almost pitying. "Don't worry, I'll give you regular updates," he reassured her. "I'll keep you in the loop."

"Thanks," Imani said, genuinely grateful.

"Talk, white boy."

Victor Davenport sat coolly in his chair as Aaron Moses paced the floor in the interrogation room at the police station. His slate-colored eyes were emotionless as they followed the detective, and the pale hand that rested upon the table was steady as a rock. He lifted his bony shoulders in an unaffected shrug. "I got nothing to say, Detective," he drawled. "Not without a lawyer present."

"Why do you think you need a lawyer?" Moses sneered. "Got something to hide?"

Davenport studied his fingernails, looking bored. "I'm not stupid. I know my rights, and you can't question me without a lawyer."

"We called him already," Moses bluffed. "He said he's on his way."

"Then we'll just have to postpone our little chat session until he gets here, won't we?" With that, Davenport folded his arms across his chest and closed his eyes. Moses shot an agitated look toward the mirror on the wall.

On the other side stood Garrison and Chief Taggert, watching through the glass. They had been there ten minutes, waiting, observing, biding their time until Davenport cracked under the strain or gave them the slightest reason to detain him.

Yesterday morning, a bartender from a popular College Park nightclub had called the command post to report seeing Althea there with a couple of her classmates four nights before she disappeared. When they left the nightclub on that particular occasion, the bartender swore he saw a man follow them out. The same man, as it turned out, who had been staring at Althea the entire night. The bartender hadn't thought much of it until he heard that Althea was missing.

Twenty-four hours after receiving the tip and armed with a police composite sketch, Garrison and Aaron Moses tracked Victor Davenport down to a seedy apartment building twenty miles from campus.

"What do you think?" Chief Taggert asked Garrison.

Standing with his legs braced apart, Garrison stroked his chin thoughtfully. "Doesn't rattle very easily, does he?"

"No kidding. And that's saying a lot, considering Moses usually has them crying by now."

"Nah, we don't want him to cry," Garrison drawled softly, almost to himself. His eyes narrowed on the gold cross suspended from Victor Davenport's neck. "We just want to see if he'll sweat a little, that's all. Then we'll let him go."

"Let him go?" Taggert repeated, stupefied. "He's the closest thing we've had to a real suspect."

"You know as well as I do that we've got nothing on him," Garrison said.

"He's got a record. That's good enough for me."

"Some parking tickets and a couple of misdemeanors two years ago don't automatically make him our perp."

Taggert's breath hissed out impatiently. "For chrissake, Wade, were you sent here to help us or sabotage us? You dismissed Toomer as a suspect, and now you're ready to send this smug little bastard along on his merry way."

Garrison didn't flinch. "We'll watch him a few more minutes, then ride his tail the second he leaves. See what he does, where he goes, who he talks to. If he acts spooked, you might get a search warrant out of it." His succinct tone brooked no argument.

Taggert sighed and fished in his pocket for his trusty roll of Tums. Thumbing one off, he popped it into his mouth and shook his head, grimacing. "This case is eating a hole through my gut," he complained. "I've got reporters calling me left and right, Pritchard on my back—"

"You arrest Davenport without probable cause and an ulcer will be the least of your concerns." Jaw clenched, Garrison reached for the doorknob. "Enough of this."

Moses glared at him as he entered the interrogation room. Ignoring him, Garrison pulled up a chair at the table and straddled it. Victor Davenport sat up straighter, regarding him warily.

"Mr. Davenport," Garrison got right to the point, "you're a smart man. I'm sure you realize we're grasping at straws by hauling you in here."

Across the room, Moses made a choking sound and started forward. Garrison silenced him with a deadly look before returning his attention to Davenport, who'd been caught off guard by Garrison's opening statement. He looked from Moses to Garrison before his mouth curled upward in a slow grin.

"Oh, I get it," he said. "You guys are gonna do the old good cop–bad cop routine, like you see on *NYPD Blue* or something. Jeez, this is unreal."

"Truth is stranger than fiction, isn't it?" Garrison murmured.

"What?"

"You've heard that expression before, haven't you? It's one of Mark Twain's finest." Garrison chuckled, shaking his head as he leaned back in his chair, posturing like he had all the time in the world. "I'm sorry, Mr. Davenport. You struck me as a well-read man for some reason. In fact, I found it odd that you like to pass your time in nightclubs surrounded by drunk college students."

"It's a free country," Davenport said disdainfully. "I can go where I want."

"Of course. It just doesn't seem like your thing, know what I mean? You seem more like the coffee shop type."

Davenport made a face. "Sitting around with a bunch of pretentious intellectuals discussing Van Gogh and Nietzsche? I don't think so."

Garrison grinned. "Guess if you put it that way, it doesn't sound so appealing. Not enough pretty women in coffee shops, anyway."

"You got it."

"So that's it, huh? That's why you like The Vous."

Davenport stiffened. "A lot of people go to nightclubs. It doesn't make them criminals."

"Only the underage drinkers," Garrison quipped.

Victor Davenport smirked. "I can assure you I'm legal. Not that it matters, though. I wasn't drinking that night."

Garrison raised an eyebrow. "No alcohol?" He leaned

forward in his chair. "So let me get this straight. You went to a nightclub, didn't dance, didn't drink, didn't mingle with anyone . . . What *were* you there for, Mr. Davenport?"

Davenport shifted uneasily in his chair. "Is my lawyer here yet?"

"You like looking at pretty college students, Vic?" Garrison prodded, his voice deceptively soft. Abbreviating Davenport's name like they were old buddies. "Is that why you went to The Vous that night?"

"Even if that were true, it still doesn't make me a criminal."

"Ever heard of voyeurism, white boy?" Moses snarled, tired of watching passively from the sidelines. "That's how the Boston Strangler got his start, staring at pretty women, peeping through windows."

"I'm not a serial killer," Victor Davenport said indignantly.

"Is that what you do, Davenport?" Moses sneered contemptuously, ignoring his protest. "Sit in your little corner and watch the honeys gyrate on the dance floor until you're so turned on that you can't wait to get home and service yourself?"

Davenport turned crimson. "I don't have to take this. I'll sue your—"

Garrison lifted a hand, signaling Moses to back off. "That won't be necessary, Mr. Davenport," he said coolly. "We're finished here." To make his point, he stood and started from the room.

But Victor wasn't finished. "If admiring beautiful women qualifies as criminal behavior, every heterosexual male should be behind bars." His harsh crack of laughter reverberated against the plaster walls. "Just because I was checking out the Pritchard chick doesn't mean I abducted her, for God's sake. And if I was gonna take anyone, it would have been that sexy little professor Pritchard's always hanging around. Now *she's* a hot number."

Garrison had nearly reached the door when Davenport

ended his tirade. At the unmistakable reference to Imani, something akin to fear gripped him. On its heel was outrage, hot and swift. He spun around, practically knocking aside Detective Moses as he crossed the room and grabbed a startled Victor Davenport by the shirtfront, hauling him unceremoniously out of the chair.

"Now you listen to me, you arrogant little piece of garbage," he said in a low, controlled voice. "I don't take kindly to threats, and that sounded an awful lot like a threat to me. If you don't think I have enough to pin you with Althea Pritchard's kidnapping, think again. All I have to do is make one phone call, and you'll be buried to your ears in incriminating evidence and on your way to a federal penitentiary so fast your head will spin." His eyes narrowed, a lethal promise. "If you think I'm bluffing, just try me."

And just as suddenly as Garrison had grabbed him, he released his hold. Davenport lost his balance as he reared backward, flailing his arms and nearly missing the chair.

Garrison stood over him, his expression filled with contempt. "You should have quit while you were ahead, Davenport. Now get out of here before I change my mind."

This time Victor didn't hesitate, scrambling to his feet and beating a hasty retreat from the room. Garrison blinked in the wake of his departure, felt the blinding fury slowly ebb from his body.

Chief Taggert stood in the doorway openly gaping at him. Detective Moses shook his head in amused disbelief. "And you thought *I* was a loose cannon," he muttered to his boss.

"Get a tail on him," Garrison ordered, jerking his silk tie loose as he strode from the room, which suddenly seemed too suffocating. Taggert and Moses started after him, flanking him on each side.

"What in the world just happened back there?" Taggert demanded, struggling to keep up with Garrison's long strides. "Why aren't we booking that son of a—"

"He didn't do it," Garrison bit off.

"What? He practically admitted it!" Moses roared.

Garrison's smile was cold, narrow. "What interrogation room were you in, Detective?"

"Wait a minute," snapped Moses, placing a detaining hand on Garrison's arm. The two men squared off in the middle of the corridor. "Are we talking about the same suspect here? He just threatened to kidnap the professor. You went off on him, for God's sake!"

"I lost my head," Garrison conceded. "But Davenport's clean. He's cocky as all get out, but he didn't take Althea."

"He didn't deny going to the club to watch her," Taggert countered.

"He's a Peeping Tom. He enjoys watching women, fantasizing about them. But he doesn't have the guts to act on anything, nor does he want to. He feels above it all, almost divinely superior. You see the cross around his neck? He probably attends church faithfully every Sunday, tells himself he's a decent guy with harmless fetishes. He wears a wedding band, even though he's never been married or engaged. It excites him to be at the club, like he's cheating on his imaginary wife or something."

Moses crossed his arms, one cynical eyebrow arched. "And how do you know all this, Sigmund Freud?"

"Training. And instincts. Or did you think I was just making small talk with him?"

Taggert and Moses exchanged considering glances. "If you're so confident he's not our perp, why do you want him tailed?" Moses persisted.

Garrison gave him a bemused smile. "I always allow myself a margin of error." Without another word, he turned and continued down the corridor.

"Where are you going?" Taggert called after him.

"You know how to reach me."

Imani was surprised to find Garrison standing on her doorstep that evening. She'd just finished on the treadmill, and wore nothing more than a spandex halter and shorts with a pair of sneakers. A fine sheen of sweat clung to her skin and dampened her curly hair.

"Garrison." Her pulse quickened, and it had nothing to do with the thirty-minute workout she'd just pushed herself through. Self-consciously, she dabbed at her face with the towel draped around her neck.

Garrison said nothing as he thrust his hands deep into his pants pockets. He had shed his suit jacket, and the sleeves of his starched indigo shirt—a very flattering color for his complexion—were rolled up, exposing powerful forearms. His tie was loosened and his shirt collar open, revealing the strong column of his throat. Tension radiated from every muscle in his body.

She stared up at him. "Is something wrong?"

His dark gaze was intense, his voice soft. "No, not really." Garrison had considered, then decided against telling Imani about Victor Davenport's veiled threat. He didn't want to alarm her unnecessarily or prematurely. And not for the first time, he wondered about this strange, overwhelming need to protect her. What had caused him to snap in that interrogation room? The rage had been swift and unmerciful, beyond his control or comprehension.

"Would you like to come in?" Imani asked softly.

"No, thanks. I just came to . . ." *Make sure you were all right. To see for myself that no harm had come to you.*

Imani was watching him expectantly, curiously. "You just came to . . . ?" she prompted.

"Do surveillance. I volunteered for the first shift."

A flicker of wariness touched her eyes. "Is this because of yesterday? Because you found Althea's backpack, and the note?"

Garrison's gaze zeroed in on her face. They had not released any information about the note. He'd made that explicitly clear. No details, not yet. "How do you know about that?" he demanded.

Imani bit her lower lip, looking sheepish. "My cousin told me when I got home this evening. Apparently there's been a leak to the media and—"

Garrison swore savagely under his breath.

"They're going to air it this evening," Imani finished almost apologetically.

He nodded curtly, turned, and headed back toward his truck parked beneath the hanging shroud of sycamore trees near her house. Close, but not close enough to be detected by the casual observer.

"I thought you were taking the first shift," Imani called after him, striving to keep the disappointment from her voice at the thought of him leaving.

"I'll be here."

Over the next two hours, between grading papers and preparing discussion notes for Friday's class, Imani tried to forget about Garrison Wade's presence just beyond her front door. But no matter how hard she tried, she couldn't get him off her mind. She made excuses to wander over to the window in her upstairs office, stole peeks at the GMC truck through the venetian blinds. Comforted somehow by his presence, wanting him so much nearer.

Stupid girl, silly girl. Didn't you learn your lesson on Monday night?

David called her around seven as she was making coffee after her shower. "Hey, stranger. We've been playing phone tag all week. If I didn't know any better, I would think you were avoiding me."

"Of course not," she said quickly. "It's just been one of those weeks."

"Tell me about it. I've been swamped here at work. I can't even imagine how many billable hours I've logged these past two days alone." He heaved an exhausted sigh. "I had planned to drop by this evening, but it looks like I'll be stuck here all night, unfortunately."

Something suspiciously akin to relief flooded her, followed quickly by guilt. "That's okay. I have a lot of paperwork to finish up myself."

"Hey listen, I was thinking we could go somewhere nice this Friday night. Someplace exotic, romantic, and sinfully expensive."

"Umm. I'll have to get back to you on that." Between David's unexpected visits to her house and the recently planned—and canceled—dates, they had been communicating more frequently lately. Imani knew David was trying to work his way back into her life, and she wasn't sure how she felt about that.

But they were still good friends, a tiny inner voice reminded her. What was the harm?

"Look, baby, I have to go," David said. "This Friday we'll definitely get together, how does that sound?"

"Okay. Why not?"

"Good. Oh, and before I forget, how was the play?"

Imani closed her eyes briefly. "It was fine," she answered lamely.

"I really hated to bail on you like that, but you know it was only out of sheer necessity. One day all of these sacrifices I'm making are going to pay off major dividends, you'll see. Call you tomorrow?"

"Sure. Good night, David." She replaced the phone slowly, her heart heavy. She felt like she was drowning, flailing and kicking her legs against a powerful current, trying desperately to surface from the deep. But there was no relief in sight, and she kept being pulled under.

Mechanically, she stirred cream and sugar into her coffee and took a tentative sip. Then before she could stop herself, she poured some coffee into a thermos, left it strong and black. And strode purposefully from the house in her bedroom slippers.

Garrison was bent over a stack of reports in the lit interior of the truck. His expression registered surprise when she tapped on the glass. He hesitated, then pushed the button to roll down the power windows.

"What's going on?" he asked quietly.

"Nothing." She paused, then thrust the steaming thermos at him. "I made coffee, thought you might like some."

Something soft flickered in his dark eyes. "Thank you." Their hands brushed as he accepted the offering from her. It was only for a second, but Imani's body reacted like he had actually reached out and caressed her skin.

He watched her over the rim as he took a sip. "This was very thoughtful of you." His mouth curved in a rueful half grin. "You make better coffee than I do."

She smiled. "I'm glad you like it."

"I do. Very much." Their gazes held for a moment, and she wondered when they had stopped talking about coffee. Because it was apparent that they had.

Garrison cleared his throat, returned to his paperwork. "You'd better get back inside," he said gruffly. "It's kinda cold for you to be out here barely dressed."

A defiant chin went up. "I'm not *barely* dressed."

He lifted his head and raked his assessing gaze across her freshly showered form, starting from the sleeveless Old Navy T-shirt to her slender legs snugly encased in low-rider denim jeans, to the furry pink slippers on her feet. It was a slow perusal that left her feeling hot and breathless.

"You are if I say so," Garrison murmured, daring her to contradict him. "And I say you are."

She backed up a step, her legs wobbly. "Fine. Enjoy your coffee." She started away, then turned around again, hands on hips. "You know, if you wanted to get rid of me, you should have just said so."

His mouth twitched. "I thought I just did."

She threw her hands up in mild exasperation, spun on her heel and stalked back toward the house. Chuckling, he shook his head after her departing form before returning to the reports he needed to catch up on from his other cases. As grueling as law school had been, it had at least prepared him, in part, for the extensive paperwork required of FBI special agents. An endless procession of reporting procedures to rival three years' worth of assignments given in any constitutional law course.

A minute later she returned, wearing her wool coat that always reminded him of peanut butter. She marched right up to the truck.

"Better?"

"Uh-huh." His amused glance flicked downward. "Except for the shoes."

She looked down and scowled because she'd forgotten to change her bedroom slippers. She didn't know what she was doing out there, what kind of game she was playing with him. It made no sense whatsoever.

She didn't care.

Skirting the fender, she opened the passenger door and climbed in beside him. Garrison looked at her like she'd lost her mind.

"What're you doing?"

"Keeping you company."

He frowned. "Did I miss something? When did I ask for company?"

Her shrug was elegantly dismissive. "You didn't. I just took it upon myself, like with the coffee." She nodded toward the pile of paperwork on his lap. "What're you reading?"

"It's classified." Her fresh scent swirled around him, filling his nostrils with soap and jasmine. If he just closed his eyes, he could still taste her sweetness, could remember the way her warm body had felt in his arms, a perfect fit. He would much rather be captured and tortured by terrorist operatives than endure the torture he now faced at this woman's hands.

"Was there something you wanted?" he inquired evenly.

You! I want you, but I can't have you! Imani blinked, felt an embarrassed flush creep over her cheeks. What was wrong with her? She was behaving like some lovestruck teenager

fawning over the high school football star—something she
had never done. It was so absurd, what she was doing. Flirting
and carrying on this way. Garrison Wade must think her a
total flake, and rightfully so.

She looked at him, met the puzzlement in those midnight
eyes. As fine as he was, he was undoubtedly used to women
throwing themselves at him. He probably received proposi-
tions the way most people received junk mail. Desiree Williams
had looked ready to slay dragons to lay claim to him. There
were probably countless others like her in his life.

"I'm sorry," Imani mumbled, her hand inching toward the
door handle as she wondered how she was going to make a
dignified exit. "I didn't mean to interrupt your work."

"That's all right." His gaze was probing. "Are you sure
there wasn't something you wanted?"

She bobbed her head quickly. "Positive. Good night."

"Good night, Imani." She thought she heard a soft trace
of regret in his voice, but promptly decided she'd only imagined it. She climbed down from the truck and returned to her
house without a backward glance.

Five minutes later, Garrison rang the doorbell and asked
to use her bathroom. She gestured vaguely to the powder
room and returned to the kitchen table where she'd been trying to write out her bills. She pretended not to notice when
he appeared in the arched entryway a minute later. As if her
heart rate hadn't accelerated when she heard the toilet flush,
heard him washing his hands in the sink.

"I've got an agent coming out to continue surveillance."

"Okay." She didn't look over her shoulder. "So I guess
this means you can start heading out."

To her surprise, he didn't take his leave. Instead, he walked
into the kitchen and pulled out a chair beside her. Their
knees brushed as he sat down, bracing his elbows on his
muscular thighs as he leaned toward her.

Liquid warmth erupted in her belly, made her look away. She floundered for something to say and pounced on the first inane thing she could come up with when her eyes fell on the Spanish-translated payment instructions on the back of her electric bill.

"So, Garrison, are you bilingual? I've heard that the FBI likes their agents to be fluent in other languages. Something about terrorism and counterintelligence."

His mouth twitched. Like he knew she was grasping at straws for conversation. "That's correct."

"So do you speak another language?" she prodded.

"Russian."

She stared at him in surprise. "Really?"

The look he gave her was amused. "You find it strange for a black man to be fluent in Russian?"

"Not strange at all. Impressive. I've always heard what a difficult language it is to learn. What made you choose Russian? Why not, say, Spanish?"

He lifted those broad shoulders in a lazy shrug. "I took a Russian studies course in college that got me interested in the Romanov period and that whole culture. So I decided to follow up with some language courses and a visit to Russia. It worked to my advantage that the FBI considers Russian a critical language."

"Say something in Russian."

A wry smile curved his sensuous lips. "How'd I know that was coming?"

"Come on, Garrison. Be a sport. I'll say something in French if you want," she offered as a bribe.

"Russian isn't like French, Imani. It doesn't sound pretty."

"I don't care."

He looked at her, his gaze lowering subtly to her legs. *"Ty neobychaino seksual'na v etikh dzhinsakh,"* he murmured in a low, surprisingly fluid voice.

Imani blinked, and wondered why her cheeks felt hot. "What does that mean?" she asked, a touch breathlessly.

He shook his head, chuckling softly. "Some things are better left untranslated."

She decided he was probably right. But Lord, if the man could make the Russian language sound sexy, she was in for a world of trouble. She looked at him suspiciously. "Did you say something insulting?"

"Not in the least," he drawled.

The directness of his gaze sent heat pulsing through her. She got up abruptly, intending to do something productive. Like empty and clean the coffeemaker, replenish Shiloh's water dish.

Garrison's arm snaked out, curving possessively around her waist. She didn't resist as he pulled her gently, firmly, onto his lap. Her breath lodged in her throat as she gazed into his face, hard angles and planes softened only by those incredibly long lashes.

His eyes were smoldering. "Why are we playing these games?" he murmured.

She swallowed with difficulty. "I don't know what you mean," she lied.

"Tell me you didn't come outside because you wanted to see me," he said, a husky command.

"You know I can't do that."

"And I can't tell you that I didn't come over here to see you. Because I did."

His words, as potent as whiskey, sent waves of pleasure coursing through her. Shame followed swiftly on its heels. "I've always been good about—"

"Staying faithful?"

She nodded slowly. "I don't want to hurt David. I don't want to want this. I don't want—"

He cupped her face, slanted his head over her mouth. She closed her eyes on a deep, involuntary sigh. Surrendering. Powerless against the masterful pressure of his lips on hers, the heat and need between them not to be denied. She flattened her hands against his solid chest, felt the rapid beat of his heart beneath her palms. As erratic as her own.

"This is what you want," he whispered into her mouth. His tongue delved inside, hot and sweet, and she met it hungrily with her own. She didn't know where he began, where she ended. They held each other tightly as their mouths opened and closed over one another, urgently, with an intensity that rocked her to the core. She could not remember why this was wrong, only that she needed him, wanted him like nothing she had ever wanted before.

His hands kneaded her back, roamed down her spine before he slipped one big hand between her thighs. The heat spread, stretching the length of her body, pooling between her legs. She clamped her thighs together, keeping his hand there near her pulsing center, arching into him. Accepting the unspoken invitation, his other hand worked its way underneath her T-shirt and deftly unhooked her satin bra, stroking the pad of his thumb across her nipple. She gasped sharply as her body went up in flames.

"Garrison," she whimpered his name. "Please . . ."

He captured the rest of her plea in his mouth, kissing her deeply, drugging her senses. She was still spinning as he lifted her T-shirt, lowered his head to her breast. His moist mouth played around the edges of her dark nipple, then closed in. She shuddered and clung to his neck as her head fell back. A low moan erupted from her throat as he caressed the sensitive peak with his tongue, slow and intoxicatingly erotic. Torturing her, driving her toward the edge.

The phone rang, sounding like an explosion in her head. She jumped up at once, her legs perilously wobbly. Garrison met her flustered expression with a calmness belied only by the smoky desire still burning in his eyes.

"Saved by the bell," he murmured with a trace of wry humor.

She walked over to the phone and snatched it up on the final ring. Fearing it might be David, that he would hear the betrayal in her voice, she tried to sound normal. A feat, considering she could barely catch her breath. "Hello?"

"Hey, Mani. It's me again." *Jada. Thank God!*

"Hey, girl . . . What's up?" Imani watched as Garrison stood, straightened his pants. His gaze held hers as he sauntered toward her. She looked up at him as he stopped before her. He reached out, brushing his thumb across her lower lip. She trembled hard, closed her eyes as he bent, kissing her softly, briefly, with enough tenderness to melt her insides.

Come lock up, he mouthed as he drew away. She nodded wordlessly, followed him to the door with the cordless phone pressed to her ear. She barely listened as Jada ranted about her mother's absurd determination to wear burgundy to the wedding.

Imani stood in the open doorway admiring Garrison's relaxed, powerful strides as he strolled into the night. The fluid grace of a panther. He stopped to greet the special agent who had arrived for surveillance duty before climbing into his truck and driving off.

Jada's irate voice finally penetrated the fog of her brain. "Imani, have you been listening to a word I've said?"

"Absolutely," she lied, closing and locking the door. Feeling inexplicably warm and giddy, she crossed to the sofa and plopped down. "Now finish what you were saying, girl, so I can get my tired self to bed."

She knew her dreams, at least tonight, would be sweet. She would save the recriminations for tomorrow.

Chapter 12

Cole Porter had always wanted to become an FBI special agent.

Long before the hit show *The X-Files* popularized the profession, Cole had dreamed of being a Glock-toting secret agent in a double-breasted suit. A legitimate assassin. He'd grown up devouring spy movies, his diet consisting of James Bond flicks, shows like *I Spy, The Avengers,* and *The Saint.* Even the comedic sitcom *Get Smart* had fueled his wannabe jones.

He had gone to college to appease his parents and to fulfill the four-year degree requirement imposed upon special agent applicants. As soon as he graduated, he'd applied for a position with the Federal Bureau of Investigation, confident that his good grades as a criminal justice major and internship with the county police department would guarantee his status as a strong candidate. The application process was rigorous, the competition fierce, and the mandatory written test was an absolute beast. Mathematics, biodata inventory, cognitive ability testing, situational judgment—each portion was ingrained in his memory because he'd had to take the exam twice. After passing it by the skin of his teeth the second time around, he was elated. He'd gone out to celebrate with his homeboys, had bragged that the next time they saw him, he'd be a bona fide special agent for the *F-B-I*. He had enunciated the letters with pride.

Everyone was impressed, because no matter how much people liked to grumble about corruption in law enforcement—criticizing Hoover's regime for wrongfully wiretapping Dr. King's phones during the sixties, not to mention the more recent PR disasters resulting from the Waco and Ruby Ridge standoffs—most folks had mad respect for federal agencies like the CIA and FBI. Whether or not their respect resulted from fear didn't matter. In Cole's estimation, being an FBI special agent put you in an elite class. Not necessarily in monetary rewards, but in other ways. People sat up straighter, took notice when an agent walked into a room and flashed his badge. It was a position that carried weight, clout. Power. Membership definitely had its privileges.

He was utterly devastated when he received the official letter thanking him for his interest, but informing him that his application had been rejected because it wasn't deemed "competitive enough." His qualifications didn't fulfill the Bureau's demanding "critical needs." The ultimate kiss-off had been the one-liner at the end of the letter, encouraging him to reapply in the future after broadening his skills base.

Cole felt like his world was coming to an end, like a giant fist had reached into his life and maliciously shattered his pipe dream. He immediately began calling around, pleading his case to anyone he could reach. He'd even contacted Supervisory Special Agent Irvin Maxwell, well respected among his peers, a man who reportedly mentored new special agents and believed in giving back to the community. Cole figured a brother would be willing to help him out, maybe hook him up with some bigwig in personnel. Why not? White folks in Corporate America always had an inside track to the Good Ol' Boy network. But Irvin Maxwell wasn't about all that. He told Cole that the Bureau was different, that their primary concern was in hiring only the most highly qualified individuals, for the "good of this great nation we are sworn to serve and protect." Cole couldn't believe that Maxwell actually bought into all that rhetoric—although, secretly, so did Cole. Law enforcement was in his blood, and on most days he liked to believe his motivations for becoming a cop were noble.

At any rate, Maxwell had given him some career advice, then sent him on his way. Just like that. No special favors, no hook-a-brother-up promises.

Cole had seized upon the opportunity to work with Garrison Wade on the kidnapping task force. He had heard good things about the special agent, had even run a history report on Wade in his eagerness to learn more about him. And Cole had to admit, albeit grudgingly, that the brother's qualifications spoke for themselves. With a J.D. from Columbia University, Garrison Wade had entered under the FBI's law program, although his fluency in Russian would have easily qualified him for the foreign language entry program. If the law degree and bilingualism didn't make him a valuable asset to the Bureau, the fact that he was an expert marksman certainly did. He could reportedly shoot a moving target from a thousand yards without breaking a sweat, could assassinate with the lethal accuracy of the most skilled sniper. He had started his career specializing in foreign counterintelligence, monitoring communications between Russian operatives and engaging in covert missions that periodically took him overseas—the stuff of Cole's dreams. After two years, however, Wade had switched tracks, joining the Bureau's Joint Violent Crime Fugitive Task Force to fight the villains on domestic soil. Cole had searched for the reasons behind the sudden move, but the records were sealed to those without top-secret security clearance.

And then there were those other intangible things about Wade, things that couldn't necessarily be found in some file. Like the methodical mind and sharp, cunning instincts that had, undoubtedly, served him well in his counterintelligence duties. Skills that could make him an adept profiler one day.

He could read people like a book, an uncanny knack that made even Moses sweat a little, although he'd sooner die than admit it. Cole had observed Garrison Wade in action, saw the way he took control almost effortlessly, with a certain reckless disregard for other people's feelings or opinions. His presence commanded respect, cooperation and, yes, oftentimes fear. He made folks sit up and take notice. Cole knew he could learn a lot from Garrison Wade although, at thirty-two, Wade was three years younger than him.

If they ever found themselves on opposite sides of the law, Cole knew that Garrison Wade would be a formidable adversary, a serious force to be reckoned with.

The tap on his window gave him a start, breaking into his thoughts. He looked up and saw the special agent assigned to surveillance that night standing beside his car, his expression inquisitive. A white boy, probably barely out of college, Cole thought a bit resentfully. Definitely fresh from the Academy. California beach boy looks, blond hair, and Nordic blue eyes. What qualified *him* to be a special agent over Cole?

Cole rolled down the window in his Taurus and flashed his best nonthreatening smile, knowing that his baby face helped a lot. "Everything okay?"

"That's what I was going to—" Recognition filled the blue eyes. "Oh, it's you, Detective Porter. I didn't recognize you at first."

"That's all right. I know we all look alike." Agent Spencer faltered, unsure how to respond to the thinly veiled insult. Cole laughed, letting him off the hook.

"Kinda cold out tonight, isn't it?" he asked, eyeing the agent hunched inside his black trench coat.

"No kidding. You never know what the weather's going to be like from one day to the next. Monday night felt like springtime."

"Welcome to fall in Maryland," Cole quipped, and both men laughed easily. "Listen, if you need to take a quick breather, I could watch the house for you. Just for a few minutes, of course."

The agent looked tempted, throwing an uncertain glance over his shoulder at Imani Maxwell's darkened house. Then he turned back, shaking his head firmly. "No, that's okay. But thanks."

"Are you sure?"

"Absolutely." He chuckled nervously. "Wade would chew my head off and spit it out like a wad of tobacco if he knew I left my post."

"Right, right." Cole forced a sympathetic grin. "Don't wanna get on *his* bad side."

"No kidding."

"All right then." Cole rapped his knuckles lightly on the side of the car door, eased his foot slowly off the brakes. "Have a good evening, Agent Spencer. And don't fall asleep on the job."

"I wouldn't dare." Agent Spencer gave a tiny mock salute. He stood watching until Cole's Taurus had rounded the corner and left the neighborhood.

One of the first things Garrison had learned to appreciate about his job was the autonomy. Although he answered to a special agent in charge, he was, for the most part, his own boss. He'd also quickly discovered that there was no such thing as a "typical" day for a special agent. His daily routine varied depending on the nature of his work assignments. One day could find him assigned to a squad where his workday could begin with either an early morning raid, an interview, or a surveillance.

On that Thursday morning, he rose at five A.M. as usual. But there was nothing usual about the way he felt when he rolled out of bed. Lighter, almost weightless, a feeling that stayed with him as he took his morning jog around the Inner Harbor, savoring memories of a stolen moonlight kiss just three nights earlier. He stopped at Lexington Market on the way back, bought fresh peaches, and had eaten two by the time he got home. Before dressing for work, he actually took a moment to enjoy the view of the city skyline from his living room window, which he rarely did, despite the fact that the added feature was largely responsible for the exorbitant rent.

He strolled into the Baltimore field division, which served as headquarters for Maryland and Delaware. He nodded briskly to the greetings called out to him as he passed the sparsely furnished government offices and cubicles. As he approached his own area, he overheard the secretary on the phone, presumably talking to a reporter who had called about Althea's recovered backpack and the accompanying note. She made a face at Garrison as he passed her desk, her voice perfunctory as she informed the reporter, "I'm sorry, Special Agent Wade is on a special," which was Bureau jargon for being on a special assignment—which, technically, he was. He'd only come in to check his messages and set up his agenda for the day.

He sent the secretary an approving nod, winked conspiratorially. She grinned, her gaze retreating in shyness. He stopped to see Eddie first, sauntering into his office and plopping down in the chair opposite the government-issue metal desk.

After a minute, Eddie ended his phone call and swiveled around in his chair to face him, grinning with droll humor. "Make yourself comfortable," he drawled sarcastically.

Garrison's mouth twitched. "Thanks." He stretched out his long legs as if preparing to settle in for a long while. "What's going on?"

"That's what I should be asking *you*." Eddie's astute gaze narrowed on his face. "You get laid or something last night?"

Garrison shook his head in mild disgust. "Is that all you ever think about?"

Eddie arched an amused eyebrow. "So a woman *isn't* the reason you've got an extra spring in your step this morning?"

Garrison ignored him. "Got anything for me?"

Eddie shook his head, chuckling as he reached for a file folder on his desk. "All work and no play, Wade. . . ."

"Yeah, yeah, yeah," Garrison grumbled as he accepted the folder. He flipped it open and began scanning the contents.

"Seems Althea made a couple of friends in one of those chat rooms," Eddie remarked, reclining easily in his chair. "The first went by the screen name HOLLY010, and went to great lengths to conceal his identity. We're still waiting on the service provider to give us a positive ID. The second wasn't as ingenious. Either that, or he simply didn't care about being discovered." He paused for effect. "I'll give you two guesses who our second chat room pal is."

Garrison didn't have to guess. Somehow he just knew. "Davenport."

Eddie grinned. "So getting laid *hasn't* dulled your brain. And all this time you deprived yourself for nothing."

Garrison scowled at his partner as he rose from the chair, folder in hand. Victor Davenport hadn't even bothered with an inventive screen name. VICDAV.

Halfway to the door, Garrison said over his shoulder, "Thanks."

"Your gratitude is overwhelming," Eddie said dryly, knowing full well how much he was appreciated. "Oh, and something else you may find interesting."

Garrison turned, one eyebrow raised.

"Your friend Cole Porter. Applied for a special agent position with the Bureau about twelve years ago—didn't really qualify."

"Interesting," Garrison murmured.

"I figured you might think so."

Garrison knew it was probably nothing. The Bureau was inundated with special agent applicants every year. The revelation that Cole Porter had once sought employment with the FBI carried about as much significance as stating the sky was blue.

Nonetheless, Garrison processed the information and filed it away. Right then he was more concerned with finding out why Althea Pritchard, a young woman reportedly devoted to her boyfriend, had felt compelled to correspond with strange men in Internet chat rooms.

Thursday afternoon at the command center was not as busy as the first day had been. The volunteers who showed up consisted primarily of stay-at-home mothers, some retired and unemployed citizens, and a few students from the university.

Imani had ended her office hours early to put in some time at the command center, staffing the phones and overseeing the volunteer efforts. She had enlisted the help of one of her students, an information technology major, to create a Web site for Althea. Visitors to the site viewed a full-color image of Althea, the same photograph being circulated throughout the country. There was a message board to intercept tips from the public, although most of the posts so far were from concerned citizens offering their thoughts and prayers. Only legitimate leads would be passed along to Garrison and the police.

"Through the Web site," explained Wendell Theodore, eager to impress his professor, "we can also connect with a number of missing persons networks and foundations around the country. You'd be amazed how many there are, Professor Maxwell."

"Saddened is probably more like it," Imani countered, gazing at Althea's smiling image on the computer screen and trying, unsuccessfully, to force the knot of sorrow from her throat.

Wendell, a junior with bad acne and a mouthful of braces, ducked his head and continued sifting through messages. Imani patted his shoulder and murmured her appreciation before moving off.

Much to her amazement, Elizabeth Torres had shown up

that afternoon, dressed in skintight black leather pants and a scarlet red angora sweater with a plunging neckline. She met Imani's surprised expression with a look of haughty defiance. "What, I can't be here? She *was* my best friend, you know."

"Of course," Imani said. Striving to put aside her personal aversion for Althea's sake, she added graciously, "We need as many helping hands as we can get. Excuse me."

One of the volunteers had arrived with refreshments for everyone, and she and Imani laid them out on the table in the rear of the main center. The woman stayed long enough to serve coffee and stuff some envelopes before her daycare provider called; then she was off to tend to a minor crisis involving her rambunctious toddler.

Imani knew the exact moment Garrison arrived. As if her body had grown attuned to his, she sensed his presence before she actually saw him.

He and Detective Moses had spent a great deal of the afternoon canvassing the community, covering some of the same ground in hopes of uncovering new leads.

The first time he and Imani made eye contact was when she was giving instructions to a group of volunteers. Using the Internet, she had compiled a list of gas stations within a thirty-mile radius and was preparing to dispatch the volunteers in cars, armed with flyers to take to each gas station. "We have to consider the possibility that Althea was taken somewhere far," she reasoned. "Potential witnesses coming from out of town may stop at the gas station and see the flyer, and it might trigger a memory."

A few feet away, Garrison looked up from his discussion with Chief Taggert and locked on her, as if he'd picked up her comments on his radar. Imani felt a jolt, as if he'd actually reached out and touched her.

Although his expression didn't change, there was an imperceptible glint in his eyes that was a combination of pride and tenderness.

It didn't escape Imani's notice that Elizabeth, who had

presumably shown up to assist with the volunteer efforts, spent more time watching Garrison than actually helping. Her dark, possessive gaze followed him everywhere. As he spoke on the phone. As he leaned over the computer where an animated Wendell re-explained the contents of the Web site—even more eager to impress the FBI agent than he'd been to impress Imani.

When Garrison emerged from a briefing session with members of the task force, Elizabeth hustled across the room in her stiletto heels to greet him.

"Hello there," she said demurely.

Garrison barely spared her a glance. "Miss Torres."

She fell in step beside him, striving to match his long-legged strides. "I was wondering if there was anything I could do for you. To help with the investigation," she clarified with a sly smile.

"Yeah," Garrison answered brusquely. "Stay out of trouble."

She stopped midstride, looking dejected.

Imani looked away as Garrison headed in her direction. Not ready to face him just yet, she turned and started toward the back of the volunteer center where the supplies were stored. She needed copy paper to run off more copies of flyers.

"Imani."

She stiffened as he came up behind her, cursing the way her heart raced at the deep timbre of his voice. She turned to face him slowly, reluctantly. She felt hot with shame over the way she'd allowed him to kiss and caress her yesterday. Embarrassed because she'd enjoyed every last moment of it.

"Garrison. What can I do for you?"

His eyes swept across her face in one encompassing motion. "I just wanted to tell you what a good job you're doing," he said quietly.

She inclined her head, resisting the warm pleasure his words brought. "Thanks, I appreciate that."

He moved a fraction closer and almost reflexively, Imani stepped back. His dark gaze, gleaming with wicked satisfaction, pinned her to the wall she suddenly found herself against. He was like a predator who knew he had successfully cornered his prey.

"I haven't been able to stop thinking about you," he said huskily.

Heat flooded her cheeks, spread through her belly. "Garrison," she murmured in protest, glancing around self-consciously for eavesdroppers.

He didn't seem to care. "I'd be lying if I said I didn't enjoy our encounter yesterday."

Imani hesitated, bit her bottom lip guiltily. "Did you?"

Garrison's gaze followed the innocently provocative gesture, felt desire stir to life in his groin. He wanted to kiss her. Wanted her with an intensity that was becoming less foreign to him the longer he knew her.

The flicker of awareness in her dark eyes told him she had read the hunger in his gaze. Read it, and felt the same. "What I feel for you, Garrison," she said quietly, "is so wrong. So completely wrong."

"Keep telling yourself that," he said, his voice low and soft. "Maybe you'll eventually start to believe it's true."

She closed her eyes on a wave of helpless frustration. He traced his thumb lightly across her cheekbone, trailing a fiery path to her lips, which parted almost instinctively for his touch.

"Look at me," he gently commanded.

Her eyes fluttered open to meet the intensity of his piercing gaze.

"I won't take you anywhere you don't want to go," he whispered. And while she was still reeling from this seductive promise, he said, "I have to go. I'll call you later."

She nodded wordlessly and watched him walk away from her. After a moment, she turned her head as the prickly sensation of being watched crawled over her. When her gaze

landed on Elizabeth standing a few feet away, she almost recoiled from the look of pure malice on the girl's face.

Without a word, Elizabeth spun on her heel and stormed
out of the building, leaving Imani to stare after her.

It was after eight when Garrison got home that evening.
The day had been another exercise in futility, starting with
his visit to Emilia Torres's home. The diminutive woman,
still grieving the loss of her husband, had not taken kindly to
being interviewed by the FBI. And she had offered no in-
sight into her son's whereabouts.

"Joaquin is a good boy," she'd insisted, mortified at the
prospect of her firstborn having any possible connection to
Althea Pritchard's disappearance. "He wouldn't harm a
moth, much less a girl he hardly knew."

"What about your daughter?" Garrison probed.

Something like pain flitted across the woman's attractive
features. Pain and regret. "Elizabeth has her problems," she
spoke in almost hushed tones, "but she would never intentionally hurt another human being, Mr. Wade. She misses
her father terribly—we all do. That doesn't make her, or any
of us for that matter, kidnappers."

He'd thanked her for her time, instructed her to contact
him if she heard from her son. And then he'd followed her
from a discreet distance as she went to Mass to light a candle
for the soul of her departed husband. And for two others
whose identities he could only speculate about.

Cole Porter, who'd been assigned to tail Victor
Davenport, had returned with the same report: "No suspicious activity. He goes to work every day like he's supposed
to, eats lunch at the same deli, gets home by five-thirty on
the dot and doesn't go anywhere. He's almost *too* normal, if
you ask me."

"Well, at least he's staying away from the nightclubs,"
Taggert had groused, adding with a snort, "Wade pretty
much guaranteed that."

"Should we question him about those chat transcripts?" Porter asked Garrison.

"Not yet. Let's give it more time."

Garrison wasn't as interested in questioning Victor Davenport as he was in discovering the identity of Althea's other chat buddy. Althea had seemed much more drawn to HOLLY010, had even confided in him about her sometimes-rocky relationship with Malik. Her correspondence with Victor Davenport, in contrast, had been very limited, progressing no further than polite small talk. It was likely that Davenport didn't even know who Althea was when he saw her at The Vous.

Likely, Garrison reminded himself. But not impossible.

Just as it wasn't impossible that Elizabeth or Joaquin Torres had called his cell phone that night, using a scrambler manufactured by their father's former electronics firm. Armed with his subpoena, Garrison would pay the company a visit tomorrow and obtain a record of all scrambler product sales for the fiscal year.

His frustration with the stalled investigation was mounting dangerously. And then to top it all off, his supervisor had informed him that, due to budget constraints, they had to pull the plug on all surveillance assignments not deemed critical. Imani Maxwell's was the first to get axed, regardless of Garrison's terse recommendations to the contrary. The bureaucrats at the top, buried behind miles of their own red tape, always got their way.

So the good mood Garrison had awakened in that morning went down the proverbial toilet, leaving him surly and restless. He took a long, hot shower and finished some paperwork while Sade crooned softly in the background.

Mellowed by the music, he picked up the cordless phone and wandered to the living room window. "It's me," he said when the voice on the other end answered.

There was a low chuckle. "Like clockwork. I knew you'd be calling soon."

Garrison hesitated. "How is he?"

"He's doing okay. None the worse for wear after the little

barroom skirmish he had the other night. Still tough as nails. Like father, like son, huh?"

Garrison's eyes flickered, then closed. Like father, like son. That was exactly what he was afraid of. "Does he need anything?" he asked quietly. "I was going to send more—"

"No need, son. It'll be a while before he finishes spending that last stash you sent." Again the low, gravelly chuckle. "What are they paying you boys nowadays? Maybe *I* need to come out of retirement. What do you say? Think the Bureau will lift their mandatory retirement age? It's kind of unfair to shove a guy out the door at fifty-seven."

Garrison's mouth curved wryly. "For you, Ross, I think they'd make an exception. But you don't want to get back in the fray. You're enjoying retirement too much. The fishing and camping trips, waking up at your own leisure."

"Yep, it's the high life all right," Ross agreed, with the faintest trace of melancholy that only a fellow comrade could understand. "How's the abduction case coming along?"

"Slowly."

"Well, don't be too hard on yourself. Quiet as it's kept, you know we have no control over these things when it's all said and done."

Garrison said nothing, his jaw clenching with a new wave of frustration.

"But don't hesitate to call me if you need to bounce ideas off someone. You know I'm always here for you."

"I know," Garrison said. "I appreciate that."

Both men fell silent a moment, cognizant of the bond that knitted their lives together. "He asked about you, you know," Ross gently informed him.

Garrison's heart constricted, swelled in his chest. Pain wrestled with the familiar bitter longing, a relentless ache that had not diminished with the years.

His voice rough with emotion, he said, "Thanks again, Ross. I'll be in touch."

"I wouldn't expect otherwise. Take care, son."

After Garrison disconnected, he remained at the window, gazing blindly out at the city skyline. A view he had enjoyed only that morning now meant nothing.

He was ten years old when he realized that his father had a problem that could not be cured, no matter how much Garrison willed it, by the love and adoration of his family.

As if it were yesterday, Garrison still remembered the final time his father had walked out on them, unable to battle his demons any longer. Garrison remembered hearing the front door close in the stillness of that fateful night, a sound that had reverberated in his young mind like the sharp crack of a rifle. He shot up in bed, peering through the darkened room that he shared with his brothers. But both were fast asleep. Damien, still tender at age four, sucking on his thumb in the bunk above his, Reginald snoring lightly in the twin bed opposite theirs. Garrison flung aside his covers and crept from the room to his parents' bedroom across the narrow hall. Light seeped from beneath the crack in the door, beyond which were the muffled sounds of crying.

He opened the door, dread sitting heavy on his chest. And the moment he saw his mother's tearstained face, he knew with the intuition of a world-weary child that he had probably seen his father for the last time.

And still he needed to hear her say it, confirm his worst fears. His voice was a low whisper. "He's gone for good this time, isn't he?"

Rosemary Wade hesitated, regarding him warily with bloodshot eyes. "Your brothers still asleep?"

Garrison nodded mutely.

She patted the bed beside her, and he crossed the room to climb in, although it had been years since he'd done this. Only babies slept with their mothers. But that night was an exception, and something told him their lives would never again be the same.

His mother held him against her fragrant body, kissing

the top of his head as she rocked him gently. "I knew you'd be the one to come."

The tears fell fast, rolling hot and bitter down his cheeks. "What's wrong with him, Ma? Why can't we make him happy?"

"Oh, baby." Her voice hitched at his brokenhearted plea. "You *do* make him happy. You know he loves you and your brothers more than anything."

"Then why does he keep leaving us? And why did he lose his job? He was the best cop in the city."

"Your father has a problem, baby. He suffers from a condition called manic depression. A lot of people do. It makes it very hard for them to lead normal lives, no matter how much they may want to."

Garrison lifted his head to gaze at her. "How'd he get it?"

"We don't know for sure, baby. Doctors and researchers are still looking for answers. Some say it's a chemical imbalance in the brain."

"Maybe it was his job. Maybe he got depressed from seeing so much crime, seeing so many dead people."

"Shh." She tightened her hold on him protectively, instinctively. "Don't think about that. I don't want you thinking about those things, Garrison. You're too young."

"But I want to be a cop, too. What if the same thing happens to me?"

"Oh, baby." Rosemary's eyes filled with tears that slipped down her cheeks to replace the streaks left by the previous ones. She cradled Garrison's head in her arms. "I want to tell you something. You know how Pastor Moody is always quoting the scripture about bearing the infirmities of the weak?" At Garrison's slow nod, she continued, "Well, that's what we have to do with your father. We have to be strong for him when he can't be strong for himself. Can you do that for him, baby?"

Garrison was crying again, silent, racking sobs absorbed by his mother's body. All he wanted was his father back home with them, safe and sound where he belonged. Without his father, Garrison didn't think he could ever be strong again, and he said so.

"You're wrong, baby. Do you know what your name means? It means defender, reinforcement. While I was pregnant with you, I taught my students about soldiers stationed at town borders during the Civil War. Garrisons, they were called. There to protect the people from invaders." Her chuckle was soft, bittersweet. "When you were born, I just looked into your eyes, saw the determination there, the strength in your tiny fists. And I decided right then and there that your name had to be Garrison. Everyone thought I was crazy, told me I couldn't name no baby Garrison. But your father agreed. He saw the same strength in you that I did."

She stroked a hand over his head, kissed him again. "Some people are just born leaders, baby. It's the natural order of things. Yes, Reginald is my firstborn and Damien is my little angel. But you, Garrison, you're my strength. My rock. Don't you ever forget that."

And he hadn't, stepping in to fill the shoes left by his vacant father. Forced into manhood by circumstances beyond his control or comprehension. When he joined the FBI, the first thing he did was establish a trusted contact to monitor his father's movements as he drifted from one city to the next. Living with distant relatives, occasionally checking himself into mental-health clinics before the walls invariably began to close in on him. And then he would be on the move again. A tormented spirit trapped in a nomadic existence, a shell of the proud man he had once been. Unwilling to return home to those who loved him, who weren't ashamed of him.

Rosemary Wade rarely, if ever, mentioned her husband. She knew that as long as Garrison was keeping careful tabs on him, no harm would come to him. And if something did happen, she would be the first to know about it. She mourned for him behind closed doors, didn't know that

Garrison overheard her embittered cries to God. They never spoke of it, haunted by their own demons, fears too unspeakable to voice aloud.

Rousing himself from these painful reflections, Garrison left the living room and walked down the hall to his bedroom. He crawled beneath the covers, clasped his hands behind his head, and willed sleep to come.

But an hour later it still eluded him. Without a second thought, he reached across the nightstand for the phone.

Imani was just drifting off to sleep when the phone rang. Frowning in the darkness, she peered at the clock on the nightstand. The lateness of the hour sent a hot alarm racing through her and she snatched up the phone, breathless with familiar dread. "Hello?"

"Hey," drawled the deep, masculine voice.

She sat up immediately. Her heart drummed. "Garrison?"

"Did I wake you?"

"That's okay. I just turned in a few minutes ago, actually." A silly smile she couldn't contain curved her lips. She fell back against her pillow, flung an arm across her eyes. She held the phone closer, wishing it were him. "What's up?"

"I couldn't sleep," he murmured. "You want to get some coffee or something?"

Imani chuckled in surprise. "It's almost midnight, Garrison. And I have perfectly good coffee right at home."

"Please?"

Something in his soft tone made her sit up again, her smile faltering. "Is anything wrong, Garrison?"

On the other end of the phone, Garrison marveled that this woman could read him so easily. He was certain his voice had betrayed nothing. He was, after all, the master of disguise—or so his colleagues at the Bureau had dubbed him.

He smiled in spite of himself. "Nothing's wrong, except

the fact that you're there, and I'm here. I want to see you," he said huskily. "Is that going to be possible?"

And that was all it took. "Okay," she acquiesced. The truth was, she wasn't about to turn down an opportunity to be with him, no matter what time it was. Or how wrong it was.

"Meet me outside in twenty minutes," said Garrison. "And dress warm. It's cold tonight."

Chapter 13

Twenty minutes later, it was a laughing Imani who climbed into the truck beside Garrison. He flashed her a warm smile, amazed by the way his heart constricted at the sight of her. Who *was* this woman? And where had she been all his life?

"This is so crazy," she muttered under her breath, her dark eyes glittering with excitement. "I can't believe you came all the way from Baltimore in the middle of the night just to get coffee." She slanted him a mildly reproving look. "And I thought you said you liked my coffee."

Garrison's mouth twitched as he pulled away from her house. "I do. But if you invite me inside your house at this late hour," he drawled, "I don't trust myself to stop at having just coffee."

Imani's cheeks flamed at the implication. When she shivered, it had nothing to do with the cold weather. She tried to make light of his remark, knowing she was playing with fire. "So this *wasn't* an elaborately disguised booty call?"

His grin was slow, wicked. "I don't play those games. Believe me, Imani," he said softly, deliberately, "when I'm ready to make love to you, you'll know."

A melting warmth rushed through her belly, making her legs tremble beneath the snug boot-cut Levi's jeans she wore. She tried to summon some feisty comeback, something along the lines of "What makes you think we'll be making love any time in this millennium?" But the words failed her, and all she could do was turn her head and stare out the darkened window, tapping her foot to the mellow beat of Maxwell's "Ascension" pouring from the speakers.

They went to an all-night Starbucks a few miles from her house. Garrison ordered two espressos with foam, and they slid into a private booth in the corner of the near-deserted shop. They sipped their hot, frothy drinks in contented silence for a few minutes, gazing at each other across the Formica table. Garrison's inky black hair was cut very close to his scalp and appeared to be the same smooth grain as his heavy eyebrows. His jaw was covered in a faint five o'clock shadow that made him look even more roguishly appealing than usual. Rugged and sexy.

Imani's palms grew moist. She felt like a schoolgirl sneaking out for a late-night rendezvous with the neighborhood bad boy. She couldn't remember the last time she and David had done anything as spontaneous as this. Come to think of it, she didn't think they ever had.

Garrison was watching her carefully, wondering about the troubled frown that marred the smooth line of her brow. "What're you thinking about?"

"Nothing." She took another sip of her espresso, avoiding his penetrating gaze. She always had the unnerving sensation that the man could read her mind, could look deep into her soul and discern her innermost secrets.

"So why couldn't you sleep?" she asked, quickly changing the subject.

He lifted his shoulder in a shrug, idly stroked his stubbled chin with his thumb and forefinger. "No particular reason." His gaze remained fixed on her. "So you grew up around here?" With practiced ease, he had turned the tables back on her.

Imani nodded. "Upper Marlboro, to be more exact. My parents were both born and raised in this area, although they never met growing up. They practically lived in each other's backyards, but never crossed paths. They went away to different colleges and still managed to find their way back to each other." A poignant smile touched her lips. She was always moved by the tale of how her parents had met and fallen in love. "Guess when it's meant to be, it's meant to be."

"Do you believe in that?" Garrison asked softly.

"What?"

"Fate. Being destined for someone you've never met. Or have just met."

"Definitely." Suddenly reminded of her silent declaration during their first kiss, Imani blushed, still shaken from that near-revelation. *I love you.* Where had it come from? And why such strong sentiments for a man she hardly knew?

"What do your parents do?"

"My mother is a human resources director, works for a CPA firm." She hesitated, her throat closing on the familiar ache. "My father passed away almost six years ago."

"I'm sorry," Garrison offered softly.

"Thanks." She waved off his sympathy and shook her head ruefully. "You know, I'm always amazed when you ask me questions about myself. I keep expecting you to just go into your database and look up everything there is to know about me. You're FBI. You probably know what I'm going to eat for breakfast before *I've* even decided."

Garrison shook his head slowly. "I have a policy."

The look she gave him was suspicious. "What kind of policy?"

"I don't use my job to access personal information about women I'm interested in. Unless, of course, they're considered potential suspects in an investigation," he added sardonically.

Imani didn't know which part of his statement to react to

first. She arched a teasing eyebrow. "How many women have you been interested in that were potential criminals?"

He grinned. "None that I know of. Something you want to tell me?"

"No." She laughed, then added wryly, "On a somewhat unrelated note, I think Elizabeth Torres has a serious crush on you. She must have been watching us earlier at the command center. When you left, I caught her glaring daggers into me. If looks could kill . . ."

Garrison grimaced, raising his cup to his mouth. "She's a troubled kid."

Imani gave a delicate snort. "That's putting it mildly."

He raised an eyebrow. "Meaning?"

"For some odd reason, I think that girl has it in for me." His gaze sharpened and Imani hesitated, wondering at the sudden urge to confide in him when she hadn't even told David about her problems with Elizabeth Torres.

But it was too late. Garrison's curiosity was aroused and, like the man himself, would not be dismissed until it had been appeased. As briefly as possible, Imani relayed the circumstances surrounding her removal from the minority recruitment program committee. Garrison listened silently, attentively, and Imani could almost imagine the wheels clicking, turning in that methodical mind of his. Always the investigator, a slave to his profession.

But when she finished her account, he didn't bombard her with more just-the-facts-ma'am questions. Instead he reached across the table, covered her hand with the solid warmth of his own. His expression was genuinely sympathetic.

"I'm sorry that happened to you," he said quietly. "It's a rotten judgment call on Dr. Yusef's part."

He'd even remembered the name of the director, which she had purposely mentioned only once. Apart from Jada, Imani was so used to being the listener in her relationships, so used to providing abbreviated versions of events for the sake of time, that she often omitted names and details. That Garrison Wade had recorded Dr. Yusef's name, and had responded to her dilemma with such compassion, meant more to her than she cared to admit.

"His decision was a tremendous blow," she confessed. "But what was more stunning was that it happened in the first place. I mean, I'm not idealistic enough to think that every student is going to like me. But I just never saw it coming with Elizabeth. I don't know," she added with a shrug, "I thought we might have had something in common, both of us losing our fathers. Guess I was wrong."

"You just never know what's going to set an individual off," Garrison said, watching her and feeling the now-familiar protectiveness. He tried to make light of it, flashing a playful wink as he took another sip of his espresso. "Want me to rough her up for you?"

Imani chuckled dryly. "No, thanks. Besides," she added peevishly, "something tells me that being roughed up by you would only turn her on." When Garrison choked on his drink, she was instantly contrite. "I'm sorry, that was catty of me," she mumbled, shamefaced.

Garrison wiped his mouth with a napkin, his dark eyes dancing with mirth. "That's okay." His lips curved in a slow, teasing grin. "I know how you females get when your territory feels threatened."

"Territory?" Imani's eyes narrowed, and she rolled her neck with mock indignation. "That's what you think, jive sucka."

At first Garrison was speechless. "Wait a minute. What did you just call me?"

"Jive sucka," Imani sassed.

To her surprise, he threw back his head and roared with laughter. The deep, rumbling sound was so pleasant, so infectious, that she started laughing without really knowing why. A couple seated at another table glanced over with curious smiles, as if they wanted to be let in on the joke. Imani didn't even know what the joke was.

But Garrison was reliving their first meeting at the police station, and his startled reaction to her Cleopatra Jones appearance.

When their laughter finally subsided, she looked at him with merriment shining in her eyes. "What was so funny?"

Garrison shook his head, still grinning. "Inside joke. I'll tell you about it later." He reclined in the booth, regarding her with lazy indulgence. "I can't remember the last time I laughed so hard. It felt good. Really good."

Imani smiled with pleasure. "It did, didn't it?"

Their eyes locked and held. Garrison's gaze slowly traced her features, as if to commit each detail to memory. As if he hadn't already. The exotically slanted dark eyes, the high cheekbones, the lushness of her mouth bearing traces of the raisin lip gloss she liked to wear, and the brown-sugar skin that melted like candy on his tongue. Everything about her was soft and feminine, as effortlessly natural as the earthy tones she often wore. He absolutely loved her retro look, from her curly Afro to the brown leather handbag with hanging tassels, to the funky four-inch heeled suede boots that gave her a sexy swagger when she walked.

"I think I'm falling hard for you, baby girl," he whispered before he could check himself.

Imani's toes curled inside her boots at the surprising admission, at the low, intimate quality of his voice. She averted her gaze and toyed with the plastic lid on her empty cup. "I don't know what to say, Garrison." *Because God help me, I feel the same.*

"Don't say anything," he murmured. "It's enough that you're here with me."

Her treacherous heart soared. She blurted impulsively, "I honestly can't think of anywhere else I'd rather be."

Garrison felt his own heart slam against his rib cage. He was afraid to want this any more than he already did. Clearing his throat, he began pulling on his leather bomber over his black sweatshirt. "I'd better get you back home. Don't want you falling asleep on your students in class."

A look of disappointment flashed in her eyes, but she nodded her consensus.

Garrison left a generous tip on the table before ushering her gently outside. A cold, brisk wind whipped at their faces, and Imani burrowed deeper into her wool coat. She warmed with pleasure when Garrison, walking closely behind her, curved his arms around her waist and pulled her back against the solid length of his body. They walked to the truck like that, their steps matched in perfect synchrony.

Like two halves of a whole, Imani thought with a bitter-sweet smile.

The following afternoon, Imani left campus immediately after class so that she could put in a few hours at the command center before her evening outing with David. After a restless night spent tossing and turning, she had awakened with Garrison's name on her lips. And she knew right then and there that she had to do something. Soon, while she still had an ounce of integrity left.

She decided to stop home first to change clothes. As she neared her house, she noticed a white Infiniti Q45 sitting at the curb. With a puzzled frown, she parked in the driveway and climbed out, cautiously approaching the car.

"May I help you?"

A thirty-something white woman opened the door and stepped from the car. She was tall and slender, with ash blond hair and cool green eyes. "Perfect timing," she said. "I just pulled up and was wondering if anyone was home."

"Are you looking for someone?"

"Actually, I'm here to pick up my mail. Julian failed to notify some of our creditors about my change of address."

Comprehension finally dawned. "Oh, you must be Sylvia Jerome, Julian's wife," Imani concluded.

"Ex-wife," the woman corrected with a tight smile. "And you must be the renter."

"Imani Maxwell. Nice to meet you."

"A pleasure," Sylvia said, looking Imani up and down a little longer than necessary.

"Your mail's inside," Imani said. "If you'll wait here, I'll just be a minute."

Sylvia's expression brightened. "Would you mind if I came in? I'm dying to see how much the house has changed since we left. Call me a sentimental fool," she added on a wistful note.

Imani hesitated. "Sure, I don't see why not." She turned and started up the porch steps, unlocked the front door, and gestured the woman inside. Sylvia Jerome walked into the house as though she still lived there, taking in the simple furnishings with those jade eyes of hers.

"It looks completely different." From her tone, it wasn't clear whether or not she thought the changes were an improvement. Then suddenly she smiled with unaffected warmth. "I like it. Oh, why didn't we think of that?" she exclaimed, crossing the room to the symmetrical bookshelves framing the fireplace, which Imani had installed shortly after moving in. "What a charming touch. Adds character and ambiance."

"Thank you," Imani said.

"Julian should have thought of that. He had so many books, most of which were piled haphazardly on his desk or in any available corner he could find." Again the wistful note crept into her voice, and her short laugh was forced, brittle.

Imani smiled to ease the woman's obvious discomfort. "I'll get your mail." She started toward the kitchen where she'd designated a drawer specifically for her landlord's misdirected mail. There were only two letters addressed to Sylvia Jerome. One was an offer for discounted carpet cleaning, and the other was for a low-interest credit card. She'd come all this way for junk mail.

"Mind if I see the kitchen?" Before Imani could give her consent, Sylvia appeared in the doorway. "I wanted to see how it looks. Thank you," she said as Imani handed over her mail. She barely glanced at the letters, shoving them into her Gucci purse as she gazed around the room.

"You haven't changed much in here." She slanted Imani a mildly chastising look. "Don't tell me you don't cook, either?"

"Actually, I enjoy cooking."

"That's good. I couldn't get Julian to spend more than five minutes at a time in the kitchen. I suppose he thought he was too brilliant to be bothered with the mundane details of domestic grudgery. That was *my* job."

Feeling slightly awkward, Imani quipped, "Well, you know how men can be."

Sylvia Jerome snorted. "Tell me about it." Her assessing gaze returned to Imani. "Are you married, Ms. Maxwell?"

It was an unwelcome reminder of the difficult dilemma she found herself in. Imani swallowed, shook her head numbly. "No, I'm not."

Sylvia's expression turned soft, almost sympathetic. As if she had read Imani's mind. "Well, count yourself lucky," she muttered. "Marriage isn't all that it's cracked up to be. Take my word for it. I'm sorry," she hastened to add at Imani's pained grimace, "I realize how awkward this must be for you. Julian is your colleague, and here I am bashing him like some bitter shrew."

"It's all right," Imani murmured. "I can only imagine how difficult these past several months have been for you. For both of you."

Moisture shimmered in Sylvia Jerome's eyes, making them iridescent emeralds. "You just never think your marriage is going to end so abruptly," she whispered. "We took a lot for granted." She swept a reminiscent gaze around the room, at the familiar surroundings once so cherished. "That's why I didn't want the house. I couldn't have stayed here. Too many memories, too many ghosts."

Imani nodded in respectful silence.

After a moment, Sylvia drew a deep, steadying breath

and flashed a self-conscious grin at her hostess. "Will you just look at me, falling apart in front of a complete stranger like this. I swore I wouldn't do this. You must think I'm a complete basket case."

"Not at all," Imani said gently.

Sylvia's grin turned rueful in contradiction. "Thank you. You're far too kind. Now I see why Julian always spoke so highly of you." She glided a manicured hand forward. "It was a pleasure meeting you, Ms. Maxwell. Thank you for my mail."

"You're welcome," Imani said, accepting the handshake.

"Don't hesitate to let either of us know if you have any problems with the house. I believe Julian had the leaky faucet upstairs repaired before you moved in?"

"Yes, thank you. He took care of everything."

Imani stood in the doorway watching as Sylvia Jerome climbed into her Infiniti and pulled off with an elegant wave. Then, her thoughts turning reluctantly to the evening ahead, she started upstairs to change her clothes and was met halfway by Shiloh, who had been napping in her bedroom. He licked the back of her hand quietly, as if to offer his sympathy and support.

"Thanks, boy," she muttered under her breath. "I'll need all the help I can get."

Two hours later, Imani was printing out messages from Althea's Web site when she happened to glance up.

Her heart lurched sickeningly at the sight of Garrison and David striding through the doors of the command center together, casually conversing. Garrison was the first to see her. His enigmatic expression was a stark contrast to her own stricken gaze.

David caught sight of her and strode over quickly, a huge grin on his handsome face.

"David," she greeted him weakly, "I thought we were meeting at my house for—"

Before she could finish the sentence, he grabbed her around the waist and lifted her high in the air. She emitted a startled laugh as he spun her around.

"What was that for?" she asked as he set her down. Over his shoulder, she saw Garrison speaking with Aaron Moses and Cole Porter. Their eyes met and held for a moment before Garrison's impenetrable gaze slid away.

"I have great news," David exclaimed, "but it'll have to wait until we get to the restaurant. This announcement has to be followed with a champagne toast."

Imani grinned, tugging down the hem of her black jersey dress. "Sounds pretty important."

"Oh, it is, believe me." His gaze roamed hungrily across her face. "God, you're a sight for sore eyes. I feel like it's been ages since we last saw each other."

In more ways than one.

"Come on," David said. He grasped her hand and began leading her toward the exit. "We have dinner reservations in Georgetown."

"Let me get my coat first. I'll meet you in the car."

"Don't take too long," David called over his shoulder.

Imani found her coat in the back room that doubled as the supply closet. She struggled to put it on quickly, clumsily, her hands trembling uncontrollably.

"Here, let me," offered a deep voice behind her. She squeezed her eyes shut as Garrison helped her easily into the coat. When his fingers accidentally skimmed the smooth column of her throat, hot tears of frustration bit beneath her eyelids.

She turned around slowly, almost against her will, like a prisoner facing the firing squad. She kept her eyes lowered as she mumbled, "Thanks."

"No problem. Hey," he said softly, tipping her chin up and forcing her to meet his dark, probing gaze, "don't do this to yourself."

Imani swallowed past the walnut-sized lump in her throat.

Her tone, when she found her voice, was full of self-deprecation. "I'm not normally like this. So dishonest and pathetic. I don't want you to think less—"

"I don't." Garrison shook his head slowly. "I could never."

"I'm so confused," she whispered, searching his face desperately. For answers, for absolution, she didn't know which. "I just want things to go back to the way they were before all this happened, before you came—" His eyes flickered. Realizing belatedly what she'd been about to say, she tried to make amends. But it was too late.

Garrison had stepped back, his expression suddenly veiled. Closed.

"Garrison—"

"You'd better go." His voice was low, even. "Don't keep David waiting."

She ventured again. "Garrison, I didn't mean—"

"Have a good evening, Imani."

She hesitated, then hurried past him from the room, the bitter ache of regret sitting like lead on her stomach.

David awaited her inside the warmth of his Mercedes. "I thought I'd have to come get you."

"Sorry," she mumbled guiltily, settling into the buttery leather seat and staring blindly out the window.

"That's okay." David was still brimming with excitement over his news. "By the way, did you know that Agent Wade and I both graduated from Columbia? We were pulling into the parking lot at the same time, and I told him that he looked familiar to me and asked him where he'd gone to school. Columbia, undergrad and law school. Isn't that funny? We were there at the same time and never even met, two brothers at a predominantly white Ivy League university." David chuckled and shook his head at the irony.

"Imagine that," Imani murmured.

"Wonder what made him go into law enforcement. With a law degree from Columbia, he could have had his pick of any prominent firm."

Imani closed her eyes tightly and tried to inject neutrality into her voice. "Guess he didn't want to practice law from behind a desk."

David snorted in disbelief. "Yeah, he'd rather risk his neck on the streets." Belatedly remembering Imani's own personal tragedy, David hastened to soften his careless remark. "But, hey, being an attorney isn't for everyone. God knows there are some days that I question my own sanity. Not today, though. Today it has finally paid off." When Imani turned her head to look at him, he grinned broadly. "I was going to wait until we reached the restaurant, but I guess now is as good a time as any." He paused for dramatic effect. "I made junior partner!"

"You did? Oh, David, that's wonderful!" And she was genuinely thrilled for him. Lord knows he had more than earned the long-awaited promotion. She leaned across the seat and kissed his smooth-shaven cheek. "Congratulations. You really deserved it."

"That's what Flannery and the others said when they called me into the conference room. They were going to wait until Monday to make the announcement, but they figured I could use a nice celebration over the weekend." He watched her out of the corner of his eye as he continued almost hesitantly, "Especially considering that they'll be sending me to California for a whole week."

"What for?"

David grimaced. "Our new corporate account. The client's some software tycoon who doesn't fly, wants us to meet him on his own turf. Flannery wants me to go. He said that's where a lot of my accounts will be based from now on, anyway."

"Really?"

"I know, I know. It means more business trips for me, more frequent-flyer miles." The look he sent her was almost beseeching. "I wish you could go with me, Imani."

"You know I can't. Besides, it's right in the middle of the semester."

"I know." A trace of resentment tightened his generous

mouth. "You know, I've been doing a lot of thinking lately. With me making partner, there really won't be a need for you to continue spinning your wheels at the university. I already make more than enough for both of us—"

Imani was gaping at him. "I cannot believe that you would even suggest that I quit working. How archaic is that, David?"

"Oh, come on, Imani. Don't go getting all feminist on me. There's nothing wrong with being a homemaker. It was good enough for *my* mother."

"You know very well I have nothing against stay-at-home mothers," Imani hissed, her hackles rising. "How dare you try to turn the tables on me like that? As long as you've known me, what have I always wanted to do? You know how much I love teaching."

"Yes, but does teaching love *you*?" David shook his head, his expression baffled. "They put you through so much politics at that school, Imani. Even you admitted that you're probably a long way from making tenure unless you apply to another university."

"It's not just about that," she argued.

"Then what *is* it about? I mean, how long will you be satisfied with associate professor status?"

"I'm twenty-nine, David," Imani reminded him tersely. "It takes some people years just to get where I am. I can't believe—"

He held up a hand, silencing her heated rebuttal. "Let's not argue about this tonight. We're supposed to be celebrating my good fortune and nothing else. Can we do that?"

"You started it," Imani grumbled, crossing her arms like a petulant child and staring straight ahead.

David glanced at her, reached over, and lightly chucked her chin the way he'd done when they were children. "You're not mad. You could never stay mad at me for very long."

"There's a first time for everything," she said archly.

* * *

"So, anyway, I told him it couldn't be done. No way, absolutely not." Pausing in the middle of his animated rendition of a conference call with an ornery client, David watched as Imani absently dragged her spoon through the bowl of vichyssoise she hadn't finished before the waiter brought their meals. "Is something wrong with your entreé?"

She looked up quickly and shook her head. "No, it's fine." The vichyssoise was a creamy soup of leeks and potatoes that she actually enjoyed. The veal loin David had ordered for her was tender but had little taste. Which was just as well since she had no appetite.

David picked up his wineglass and took a sip of chardonnay. "Am I boring you with my story? I don't think you've been paying attention to a word of it."

Indeed, Imani had not noticed anything since their arrival. She had allowed herself to be escorted into the plush interior of the Four Seasons Hotel like a docile lamb, not seeing the lavish drop rugs, cherrywood furnishings, and abundant chandeliers that signaled each guest's acceptance into a world of unparalleled wealth and grandeur. Even as she sat across from David at the linen-covered table in a private corner of the luxurious restaurant, she paid no mind to the exotic Hawaiian flowers and plants meant to enhance the ambiance, did not hear the soft strains of music drifting from a baby grand piano. Although the atmosphere was romantic and relaxed, the restaurant filled with affluent patrons entertaining clients and celebrating anniversaries, they might as well have been dining at McDonald's for all it mattered to Imani. She suddenly felt very tired and emotionally spent.

"I'm sorry, David. I just have a lot on my mind." She forced herself to sip the expensive chardonnay he had ordered in honor of his promotion. The wine tasted bitter on her tongue, sour in her belly.

"Like what?"

"Hmm?" she murmured distractedly.

"You said you have a lot on your mind. What?"

Imani set down her wineglass slowly, carefully. She felt

like Judas Iscariot before the ultimate betrayal. Here they were supposed to be celebrating David's hard-earned success, and all she could think about was another man. A man who wasn't even right for her. Guilt welled up inside her and threatened to overwhelm her.

"Imani?" David was frowning at her, his concerned expression compounding her guilt. She deserved to be hauled outside and flogged.

"Have you ever wondered what would happen if . . ." She trailed off for a moment. Finally she forced herself to persevere through the vicious tangle of nerves. "What would happen if we didn't get married after all?"

David's frown deepened, grew perplexed. "You mean if we just lived together? Like a common-law arrangement?" Before she could answer, he shook his head adamantly. "We're not going to half-step that way, Imani. If we're going to be together, we're doing things the right way. Traditional church wedding, our own house in the suburbs with a backyard big enough for a pool—the whole nine yards, the way our parents did it."

Imani reached across the table and covered his hand gently with hers. "That isn't what I meant, David."

He grew very still, his eyes fastened on hers. "Then what *did* you mean?"

"I meant," she began with difficulty, her throat tightening, "what if we wound up with other people? Have you ever considered that possibility?"

Something inscrutable flickered in David's gaze before he averted it. He wiped his mouth with the linen napkin and signaled for the waiter.

Imani's heart constricted. "David—"

"I don't want to discuss this right now," he said in a harsh whisper.

They were both silent as the valet retrieved his Mercedes, as they began the long journey toward College Park. Imani watched David at stolen intervals, noting the way his hands tightly gripped the steering wheel, the way the muscles bunched and rippled in his jaw. It was only as they neared the deserted command center where Imani's Jeep was still parked that he broke the tense silence that hung between them.

"So much for celebrating my promotion with the love of my life," he said bitterly.

Tears of regret sprang to her eyes. "Oh, David. I didn't mean to ruin your evening, you know that. I'm so proud of you, so happy that you made partner."

"Are you?" he countered skeptically.

"Of course I am. How can you even question that?"

"I don't know. I guess the same way you can question the future of our relationship."

"Why haven't *you*?" She shook her head, torn between exasperation and sympathy. "David, even before our separation, we hadn't made love in months. Don't you think there's something strange about that?"

"We'd both been very busy." He stared at her, incredulous. "Is that what this is about? You were worried about our sex life?"

"No." A mirthless laugh bordering on hysteria bubbled up and spilled from her mouth. "That's not it at all."

"Good. Because our relationship is a lot more solid than what goes on between the sheets."

"This isn't about that, David."

"Then what? Is this about the argument we had earlier? You're mad because I want you to stay home once we're married? What's wrong with that? If a man can provide for his family, I see nothing wrong with asking his wife not to work. We've discussed this before, Imani. You know my views."

"And you know mine," Imani said hotly, indignantly.

They glared at each other, squaring off across the confined space of the car. Then suddenly, to Imani's utter surprise, David's lips spread in a slow, self-assured grin.

"What's so funny?" she snapped.

He shrugged dismissively. "You. Me. This entire discussion. I don't even know what we're arguing about, and I don't care. I'm not going to let anything rain on my parade, not until I'm ready to come down off this high." He leaned over, kissing her soundly on the mouth before she had a chance to react.

When he drew away, his grin was full fledged. "I know you're just trying to punish me for working late these past few days, canceling dates on you left and right."

"David—"

"It's all right, I forgive you. You chose a rotten night to get your revenge, but I understand. I know how sensitive you women can be." He climbed out of the car and came around to open the passenger door for her. He helped her out, bowed gallantly before skirting the fender to get back inside his car. He rolled the windows down as he peered out at her. "Get inside your Jeep so I can follow you home, make sure you get there safely."

Imani stood staring at him in openmouthed shock. "David, we really need to—"

He shook his head. "Not tonight, Imani. My flight leaves early in the morning, and I haven't even packed yet. Now come on, I'm letting all the heat out."

She unlocked her Jeep and climbed in mechanically, unable to believe this strange turn of events. She immediately rolled down the driver's side window. "David—"

But he had rolled his windows back up, sealing off her voice. Imani had no choice but to start the engine and pull out of the parking lot, frowning darkly. She had always known David Scott had a stubborn streak to rival hers, but this was downright ridiculous.

At her house a few minutes later, she practically leapt from her vehicle and hurried to his car. "Will you at least call me once you get there? We really need to talk."

He flashed the familiar warm smile. "Of course. I'll see you in a week, baby."

"All right. Have a good trip."

He waited until she was safely inside her house before driving off. Bolting the door behind her, she let out an exhausted wail that sent Shiloh bounding toward her from the kitchen. She ignored him, trudged upstairs without removing her coat, and flung her body across her bed, where she allowed herself a long, hard cry.

An Important Message From The ARABESQUE Publisher

Dear Arabesque Reader,

Arabesque is celebrating 10 years of award-winning African-American romance. This year look for our specially marked 10th Anniversary titles.

Why not be a part of the celebration and **let us send you four specially selected books FREE!** These exceptional romances will be sent right to your front door!

Please enjoy them with our compliments, and thank you for continuing to enjoy Arabesque.... the soul of romance bringing you ten years of love, passion and extraordinary romance.

Linda Gill
PUBLISHER, ARABESQUE ROMANCE NOVELS

P.S. Watch out for our upcoming Holiday titles including *Merry Little Christmas* by Melanie Schuster, *Making Promises* by Michelle Monkou, *Finding Love Again* by AlTonya Washington and the special release of *Winter Nights* by Francis Ray, Donna Hill and Shirley Hailstock—*Available wherever fine books are sold!*

New Holiday Titles

ARABESQUE

BET BOOKS

www.BET.com

SPECIAL OFFER! 4 BOOKS FREE!

A SPECIAL "THANK YOU" FROM ARABESQUE JUST FOR YOU!

Send this card back and you'll receive 4 FREE Arabesque Novels—a $25.96 value—absolutely FREE!

The introductory 4 Arabesque Romance books are yours FREE (plus $1.99 shipping & handling). If you wish to continue to receive 4 books every month, do nothing. Each month, we will send you 4 New Arabesque Romance Novels for your free examination. If you wish to keep them, pay just $18* (plus, $1.99 shipping & handling). If you decide not to continue, you owe nothing!

- Send no money now.
- Never an obligation.
- Books delivered to your door!

We hope that after receiving your FREE books you'll want to remain an Arabesque subscriber, but the choice is yours! So why not take advantage of this Arabesque offer, with no risk of any kind. You'll be glad you did!

In fact, we're so sure you will love your Arabesque novels, that we will send you an Arabesque Tote Bag FREE with your first paid shipment.

* PRICES SUBJECT TO CHANGE.

YOU'LL GET 4 SELECT ROMANCES PLUS THIS FABULOUS TOTE BAG!

ARABESQUE

**Visit us at:
www.BET.com**

THE "THANK YOU" GIFT INCLUDES:

- 4 books absolutely FREE (plus $1.99 for shipping and handling).
- A FREE newsletter, *Arabesque Romance News*, filled with author interviews, book previews, special offers, and more!
- No risks or obligations. You're free to cancel whenever you wish with no questions asked.

INTRODUCTORY OFFER CERTIFICATE

Yes! Please send me 4 FREE Arabesque novels (plus $1.99 for shipping & handling). I understand I am under no obligation to purchase any books, as explained on the back of this card. Send my free tote bag after my first regular paid shipment.

NAME _____

ADDRESS _____ APT. ____

CITY _____ STATE _____ ZIP _____

TELEPHONE (____) _____

E-MAIL _____

SIGNATURE _____

Offer limited to one per household and not valid to current subscribers. All orders subject to approval. Terms, offer, & price subject to change. Tote bags available while supplies last.

AN104A

Thank You!

ARABESQUE

Accepting the four introductory books for FREE (plus $1.99 to offset the cost of shipping & handling) places you under no obligation to buy anything. You may keep the books and return the shipping statement marked "cancelled". If you do not c   about a month later we will send 4 additional Arabesque novels, and you will be billed the preferred subscriber's price of just $4.50 per title. That's $18.00* for all 4 books for a savings of almost 30% off the cover price (Plus $1.99 for shipping and handling). You may cancel at any time, but if you choose to continue, every month we'll send you 4 more books, which you may either purchase at the preferred discount price. . . or return to us and cancel your subscription.

* PRICES SUBJECT TO CHANGE

THE ARABESQUE ROMANCE BOOK CLUB
P.O. BOX 5214
CLIFTON NJ 07015-5214

THE ARABESQUE ROMANCE CLUB: HERE'S HOW IT WORKS

PLACE
STAMP
HERE

Chapter 14

Louis Pritchard stood at the French windows in his study gazing out into nothingness. His study, normally used for conducting business meetings when he was home, had now become his retreat as well. He needed an escape from the endless stream of visitors bearing sympathy cards and armloads of hot meals, the round-the-clock presence of an FBI agent posted by the phone in anticipation of a ransom demand, not to mention the constant herd of reporters camped out at the entrance to the gated community, peering through the high iron bars like starving hyenas on the prowl for fresh kill. They were waiting to pounce on anyone with even the remotest connection to the case for a scrap of news, some trophy to take back to their warlord producers. Louis knew it was an unfair assessment, considering he had often used the media for his own political gain. He knew it was his high-profile status that kept the kidnapping case in the news, kept Althea's smiling image front and center in the minds of every viewer across the country. In all honesty, Louis couldn't begrudge the media presence, especially if their coverage led to a crucial break in the case. But as the days passed with no concrete leads or suspects, it became more of an effort not to view everyone—members of the press included—as a painful reminder of this nightmare.

Sighing heavily, Louis shoved his hands into the pockets of his wool gabardine trousers, his expression bleak. Today marked exactly two weeks since Althea had disappeared. Two weeks of fear and desperate uncertainty, a hell he wouldn't wish upon his worst enemy.

He had felt like a fraud in church that morning. Like an automaton, he had gone through the motions of greeting his friends and supporters with smiles and handshakes, responding to their concerned inquiries with firm assurances that his faith was not shaken, that he was trusting God to return Althea home safely. The reality was that just last night, as he lay beside his sleeping wife, he had come perilously close to cursing his Maker. It was bad enough that he had lost his baby sister to the insidious underworld of drug addiction, and that he and Barbara had struggled for years with infertility. To suddenly lose the only child they had ever known was too much. With tears squirting from his eyes, he had succumbed to all-consuming outrage and self-pity, and had stopped just short of shaking his fist at the darkened ceiling.

Daylight had brought some clarity, a sense of remorse, and now as he wandered over to his collection of photographs— his Wall of Fame, as Althea jokingly called it—he acknowledged that he had a lot to be grateful for. He had accomplished much in his life and had enjoyed a successful political career that many felt could carry him all the way to Congress, maybe even higher. And he had done everything by the book, through old-fashioned hard work and persistence. His conscience pricked him a moment, reminding him of the one blight on his otherwise spotless record.

If he had to do it over again, perhaps he wouldn't have agreed to plant the informant in the Torres political camp. His campaign aide's discovery of fundraising discrepancies, and Louis's decision to go public with the information, had secured him the election in a race many had favored him to win, anyway. The victory had been bittersweet. His conscience was tinged with guilt as he was sworn into office.

Louis sighed once again and shook his head. He wasn't proud of the way he'd handled the Torres scandal. And if one of his late rival's children had abducted Althea for revenge, as Detective Cole Porter had implied on his last routine visit, then Louis wouldn't have to worry about earning Carlos Torres's forgiveness. He would never forgive himself.

He gave a start at the sudden jangling of the phone on his desk. In mute terror he stood stock still, staring at the instrument as if it were a foreign object. A moment later, the door swung open and the blond-haired special agent who had been assigned phone surveillance duty stood there. He gave a subtle nod for Louis to answer the call.

Louis crossed to his desk and picked up the receiver with a hand that trembled violently. The static of a bad connection crackled over the line. Then came a small voice, ghostly faint and barely audible.

"Uncle Louie? Help me . . . please . . . ."

Garrison stood before the map of Prince George's County tacked to the bulletin board in the War Room. Using his finger, he traced a path from Althea's last known sighting across the street from the university, to the Laurel restaurant where the first note had been found, then back to College Park for the location of the second note. It was a small perimeter of area, yet for all the progress they had made thus far, he may as well have been looking at a map of the entire state of California. He stared at the message board until the photocopied notes from the kidnapper began to swirl together, a dizzying jumble of words and veiled insinuations. A madman's warped riddle.

Closing his eyes, he scrubbed a hand over his face as if to rub out the fatigue, but it was no use. The fatigue came from deep within, beating at him relentlessly, unmercifully. Threatening his razor-thin grip on logic, objectivity. Chipping methodically at his hard, protective shell of control, and permitting guilt and uncertainty to creep in. It had been two weeks since Althea Pritchard disappeared, and they were no closer to finding her than they had been the first day.

It took a supreme effort of will for him to force the horrific scenarios from his mind, many of them drawn from actual events he'd been unlucky enough to witness firsthand.

Almost invariably, his mind returned to the night Kayla Dyson was taken to the emergency room, critically wounded from a gunman's stray bullet. Garrison had stood at the window watching the ER medics work frantically on the little girl as they fought to resuscitate her lifeless form. Garrison's body had grown cold and rigid as Kayla flatlined, as the surgeon wearily pronounced the time of death. Garrison had wandered the streets aimlessly for hours that night, castigating himself for his role in the little girl's death. He couldn't help wondering if the outcome might have been different if he hadn't challenged the armed robber, drawing his accomplice from the waiting car where he had started firing on them in mad desperation before Garrison put a slug between his eyes.

"Garrison."

Garrison jerked his hand away from his face and turned his head to glance over his shoulder. He didn't know how long she had been standing in the doorway watching him, quietly observing him as he wrestled with his inner demons. As he hovered dangerously on the brink of self-destruction.

She stepped into the room hesitantly, her steady gaze fixed on his face. He balked at the unmistakable softness of concern in her dark eyes. He didn't want her concern, didn't need it.

"What're you still doing here?" he asked gruffly. "I thought everyone was gone."

"I was about to leave, and then I saw the light on in here and . . ." Imani trailed off uncertainly, still watching him carefully. "Are you okay?"

"Fine," he said curtly, turning his back on her. He tensed

at the soft approach of her footsteps. She stopped beside him, and he looked at her sideways from beneath his lashes.

She nodded at the bulletin board. "Do you mind?"

He hesitated, then nodded shortly. "You're in here now."

Ignoring his brusque tone, Imani studied the map with the red pins marking search territories. Her frown grew as she read the kidnapper's sinister messages. After a moment she folded her arms across her chest and hugged herself, an instinctively protective gesture.

"If only walls could talk," she said in a low voice. "They could tell us where she is, what's been done to her."

Garrison was silent, sharing the sentiment. As useless as it was.

"How many abductions have you done, Garrison?"

Already anticipating her train of thought, he tried to divert her. His response was brief and noncommittal. "I don't keep track."

"Garrison."

He met her stubborn gaze with his own. "Too many."

Undeterred, Imani felt compelled to ask the question she dreaded hearing the answer to. "How many of the victims were found . . . alive?"

He said nothing, but his stony expression spoke volumes about tragedy and loss, the bitter defeat and disappointment he'd suffered alongside the devastated families. The hard-life lessons of law enforcement officers, lessons she herself had been privy to more often than she cared to remember.

Garrison felt, rather than saw, Imani shiver. "Althea's going to be found," she said resolutely, as if willing it by sheer determination. "We're not going to lose her. She still has so much life left to experience."

So did the others, Garrison thought. But he kept the grim warning to himself, deciding—once again—that it was okay to protect Imani from the truth. To leave her to her illusions.

Unable to resist, he allowed himself to look her fully in the face and saw, for the first time, the dark shadows beneath her eyes that could only be caused by lack of sleep. He wondered what had been robbing her of rest for the past two nights since he'd last seen her. He already knew the source of *his* insomnia.

Imani's eyes lowered from the map and settled blankly on a point before her. Then slowly, almost against her will, she turned her head to meet his probing gaze. They stood like that, side by side, not touching, not speaking, for a prolonged moment. Questions that had nothing to do with the case, that were too painful to contemplate, much less voice aloud, hung between them.

Suddenly Garrison's cell phone rang and he snatched it up, turning away from her. His voice was rough. "Wade."

"Wade, this is Spencer. I'm at Pritchard's house . . . You'd better come quick."

Garrison frowned, dread resettling in his gut. "I'm on my way."

Louis Pritchard was badly shaken, slumped forward with his head cradled between his hands. "I *know* it was her," he insisted. "She's the only one besides my late sister who called me Louie."

Seated next to him on the ivory sofa in their parlor, Barbara Pritchard ran a soothing hand up and down his back. She had been napping upstairs when the call came and had been jarred awake by the sound of her husband's agonized wail.

"She's alive," Louis moaned again, torn between anguish and relief. "At least we know that our baby is still alive."

Tears welled in Barbara's eyes, and she buried her face in the crook of his shoulder.

Above their heads, Kirk Spencer met Garrison's gaze, and the two men left the room silently, as much to confer as to give the couple their privacy. They stood outside the closed parlor door.

"We traced the call to a pay phone in College Park,"

Spencer announced without preamble. "And you'll never guess where."

Garrison's expression was grim. "Outside the 7-Eleven." The same place where Althea's backpack with the note had been found. Anger twisted inside him. "It's some kind of game."

Spencer nodded in agreement. "We don't know for sure that it was Althea who called. Could have been some students playing around, nothing better to do on a Sunday afternoon. Cruel, but entirely possible."

Garrison nodded. "I'll head back up there, canvass the area and see if anyone noticed anything. How was the connection?" he asked, thinking about the scrambled voice on the call he'd received. He was expecting subpoenaed purchase receipts from Carlos Torres's former electronics firm by tomorrow afternoon.

"It was bad, could have been a tape. The boys in audio will be able to tell."

Again Garrison nodded, suppressing the thought that if the kidnapper had used a tape of Althea's voice, it was likely because Althea herself couldn't be used. It was a grim possibility.

"What I don't get is," Spencer said, "why call at all if it's not to make a ransom demand?"

"Because this isn't about a ransom," Garrison muttered. This was personal.

He had started toward the door when Spencer added, "Oh, you might want to have a little chat with Detective Porter."

Garrison turned, one eyebrow lifted. "About?"

"Pritchard says Porter told him that one of Torres's kids is our perp, and now Pritchard is on a rampage, blaming himself for what's happened to Althea, saying he'll never forgive himself for what he did during the campaign."

Garrison clenched his jaw, coolly digesting the information. "Anything else?"

Spencer hesitated. "I saw Porter talking to some reporters when I got here earlier. We were wondering how the media uncovered the contents of the second note? Something tells me we don't have to look too far to find our leak."

Chapter 15

"What do you mean he wouldn't let you end things for good?" Jada's frown was bewildered. "How can he not *let* you? What did he do?"

Imani described David's odd behavior on Friday night and his refusal to stay on the phone longer than five minutes when he called her from his San Francisco hotel room on Saturday evening.

"It's like he's trying to avoid me," she finished on a frustrated note.

"Interesting." Eyes narrowed in speculation, Jada regarded Imani across the table in Channel 13's bustling cafeteria. She had just returned from a weekend getaway with Marcus and had called Imani that morning to have an early lunch with her before class.

"Did I miss something?" Jada demanded. "When did you finally decide to end the charade between you and David?"

Imani winced, guilt searing her cheeks. "You're the one who told me that I'm not in love with him," she rejoined evasively.

"Yes, and as I recall, you disagreed. Quite vocally, I

might add. So my question is," she leaned forward deliberately in her seat, "what happened to change your mind?"

And in the time it took Imani to blush and drop her gaze, comprehension dawned. Jada's eyes sharpened, widened. "Oh my God. You met someone else!"

"Not so loud," Imani muttered, casting a self-conscious glance around the crowded cafeteria.

Jada waved off her cousin's embarrassment, grinning from ear to ear. "Who is he?"

Imani covered her face with her hands and shook her head. "It's so crazy," she groaned unhappily. "So wrong."

Now she really had Jada's undivided attention. *"Do* tell."

Imani looked everywhere but at her relentless inquisitor. "It's a long story, Jada. And complicated."

"Start from the beginning."

But Imani's gaze had found and settled on a tall, dark-skinned young man rising from a table across the room. He wore a crisp denim shirt over a pair of khaki Dockers, and when he laughed at a joke his companion made, his teeth were strong and white, dimples flashing in his lean cheeks.

"Imani?" Jada glanced over her shoulder, following the direction of her cousin's distracted gaze. "Who are you staring at?"

"That guy over there in the denim shirt. He looks familiar. Who is he?"

"Oh, that's Damien, one of our interns. Sweet kid." She turned back with a mischievous grin. "If you think he's cute, you should see his brother. Wait, you already have. Garrison Wade, the FBI agent?"

Imani swallowed, tried to look casual. "Oh yeah? That's his brother?"

"Um-hmm. Girl, that man is orgasm fine."

Imani chuckled in spite of herself. "That's a new one. What's it supposed to mean?"

"You know, he's so fine that when you look at him, you just . . ." Jada trailed off, wriggling her eyebrows suggestively.

Imani shook her head in mild disgust. "I don't know about you, girl. Are you sure you're ready to get married?"

"Oh, don't act like you didn't think the same thing when you saw Garrison Wade for the first time. Anyway, don't try to change the subject. You were going to tell me the identity of your mystery man, the one who stole your heart from David."

"I never said anything about my heart being stolen." But even as the denial left her mouth, the words rang hollowly with untruth. She glanced quickly at her watch. "Don't you have a meeting with your producer in five minutes?"

Jada consulted her own wristwatch and scowled. She jabbed an accusing finger at Imani. "This ain't over. I want answers, Imani Maxwell. Tonight. I'll be calling you, and don't you dare ignore that phone."

As Imani was leaving the television station a few minutes later, she checked her voice mail messages to make sure none of her students had tried to schedule an appointment with her. Although she seldom took lunch breaks and still had two hours before her afternoon class, she felt guilty about spending more time away from campus than neces- sary—although her colleagues did it all the time.

She had just reached the parking lot when she saw Damien Wade peering under the hood of an old Nissan Sentra that had likely seen better days.

"Need a jump?" she asked, approaching him.

He jerked at the sound of her voice, bumping his head on the roof of the car.

"Sorry," Imani said with an apologetic grin. "Didn't mean to startle you."

He grinned sheepishly, rubbing the back of his head. "That's okay," he mumbled ruefully. "I probably would've done that eventually, anyway."

For some reason, she was touched by the note of self- deprecation in his voice. "Do you need a jump?" she asked again. "I have some jumper cables in my truck, and I could just pull into the vacant spot next to yours."

"Thanks, but unfortunately the battery's not the problem. It's the transmission. It's finally given up the ghost on me."

"Bummer," Imani murmured sympathetically. She'd been there, done that. Last year her Corolla's transmission had heaved its last breath, prompting her to splurge on the Jeep with her savings. She had paid her dues with used-car blues long enough.

"Would you like to use my cell phone to call someone?" she offered.

Damien looked surprised by her generosity. "You don't mind?"

"Not at all." She chuckled. "You're not calling anyone in China, are you?"

Damien grinned and shook his head. "No, ma'am." He slammed the hood shut, then wiped his hands on a cloth rag before accepting the compact phone from her.

Imani took a few steps away, giving him his privacy. When he had ended the call, he handed the phone back to her. "Thank you."

"No problem. Someone coming to get you?"

He grimaced. "Nobody was home." He flicked a worried glance at his watch. "I had hoped my mom would be back by now, but she's not. I'm supposed to meet someone in twenty minutes, too."

"Well," Imani stuck her cell phone back inside her handbag, "I have some extra time. Would you like a ride?"

"Aw, no, that's okay. I couldn't impose on you like that."

"No imposition. Where do you live?"

He hesitated. "East Baltimore, about fifteen minutes from here."

"Come on, I'll take you home, and then you can come back later with a tow. Lock up your car." Imani started away before he could utter another protest. After a moment he fell in step beside her, walking quickly.

"Are you always this nice to strangers?" he asked.

"Usually." Imani smiled, stuck out her hand. "Imani Maxwell, by the way."

He shook her hand almost timidly. "Damien. Damien Wade."

"It's nice to meet you, Damien. Damien Wade."

He grinned, and if he weren't so dark skinned, she would have sworn his ears turned red. She marveled at the contrast between the two brothers. Where Garrison was confident and self-assured almost to the point of downright cockiness, Damien Wade was shy and unassuming, qualities she found quite endearing in the handsome young man.

Other than to compliment her Jeep, he spoke very little during the ride across town. Imani quickly discovered that it was like pulling teeth to extract more than monosyllabic responses from her passenger.

"So you're an intern at Channel 13. Where do you attend school?"

"Towson University."

"Really? I teach at the University of Maryland College Park."

"For real?" He smiled, but offered no more.

"Do you like it at Towson?"

He shrugged. "Sure, it's cool."

"So I guess it's a safe assumption that you'd like to go into broadcast journalism one day."

"Maybe."

She slanted him a teasing look. "Maybe?"

"Well . . ." She practically held her breath in anticipation of the longest response he would give—for naught. "I think so."

"Don't tell me. They're working you to the bone over there at Channel 13. Uh-huh, that's what it is," she concluded as Damien grinned. "I know what a slave driver my cousin can be."

"Your cousin?"

"Jada Jamison."

"*That's* your cousin?" He studied her profile and nodded after a moment. "Yeah, you both look alike."

"Yep, but I can assure you that we're nothing alike." Imani grinned. "You just let me know if she gives you a hard time and I'll get her for you."

Damien laughed, flashing those dimples again. "That won't be necessary, Ms. Maxwell. Jada—I mean Ms. Jamison—is real cool. She's nice to me." He ducked his head, suddenly self-conscious, and Imani smiled inwardly at the telltale signs of a crush.

"So if you didn't become a news anchor," she began conversationally to ease his embarrassment, "what would be your second choice?"

His expression brightened. "Oh, that's easy. An FBI special agent."

"Really?" Not that she was the least surprised.

"Yeah." Damien turned his head and stared out the window. "But my brother won't let me. He says he doesn't want that life for me."

Imani arched an eyebrow, opened her mouth to ask Damien what *he* wanted, then decided against it. After all, hadn't her own father made her promise not to marry someone in law enforcement? Wouldn't it be hypocritical of her to impugn Garrison for barring his younger brother from the FBI for the very same reason?

"You must really respect your brother's opinion," she remarked instead.

Damien nodded vigorously. "Definitely." His tone softened. "He looks out for me."

"You're lucky," Imani said, touched by the quiet admission.

At Damien's prompting, she turned onto a narrow side street lined with aging but well-maintained brick row houses. They pulled in front of an end unit featuring a bay window that overlooked a profusion of vibrant colors in a flowerbed and neatly trimmed shrubbery.

A petite brown-skinned woman was just climbing out of a midnight blue Lincoln Town Car parked before the house. She smiled into the truck and waved at Damien.

"That's my mom," Damien supplied, unfastening his seatbelt. "Thanks for the ride, Ms. Maxwell. I really appreciate it."

"You're welcome, Damien. What're you doing?" she demanded as he dug into his pocket and fished out some wrinkled bills. She rolled her eyes heavenward. "Put your money away, Damien Wade."

He looked anxious. "Are you sure?"

Imani feigned insult. "Do I look like a cabbie to you?"

"No, ma'am," he said with a shy grin. "Thanks again."

As he climbed out of the Jeep, his mother met him with a hurried kiss. "What happened to your car, baby?"

"Broke down. Ms. Maxwell was nice enough to give me a ride."

His mother looked beyond his shoulder into the idling Jeep. She met Imani's friendly wave with a warm smile. Before Imani could pull off, the woman approached.

"Thank you so much for giving Damien a ride home. I was running late and didn't realize what time it was." She thrust a manicured hand through the window. "My name is Rosemary Wade."

Imani accepted the warm handshake with a smile. So this was the strong black woman who had given birth to Garrison Wade. She liked her immediately. "Nice to meet you, Mrs. Wade. Imani Maxwell."

Rosemary Wade beamed with pleasure. "What a beautiful name. Are you in a hurry? I baked some coffee cake just this morning. Would you like to come in for a few minutes?"

Imani hesitated, glancing at the digital clock on her dashboard. "Well, actually, I have to—"

"Just for a little bit," Rosemary coaxed. "You gave my son a ride home. The least I can do is offer you a cup of tea and refreshments."

Imani hesitated a moment longer before nodding. "All right. It's very kind of you."

"One good turn deserves another. Go on and park, baby. There's an open spot right up ahead."

Damien Wade was grinning at Imani as she joined them on the steps a minute later. "She can be very persuasive when she wants to be," he whispered conspiratorially behind his mother's back.

Imani grinned. "So I see."

The interior of the house was warm and inviting, impeccably furnished with the pleasant fragrance of apple-scented potpourri clinging to the air. Imani had only a glimpse of framed portraits of Garrison and his brothers and a cherry-wood curio cabinet displaying rows of trophies before she was ushered into the kitchen and gestured into a chair at the gleaming oak table.

"Do you like coffee cake, Imani?" Rosemary Wade asked, moving about the kitchen with practiced efficiency. "You don't mind if I call you by your first name, do you?"

"Not at all."

"Good. But you can call me Mrs. Wade." She chuckled, adding unapologetically, "I'm from the old school. I don't believe in allowing young folks to call their elders by their first name. It opens the door to disrespectful behavior, don't you agree?"

"Yes, ma'am. Absolutely."

Rosemary Wade smiled and gave her an approving nod before slicing into the coffee cake. "I'm sorry, did you tell me whether or not you like coffee cake?"

"I do." Even if Imani didn't, she wasn't about to risk offending her formidable hostess. But a moment later when she sampled the home-baked good, she knew she needn't have worried, anyway. It was by far the best coffee cake she'd ever had, and she said so.

Rosemary Wade beamed. "Why, thank you, baby. I'm glad you like it. Now that I'm retired, that's all I've been doing with my time. Which probably explains this," she added jokingly, patting the gently rounded swell of her hips.

She carried two steaming porcelain teacups over to the

table and sat down across from Imani. "Hope you like chamomile tea. My doctor has prohibited me from caffeine products, namely coffee." She made a face, her pert nose wrinkling prettily with the gesture. "I used to drink ridiculous amounts of the stuff every morning to deal with those tyrants I called students."

Imani laughed. "That sounds like me."

Rosemary smiled, her interest piqued. "You teach, too?"

"At the University of Maryland College Park."

"A professor? How wonderful. You must enjoy it."

"On most days," Imani said with a rueful smile.

Rosemary grinned, sipping her tea. "And all this time I thought it was just because I taught middle school."

"Nope. It's a challenging job at any level, just in different ways. How long did you teach, Mrs. Wade?"

"Thirty-five years. Retired from the Baltimore City Public School system three years ago," she said proudly.

"Thirty-five years? Wow, that's impressive. Do you miss it?"

"Sometimes. Being retired doesn't mean you stop being a teacher. It's something that's in your blood, know what I mean?"

"I do," Imani said softly. And she really did.

"Anyway, I spend most of my time nowadays volunteering at a nursing home. And looking after my boys when they let me," Rosemary added with a laugh. "Do you have any children, Imani?"

"No, ma'am." Imani took a sip of the fragrant tea, washing down the rest of the incredibly moist coffee cake. She was afraid to appear greedy by asking for another slice.

"I have four beautiful grandchildren between my two sons."

"Oh?" Imani set down her cup carefully, wondering why it should bother her that Garrison had children. It was certainly none of her business.

"Reginald and his wife have three children," Rosemary explained with the glowing satisfaction only a mother could know. "And Damien has an adorable three-year-old daughter. Although," she added, oblivious to the way Imani practically sagged against her chair in relief, "as much as that child adores Garrison, you would think he was her father."

Imani smiled.

"Garrison's my second oldest," Rosemary continued. There was no mistaking the deep pride in her voice and the affectionate softening of her features. "See all those plaques and certificates in the living room? Those are all his—commendations from the FBI and CIA, from Columbia University, from various civic organizations. He refuses to hang them up in his own apartment, so I'm only too willing to display them here."

"You must be very proud."

"Absolutely. Proud of all my boys, actually." She smiled at Imani. "Are you from around here?"

"Not quite. I live in College Park, but I'm originally from Upper Marlboro."

Rosemary nodded, pursing her lips in thought after a moment. "Isn't that also where the missing girl is from? The county executive's niece?"

Imani nodded, stifling the sharp stab of pain that always accompanied the reminder of Althea's disappearance. Last night, she had wanted to call Garrison to find out what had sent him hurrying from the command center with that ominous expression, but she knew such an inquiry would be inappropriate. She was no more entitled to inside information about the investigation than the average concerned citizen.

"Garrison's been working day and night on that case," Rosemary murmured, her expression suddenly remote and reflective. "Sometimes I worry about him. And I wonder if . . ."

Imani waited, her heart in her throat, for the woman to complete her thought. But Rosemary Wade only shook her head, forced a bright smile. "Pay me no mind. If Garrison were here, he'd give me that thunderous scowl of his and tell me I worry too much. And he'd be right. I worry myself sick over these boys like they're not all grown men. Even this one," she grunted as Damien entered the kitchen. He rummaged around in the refrigerator before removing a can of Pepsi. "Is that room of yours clean, boy?"

Damien ducked his head with a shamefaced grin. "As soon as I finish studying, Ma. I promise."

"Where's Angelique?" Rosemary called after his retreating form. "I thought she was supposed to be dropping India off this afternoon so that she could go on that job interview."

"That's what I thought, too," he called back.

Rosemary shook her head, her smile indulgent. "A mother's job never ends. Remember that, Imani."

Imani chuckled. "I'll try, but it'll probably be a while before I get to put that theory to the test."

Rosemary's dark eyes twinkled as if she held a secret Imani was not privy to. "You never know."

Imani's cheeks grew inexplicably warm. She quickly checked her wristwatch. "Well, I'd better start heading back. I teach a class at two."

"Oh, that's too bad. I was really enjoying our conversation."

"Me, too," Imani said sincerely.

Rosemary stood with their empty teacups and saucers, crossed to the double sink. "Take some more coffee cake for the road. And if you're ever in the neighborhood, feel free to stop by." She smiled over her shoulder. "Maybe Garrison will be here, and you could meet him. Something tells me the two of you would really hit it off."

And therein lies the problem, Imani thought as she beat a hasty retreat a few minutes later. She felt like a fraud for not telling Rosemary Wade that she was already halfway in love with her son.

Garrison's worst suspicion had been confirmed.

"It's definitely a tape," announced the bespectacled FBI audio technician after listening to the previous day's recorded phone call. Before him was a bank of black-faced electronic equipment studded with a complicated array of knobs, levers, lights, and gauges. Garrison stood behind him, arms crossed and legs braced slightly apart, his expression grim. Beside him Aaron Moses, Cole Porter, and Kirk Spencer looked on with wide-eyed fascination.

"Are you absolutely sure?" Garrison demanded, the ramifications of the tech's verdict registering with the force of a heavyweight blow to his gut.

Bruce nodded, turned one knob down and pushed two small levers up. "I isolated and muted Pritchard's voice to pull out any other sounds. What you hear is light background noise from the street, but here's the interesting part. The noise doesn't blend into Pritchard's voice, as it would if the original call were made from the pay phone. The background sounds *overlap* Pritchard's voice, as if they are independent of each other. This is how they measure on the machine." Bruce paused, proud of the advanced technology available at his disposal. "It's like the message was recorded in a hollow sound-proof box, then played at the pay phone."

Garrison's frown deepened. That Althea's kidnapper would go to such lengths as to record a tape suggested premeditation. A sinister, calculating premeditation that didn't bode well for the outcome.

"So it's definitely Althea's voice?" He wanted to confirm.

Again Bruce bobbed his head affirmatively. "I compared this tape with the one you gave me from her voice mail. It's a match, no question about it."

Garrison stifled the harsh profanity that rose to the back of his throat, burned like sour bile. He wanted to let loose a string of expletives, for all the good it would do.

"Thanks, Bruce."

"Any time, Garrison." The tech had already turned back to his blinking machines, more comfortable with the impersonal technology than with fellow human beings. But he was the Bureau's best, which was why Garrison had personally delivered the tapes to him for analyzing.

Garrison led the way back into the hall, his mind already

clicking with plans for the next move. Four pairs of eyes were settled expectantly on him as he shut the door behind them.

"What kind of psycho gets off on making tapes of their victims begging for help?" Moses angrily demanded.

"The kind who wants to send a message," Garrison answered in a low voice. "A very personal one."

"So it has to be someone connected to the county exec," Cole concluded. "There's just no other reason for the perp to make a call like that, taunting and yanking the man's chain. Playing mind games."

Garrison regarded Cole in shrewd silence for a moment. He was testing the waters, trying to see if the other man would blink, start fidgeting, anything to give away his position. After a moment, Cole's uncomfortable gaze slid away from his.

Garrison glanced at the others. "We need to talk to more eyewitnesses in College Park, see if anyone saw our phantom at the pay phone. I had little success yesterday, but maybe we'll have better luck today finding someone who was around at the time."

"I'll go," Spencer volunteered.

Moses flicked an impatient glance at his watch and saw that it was nearly four o'clock. Reading his mind, Garrison raised a sardonic eyebrow and drawled, "Hot date tonight, Detective?"

"No," Moses grumbled. "Cole and I will ride with Spencer."

"Thank you, gentlemen." As they started off, Garrison said, "Detective Porter. A moment of your time please."

Cole hesitated, exchanging glances with Moses before turning and retracing his steps back to where Garrison stood, his shoulder propped against the wall. The hall was dim with a low ceiling and didn't have much traffic this time of day. Two technicians in lab coats walked past, murmuring greetings to Garrison. He responded with a polite nod for each.

"What's up?" Cole asked.

"You tell me," Garrison said quietly.

Cole frowned. "I don't understand."

"Is there any particular reason you felt compelled to tell Pritchard we had established Joaquin or Elizabeth Torres as a suspect?"

"I didn't—" Cole's mouth tightened as Garrison shook his head slowly, a subtle warning. He quickly changed his story. "I may have told him, yes. But only because he seemed so desperate for answers. Face it, we're not making any progress on this case, and those of us in the police department are the ones taking the heat. No one's gonna point a finger at the mighty feds and say *you're* not doing your job." He clamped his mouth shut suddenly as if realizing, too late, that he had revealed too much.

Garrison's expression remained impenetrable. "Is that why you went to the media about the contents of the note?"

Cole flushed deeply. "I never t-talked to any reporter."

"Please don't insult my intelligence, Detective Porter," Garrison said in a terrifyingly sober voice. "It's been a long day. I'm not in the mood for games."

"I didn't think it was a big deal," Cole said defensively.

Garrison raised a skeptical eyebrow. "After I specifically told everyone not to provide details about the note because it might compromise the investigation. Because it might set off a floodgate of copycats, and then instead of focusing on the legitimate leads, we'd be spending our time sifting through piles of red herrings." He paused, eyes zeroing in on the single bead of perspiration that trickled down the side of Porter's face. "What part of that didn't you understand, Detective?"

Cole thrust his hands on his hips, his voice rising with indignation as he protested, "Look, Agent Wade, I'm a darned good cop—"

"I never implied otherwise," Garrison countered calmly.

"I may not be some hotshot special agent like you, but—"

Slowly, deliberately, Garrison came off the wall and stood directly in front of Cole. His voice was eerily soft as he leaned down and murmured in the detective's ear, "I think

I asked your partner this question before, and now it's your turn. Are you going to have a problem working with me? Because if you're looking to have your ego stroked, I suggest you look elsewhere. I'm not the one." He paused, letting his words sink in. "Do you read me, Detective?"

Cole hesitated, then nodded slowly. "Loud and clear."

"Good." Garrison drew back, keeping his deadpan expression trained on the other man's taut face. "I'm not here to bust your chops, Detective. Unless you give me a reason to."

Something like resentment flickered in the detective's eyes. "Are we finished?" he inquired tightly.

"Time will tell," Garrison said softly.

Without another word, Cole turned on his heel and stalked off down the corridor. Garrison watched him go, knowing he had probably made an enemy and not caring. He stood there a moment, allowing the coiled tension to ebb from his body before starting in the opposite direction, taking the elevator to his office.

"This just came for you," the secretary announced, handing him a sealed FedEx envelope marked CONFIDENTIAL.

"Thanks," Garrison murmured, never breaking stride as he accepted the envelope and headed for his office. He closed the door and settled behind his desk with the contents of the envelope, prepared to find the needle in the haystack he'd been searching for.

An hour later, he was not disappointed.

Much to Imani's relief, Jada did not call her that evening as threatened. Imani welcomed the temporary reprieve, as it not only rescued her from having to answer questions about Garrison but also freed her time to catch up on some work. She had promised Dr. Yusef that she would have a rough draft of her essay for the anthology by the end of next week, and to date she hadn't conducted enough research to write more than a paragraph.

"You should boycott," Jada had suggested crossly. "In protest of his cowardly decision to remove you from the program committee."

Imani had laughed. "What? Cut off my nose to spite my face?"

In the world of academia, she knew the importance of getting her works published, especially as an associate professor seeking a tenure-track faculty position. The recognition she would receive as a result of being included in the African-American Studies department's anthology would go a long way toward achieving her long-term goals. Not only that, but Imani took great pride in working with the department's accomplished faculty members. Their diverse backgrounds and commitment to fostering academic excellence in teaching and research on African-American life were exemplary.

The objective of the anthology was to share the results of collaborative research projects focusing on the economic, political, cultural, and literary role of African-Americans throughout history. The contributing authors consisted of a carefully selected team of scholars and policy analysts from several historically black colleges and universities. The publication of the anthology would be followed by a symposium supported by the prestigious Ford Foundation grant, and promised to draw attendance from writers, professors, public policy makers, and artists across the nation.

Imani's essay was to explore the literary representation and societal impact of working women of color. Armed with her research tomes and photocopied articles, she plunked down on the floor in the great room and began drafting an outline. Shiloh trotted downstairs to join her, and she passed an absent hand over his fur as she scribbled notes.

Suddenly the golden retriever's head lifted, his back growing rigid as he stared toward the front door.

Imani glanced over at him. "What is it, boy?"

Shiloh rose on all fours and crept to the door. A low growl that started as a rumble in the back of his throat grew louder, more insistent. The fine hairs on the back of her neck rising, Imani stood and cautiously approached the door.

"Who's there?" she called, not really expecting an answer. When her query was met with silence, she added with false bravado, "If someone's out there, you're trespassing on my property, and in five seconds I'm going to call the police."

She waited, heart hammering wildly in her chest. Then suddenly Shiloh settled on his hind legs and gave his tail a vigorous swish.

She reached out, ran a trembling hand over his neck. "Okay now?" she murmured.

Shiloh looked at her with solemn amber eyes, then emitted a short bark.

"All right." He followed Imani to the window, peered out into the shadowy darkness with her. After a moment she announced, "I don't see anything, Shiloh. False alarm."

But long after she returned to her research, she couldn't dismiss the vague sense of foreboding that whispered across her skin, invaded her senses like icy fingers of dread. *The players have been selected. Let the games begin....*

During his previous visit to Emilia Torres's home, Garrison had helped himself to a paperback horror novel belonging to Joaquin Torres. Shortly after running the fingerprints through the Bureau's National Crime Information Center, a computerized database accessible to law enforcement agencies nationwide, he had received the criminal history report he was looking for. Three years ago, at the age of eighteen, Joaquin had been charged with two counts of sexual assault against a classmate, charges that were later dropped when the victim suddenly, without warning, recanted her story. One year later Joaquin faced stalking charges, and once again escaped serving prison time when he was acquitted. There was no doubt in Garrison's mind that Carlos Torres, a prominent businessman, had exerted his influence to get his son out of trouble. Garrison wondered how many other scrapes

Daddy Dearest had rescued Joaquin from, how many incidents were never reported.

Today's confirmation that Joaquin had purchased a voice scrambler from Torres Electronics, now Intracom Technology, was another building block in Garrison's growing theory. The model Joaquin had bought just two months ago was a state-of-the-art analog voice scrambler meant to secure the privacy of phone conversations. When he made phone calls, what the recipient heard was a metallic, disembodied voice that disguised the identity of the caller. The model Joaquin had purchased was also equipped with a device to protect his calls from being bugged or tapped.

Voice scramblers were essential for use by law enforcement agencies and fire departments, as well as business executives who didn't want their sensitive communications to be overheard. The question was, what would an unemployed twenty-one-year-old need one for? And not just any scrambler, but an expensive top-of-the-line model to rival even those used by the Bureau.

At Garrison's urging, the FBI was intensifying the search for Joaquin Torres. Now that his name and identifying data had been entered into the NCIC, Garrison hoped it would only be a matter of time before Joaquin was brought in for questioning. In addition, a "stop" had been placed against his fingerprints in the FBI's Criminal Justice Information Services Division so that local police would be notified immediately upon the receipt of any additional fingerprints, making it easier to track Torres's location.

"I want this kid found," Garrison growled into his cell phone on the way home.

On the other end, Eddie concurred. "So, the mother has no idea where her only son is?"

Garrison frowned. "That's her story, and she's sticking to it."

Eddie sighed heavily, impatiently. "Good thing her alibi on the night of Pritchard's disappearance checks out," he said, "or we'd be looking at an entire family of suspects.

What're you doing about Elizabeth Torres's possible connection to the backpack? You buying her story about someone else removing it from the room?"

Garrison thought fleetingly of Cole Porter and Elizabeth's suggestion that the police may have recovered Althea's backpack during their search of the dorm room. After today's tense confrontation with the detective, Garrison, already suspicious by nature, knew anything was possible.

"I'm keeping an open mind," he muttered finally.

"Smart man. You meeting for Monday Night Football at the Zone?" Eddie asked, switching gears.

Garrison glanced at the clock on the dashboard, saw that it was nearly eight o'clock. He thought about the cold leftovers and stark emptiness awaiting him at the apartment, and decided he needed a break from the loneliness and recriminations at least for one night.

"Be there in a few."

Eddie didn't hide his approval. "There's hope for you yet, Wade."

After Garrison hung up, he dialed voice mail to retrieve his messages. His mother's plaintive voice rolled on first. "Hey, baby, just wanted to see how you were doing. Haven't heard from you in a few days. Oh, and I met the loveliest young woman today—wish you had been there. Give me a call soon."

Garrison shook his head at his mother's unrelenting matchmaking attempts. He wondered idly about the identity of this latest hapless victim, a woman with the potential to dethrone Desiree Williams in his mother's grand schemes.

The next call was from Nate, brimming with joyous wonder over his and Nakia's very first sonogram. "It was amazing, G-man. Don't tell anyone, but I got all choked up."

Garrison was smiling as he deleted the messages and disconnected. He was genuinely happy for his childhood friend, whom he'd never envisioned settling down with a wife and kids. Sometimes it seemed that everyone around him was doing the domestic thing; even Eddie had recently hinted at wanting something more permanent with his longtime girl-friend, Annabella.

As Garrison pulled into the parking garage across the street from the Inner Harbor, he told himself that the bitter ache of regret he felt had nothing to do with a certain unattainable college professor.

Chapter 16

They were huddled around the classroom door as Imani approached that Wednesday afternoon, two of her students standing in a cluster with Elizabeth Torres as the center of attention.

"Hello, ladies," Imani murmured, adding curtly, "Elizabeth."

"Hey, Professor Maxwell," Yvette and Denise chorused in unison. Elizabeth greeted her with the predatory smile of a wolf.

"Oh, Professor Maxwell," she purred, "did you hear the good news? The program committee has selected me to replace Althea as the student panelist. Isn't that wonderful?"

Imani refused to rise to the bait, no matter how surprised she was. "Congratulations, Elizabeth," she said neutrally.

Yvette laughed. "She thinks she's on a roll now, Professor. She was just telling us how she plans to seduce that FBI agent from the news."

"Oh?" Imani met the smug satisfaction in Elizabeth's dark eyes with the barest hint of amusement, even as she felt something ugly and territorial stir to life within her. "Well, good luck."

"I don't need luck, Professor Maxwell," Elizabeth drawled

with a confident toss of her head. "I always get what I want. You should know that better than anyone."

Not missing the deliberate barb, Imani flashed a narrow smile. "And look how easily I forgot." Without another word, she turned and headed into the classroom, refusing to be rattled by a vindictive child whose pretty little neck she would have wrung were it not against university policy.

"She had the best essay out of the remaining submissions," Julian Jerome defended himself as he and Imani stood in line to pay for their salads in the South Campus dining hall.

"I didn't say a word," Imani countered evenly.

Julian chuckled mirthlessly. "You don't have to. Disapproval is written all over your face. Look, we had to reach a decision soon. The date of the recruitment program is closing in fast, and we really couldn't afford any more delays. With all due respect to Althea Pritchard," he added guiltily.

Imani winced. "You don't have to explain anything to me, Julian. I'm no longer on the committee, remember? What are you doing?"

He had bumped her aside in order to pay for both of their meals. He flashed his trademark poster-boy smile at the ill-tempered cashier and was rewarded with a warm answering grin.

"You didn't have to do that," Imani protested.

"What? She looked like she could use some cheering up."

"Not the cashier," Imani groused, "I'm talking about me. You didn't have to buy my lunch."

"Why not? This is probably the closest I'll ever come to having a date with you."

"Oh, Lord." Imani rolled her eyes heavenward as he followed her to a vacant table in the corner and sat down beside her.

"You wound me, Professor Maxwell. I think you've given too much credence to my reputation as some sort of lady-killer. I'll have you know that I've suffered through many solitary meals since my divorce, and believe me, it's not fun."

"That's unfortunate. I happen to enjoy my own company."

"Is that a subtle hint for me to get lost?" he teased.

"I wouldn't dare."

He laughed, spearing a cherry tomato with his plastic fork and popping it into his mouth.

"Speaking of your ex," Imani said, "she stopped by the other day to pick up her mail."

Julian frowned. "Sylvia?"

"Got any other ex-wives I don't know about?"

His smile was distracted. "Wonder what that was about," he muttered, half to himself.

"She said you forgot to send her forwarding address to creditors."

He paused, then gave a dismissive shrug. "It's possible. It hasn't been high on my list of priorities. Speaking of priorities," he began, "how's the writing for the anthology coming along?"

Imani chewed slowly, buying time. She knew how much Julian had wanted his work to be included in the publication; he'd spoken of little else after his department announced the project. They were both more than surprised when Anthony Yusef solicited her involvement over the multipublished Julian's.

"It's going well," Imani answered impartially.

Julian nodded, his smile a bit forced. "Well, just let me know if you need any help on the research end. You don't write seven books without becoming a bit of a research guru."

"Thanks, I may just take you up on that," Imani said, knowing she never would.

"But getting back to Elizabeth Torres," Julian said, returning his attention to his garden salad. "She really has a lot of great ideas for the program. You'd be impressed."

And so for the next half hour, Imani had to sit with a tight smile as Julian enthusiastically described Elizabeth's "great" ideas.

All of which had come from Althea.

Imani was subdued as she drove to her parents' house that evening.

She found her thoughts drifting to Jada's upcoming Thanksgiving wedding and all of the preparations surrounding the event. There seemed to be so much to do in so little time. But no matter how hectic the planning became, Jada and Marcus always maintained an air of blissful contentment. They understood that there was more to marriage than the ceremony itself, and Imani commended them for that.

Being around the couple often awakened feelings inside her, feelings and desires she had thought were long buried. It was unsettling to discover that somewhere deep within her, in the darkest, innermost recesses of her heart, she still entertained those childhood fantasies of love and happily ever after. It was almost as unsettling as the realization that she had intended to marry David without any real expectations of either. The reality was that as much as she admired and respected him as a friend, she instinctively knew that he could never bring her the kind of radiant happiness Marcus obviously brought Jada. And conversely, it was unfair of her to deprive David of the love and devotion of a woman who would melt in his embrace, who would regard him as the one and only man she could ever hope to spend eternity with.

The identity of Imani's Prince Charming whispered across her mind like a cruel taunt, baiting her with things she could never allow herself to want. Hopes and desires that would remain relegated to the lonely hours of the night, to be dismissed as dreams when daylight dawned with its inevitable reality check.

Forcing these gloomy thoughts from her mind, Imani

headed toward her parents' house, hoping to grab a quick meal with her mother and catch up on each other's lives.

Even before she crossed the threshold, she knew something was terribly wrong. Foreboding descended upon her in nauseating waves, and she bounded up the stairs as ghosts from the past followed in hot pursuit.

Vivienne Maxwell sat propped against the nightstand, on the floor, tears pouring down a face contorted with unspeakable grief. Beside her, where the phone had fallen, the receiver was off the hook. With a strangled cry, Imani rushed across the room to her mother and knelt quickly at her side.

"Mom! It's me, I'm here—" In horror, her eyes fell on the prescription bottle of antidepressants clutched tightly in her mother's hand. Imani screamed as panic surged within her, swift and unmerciful. "What did you do? What have you done?"

Vivienne shook her head from side to side, squeezed her eyes shut. "I-I couldn't, baby—"

But Imani had snatched the bottle, shook it vigorously to confirm the contents. It was still relatively full, and in dizzy relief she flung it aside and scooped her mother into her arms. Vivienne's frail body shuddered with sobs, tortured sounds erupting from the very depths of her soul.

"I miss him so much," she wailed into her daughter's chest. "Why did he have to leave us? *Why?*"

Imani lost the battle to her own carefully restrained grief. She surrendered to the bitter flood of tears that spilled down her cheeks and seeped into her mother's hair. "You have to get help, Mom," she cried. The pleas began in desperate succession. "We'll start going to the support group meetings again. I'll start going with you to see the psychiatrist again. Anything you need. We'll get through this together, I promise you."

She held her mother tightly, rocking her back and forth like a small child, needing the proof of Vivienne's warm, living body as much as she needed to comfort and protect her.

She didn't know how long they remained there, how much time passed. It was as inconsequential as words or explanations. Imani knew what had triggered her mother's near act of desperation. The approaching anniversary of Irvin Maxwell's death, a date Imani had been trying unsuccessfully to force from her mind for weeks.

When at last the emotional storm subsided, Vivienne drew back and rested her head weakly against the nightstand. "I'm sorry, baby," she whispered brokenly. "I'm trying so hard."

"I know." Imani swiped determinedly at her own tear-soaked face. "That's it, I'm moving back in. You can't stay here alone any longer."

Vivienne shook her head. "No—"

Anger welled up inside Imani's chest, made her speak more severely than intended. "It's not up for debate, Mom!"

Vivienne laid a soothing hand over her daughter's. "What I'm trying to say is, you don't have to move back home because I won't be here. I'm going to stay with Vanessa for a while." A rueful grimace touched her lips. "I guess there *is* some truth to twins having some sort of telepathic link. Vanessa called right as I was about to take my medicine, as if she could sense what crazy thoughts were going through my head."

Imani exhaled a deep breath that burned. Feeling dangerously lightheaded, she leaned back against the wall and closed her eyes for a moment. "Thank God for Aunt Vanessa," she whispered, shaken by how close she had come to stumbling upon a more disastrous scenario.

"I'm so sorry for scaring you, baby," Vivienne murmured dejectedly. "It's going on six years now. I know I should be over these feelings, this overwhelming despair. But I just find it so hard to move on, to put the past behind me. I—" Her voice caught, fresh tears filling her mournful eyes.

Imani had never seen sadder eyes. It broke her heart into shattered halves. She crawled back over to her mother, laid her head on her shoulder the way she'd done as a child. "On one hand, Mom, I want to tell you to grieve at your own pace, not to put restrictions on yourself because everyone deals with loss in different ways. But on the other hand . . ." She sighed, drew a shuddering breath. "On the other hand, I'm so scared for you. Scared of what you've become, what you may do to yourself. And yes, scared for myself. I don't want to lose another parent."

"I know, baby." Vivienne rubbed her cheek against the softness of Imani's hair. "And that's why I couldn't go through with it. I thought about you and Vin, about the devastation it would cause you."

"But are we your only reasons for wanting to live, Mom?" Imani asked with painful honesty. "Isn't there anything else at all?"

Vivienne grew still, and when Imani lifted her head to look at her, her mother wore a remote, haunted expression. "I don't think you know what it's like to love someone as much as I loved your father," she said softly. "I was involved with another man when I met him. The moment I saw Irvin, I knew I would always love him. You can't know how scary that feels. To fall in love so quickly, with such reckless abandon."

Imani ignored the inner voice that contradicted her mother's words, whispering the unwelcome reminder that she *did* know what it felt like to fall for someone so quickly, with such reckless abandon.

"He was my world," Vivienne continued, "and sometimes I regret that fact, that I opened myself up to such hurt by loving him so deeply. But it's the same with motherhood. I love you and Vin just as much as I loved your father. I would probably lose my mind if anything happened to either of you." She sighed, forced a wan smile as she gazed at Imani. "Do you know what brings me consolation sometimes? The fact that you and David have each other, that you have so many wonderful years ahead of you. I know your father is smiling from heaven."

Imani managed a wobbly smile even as her traitorous heart clutched, constricted with guilt.

Ten minutes later, Vanessa Jamison hurried into the house with the sweeping authority of a miniature tornado. A registered nurse at Heartland Health Care Center in Hyattsville, she was crisp in her white uniform with a floral-patterned jacket, her stethoscope still dangling from her neck. Thick, neat braids hung past her shoulders and gave her an exotic look. She kissed her niece, then wrapped her briefly in a comforting hug before turning her attention to her sister. Without a word, both women gravitated together in a fervent embrace, swaying back and forth in each other's arms. When they at last drew apart and gazed at one another, their features were as identical as the tears streaming down their faces.

"We're going to get through this," Vanessa vowed, her voice husky with emotion. "Do you believe me?"

Vivienne hesitated, then bobbed her head meekly. "Thanks for coming," she whispered.

Vanessa waved off the gratitude, began opening dresser drawers to pack her sister's clothes. "I should have done this a long time ago. I'm two minutes older, I'm supposed to protect you. Mani, find me your mother's suitcase, and then I want you to go home so that your mother and I can have a long heart-to-heart."

Imani didn't even think about opposing her spirited aunt, who used to deliver the worst punishments she, Vin, Jada, and Jada's older sister Jacqueline had ever experienced. Aunt Vanessa distributed discipline as liberally as the love she showered upon them, didn't discriminate between her own children and those of her sister's when it came to doling out gifts and butt whippings. The neighborhood gossips had whispered that Vanessa Jamison's formidable nature was to blame for her divorce, although close family members knew that it had more to do with Darrell Jamison's wandering eye than anything else.

"Will you call me later once you're settled in?" Imani asked her mother after returning from the guest room with the suitcase.

"Of course." Vivienne smiled softly. "Go home and get

some rest, you look tired. Don't worry about me, I'm in good hands."

"I know." Imani kissed her mother's cheek, then Aunt Vanessa's, before slipping quietly from the house.

Garrison was waiting for her when she arrived home.

He stepped from the shadows of his truck, appearing like a mirage on the desert of her despair. Emotion seized her, and she squeezed her eyes shut as if to make him disappear. Images flashed behind her closed lids: her father lying in a pool of his own blood, then Garrison, then her father again. Horrifyingly vivid, the visions rewound and repeated in her mind's eye until she wanted to scream out.

He met her as she stepped down from her Jeep and locked the door. "What're you doing here?" she asked in a low voice without looking at him. "This really isn't a good time."

"I needed to see you," he said softly.

"Why?"

He lifted those broad shoulders in an almost helpless shrug. "I don't know."

She whirled on him, something inside of her snapping. "You don't know? You don't know? You haven't had two words for me all week, and suddenly you show up on my doorstep because you *needed* to see me?" Her tone turned scornful, mocking. "Wait, don't tell me. You sensed my distress, sensed that I needed you. Is that it?"

"Would that be so crazy?" he murmured.

"Yes, because I *don't* need you. And the sooner you get that through your head, the better." She knew she was lashing out at him, perhaps unfairly, but she felt utterly powerless against the tide of her own erratic emotions and fears. How she longed to go to him, confide everything, and draw strength from him.

But she couldn't. She wouldn't.

Garrison was silent, watching her with that dark, intuitive gaze.

"And for God's sake, stop looking at me like that!" she snapped.

"Like what?"

"Like *that*. With those, those *eyes* of yours," she hissed, and immediately realized how moronic she sounded.

There was a hint of wry humor in the twitch of his mouth, in his voice. "I don't know how else to look at you, Imani."

Teetering precariously on the brink of hysteria, Imani spun on her heel and started up the walk. Garrison reached out quickly, grasping her upper arm and pulling her around to face him. She struggled against him, tried to kick him, but was hopelessly outmatched. He pulled her close against him, so close that she couldn't hurt him or escape from him. She glared up at him, the wild racing of her heart a combined result of her exertions and their sudden proximity.

His eyes roamed across her face, a smoldering examination. "Why are you doing this?" he demanded in a voice roughened with anger, confusion.

"What do you want from me, Garrison?" she shouted. "You appear out of nowhere one day and expect me to reorganize my entire life for you, no questions asked. I'm sorry, but it doesn't work that way! You may recall that I was in a relationship before you came along."

It was a weak argument in the face of all that had transpired between them. She knew it as well as he did. But it was all she had, her ace in the hole, and she grabbed onto it with both hands.

"David and I may have our problems," she continued vehemently, "but we're committed to making things work." Tears stung her eyelids, straining for release. She nearly choked on the lie, knew she would if she didn't get away soon.

Garrison tightened his hold on her, his eyes blazing into hers. "Look me in the eye and tell me you love him," he commanded fiercely.

Imani glared up at him, hating him for forcing her hand,

hating herself for being so utterly weak and deceitful. "I love him," she said defiantly. "I always have, and I always will."

Something like pain flickered across his face before his expression hardened. "Liar," he snarled, but he released her. Not sparing her another word, he turned and walked back to his truck without a backward glance.

Imani stormed into the house and slammed the door, trembling so violently she thought she would go into convulsions. She stood there with one hand on the doorknob, every fiber of her being clamoring to fling the door open, run after him, and beg his understanding. She swore bitterly under her breath, pounded her fist against the door. Her fury was useless, as futile as the tears that finally erupted and sent her sliding to the floor in a crumpled heap of regret.

Garrison spent the better part of the next morning in a meeting at the federal courthouse in Baltimore with Assistant U.S. Attorney Bill Moynihan, who would be prosecuting the case against serial child rapist John Beaufort. Garrison had testified in the preliminary hearing and was now, at Moynihan's special request, meeting to compare notes on prosecution strategies. Although the role of FBI agents was customarily limited to preparing prosecutive reports and testifying in court once the criminals were apprehended, Garrison was never surprised when he was called upon to provide additional support to the U.S. Attorney's office, nor did he particularly mind. Given his bloodlust determination to see the violent offenders punished to the full extent of the law, he would do just about anything to help make it happen, would try the case himself if necessity warranted it. And more than anything, he wanted to see John Beaufort sent straight to hell in a handbasket, even if he had to personally make the delivery.

So it was with extreme self-loathing that Garrison found himself preoccupied with thoughts of Imani Maxwell as he sat across the conference table from Bill Moynihan. He hadn't been able to stop thinking about her since the previous night's confrontation, had been tortured with instant replays of her declaration that she loved David Scott. As much as Garrison refused to accept this as truth, he couldn't help questioning how much was wishful thinking on his part. Did he have a hard time believing that Imani was in love with David because her actions suggested otherwise, or because Garrison wanted her for himself? Because there was no denying the latter fact. He wanted her, wanted her with a vengeance that was slowly, painstakingly, driving him insane. Wanted her body, soul, and mind. *Thou shall not covet.* He had obviously missed that lesson in Sunday school, and now he was paying for it. In spades.

"Everything okay?" the prematurely graying Moynihan asked, noting Garrison's thunderous scowl.

"Fine," Garrison said gruffly.

Moynihan adjusted his horn-rimmed glasses on his aquiline nose. "We can wrap this up soon. I know you're also working the kidnapping case."

"It's no problem." Garrison forced thoughts of Imani from his mind and focused on the matter at hand. The successful prosecution of a violent predator was far more important than his love life, or lack thereof.

An hour later when he emerged from the federal courthouse, he drove straight to the office. He had just finished checking his voice mail messages when Eddie appeared in the doorway, studying him in shrewd silence for a moment.

"Don't tell me. Lovers' quarrel?"

As always, Garrison was annoyed by his partner's unnerving ability to discern his moods, especially considering that no one else could. Although Garrison hadn't told him a thing about Imani, Eddie remained dogged in his conviction that there was something going on between the two.

"What do you want?" Garrison growled without looking up from making notations.

"That bad, huh?" Eddie chuckled, leaning on the door

frame. "And here I thought we were making progress. But come to think of it, you've been in a pretty foul mood since last Friday night. Something must have happened."

"Are you here to psychoanalyze me, Balducci," Garrison muttered, "or do you have a better reason for darkening my doorstep?"

Eddie shook his head, grinned before his tone turned serious. "Finally got a positive ID on Althea's mysterious chat buddy. It's quite interesting, actually."

Garrison's head snapped up. "Who?" he demanded.

"Name's Julian Jerome. And get this: he's a professor at the University of Maryland. Coincidence?"

Garrison's smile was narrow, sharp. "No such thing."

Julian broke out into a sweat as soon as he saw him coming.

Not a visible sweat with rivulets of perspiration dripping down his face, soaking his clothes. This was more of an internal sweat, as if some mechanism had sent a warning signal to his brain, jumpstarting his instincts into panic mode.

He stood outside the building, conversing with one of his female students. He pretended not to notice as Special Agent Garrison Wade drew near. As if anyone could miss the imposing figure of a six-foot-four brother in a double-breasted dark suit, sauntering across a college campus with all the authority of one who belonged there, wearing no coat as if it were a sunny eighty degrees outdoors and not barely sixty.

Julian had hated guys like Wade throughout high school and college. Tough guys who called Julian a pretty boy, challenged him to fights because they thought he looked soft. Soft and high-yellow. Garrison Wade had probably been popular in school whether he wanted to be or not, while Julian had fought for the respect of his peers in the Detroit high school he'd attended, a rundown institution with the reputation of having more juvenile delinquents than budding scholars. Was it any wonder that he'd seized upon the opportunity to attend a private liberal arts college far from home, had been drawn exclusively to white women who did not perceive his green eyes and wavy hair as some sort of character flaw, some warped indicator of weakness?

"Mr. Jerome. I was wondering if I could have a moment of your time."

"Certainly. I'll see you in class next week, Tamara." Julian dismissed his student, forced a smile as he faced Wade. He was unnerved to find that the top of his head barely skimmed the agent's shoulder, and it was with a supreme effort that he tried not to crane his neck just to meet Wade's dark, assessing gaze.

Garrison noted it, although his expression never changed. "I wanted to ask you about your online correspondence with Althea Pritchard."

"That's fine," Julian said easily, "but if it's all the same to you, could we conduct this conversation inside the warmth of my office?"

Garrison inclined his head coolly. "Lead the way."

He was not surprised when Julian Jerome gestured him into a low chair before claiming the high-backed leather swivel throne behind the desk. Establishing perimeters, putting Garrison in his place.

"No, thanks," he declined, mildly amused. "I prefer to stand."

For a moment Julian looked crestfallen, like a child who'd been told he couldn't go to the circus. But then he gave a dismissive shrug. "It's probably just as well. These chairs aren't really designed for a man of your height and physique. *I* had problems with the chair they stuck me with, until I demanded something more suitable. Ergonomics, you know. Anyway," he continued a bit smugly, "they were more than willing to accommodate my request, of course."

Garrison had wandered over to examine a wall of framed plaques and certificates, the distinctions ranging from literary awards to letters of commendation from high-ranking university officials. He thought of the contrast between

Imani's sparsely furnished office and the one he now stood in. Other than to display her degrees on the wall behind her desk, Imani had chosen not to showcase the various certificates of merit he knew, for a fact, she had received. Not that he faulted Julian Jerome for doing so; it was just something he took note of, filed away in his mental cabinet.

"Impressive," Garrison murmured, turning from the wall and noting a mahogany bookshelf lined with titles bearing Julian's name. He walked over, slid out a textbook and absently thumbed through it. "Looks like you're quite an authority on African-American history."

"That's what they tell me," Julian answered glibly. The cruel taunts flitted across his mind, never completely dormant. *You ain't one of us, you just a mixed-up white boy.*

Garrison replaced the tome, propped a shoulder against the wall beside the bookshelf. He nodded toward the framed degrees displayed behind Julian's desk. "You don't have a Ph.D.?" he inquired casually.

The corners of Julian's mouth tightened perceptibly. "I'm working on it." The lips relaxed into an affable smile. "It's the price I pay for having so many books published. Takes time away from my studies."

"Of course. Which is why I'm a bit baffled that you could spend so many hours online chatting with students, namely Althea Pritchard."

Julian shrugged, glanced briefly out the window. "It was my way of relaxing, unwinding after a long day. Surely there's no crime against that, Agent Wade?"

"You obviously thought so," Garrison countered smoothly. "Or was there another reason you provided a false name and address when signing up for the chat group?"

He felt, rather than saw, the other man tense. Julian reached across the blotter, picked up the stapler and began playing with it, transferring its solid weight from one hand to another. "I had my reasons for doing that," he said stiffly.

Garrison raised an eyebrow. "And those would be?"

"Look, Agent Wade, I know what you're thinking. That

I'm some pervert who lurks in chat rooms to have illicit conversations with unsuspecting minors. I can assure you that nothing is further from the truth. I go online seeking intellectually stimulating correspondence with like-minded people. In case you didn't know," he added bitterly, "I wasn't exactly married to a rocket scientist."

"So you wanted to see if the grass was greener."

An embarrassed flush crept across Julian's high cheekbones. "You've read the transcripts," he said tightly. "There was nothing unsavory about my conversations with Althea Pritchard."

"Did you know who she was?"

Julian hesitated. "No. She used a screen name just like everyone else, didn't give away personal details about herself."

"She mentioned that she was an eighteen-year-old college student from Upper Marlboro, Maryland. Told you that she was dating the star basketball player whom she lost her virginity to. You don't consider that personal information?"

Julian met Garrison's gaze evenly. "Unless I'm mistaken, sixteen is still the legal age of consent in Maryland. So once again, Agent Wade," he said with the slow hint of a smile, "I'm within the boundaries of propriety."

Garrison nodded slowly, deliberately. "Where were you on the night of Althea's disappearance?"

The satisfied smile waned. "I-I was home."

"Can anyone vouch for your whereabouts?"

"I suppose not. I live alone now that I'm divorced. But I *was* home," he insisted. "I have no reason to lie to you."

"You sure about that?"

Once again the mouth tightened. The stapler was set down with a thud. "If there's nothing else, Agent Wade, I have an important meeting to attend for an upcoming program."

"The minority recruitment program?"

Julian hesitated, eyeing him warily. "Yes, that's correct. I took over as chairman following the removal of my colleague."

"Congratulations," Garrison said softly.

"There's nothing to be congratulated for. It was very difficult for me, and awkward. Imani Maxwell is a very dear friend of mine."

"You don't say," Garrison drawled. He straightened from the wall, started for the door. "Thanks for your time, Mr. Jerome. I'll be in touch."

"By all means," Julian muttered.

At the door, Garrison turned. "Just out of curiosity," he began offhandedly, "what does HOLLY010 stand for?"

Julian looked as if he were trying to determine if his answer could be incriminating. He answered slowly, almost cautiously, "Hollywood. It's an old nickname. And the number ten signifies how many years I was married."

Garrison nodded. "Interesting."

"What? What's interesting?"

"That you chose that number for that particular reason. Considering it was your wife you were trying to conceal your chats from."

Julian flushed. "I never said—"

"You didn't have to. I took an educated guess." Garrison tipped his head politely. "Enjoy your meeting, Mr. Jerome."

Julian waited until Garrison had been gone at least five minutes before he rose, crossed the room, and threw a quick glance down both ends of the silent corridor. Closing the door discreetly, he walked back over to the desk and snatched up the phone. He spoke tersely for only a moment before replacing the receiver with a violently trembling hand.

Outside in the hallway, Garrison emerged from the corner where he had been waiting. He nodded once to himself, turned, and exited the building. Back in his truck, he dialed Eddie at the office. "Run a background check on Julian Jerome. There's something he's not telling me, and I intend to find out what it is."

* * *

Thirty-two-year-old Irvin Maxwell, Jr. was a born mathematician. On childhood trips to the grocery store with his mother, he had dazzled customers with his ability to tally the bill before the cashier could ring it up, and he was never off by more than three cents. When he left home for college, it was a foregone conclusion that he would major in accounting. Number crunching was as much a part of him as teaching was a part of his sister.

That Friday evening as Imani stood in the tiny kitchen of his rent-controlled Northeast D.C. apartment, she couldn't help smiling absently at her older brother. He sat hunched over his laptop computer in the narrow living room that doubled as his study. Bookcases were lined with tomes for the accounting professional, titles such as *Fundamental Principles in Accounting* and *Tax Methodology for the Certified Public Accountant* stamped across the thick spines. The evening news droned from a nineteen-inch color television Vin had owned since college.

He was still in shirtsleeves, with his navy blue tie loosened, although he had been home more than an hour. His fingers flew deftly across the keyboard as he worked on a report which, in all likelihood, was not due for another two weeks. It would not occur to him to leave work behind at the office, to take time out to enjoy his weekend.

"How's Cassandra?" Imani called through the opening to the living room.

"I wouldn't know. We're not seeing each other anymore."

"That's too bad," Imani lamented. "I really liked her."

Vin hummed a noncommittal note, continued tapping away.

Imani didn't have to ask what had happened between her brother and his latest girlfriend. Since their father's death, Vin had retreated into his work like never before, seeking refuge in his world of numbers and accounting computations. Math, unlike life, was logical. The numbers fell neatly, predictably, into place and provided only one right answer. Relationships were entirely different and demanded more than Vin was willing—or able—to give. Not unlike his sister. What a pair they were.

Imani shook her head ruefully as she stirred a Crock-Pot full of the thick, aromatic chili that had always been a favorite with her father and brother. She opened the cabinet to retrieve more pepper and marveled, not for the first time, at the precision with which the contents were arranged by alphabetical order. Vin had always been a compulsive neat freak, would probably break out into hives if he saw the chaotic disarray of his sister's storage closet.

"I'm not saying you have to move back home or anything," Imani said, resuming their previous conversation as if it had never been interrupted. "I just know how much it would mean to her if you visited more often."

Vin paused in his typing. "You know why I don't," he said quietly.

Indeed, Imani did know. It was both a blessing and a curse that Vin Maxwell bore a striking resemblance to his late father, even shared some of the same mannerisms. It was difficult for Vivienne Maxwell to look at her son without seeing his father, without remembering the way he, too, had stroked his chin when deep in thought or agitated. Even the sight of Vin's misdirected mail, addressed to Irvin Maxwell minus the affixed *Junior,* brought tears to Vivienne's eyes.

"Still," Imani murmured. "I know it would really make her happy to see you."

Vin sighed deeply and removed the stylish wire-rimmed glasses he'd been forced to start wearing within the past year. He pinched the bridge of his nose tiredly. "You know I'm not trying to hurt her, Imani. It's just that . . ." His voice trailing off, he shook his head helplessly. "That house . . . so many memories."

Imani understood all too well what he meant. She also knew how hard it was for her brother to pass the J. Edgar Hoover FBI Building on his way to work every morning. Although Vin could easily have had his pick of any Fortune 500 company when he graduated *summa cum laude* from college, he had bypassed all the hefty signing bonuses and stock options thrown his way by overzealous employers and had chosen to work for the Department of Housing and Urban Development. Not necessarily because he preferred a career in public service, but because his office would be near his father's. The two had met for lunch every afternoon without fail, had turned a simple meal into a standing tradition.

"I know how you feel about the house," Imani spoke softly, reflectively. "Sometimes when I'm there, I even imagine I can still hear his voice. If I'm honest with myself, I'll admit that my reasons for moving out had more to do with the memories than needing a shorter commute to campus."

Vin met her gaze through the kitchen's alcove. Then after a moment he returned his attention to the screen before him. "I'll stop by Aunt Vanessa's tomorrow."

"Thank you," Imani said simply. She bent, sliding a fragrant pan of buttery corn bread from the oven. She cut and placed a thick wedge on a saucer, heaped a healthy serving of chili into a bowl, and piled both onto a tray.

Vin barely glanced up as she set the meal on the desk beside him. "Thanks, Mani. You really didn't have to come over and fix me dinner."

"Of course I did," she said blithely. "Otherwise you would have remained at that laptop all night, stopping only to microwave some popcorn and maybe nibble on that old spaghetti in your refrigerator, which I should have thrown out. Matter of fact," she decided, returning to the kitchen and extracting the plastic container in question. She stood over the trash bin and dumped out the mold-covered contents, shaking her head in mild disgust. Notoriously frugal, Vin had been known to eat leftovers older than the abused leather armchair he refused to surrender to Goodwill.

"There's enough chili in this pot to last you a week, at least," Imani said, washing and drying the Tupperware container, knowing it would drive her brother crazy to see any dirty dishes in the sink.

"You know I can go through your chili faster than that," Vin mumbled around a steaming mouthful.

"Well, then, I'll just have to come back next week and fix you some more." Grinning, Imani approached and draped her arms around his neck. She peered over his shoulder. "What're you working on, anyway?"

He hit a button and the screen went blank. "You know I can't tell you that."

She chuckled dryly. Between her late father, Vin, David with his attorney-client privilege mandates, and now even Garrison, it seemed that all the men in her life were involved in high-security professions on one level or another.

"Well, I'd better head back over to the volunteer center," she said, pulling on her russet leather jacket and cinching the belt around her waist, her mood suddenly dampened at the unwelcome reminder of Garrison.

Vin frowned. "Aren't you supposed to be working on that anthology essay?"

"I will. I've devoted the entire weekend to it, no exceptions." She leaned down, planted a chaste kiss on her brother's cheek. "Come lock up."

Imani was so preoccupied with painful reflections of Garrison as she left the apartment building that she didn't even notice the cold pair of eyes watching her from across the street. She thought nothing of the dark sedan that pulled out and followed her back to College Park at a slow, deliberate crawl.

Chapter 17

By Saturday morning, Garrison knew what he had to do.

For the past two days, he and Imani had treated each other with nothing more than civil reserve on the few occasions they happened to find themselves in the same room. Garrison thought he would lose his mind if he had to spend another minute exchanging cordial words with the woman he'd been trying, unsuccessfully, to purge from his system. The final straw had come last night at the command center, when she sought Aaron Moses's help with something she normally would have turned to Garrison for. Knowing how much she despised the detective and avoided dealing with him at any and all costs, Garrison realized like never before how bad things were between them.

The decision came to him as he completed his double jog around the Inner Harbor against a gray, overcast skyline as ominous as his mood. The weather forecast called for chilly temperatures and early-morning showers, neither of which Garrison heeded as he trudged back to his apartment and peeled off his sweats for a shower.

Standing under the hot spray, hands braced against the tiled walls, he analyzed his feelings for Imani Maxwell. She intrigued him, appealed to him in a way no woman ever had. She was intelligent, beautiful, giving, stubborn, vulnerable yet fiercely independent, and all at once. She challenged him, baffled him, and occasionally infuriated him. And she could seduce him so effortlessly, with only a look or a soft word or a caress. Garrison had never considered himself a home wrecker, the sort of brother to trespass on another man's territory. He respected the sanctity of marriage, believed wholeheartedly in monogamous relationships. If he honestly didn't think he had a chance with Imani, he would have backed off a long time ago.

Liar, an inner voice countered darkly. An army of maverick assassins couldn't have kept him away from her. And nothing or no one would stand in his way now.

Emerging from his shower, he quickly pulled on a beige-colored cableknit sweater over a pair of dark jeans, and had barely laced up his Timberland boots before he was heading out the door.

He arrived at Imani's house before noon and saw with a sinking heart that her Jeep was gone. He got out anyway, walked to the front door as if expecting to find her home if he willed it hard enough. There was a slip of paper taped to the door, and something like alarm clutched in his chest, made him tear the note down without a second thought.

When he read the contents, the dread twisted in his stomach, but not for the original reason he'd feared. This note was dictated in Imani's brassy, distinctly feminine handwriting: *David, In case you get back early, I'm at the bridal shop in Columbia. Be back in a little while. Imani.*

His expression grim, Garrison crumpled up the note and strode purposefully back to his truck, yanking out the phone book he kept in the trunk. After a quick search, he found what he was looking for, hopped behind the wheel, and sped away from the curb in a squeal of tires.

* * *

"When is this woman going to show up?"

The surly demand came from Chante Knowles, one of Jada's bridesmaids. It was the third time she had asked the question in the last twenty minutes, although none of the other five women assembled could provide any answers.

Matron of honor Jacqueline Jamison-Randolph stood before a mirror admiring her reflection, her smooth terra-cotta complexion a flattering contrast against the straight-cut silver gown she wore, wide hips made for childbearing flaring nicely beneath the fitted bodice. "I must admit," she said, executing another twirl to catch a glimpse of her bared flesh in the backless dress, "my baby sister has good taste. I look positively fierce in this dress."

There were low murmurs of agreement behind her as the other bridesmaids in identical gowns gazed at their own reflections, jockeying for position in front of the mirror. Only Chante and Imani remained seated on the plush sofa provided for patrons of the exclusive bridal boutique.

"I can't believe Jada is running late for her own fitting," Chante complained.

Jackie snorted, finally relinquishing her position at the mirror to join them on the sofa. "Mama always said that girl would be late for her own funeral."

"Why didn't you bring her with you?" Chante turned her ire on Imani. "You're supposed to be the maid of honor."

"Because that wasn't the arrangement," Imani calmly replied. "She stayed over at Marcus's last night, said she'd meet us here in the morning."

Chante checked her diamond-studded watch, made a sound of disgust. "She's almost half an hour late, and that saleswoman keeps glaring at us like we're a bunch of vagrants." A corporate broker ruled by strict schedules and the frenetic pace of power meetings, Chante had little patience for tardiness and was not accustomed to passing her time waiting for others, sorority sister or not.

Imani's cell phone trilled, and she reached inside her purse and snatched it up. Jada's frantic voice greeted her before she could even utter a word. "Imani, something's come up, and I won't be able to make it for the fitting."

"Where are you?" Imani asked, straining to hear her cousin above all the background noise. Sirens, traffic sounds, loud voices.

"I'm in Philadelphia."

"Philadelphia!" Imani exclaimed, and five pairs of eyes swung in her direction. Lowering her voice, she hissed into the phone, "What are you doing in Philadelphia?"

"There was a train derailment, and Greenberg called me first thing this morning to go cover the story. It's a mess, girl."

Imani's frown turned to concern. "Was anyone hurt?"

"Yes, but we don't have an exact count yet. The police and transit authorities are still trying to contain the area. Sections of the train are still on fire, and the medics are on the scene trying to help as many passengers as they can—" She broke off, speaking to someone in the background in a strained voice. The wail of more sirens could be heard.

"Are you all right?" Imani asked when Jada came back on the line.

"I'm fine. Marcus drove me up here, and we'll probably stay overnight. Listen, I want you to do me a favor. Could you try on my gown for me?"

"What?"

"Come on, Imani. I don't know when I'll be able to reschedule a fitting, and if the dress needs alterations, the seamstress told me it might take weeks due to her workload. I don't have that kind of time with the wedding just around the corner."

"But Jada, I'm not—"

"We have the exact same measurements, girl, so don't even try it. Same bra size, same height, same weight. Just make sure you have on the shoes I'll be wearing when you try it on. Jackie has them. By the way, how does everyone look?"

"Wonderful," Imani answered weakly. "The dresses fit perfectly, and everyone's really pleased."

"Good, that's the *last* thing I need to be worrying about, disgruntled bridesmaids. Look, I have to run. You'll let me know how the gown fits when I call you tomorrow?"

"Um . . . sure."

"Thanks, Imani. Don't know what I'd do without you, girl. Give everyone my apologies."

"They'll understand. And be careful, Jada."

"What did she say?" Jackie and Chante chorused in unison as Imani disconnected.

Imani explained to everyone about the train derailment in Philadelphia.

"Lord have mercy," Jackie murmured. "Hope it's not terrorist related."

The other women fell silent, each vividly reminded of the horrific events of September 11. The entire nation had been on a heightened sense of alert since that terrible day, and could not hear about plane, bus, or train crashes without fearing the absolute worst.

Seeking to lighten the mood, Chante asked, "Well, what did she ask you to do?"

Imani bit her bottom lip. "She wants me to try on her gown for her."

The others brightened at the prospect of being able to see *someone* in the imported creation from Milan, bride or not. "Well, what are we waiting for?" Jackie demanded, signaling for the saleswoman, who glided over with a polished smile.

As unconventional as Jada was, she had chosen a traditional princess wedding gown. Sleeveless, with a form-fitting bodice that exposed a wicked amount of cleavage, the billowing skirt was made of white appliquéd silk that whispered with each movement.

Imani squeezed her eyes shut against her reflection, not allowing herself to want what the image represented. Afraid to want it.

"Imani, come on out so we can see you," Jackie called from the other side of the curtained dressing room.

Imani jerked her head in refusal. "No need, Jackie. It fits just fine," she called back.

"Come on, Imani." A chorus of other voices joined her cousin's, growing insistent with each plea.

The saleswoman smiled at her. "Just a peek," she cajoled lightly. "It wouldn't hurt."

Speak for yourself. Pushing aside her animosity, Imani relented and stepped from behind the curtain.

"Ohhh." The collective sighs made her blush, feeling foolish. "Imani, you look absolutely beautiful. Radiant."

"Step up here so we can get a better look at you," the saleswoman suggested, and before Imani could utter another protest, she was being guided onto the raised platform facing a floor-to-ceiling three-way mirror.

"You guys, I'm not the bride," she reminded the women surrounding her with expressions of rapt admiration.

"Not yet," Jackie retorted, and the others cackled in agreement.

Imani rolled her eyes, feeling like a mannequin on display.

She didn't even realize when she ceased to be the center of attention until she heard the faint stirring among the women, heard Chante murmur under her breath to Jackie, "Girl, who *is* that chocolate dream that just walked through the door?"

And somehow Imani just knew.

She turned around slowly, as if in a dream. Garrison stood near the entrance, watching her intently. And in one timeless moment their gazes connected. From across the length of the room, his dark eyes appeared smoky, almost brooding. Just the connection they made in that heartbeat was enough to suspend her, to make her forget where she was and what she was doing. All the others faded away to a hum of whispers, vague shapes and colors. He alone remained in her fixed vision, not releasing her from his gaze— silent, penetrating . . . ominous.

Imani felt her breath quicken, lodging somewhere between her throat and chest. Her stomach clenched, her skin tingled all over. The blood began to pound through her, making her feel warm and then cold, then warm again—too warm.

He started toward her slowly, purposefully, like a predatory animal stalking its prey. Or a man intent on claiming his woman.

She opened her mouth as he drew near. "Garrison—"

Before she could form another word, he grabbed her hand and began leading her down from the platform. With scandalized gasps, the others parted like the Red Sea to let them through, their faces a blur of shocked expressions. Imani, too startled to protest, had to practically run to keep up with him as he strode resolutely toward the glass doors, his jaw set determinedly.

"Sir—" the saleswoman sputtered in protest.

Heedless to the commotion he was causing, Garrison kept going. Imani felt like the starring lead in some satirical version of the *Runaway Bride*. She clutched a handful of silk, lifting the flowing skirt to keep the pristine hem from being dragged upon the ground. Jada was going to kill her if she ruined this gown.

But not before Imani killed Garrison Wade.

She gasped as the cold air outside hit her, a wintry assault upon her exposed flesh. "What do you think you're—"

Garrison turned then, sweeping her into his arms as if she weighed next to nothing. The blows she rained upon his solid chest with her fist fell like raindrops, as ineffective as a child's. He strode to his truck parked at the curb and dumped her unceremoniously inside. Before she could react, he had rounded the front fender and climbed in beside her, pulling off before he'd even slammed the door.

She gaped at him, shock mingling with fury. "Are you insane? What do you think you're doing! You can't just walk into a place and—"

"I can," he countered in a low voice, "and I just did."

"You're crazy! Stop this car right now!" When he ignored

her, she twisted her body in the passenger seat—a feat in all the folds of appliquéd silk—and tried to unlock the automatic door. But he had locked it from the driver's side control panel. Impotent with rage, she whirled on him. "*What* is your problem? Why are you doing this? And while I'm at it," she spluttered with rising hysteria, "what's with you not wearing coats? Do you have something against being warm?"

His mouth twitched, mirthless. "What's the matter? Afraid I'll catch my death of pneumonia and you'll have it on your conscience that the last words we exchanged were angry ones?"

She opened her mouth to protest, astounded by his unmitigated gall, but no words would come. At least nothing intelligible. She snapped her mouth shut and folded her arms angrily across her chest. It occurred to her, then, that she was dealing with a loose cannon. A certifiable lunatic. The stress of the job had finally made him snap. Hadn't she always heard about FBI agents who strayed from the straight and narrow path, became renegades as dangerous as the fugitives they were supposed to be hunting and apprehending?

And all this time she had been looking over her shoulder for an unseen enemy.

She eyed him warily, as if he were some wild animal whose next move she feared. His profile was stony, dark, and gloomy.

"So I guess congratulations are in order," he stated flatly.

"*What?*" Comprehension slowly dawned. "No, you don't under—"

"Don't I?"

"Wait a minute," she fumed. "I don't owe you any explanation! You just abducted me and if I'm not mistaken, that's a federal crime, *Special Agent* Wade."

That seemed to sober him. Without warning, he veered into the deserted parking lot of a closed Jiffy Lube and threw the truck into park. His expression, when he met her stunned gaze, was tumultuous.

"I didn't mean to frighten you," he said quietly.

"Well, it's a little too late for that, don't you think?" she snapped.

He reached over suddenly, hauling her across the console and into his lap. His chest rose and fell rapidly with his erratic breathing, matching her own heaving breasts. He gazed at her and she stared right back, still trembling with resentment.

Then he uttered raggedly, "Please don't marry him."

Her mouth fell open in surprise. "Garrison—"

Before she could complete the thought, much less the sentence, he slanted his mouth over hers, roughly, possessively. When her hands jerked up to his chest in angry protest, his arms tightened around her waist, a steel band that drew her firmly against him in the confined space.

"Please," he whispered desperately, his lips hot and sweet against hers. His hand held the back of her head, pushing her deeper into his hungry kiss. "Please don't do it."

She felt dangerously lightheaded on a wave of warring emotions, fury and desire swirling through her at dizzying speeds. She felt like she was trapped in a tornado, twirled and tossed every which way. As the storm raged, the anger slowly ebbed, surrendering to heat and a need that threatened to consume her. She wrapped her arms around his neck and opened her mouth fully to him, sucking his tongue, tasting his urgency.

He groaned softly in approval, holding her tighter against him like he would never let go. "See what you do to me," he rasped against her mouth. "I can't breathe without you, Imani."

She threw back her head and flattened her palm against the closed window as his lips trailed a greedy path down the plunging neckline of the gown. He rained hot kisses on her bared flesh, drawing deep shudders from her body. Her respiration couldn't keep up with her racing heartbeat. She felt perilously close to exploding.

Still cradling the back of her head, he brought his lips to hers once again, fusing them together. Imani knew she should end the kiss right then, but she felt utterly powerless against the onslaught of his passion, against her own insatiable hunger for him. Her tongue slid across the sensuous curve of his bottom lip, nibbling, pulling, wanting so much more. Needing so much more.

"Please," she whimpered against his mouth. Begging him to release her from the madness, begging him not to.

She finally mustered the strength and pulled away, resting her forehead weakly against his. Their panted breaths mingled, fogged up the windows.

For a while neither spoke, shaken by the sheer magnitude of what they had just shared. Willing her heart to return to its normal pace, Imani finally murmured, "Garrison."

His eyes were closed, the long, ebony lashes resting on his cheeks like miniature lace fans. "What, baby?" he answered huskily.

She smiled softly at the endearment, slipping so naturally from his mouth. "It's not my dress."

Opening his eyes slowly, he drew back and studied her, the smoky desire in his dark gaze gradually giving way to confusion. "What do you mean?"

"It's not my wedding dress. Jada's the one getting married, not me."

His eyebrows furrowed. Then, as her meaning slowly registered, relief—indescribable in its intensity—surged through him, followed quickly by a touch of embarrassment. His mouth curved upward in a shamefaced half grin. "Jada?"

"Uh-huh," Imani replied, giving him an amused don't-you-feel-stupid look.

He did. His gaze dropped to the gown twisted around her body. He remembered how the vision of her standing there in a hypnotic swirl of white silk had taken his breath away, emotion clogging in his throat. It was followed swiftly by desperation and a possessive fury, hot and blinding.

"It's a beautiful dress."

"Mmm-hmm. Jada thinks so, too. And something tells me she'd like to keep it that way."

His sheepish grin widened, the sexy half dimple flashing in his right cheek. "Tell her to send me the cleaning bill."

"Oh, you can bet your life on that. Now please take me back before those people call the police on you."

It was with shocked silence that Imani was greeted at the bridal boutique a few minutes later. She mumbled an uncomfortable apology to the saleswoman, met the open speculation in her friends' stares with a defiantly arched eyebrow as if to say, *What?* As if nothing out of the ordinary had just occurred.

And then out of the stunned silence, her cousin spoke. "Well," Jackie drawled with wicked amusement, "I guess we all know what's going to happen at *her* wedding if she tries to marry David."

For a moment no one spoke. And then, one by one, they all dissolved into fits of laughter. Even the saleswoman hid a guilty smile behind her hand.

With as much dignity as she could muster, holding her head high, Imani started for the dressing room to remove the gown, vowing to make Garrison pay dearly.

Afterward, Imani declined an invitation to go shopping with the girls who would, in all likelihood, spend the entire time bombarding her with questions about Garrison. Jackie had already threatened to tell David if her cousin didn't "give up the goods" on the handsome FBI agent, and Chante had instructed Imani to give Garrison her phone number if Imani didn't want him—which she'd have to be dumb and blind not to, Chante had added tartly.

The message light was blinking when Imani arrived home, kicking off her sodden shoes that had gotten drenched in the cold downpour. Grumbling because she had forgotten to take her umbrella that morning, she listened to the only voice mail message she had.

"Hey, Imani, it's me. Just wanted to let you know that I'll be staying in San Francisco one more day; something came up unexpectedly. Anyway, I'll call you later if I can."

Imani groaned as she deleted the message and hung up. She had really hoped David would return today so that they could have their talk. The longer it was postponed, the more deceitful she felt. And although she dreaded causing him any pain, she knew in the long run it was best for both of them.

Distracted by these thoughts, she treated herself to a hot bubble bath, hoping to dispel some of the chill from the rain. Lulled by the warm water and lavender-scented bath crystals, she soon drifted off to sleep. She dreamed of Garrison, something so steamy and erotic that she snapped awake, blushing furiously. With a frustrated scowl, she climbed from the clawfoot tub, grabbed her towel, and stomped into her bedroom. Shiloh, fast asleep in his favorite corner, didn't even stir. Rain always knocked him out, made him so tired he could sleep through a catastrophe.

Imani dressed quickly, yanking on a pair of black leggings and her father's old FBI T-shirt, which she often wore around the house to feel closer to him.

For what she was about to do, she would also need his strength. She dialed the number to David's hotel room. "Hello?" a woman answered, her voice sultry with sleep.

Surprised, Imani hesitated. "I'm sorry, I must have the wrong room. I'm looking for David Scott?"

There was a heavy pause on the other end.

"Hello?" Imani prompted.

"This is David's room. May I ask who's calling?"

"Is this Suzanne?" Imani answered with a question, recognizing the voice of David's longtime secretary, a beautiful Asian woman.

"Yes, it is. Uh, hello . . . Imani." David's voice could be heard in the background, angry and surprised, and then he came on the line.

"Imani?"

Imani's heartbeat was a deafening roar in her ears. "David," she greeted him mildly. "I got your message earlier, thought I'd try to reach you."

"Imani—" David began desperately.

"I was going to suggest that we start seeing other people," Imani murmured, "but I guess that's a moot point, isn't it?"

"Imani, listen to me. You don't understand."

"Just tell me the truth, David. Are you sleeping with Suzanne or not?"

He hesitated so long she thought he wouldn't respond. But it didn't matter. She had her answer. "It all makes sense now," she said softly, half to herself. "All those months before we broke up, you didn't want to sleep with me because you were already getting what you needed elsewhere."

"Imani, I still love you. I never meant to hurt you."

"I know," Imani said, surprisingly calm. "Things just happen sometimes, no matter how good our intentions."

David paused, taken aback by her composure. "I don't want it to end this way, baby girl. We have so much history. We're *friends*—"

"And we'll always be, David."

"I'll be home tomorrow," he said quickly. "I can come over, we can sit down and discuss this together."

"That really won't be necessary, David."

"Please, Imani? Just hear me out one last time, and then I'll leave the decision up to you. Please?"

"I think you've humiliated yourself enough in front of Suzanne. And David," she added quietly, firmly, "it *is* over between us. Nothing you have to say will change that."

There was a muffled sound on the other end that could have been a groan, a profanity, or a combination of both. She closed her eyes, said goodbye, and replaced the receiver.

She didn't know what to make of the strange tranquility that descended upon her. She felt incredibly relieved, as if a giant burden had been lifted from her shoulders. David's betrayal had made it easier for her to sever the ties between them once and for all.

Imani went downstairs and fixed herself a cup of chamomile tea, smiling a little when she thought of Rosemary Wade. She wished she had some of her coffee cake.

Walking into the great room, Imani built a fire, put Celine Dion's *Greatest Hits* CD on a loop, and pulled out her research materials. A sense of melancholy settled over her as she tried to concentrate on her work. Although she was relieved that the charade had finally come to an end, she would miss the friendship she and David had enjoyed for most of their lives. Because she knew, instinctively, that no matter what either of them said to the contrary, things would never be the same between them again. Just as they had known they couldn't go back to being mere friends once they shared that first tentative kiss, so long ago it seemed. She honestly hoped that what David and Suzanne had was about more than just sex; she hoped it was something more meaningful for both of them.

She had just finished her outline when the doorbell rang. Laying her books aside, she padded to the front door in her bare feet.

Garrison stood there holding a newspaper over his head. His eyes touched briefly on her shirt before sliding back up to her face. "May I come in?"

Imani crossed her arms, arched an eyebrow even as her heart began racing. "If I don't," she teased, "are you going to toss me over your shoulder and cart me off like some caveman?"

His lips curved in a lazy grin. "Only if you want me to," he drawled.

Resisting the tug of a smile, Imani opened the door wider and gestured him inside. He tossed aside the sodden newspaper and brushed past her, stomping his big, booted feet on the welcome mat.

"Don't tell me," Imani said dryly, closing the door. "You don't believe in umbrellas, either."

"An extravagance."

Imani shook her head in mild exasperation. "You are impossible, Garrison Wade. Well, at least remove your boots so you don't track any mud onto my carpet."

"Does this mean I can stay a while?"

She didn't like the husky intimacy she heard in his voice. She turned away, starting toward the kitchen. "Would you like some coffee?" she asked, instead of answering his question. "I'm having tea, but I'll make a pot of coffee if you want some."

"Thank you, I'd appreciate that." Setting his boots by the door, he followed her into the kitchen. "Where's Shiloh?"

"Upstairs fast asleep. The rain gets him every time." She measured Folgers into the coffeemaker and pulled a ceramic mug from the cabinet.

Garrison noticed the box of chamomile tea on the counter and made a face. "My mother drinks that stuff."

"I know," Imani spoke without thinking, and at Garrison's puzzled look, hastened to add, "I mean, a lot of women do. It can be very relaxing. Want to try some?"

"No, thanks," he said. "Give me the straight black stuff any day."

Imani rolled her eyes at him. "Have you always been such a macho man?"

He leaned back against the counter, dark eyes twinkling as he folded his arms across his wide chest. "Always."

And because Imani couldn't help admiring the way he looked in his sweater, how nicely the fawn color blended with his deep, mahogany skin, she busied herself with wiping the counter of imaginary coffee crystals. "Were there a lot of people at the volunteer center?"

"Not a lot. I sent them all home, told them to go be with their families."

Imani glanced up, her expression softening. "That was very kind of you."

Garrison shrugged, frowning slightly. "Don't know how much kindness had to do with it," he said grimly. "There wasn't much for them to do."

He didn't have to elaborate. Imani knew that with no solid leads or suspects, the investigation—as well as the volunteer efforts—had nearly come to a standstill. No one wanted to voice aloud their worst fears, that no matter what they did from now on, it was too late for Althea. The memory of what had happened to Washington, D.C. intern Chandra Levy three summers ago was never far from anyone's mind.

"Hey," Garrison spoke softly, "don't go losing hope on me. Remember what you told me in the War Room last Sunday, about Althea still having so much life left to experience? I took your words to heart."

"You did?" For some reason, that meant a lot to her.

"Yeah," he said quietly. "I need your optimism on this case, Imani. Maybe to balance my cynical nature, I don't know. But I've come to depend on it. So," he tipped her chin up, gazed into her eyes, "could you hang in there with me?"

Imani nodded, knowing she would have gone to the ends of the earth and back for this man. She was certain her eyes told him so. "I will."

His gaze flickered, drifted to her mouth. The coffeemaker percolated, and she turned away almost in relief.

They settled into the cozy warm great room with their coffee and tea, sitting at opposite ends of the camelback sofa before the crackling fire. The logs made a soft hissing sound as they burned, sending up an occasional spray of bright embers. Celine Dion crooned softly in the background about the power of love.

Imani realized how incredibly romantic the scene would appear to an outsider. She wondered if Garrison had noticed as well. Of course he had. The man noticed everything.

To prove her point, he nodded toward her shirt and casually remarked, "I have a few like those at home."

Imani glanced down at herself and wanted to smack her forehead because she had completely forgotten she was wearing her father's navy blue FBI T-shirt with the yellow lettering.

Garrison was watching her quietly, intently. "Whose shirt is that?"

Her expression clouded. "It was my father's," she whispered.

Although jolted by her words, he remained perfectly still. "Your father worked for the Bureau?"

Imani swallowed, nodded reluctantly. "He was a supervisory special agent at the D.C. headquarters office before he—" Her voice hitched, as if she couldn't bring herself to utter the word.

Garrison stared down into his coffee. And suddenly everything made sense, the pieces of the puzzle falling into place. "He died in the line of duty," he concluded softly.

"Yes." Imani turned her head to hide the sheen of tears in her eyes. Her voice, when she spoke again, was husky with suppressed emotion. "If it's all the same to you, Garrison, I'd really rather not talk about it right now."

He hesitated, then nodded slowly. "I understand."

"Thank you."

They sat in silence for another moment, staring into the roaring fire, and then Garrison asked, "How did things end between you and David?"

Imani slanted him a censorious look. "What makes you so certain things have ended?"

His knowing gaze held hers. "Haven't they?"

She considered lying to him, but what would be the point? Like the stealthiest of invaders, he had infiltrated her relationship with David, exposed all of its weaknesses, and crept away with the biggest bounty of all: her heart.

"It's over," she said quietly.

"What a shame," Garrison said in a deep, velvety voice that had a dangerous effect on her heart rate. "I guess it's true that one man's loss is another man's gain."

Without answering, Imani rose shakily and began stacking her research books in a neat pile on the table. "I really need to be working on this essay," she muttered under her breath. She had told Garrison all about the anthology as he drove her back to the bridal boutique, had held his interest as if what she was describing were the most fascinating thing in the world.

He set aside his half-empty coffee mug. "You want me to go?"

She paused in the middle of folding a thick afghan and met his dark gaze. Common sense warned her to send him on his way, and for more reasons than the fact that she was supposed to be working. But deep in her heart she knew she wanted him to stay, had craved his presence for the past two weeks like an addict in withdrawal.

"You can stay," she said softly, sealing her fate.

Garrison rose slowly to his feet. His heated gaze never left hers as he stood before her. "I'd like nothing better," he murmured.

Fear coursed through her. Fear mingled with an undeniable anticipation, almost heady in its intensity. The afghan fell limply from her hands. "Garrison . . ."

"For as long as I live," he said huskily, "I'll never forget how beautiful you were in that wedding dress. Breathtaking."

"Thank you," she whispered. The anticipation wound like a spring inside her, made her heart pound dangerously in her chest.

Garrison reached for her, curving an arm possessively around her waist and drawing her gently, coaxingly, against the solid length of his body. "Tell me if you don't want this," he said, his voice low and intoxicating. "Just one word and I'll stop."

His words sent shivers through her whole body. She trembled hard, closed her eyes. "You know I don't want you to."

Garrison leaned down, touching his lips gently to her closed lids. Her lashes fluttered upward, her gaze settling on the sensuous curve of his mouth. God, how she loved that mouth. She slid her arms around his neck and leaned close, kissing him softly, sweetly.

He moaned deep in his throat. "Do you know how many times I've dreamed about this?" he whispered against her mouth.

She shook her head, her eyes growing smoky. "Not nearly as often as I have."

His eyes smoldered with pleasure before his mouth covered hers again, hot and coaxing, and she opened her mouth to welcome his probing tongue. He worked his magic, plunging deep and retreating in a primal rhythm that drew a low, guttural moan from the very depths of her being. Liquid fire began a slow, exquisite burn in her belly and spread outward in licking flames. They kissed long, hard, and provocatively.

Still wrapped in each other's arms, they sank to their knees on the floor. The heat from the fire spread like a slow, thick liquid over the hearth and into the room, no match for the heat between their bodies. Garrison cupped her face between his hands, and she let her head fall back as he trailed his mouth down her throat, nibbling and raining seductive kisses that burned her sensitive flesh.

After a moment, their gazes met and held. At Imani's subtle nod, Garrison began undressing her slowly, almost reverentially, savoring the sight of her body. She quivered everywhere he looked at her, touched her. In the firelight, his hungry gaze swept over her sleek brown body, her flat stomach, and the shapely expanse of her long legs. She was the most sublimely beautiful woman he had ever seen, and he told her so in a voice thickened with desire.

A becoming flush stole across her cheeks. "Thank you," she whispered.

She reached to undress him and he let her, watching her beneath hooded lids as she silently marveled at the fine specimen he made. Broad shoulders and a wide chest planed with hard, sinewy muscle over a taut, beautifully sculpted abdomen. She touched him everywhere, enjoying the feel of him as he trembled beneath her exploring hands. When he rose to retrieve a condom from his wallet, her eyes followed him, silently entreating him to hurry back to her. He sheathed himself quickly and returned to her.

And then they were lying naked together on the hearth rug, skin to skin, hard against soft. Frenzied need pulsed through her as his strong, capable hands roamed the length of her body, caresses that were followed with languid kisses and the exquisite torture of his tongue. She writhed against him as craving roared through her, throbbed in her moist center. She cradled his head, holding his mouth to hers.

"Now," she entreated breathlessly. "Please . . ."

Garrison pulled her on top to straddle him, and her breath escaped from her on a soft cry as he entered her, stretching her deeply. It took every ounce of his willpower not to ravage her right then and there, but he held himself in check. He lifted her by the waist and slid her back down on him slowly, inch by inch.

She inhaled sharply, biting her bottom lip so hard she thought she would draw blood. Bracing her hands on his abdomen, she began to move on him at her own pace, rotating her hips in an incredibly sensual rhythm that had him gasping for air, desperately clinging to a shred of self-control. Arching into him, Imani pushed her breasts into his face, wanting to be filled with him until she exploded into nothingness. His mouth covered one dusky nipple, suckling greedily and nearly sending her over the edge. She threw back her head, panted his name as she rode him. Outside the rain tumbled against the windowpanes in driving sheets, but it was nothing compared to the storm brewing in that room. She moved faster and faster until they were both breathless, until the heat between them condensed to a slick gloss of sweat on their skin.

With a rough, hungry sound, Garrison rolled her onto her back, and she automatically tightened her legs around him. Clutching her hips, he thrust deep and hard, devouring her, needing her, loving her as he was meant to from the beginning of time.

Wrapping her arms around him, tears shimmering in her eyes, Imani whimpered in earnest, "I love you."

Garrison could scarcely believe his ears, was afraid to accept what he had heard. "Say it again," he whispered urgently against her mouth.

She dug her nails into his back, the frantic movement of her hips beneath his driving him toward the point of no return. "I love you, Garrison."

"Baby . . ."

She cried out wildly as she erupted, burying her face in his shoulder to absorb the violent shudder that swept through her. Garrison gripped her tightly, moaning with his own powerful release.

They clung to each other as they drifted hazily back to earth, as their racing heartbeats gradually steadied, as their ragged breaths filled the air, as the real world took form around them. They laid together without speaking for several moments as Celine Dion's "If Walls Could Talk" played in the background, the lyrics hauntingly appropriate.

Garrison raised himself above Imani, absorbing his weight on both arms as he gazed down into her eyes. "Did you mean what you said?" he asked softly.

Imani stared up at him, at the face she loved more than life itself. "Every word."

With an exultant groan, he rolled them over so that her body covered his. She smiled against his chest, endeared by the simple maneuver, his concern over crushing her. When she lifted her face to his, his lips brushed her cheek and grazed her mouth, coaxing her into a stirring openmouthed kiss that left them both breathless again. They at last drew apart, their foreheads touching as they gazed at each other.

He traced her cheekbone with his thumb. "I love you so much," he said with aching tenderness.

Imani blushed with delight. "You don't have to say that just because—"

He shook his head adamantly. "If you knew how much it's been killing me to stay away from you," he said huskily, "you wouldn't doubt my feelings for one second."

Imani stared at him, saw the fiery passion in his glittering eyes, and knew he meant what he said. A surge of joy, over-whelming in its intensity, welled up inside her and brought fresh tears to her eyes.

Garrison pulled her to him and tucked her head into the hollow of his neck. He located the afghan on the floor and covered them with it. Beside them the fire crackled, and after a while both fell into a deep, contented sleep.

Chapter 18

Imani awakened the next morning feeling incredibly drugged and liking it. She stretched languorously in the four-poster bed, flooded with wickedly delicious memories of the previous night. She and Garrison had awakened several times to make love, unable to get enough of each other, their limbs twined in the darkness of the room as they gave themselves to one another with desperate abandon.

She lifted her head from the pillow and found him sitting on the edge of the bed, watching her quietly. He was partially dressed, wearing yesterday's dark jeans and his boots. The shadowed growth on his jaw, combined with the sight of his bare chest, made him almost unbearably sexy.

She blushed under his penetrating gaze, suddenly shy as she pulled the satin bedsheets protectively to her breasts. "Good morning," she murmured, her lips parting in a smile. "So I wasn't dreaming."

Garrison shook his head, his mouth quirking. "Nope, I already checked to make sure."

He could tell that pleased her. She smiled again shyly and he gazed at her, admiring her fresh morning beauty. He was hooked.

He reached out, trailing a finger lightly down the length of her spine from the top of her neck to the small of her back, drawing a low moan from her.

"How long have you been awake?"

"Not too long," he said softly. Despite the number of times they had made love, his desire for her was unabated. Her brown-sugar skin and curvaceous form outlined beneath the covers beckoned to him, filling him with images of the incredible night of passion they had shared. He wanted to climb back into that bed and make love to her again and again, until neither had any strength left. When she rolled onto her back, affording him a brief glimpse of one plump, beautiful breast, he felt a jolt of hunger.

But it wasn't just about the mind-blowing sex they had shared, or the fact that when she kissed him and wrapped those glorious brown legs around him he forgot everything else, including his own name. Submerged in her, driving deep into her overwhelming heat, his thoughts vanished into a dizzying sense of completion. For the first time ever, after having his fair share of lovers, Garrison truly understood the indescribable beauty of becoming one with a woman.

This woman, he thought as he gazed at her in the morning sun, had changed his life forever. And for as long as he lived, he knew there would never be another Imani for him.

"What time is it?" she asked.

"Seven-thirty."

She groaned. "I see you're an early riser. Don't you make exceptions on the weekend?"

"Occasionally." He smiled, toeing off his boots. "I took Shiloh for his walk."

Her eyes widened, filled with pleasure at his thoughtfulness. "Oh, Garrison, that was so sweet."

His eyes glinted wickedly. "What do I get in return for my kindness?"

She eyed him warily as he stood, removing his jeans. "Um . . . thank you?"

He shook his head slowly, deliberately, crawling back into bed with her. "Not good enough."

She giggled, scooting away from him. "Come on, Garrison. I already promised to go to the Ravens game with you, and I'm a Redskins fan." Not to mention that she hadn't yet recovered from last night's marathon. A delicious ache had settled into her limbs, her body permanently branded with his intensely passionate lovemaking.

"Yeah, you did agree to give up your entire afternoon for me," Garrison acknowledged, sounding thoughtful. He laid back against the pillow, his hands clasped behind his head. "I suppose we're even."

Imani gaped at him, torn between laughter and insult. "You're going to give up that easily?"

He turned his head to meet her affronted gaze, his dark eyes twinkling with mirth. "We should be getting up soon, anyway. The game starts at one and I still need to go home, shower, and change."

She gave him a sultry look under her lush lashes, a temptress in all her feminine glory. "Are you sure?" she purred, snaking one satiny leg between his.

Raw need ripped through him. With an agonized groan, he rolled over on top of her. "I suppose we can spare a few more hours," he uttered, bending his head to ravish her sweet lips.

Garrison's sparsely decorated downtown Baltimore apartment was a typical bachelor pad, except that it was impossibly immaculate. Stark white walls contrasted with the black leather furniture, and not a crooked angle could be found in the placement of the exquisite Indian rugs covering the golden hardwood floors. What the apartment may have lacked in abundant furnishings, it more than made up for with a wall of steep windows providing a panoramic view of the downtown skyline. It would be spectacular, she knew, to watch the sunset from there, or recline on a blanket on a sticky July evening to take in the fireworks display.

It jarred her to realize how easily she inserted herself into those scenarios, how desperately she wanted a future with Garrison, against her better judgment. Everything about her recent behavior had been uncharacteristic of her. When she emerged from the shower that morning, her body had remained hot and weak from their lovemaking, so sensitive that the mere brush of the towel across her skin had aroused her. As David was her only other lover, it was the first time she'd ever had sex with no promises of marriage.

Her mother's tearful confession whispered at the back of her mind like a warning. *You can't know how scary that feels. To fall in love so quickly, with such reckless abandon.* If "reckless abandon" didn't describe Imani's behavior over the last twenty-four hours, she didn't know what did.

Declining Garrison's sly invitation to tour his bedroom, Imani wandered through the small apartment while he showered and dressed. The black granite entertainment center held a thirty-two-inch color television and an elaborate stereo system, and she sifted through his expansive music collection before settling on Angie Stone's "Mahogany Soul," the title that described her baby to a T. She smiled to herself at the realization that she'd already come to regard Garrison as her "baby."

The kitchen was narrow, almost too small to accommodate the gleaming giant of the Sub-Zero refrigerator. Because Imani had always wanted one of her own, she pulled it open and shook her head in amazement at the spacious interior. A moment later her appreciation turned to amusement when she spied the bulk supply of Popsicles. Who stocked up on Popsicles in the middle of October?

"What's with all the frozen treats?" she called toward the bedroom, her voice tinged with laughter.

She heard Garrison's low chuckle. "It's a long story."

"Can't wait to hear it." Grinning, she closed the refrigerator and snagged a cherry lollipop from a large plastic container filled with an assortment of flavors. As she started to unwrap her contraband, she paused. A suspicious smile lifted the corners of her mouth as she glanced from the refrigerator stockpiled with Popsicles to the stash of candy. "I'm starting to notice a pattern here," she muttered under her breath. The man either had a sweet tooth or a serious case of oral fixation.

The doorbell rang, and after a few moments when Garrison didn't materialize from his bedroom, she called, "Want me to get that?"

His muffled grunt told her that he had a mouthful of toothpaste, so she went to answer the door.

The engaging smile on Desiree Williams's face quickly vanished at the sight of Imani. A slightly embarrassed flush crept over her cheeks as she thrust her hands into the pockets of her pristine white lab coat. "I'm sorry. Is Garrison here?"

"Sure." Imani opened the door wider and stepped aside to let her enter.

"I believe we've met before," Desiree said, offering a forced smile. "At the play?"

Imani nodded. "Right. Nice to see you again." She had the same knot of tension in her stomach as she'd had that night, a feeling she now acknowledged as plain old-fashioned jealousy.

Garrison emerged from the bedroom, pulling on a purple Ravens jersey over his head. "Who was at—" His words broke off at the sight of their visitor, as both women turned to look at him. Slowly he gave the jersey one final tug, settling the material over his big shoulders.

"Desiree," he greeted her, his expression neutral.

"I apologize if this is a bad time," Desiree said. "My shift just ended, and I thought I'd stop by on my way home and . . ." Her voice trailed off and for a moment, an awkward silence descended upon the room.

Imani crossed her arms and became absorbed in an inspection of her white Reeboks. Garrison watched her, carefully gauging her reaction.

"I should have called first," Desiree finished apologetically.

"That's okay," Garrison said mildly. "We were actually on our way out the door."

"You must be going to see Nate play," she surmised, gesturing to the Ravens jersey displaying Nate Jones's number fifty-six. She looked surprised. "So you're finally making use of those tickets he offers you every week."

"Something like that."

Desiree chuckled dryly. "Congratulations," she said to Imani. "We've all been trying to convince this man to get out more often, and you've managed a play *and* a football game. What's your secret?"

Imani met Garrison's inscrutable gaze. "I'll let you know when I figure it out," she answered softly.

Desiree's glance shuttled between them. "Well, don't let me keep the two of you from your plans. Enjoy the game, and it was nice meeting you again, Imani."

Imani smiled politely. "You, too."

"I'll walk you out," Garrison murmured, stepping into the corridor with Desiree and pulling the door closed behind him. He studied her face quietly for a moment. "Are you all right?"

She bobbed her head quickly, too quickly. "Of course, why wouldn't I be? I'm probably more embarrassed than anything. I swear I had no idea you had company, Garrison, or I never would have—"

"I know."

Desiree's expression was a touch wistful. "So I guess this thing between the two of you is pretty serious. She's the one you've been saving your heart for."

"Yeah," Garrison admitted softly.

Desiree tried not to look deflated. She straightened visibly and took a deep breath. "Well, then, I guess I can stop going out of my way to be kind to your mother," she teased.

A corner of Garrison's mouth twitched, but he said nothing.

She leaned close, kissing his cheek. When she drew away, she wore a bittersweet smile. "Take care of yourself, Garrison Wade. I hope that lady in there knows how lucky she is."

"I think I'm the lucky one," he said quietly. "Take care, Desiree."

He watched her start off down the hallway before he stepped back inside the apartment. Imani stood gazing out the window, her arms folded across her chest almost protectively. He crossed the living room to stand behind her.

"Quite a view," she said softly, without turning to look at him.

"Hmm," was his noncommittal response. He reached around, put his finger beneath her chin until she had to turn completely and face him. "Everything okay?"

"Sure." But her eyes dropped in contradiction. She cursed herself for being so insecure, so jealous that she felt positively ill. She thought about David and his secretary, and marveled that her reaction to his infidelity came nowhere near the level of turbulent emotions raging through her now.

"It's probably none of my business that you get Sunday morning female visitors," she began in a low voice. "Just because we slept together doesn't mean I'm entitled to make demands—"

"Look at me." Garrison coaxed her chin upward. She met the intensity of his dark gaze reluctantly. "Desiree was there for me during a very difficult time in my life, and for that I'll always be grateful. But believe me when I tell you that there's nothing between us beyond friendship."

Imani stared into his eyes, seeing the truth reflected there. "Garrison—"

"I don't sleep around," he continued with quiet gravity. "I hope you understand that what we shared last night was anything but a one-night stand because I can assure you that it meant far more to me than that. More than you'll ever know. And as for being entitled to make demands of one another," he added, his deep voice husky with promise, "you'd better believe *I'm* going to. I play for keeps, Imani. Don't ever forget that."

She swallowed hard and remained silent. He lifted her hand to his lips and gently kissed each fingertip, gazing into her eyes and watching her sooty lashes flutter. He brought his face close to hers and murmured against her mouth, "So are you going to be my woman, or what?"

Imani smiled. "I'm yours," she whispered.

Garrison cupped her face in both hands and slanted his mouth possessively over hers, effectively silencing any lingering doubts.

Chapter 19

Jada was laughing hysterically.

Seated behind the desk in her office, Imani wore a scowl that really didn't hold much rancor. "I see Jackie wasted no time calling you," she griped into the phone. "You just got back last night."

"I know," Jada gasped, struggling to catch her breath. Imani could just imagine tears of mirth rolling down her cousin's face. "She caught me the second I walked through the door. It was the best homecoming news I had ever received."

"Your gown could have been ruined," Imani reminded her dryly.

"But it wasn't. Anyway, it would have been a small price to pay to see the look on your face when that man marched into the boutique and whisked you away. I wish I had been there!"

"If you had been," Imani drawled, "I wouldn't have been wearing the wedding gown. *You* would have."

Jada laughed. "I couldn't have planned it better myself. Not that I'm glad the train derailment happened," she hastened to add. "Thank God there were no fatalities."

"Thank God," Imani soberly agreed.

"Anyway, it's the first time in my life that I'm actually grateful for my sister's big mouth. *You* certainly weren't going to tell me about you and Garrison Wade. I can't believe you were holding out on me like that, Imani. I thought we shared everything."

"Please don't lay that guilt trip on me," Imani groaned helplessly. "You know I wasn't deliberately trying to keep anything from you. Things between me and Garrison just happened so quickly—"

"*I'll* say," Jada snorted. "You just met him—what?—two weeks ago?"

"Three weeks this Wednesday," Imani mumbled. And she had already fallen madly, head over heels, in love with him.

"You know I'm the last one to talk about time frames. You may recall that it was love at first sight for me when I met Marcus. But you've always been more cautious and reserved, more levelheaded where men are concerned."

"You make me sound like a nun."

Jada chuckled. "Well, you *were* saving yourself for marriage . . . until David came back from law school and seduced you."

"For the last time, Jada, he did *not* seduce me," Imani protested. "Anyway, it doesn't matter now."

"Indeed. There's a new sheriff in town." Jada sighed deeply, appreciatively. "Garrison Wade. What a man, what a man. And to think we were just discussing him last Monday, and you never said a thing. I should have known it would take a brother like that to make *you* lose your mind. Not that I blame you one bit."

"Gee, thanks."

"How did David take it?"

"Well, he doesn't know about Garrison," Imani hedged. "I ended things with David before . . . uh . . ."

"Before you officially cheated on him by sleeping with Garrison?" Jada supplied in an amused, knowing tone.

Imani's cheeks flamed. "I never said—"

Jada laughed. "You didn't have to. And I know it was good, that man *looks* like he can handle his business in the bedroom!"

Imani couldn't stifle the private smile that tilted the corners of her mouth. What she and Garrison had shared was far too special to be reduced to girl talk, even with her best friend.

"That's probably what you were doing while I was trying to reach you last night, hussy," Jada teasingly accused.

Imani cleared her throat, straightened a pile of papers on her desk. "As much as I'm enjoying this conversation, dear cousin, I really have to get some work done."

"Uh-huh, likely story. Will you be home tonight, or do you and Special Agent Bedroom Eyes have plans?"

"Actually, I'll be at your mama's house. She's working the night shift, and I want to stay with my mother, keep her company."

"Oh." Jada's tone grew somber. "How *is* Aunt Viv?"

Imani sighed, resting her head against the high-backed chair. "She's been doing better since she moved in with your mom." A reminiscent smile touched her lips. "You know they've always had a therapeutic effect on each other."

"Not unlike their daughters," Jada said gently. "Anyway, give Aunt Vivienne my love. If I get a chance, I'll stop by. Hey, maybe we could even have a slumber party the way we used to."

Imani grinned. "You know your mama would have a fit if she missed one of those."

"You're right. Maybe next time. We'll plan it, and make Jackie leave her bad kids at home with their father. That'll teach him for insisting that they have four children."

"You're evil, girl. I'll catch you later."

After Imani hung up, she swiveled around in her chair to gaze out the narrow window, her cousin's words still echoing in her mind. Jada was definitely right about Imani being the more levelheaded one when it came to men. She had always approached relationships with the utmost caution and re-serve, which was probably the reason she hadn't had that many. But from the moment she'd met Garrison Wade, had felt that electricity when their hands briefly touched, she had sensed her carefully ingrained control slipping away. It wasn't just the chemistry, explosive as it was, that bonded them to-gether. It was an indescribable connection, an innate sense of rightness she had felt in that first stolen kiss. She couldn't have stopped herself from falling in love with him any more than she could have prevented her own birth. It didn't matter that she knew very little about him beyond what he chose to share with her, that she wondered about the brooding sad-ness that occasionally descended upon his expression when he thought she wasn't looking. She marveled that the very same man who could plead with her not to marry another, could make love to her with such fierce intensity that she wept in his arms, could be so dangerous and compelling with the flip of a coin. He was a man full of contradictions, and she found herself loving each and every one of them, perhaps to her detriment.

So absorbed was she in these thoughts, Imani nearly missed the sight of Malik and a blond-haired woman stand-ing on the sidewalk below her window. He had only been to class twice since Althea's disappearance, and had not re-turned any of Imani's concerned phone calls.

She was about to knock on the glass to get his attention when she recognized that his companion was Sylvia Jerome. Surprised and a bit mystified, Imani frowned. As she watched, Malik pointed toward her office. Sylvia Jerome raised those cool green eyes and met Imani's puzzled gaze through the window. Imani grew very still without realizing it, and after a moment Sylvia's expression relaxed into a friendly smile, her manicured hand lifting in a tiny wave. Malik followed the gesture and looked away guiltily when he spied his pro-fessor.

Returning Sylvia Jerome's smile rather hesitantly, Imani

moved away from the window. A minute later she got up to adjust the thermostat settings, hoping to ward off the sudden chill that had settled over her skin.

He had followed him for over an hour, starting from his upscale Annapolis apartment to the university campus. He parked a discreet distance from his prey—for, in a sense, that was what he had become—and waited for him to make his move.

He was not disappointed.

Garrison watched as Julian Jerome wended his way through the crowded parking lot and walked toward the dormitory, throwing cautious glances over his shoulder. He did not enter the building, but stood at the bottom of the steps, tapping a rolled newspaper against his leg in sporadic, agitated movements. He glanced up expectantly each time the door opened, frowning when she didn't appear. Garrison didn't have to guess the identity of the student he awaited. He had known even before Julian pulled into the lot behind LaPlata dormitory.

So he wasn't surprised when Elizabeth Torres finally emerged and descended the steps, strolling past Julian Jerome without making eye contact. He glanced around quickly before following her, never more than two paces behind her as they conversed. Then suddenly Julian was beside her, his face flushed with unmistakable anger.

Lowering his binoculars, Garrison's lips curved in a slow, predatory smile. *Gotcha,* he silently mouthed around a mint-flavored toothpick.

They never saw him materialize. "What seems to be the problem?" he drawled lazily.

Two startled faces swung in his direction. One quick, assessing sweep of their guilty expressions confirmed Garrison's first suspicion.

"A-Agent Wade," stammered Julian. "What brings you to campus today?"

"That's for me to know," Garrison murmured, studying Elizabeth from behind his mirrored shades, "and you to find out. Something wrong, Miss Torres?"

Elizabeth's eyes darted furtively to Julian's before she answered, "Not at all." She mustered a demure smile, swung her hair over one shoulder with less confidence than usual. "But thanks for caring enough to ask."

Garrison shifted his gaze to Julian. "The professor and I need to have a little talk, Miss Torres. Would you excuse us?"

"But—"

"Leave us," Garrison said, a terse command.

Without another word, Elizabeth hurried off. Julian watched her go, his expression apprehensive. He turned back to Garrison reluctantly. "Look, Agent Wade, I don't know what this is about, but—"

Garrison draped an arm around Julian's shoulders, steering him as they walked in the opposite direction toward the parking lot. "Do you have children, Mr. Jerome?" he began conversationally.

"No," Julian mumbled.

"Neither do I. But I have nieces and nephews that I'm extremely fond of, and I can't even imagine what I'd do if someone harmed a hair on their little heads." He paused, shook his head at the thought. "It's probably a good thing that I don't have any children, especially daughters. Not in this twisted world we live in, where unscrupulous grown men prey on young girls just for the sport of it."

Julian stared straight ahead. "What are you getting at, Agent Wade?"

"How long have you been sleeping with Elizabeth Torres?"

Julian stiffened, his efforts to move away foiled when Garrison tightened his hold. "This is an outrage," he sputtered, flushing brightly with indignation. "What gives you the right to—"

"So that *wasn't* a lovers' quarrel I stumbled upon a few minutes ago?" Garrison asked, deceptively soft.

"Absolutely not!"

Abruptly, Garrison stopped and faced Julian. Slowly, deliberately, he removed his sunglasses and slid them inside his breast pocket. "I'll give you the benefit of the doubt, Mr. Jerome, by assuming you misunderstood my question. I'm going to ask you one more time, so listen carefully." He paused, his expression growing cold. "How long have you been sleeping with Elizabeth Torres?"

Julian jammed his hands into the pockets of his tweed blazer, averted his gaze as he spat bitterly, "If you think for one second that she's some hapless innocent—"

"She's seventeen."

"So what? She hardly acts her age," he sneered.

Garrison's smile was narrow, sharp. "I hope you're not going to tell me that Elizabeth Torres seduced you, that you had no control over your own actions, because that's the oldest and weakest excuse in the book."

Julian's eyes filled with desperation. "I haven't admitted to anything. Just because you saw us walking together doesn't mean we're having an affair."

"What were you arguing about?" Garrison asked quietly.

"We weren't really arguing. It was more of a mild disagreement regarding the minority recruitment program. Elizabeth is the student panelist—"

"And you're chairing the committee," Garrison finished. His eyes narrowed shrewdly. "Why come all the way across campus to meet individually with Elizabeth? Isn't that what the committee meetings are for?"

Julian hedged, "Well, yes, but . . . She asked me to meet her, said she was thinking about resigning her involvement because she felt guilty about taking Althea's place. I came to reassure her, perhaps change her mind. That's probably what you misinterpreted as an argument."

Garrison shook his head slowly, grim humor and disgust curving his mouth. "So that's your story, and you're sticking to it."

Julian frowned. "I don't understand—"

"See, Mr. Jerome, I did some digging around, found out some very interesting things about you." Garrison cocked his head to one side, chewing his toothpick thoughtfully. "If I paid a visit to your old employer at Wesley College, what do you think they'd tell me about the real reasons behind your sudden resignation? Other than that bogus cover story about your recurring health problems?"

Julian's face reddened, his lips tightening.

"That's what I thought." Garrison reached into his pocket, extracting his business card and slipping it into the other man's breast pocket. Leaning down, he murmured in Julian's ear, "I'll give you twenty-four hours to come up with another explanation about you and Elizabeth Torres. After that, all bets are off."

As he drew away, Julian said with outright displeasure, "I don't see what any of this has to do with the kidnapping investigation."

"Don't you?" A hint of menace in his smile, Garrison lightly patted the other man's cheek, his voice a soft challenge. "Please keep me waiting. I enjoy solving puzzles almost as much as I love hunting."

Julian's green eyes flashed angrily. "This is highly inappropriate—"

Garrison slid on his sunglasses, pointing to his watch as he backed away. "Tick, tock, Hollywood. Tick, tock."

Twenty minutes later, Garrison watched from an obscure position in the rear of the dimly lit lecture hall as Imani conducted class. By the end of the hour, he honestly didn't know what impressed him more: her vast knowledge of literary works by African Americans, or her amazing rapport with her students. She not only instructed them but, perhaps more importantly, she *engaged* them. She turned an academic lecture about the historical relevance of early slave narratives into a fascinating roundtable discussion that Garrison found himself enjoying, although he hadn't read *Incidents in the*

Life of a Slave Girl since college. It didn't hurt that Imani looked downright mouthwatering in a creamy silk blouse, a straight-fitting coffee skirt that roamed the delicious curves of her body, and matching suede pumps that showed to advantage the sleek contours of her legs. Legs that had wrapped around his waist and led him straight to paradise all night long. He took it all in—the discussion and the fetching vision she made—with rapt attention, silently hoping that his cell phone wouldn't summon him away.

It was no wonder that her male students followed her movements with appreciative gazes, some perched literally on the edge of their seats as Imani paced slowly at the front of the lecture hall. As she spoke, her arms floated gracefully through the air as if she were conducting an orchestra.

"All right, everyone," she called when class was over, "don't forget that on Wednesday we're back in our regular classroom. I don't want to hear excuses from anyone missing class because we weren't here."

The admonition was met with scattered chuckles. "Don't forget to tell them about the broken heater, Professor," one girl entreated. "It's too cold in there to have class."

"I'll mention it tonight at the meeting," Imani promised, gathering her belongings as the students filed out. A few lingered behind to ask additional questions or provide further commentary on the discussion.

When the last of them were gone, Garrison descended the stairs and sauntered toward the front of the room. "I was wondering if you might be available for after-hours tutoring," he said in a low, deep voice.

Imani glanced up quickly, surprise followed by warm pleasure. Her gaze ran over him quickly, taking in the clean lines of the navy suit, the crispness of the white shirt, the absence of a tie. The cut of the suit, like all his others, emphasized the whipcord leanness of his body, hinting at masculine power and grace.

Tilting her head to one side, her lips curved in a coy smile, she murmured, "That depends."

"On what?"

"What you need assistance with. Whether it falls under my area of expertise. And then there's my busy schedule to consider." She slung her suit jacket over one shoulder, lowered her lashes as she added silkily, "Some things take longer than others, and I like to take my time, make sure you get it right."

Garrison swallowed hard, enjoying the wicked repartee immensely. "When can we get started?" he asked softly. "I think you'll find that I'm a very eager pupil."

"I don't doubt that. Follow me to my office, I'll see what I can arrange." She started for the door, briefcase swinging in one hand, hips undulating. Garrison trailed her, boldly admiring the view. They rode the elevator in silence, heated gazes locked on one another. It seemed an eternity before they reached the privacy of her office, closed and locked the door behind them.

Imani had barely set down her belongings before Garrison grabbed her, pulled her into his arms. She closed her eyes, melting easily into his embrace. He pressed the length of her body to his as he stood against the door. His mouth traveled over hers, tasting, devouring, demanding, leaving her to marvel at how powerfully erotic a simple thing like a kiss could be. When his hands glided upward to skim the underside of her breasts, she moaned her pleasure into his mouth. When he stroked his fingers across the aching tips through her silk blouse, she nearly collapsed against him.

His hands went around her hips then, dragging her against him, letting her feel the hard evidence of his need. Almost mindlessly, she ground herself into him, and it was his turn to utter a low, guttural moan.

Drawing away, she smiled demurely into his eyes. "Is this what you had in mind for tutoring?" she whispered seductively, trailing her hands across the front of his starched shirt, feeling the muscles in his broad chest tremble beneath her touch.

"You have no idea," he said huskily. He wanted to back

her over to the desk, sweep everything to the floor, and make love to her right then and there.

Reading his mind, Imani took a cautious step backward, wagging a reproachful finger. "Don't even think about it."

"Too late, I already have." He reached for her again, but she evaded his grasp, spinning and walking over to her desk. She sat down and smoothly crossed her legs, and Garrison's hungry gaze fastened on the curve of her thighs where the front slit in her skirt parted.

Her own body stirred in response, remembering the way she had coaxed him to stay last night, had practically ripped his clothes from his body in her haste to be joined with him. Halfway up the stairs she had straddled him and taken him deep inside her, drawing a husky groan of male pleasure. She'd never have imagined she could be so lustful, so aggressive, and even now she flushed at the memory. There was no denying that Garrison Wade brought out the unexpected in her, the wanton abandon she had never experienced with David.

"I think I should enroll back in school," Garrison murmured, sauntering over to her desk.

Imani chuckled softly. "If you were one of my students," she averred, "I couldn't in good conscience continue seeing you."

"No?" Garrison perched a hip on the edge of the desk. "Then I guess I'll just have to content myself with sneaking into your classes and hiding in the back."

"Is that what you were doing?"

"Something like that." He smiled down at her. "You were amazing in there. I was as riveted as your students."

"Oh, stop it." Imani laughed, waving off the compliment. But her cheeks had warmed with delight. "I just try to make learning as interesting as possible."

"Which you definitely accomplish. I don't think there was one student not participating in the discussion."

"They're a good group. Smart, thirsty for knowledge.

Opinionated," she added with a proud grin. "They remind me a lot of myself at that age."

Garrison smiled, then as an afterthought asked, "Isn't Malik Toomer one of your students?"

Imani's grin faded, her expression clouding over. "He is. He hasn't been coming to class lately, and I'm really concerned about him."

"What do you think is going on?"

"I don't know," she answered with a helpless shrug. "I mean, I realize that student athletes have a reputation for blowing off their classes, but Malik has never been like that. He takes his studies seriously, really believes in earning good grades." She lifted beseeching eyes to Garrison's. "Do you think his odd behavior has anything to do with Althea's disappearance? I know how upset he's been."

"It's possible. Have you noticed anything else unusual?"

"Now that you mention it," Imani said slowly, thoughtfully, "this morning when I happened to glance out the window, I saw Malik standing on the sidewalk with Sylvia Jerome."

Garrison's gaze sharpened. "Julian Jerome's ex-wife?"

Imani nodded. "I didn't even know that she and Malik were acquainted. And maybe they're not, maybe he was only giving her directions. It was strange, because he pointed right toward my office."

"*Your* office?"

"If I'm not mistaken. They both looked up at me, and then Malik looked away quickly, like he felt guilty about something. Probably for missing class."

"Did Sylvia Jerome come to your office?" asked Garrison.

"No. I kept wondering if she might, but she never did." Imani frowned. "So why would she have been asking where it was?"

Garrison was silent. Imani could see the wheels spinning, marveled as he made the seamless transformation from lover to investigator. "This anthology you're working on," he began in deliberately even tones, "how did Jerome feel about not being included?"

"Julian?" Imani bit her lip, pensive. "Naturally he was disappointed. I think he assumed—we both did, really—that he would be a contributor."

Dark, measuring eyes met hers. "Have you detected any changes in his behavior toward you?"

"No." Imani shook her head, her mouth curving wryly. "If anything, he's been kinder and more supportive than ever. He's letting me rent his house for virtually pennies." She cast a speculative look at him. "Why do you ask?"

"Just curious." Before she could probe further, he continued. "I heard you mention a meeting to your students."

She wrinkled her nose in distaste. "Faculty meeting tonight at five. Shouldn't last any longer than an hour, and then I'm going to my aunt's house to stay with my mother."

"Everything okay?"

She nodded quickly, too quickly as she began stacking papers on her desk. "I just like to check in on her sometimes." After the level of intimacy she and Garrison had reached, why did she still find it difficult to share details about the devastating impact of her father's death upon her family's life?

Perhaps for the same reason Garrison withheld his secrets from her.

And not for the first time, she questioned the wisdom of her decision to become involved with a man she could have no future with.

She glanced up from her task, her gaze colliding with the penetrating scrutiny in Garrison's dark eyes. "Something wrong?" he asked quietly.

"Not at all. So what about you?" she asked, hoping to distract him, unnerved that the man never missed a thing. "Where will you be this evening?"

Garrison's watchful expression did not change as he replied, "I'm on my way to a strategy meeting with the task force."

Imani nodded, smiled. "Thanks for stopping by."

His mouth curved in the slow, sexy grin that never failed to send her system into overdrive. "Believe me, Professor Maxwell," he drawled huskily, "the pleasure was all mine."

Garrison's cell phone rang as he left the building a few minutes later. He snapped it open, answered briskly, "Wade."

"Is this Special Agent Garrison Wade?" inquired a low, tentative voice.

"Who's asking?"

"My name is Cecilia Dufresne. The president's secretary left a message for me earlier." She hesitated. "I understand you wanted to speak with me?"

"That's correct. Are you available this afternoon?"

"Um, yeah. But I live in Delaware—"

"Doesn't matter." As the Baltimore FBI field office served Delaware as well as Maryland, Garrison had logged countless miles to the bordering state in the course of investigating cases.

"Why don't we meet at the Chesapeake House off the highway?" Cecilia Dufresne suggested. "That's a halfway point for both of us."

Garrison glanced at his watch, noted that it was three-thirty. Traffic, he knew, was already in full swing. "Meet you there at five."

Cecilia Dufresne was unprepossessing in appearance. Her hair was a dirty blond worn in a blunt pageboy that framed an ordinary face, her prominent nose was dusted with freckles, and her amber eyes shifted about nervously when she spoke in a slow, halting manner. The baggy cardigan sweater she wore could not disguise the beginnings of a weight problem.

She was not what Garrison had expected. For that reason, his interest in what she had to say went up a notch.

He bought her a meal from one of the eateries, then steered her to a corner table that overlooked the parking lot.

Families and couples traveling up and down the coast stopped at the Chesapeake House to refill gas tanks and fill stomachs. With Thanksgiving still a few weeks away, the crowd milling about was only a fraction of what it would soon be.

"I was a little surprised when Stella Marsden called me at home," Cecilia Dufresne confessed, shaking ground pepper onto her baked ziti. "Considering the circumstances under which I left the university, I never expected to hear from anyone there again, least of all the president's personal assistant. Truth be told, I'm still a bit unclear on how I can help you, Agent Wade."

"Start by telling me about your relationship with Julian Jerome."

"Relationship." She grimaced at the word, gazing blindly out the window for a moment. "I'm not sure that what we had could be categorized as a relationship." There was no bitterness in her voice, but rather sadness, a touch of regret.

"How would you categorize it?" Garrison gently probed.

She shrugged, contemplating her food. "An affair. A terrible mistake. Or at least that's what he called it when he broke up with me," she added, her mouth twisting ruefully as she took a bite of ziti.

Garrison arched an eyebrow. "Jerome ended things?"

Cecilia nodded, chewing thoughtfully. "He said that although I was nineteen and legally an adult, it was wrong for him to continue seeing me. I offered to withdraw from his class, but he wouldn't let me. Said I was one of his best students, a welcome reminder of why he had chosen education as a profession."

Suppressing a rude remark that came to mind, Garrison continued evenly, "Do you know what prompted his sudden attack of conscience?"

Cecilia answered slowly, "He said he didn't want to keep lying to his wife. Said she didn't deserve his infidelity."

"And how did you feel about that?"

"I understood." Her gaze lowered guiltily to the table. "I felt bad about cheating on my boyfriend, too."

"But you didn't want to end the affair with Jerome."

"No." She hesitated. "I thought I was in love with him."

"And now?" Garrison pressed.

"And now I realize that it was more infatuation than anything else. Look at me, Agent Wade," she implored, skimming a hand down the blunt crop of her hair. "I'm not beautiful by anyone's standards, but Julian made me feel like I was. He made me feel special, appreciated, like I had more to offer a man than brains and a vast knowledge of trivia." When her litany was met with silence, she continued almost desperately, "I mean, he had tons of gorgeous girls throwing themselves at him, but he chose to be with *me*."

"I'm not judging you, Miss Dufresne," Garrison said.

"But you *are* judging Julian," she countered defensively.

"I think he abused his position by taking advantage of you," Garrison said flatly. "I make no apologies for that."

Cecilia stared at him, noting the steely resolve in his dark gaze. "Maybe you're right," she whispered tightly. "Maybe he did take advantage of me. But he never forced me to have sex with him, a fact my parents refuse to acknowledge even five years later. They still blame him for the fact that I dropped out of school, that instead of becoming some brilliant scientific researcher at a major pharmaceutical firm, I'm a bank teller working my way up to manager." Her laugh was short, brittle. "To hear them tell it, everything that goes wrong in my life is Julian Jerome's fault."

"You can't blame them for their anger and disappointment," Garrison said quietly. "I imagine I would feel the same in their position." He paused. "Were your parents the ones who went to the president about the affair?"

She shook her head quickly. "They didn't find out until after the fact, when Julian had resigned."

"Who came forward about the two of you?"

Cecilia frowned. "That's just it. We never found out."

"What do you mean?"

"Right after Julian broke up with me, he was summoned to the president's office and told that an anonymous source had complained about his inappropriate conduct, specifically, his relationship with me."

"Your boyfriend?"

"It wasn't him, either. He found out the same time as my parents."

"Are you sure?"

"Positive." Guilt filled her eyes once again. "He cried."

"Had anyone else learned about the affair? A classmate or friend perhaps?"

"It's possible, but highly unlikely. I never told anyone, and Julian and I were very discreet, cautious almost to the point of absurdity." She took a sip of her diet Coke. "We always met at the old cabin all the way over in Frederick. It's been in his wife's family for years, but no one ever used it," she explained. "When he first took me there, the cabin was in a total state of disrepair. It sort of became our special project to fix up the place, make it our little hideaway." A soft, reminiscent smile flitted across her face. She looked at Garrison, her expression one of undiminished longing. "How is he, anyway?"

"He seems none the worse for wear," Garrison muttered grimly. Anger coiled in his gut at the fact that Julian Jerome had gone on with his life with no thought to the besotted young woman he'd left behind, whose future he had cavalierly destroyed. On the heels of his anger was the desire to make Jerome pay for his actions, what Eddie referred to as Garrison's "bloodlust tendencies."

"Are he and Sylvia still . . . ?" Cecilia trailed off hopefully.

"Divorced."

"That's a shame," she murmured, although her tone suggested anything but regret. "You know, I've always believed that it was Sylvia who got Julian in trouble."

"Didn't you just say no one else knew about the affair?" Garrison countered.

"Yes, but a part of me has always wondered if she suspected anything. There was one occasion, in particular, that struck me as odd. I never told Julian about it because I told myself I was probably being paranoid."

"What happened?" Garrison demanded.

"I was coming back from class one afternoon when I saw Sylvia Jerome standing outside the dormitory. She didn't go in or anything. She just stood there on the sidewalk, staring right up toward my room. I panicked, thought she was there looking for me and was waiting to confront me. But as I got closer, she just turned and left. And that was it, the last I ever saw of her."

Garrison said nothing, recalling Imani's account of a similar episode earlier that day.

"Agent Wade," Cecilia ventured hesitantly, "what is this all about? Is Julian in some kind of trouble?"

"Not quite."

"I've seen you on television. I know that you're investigating the disappearance of that missing student." She paused as something akin to horrified denial filled her expression. "Do you think Julian had something to do with it?"

"I'm exploring all possibilities," Garrison said without inflection.

"Julian couldn't do anything like that. Say what you want about him, Agent Wade, but he's no kidnapper. He doesn't have a violent bone in his body. He was the most tender, compassionate man I knew, everyone loved and respected him. Nothing was the same after he left. You're making a big mistake if you suspect him of this abduction."

"I'll take that under advisement," Garrison drawled. He reached into his breast pocket, withdrew his card, and passed it to her. "Thanks for your time, Miss Dufresne. If you think of anything else, give me a call."

Back on the road, Garrison examined the new information Cecilia had provided. Julian Jerome had engaged in an extramarital affair with one of his students, then resigned from the small private college to avoid scandal. Now, five years later, it appeared that he was up to the same old tricks, and this time his victim of choice was Elizabeth Torres. Garrison grimaced at the notion of Elizabeth being a victim. She was a scheming, manipulative Lolita who preyed on the weaknesses of others, who trampled on friends and enemies alike to suit her own needs. But the fact remained that she was still a seventeen-year-old student. And if Jerome had crossed the line by sleeping with her, how many others were there? Had he also slept with Althea Pritchard, then gotten rid of her to avoid another scandal and termination from the university? Remembering the heated exchange between Elizabeth and the professor earlier, Garrison knew anything was possible.

And what about Sylvia Jerome? Had she known about her husband's affair with Cecilia Dufresne and alerted college officials? Would she have taken such action without confronting her husband first? If her motive was revenge, then it was highly likely. But to what extent would Sylvia Jerome go to get even with her husband for his infidelity? Would the tentacles of her malevolence extend to Julian's lovers and those she suspected of being involved with him?

If so, Garrison thought grimly, then perhaps it was time to start taking a hard look at Julian Jerome's ex-wife.

Chapter 20

It was after seven by the time Imani emerged from the faculty meeting. She had paid scant attention as her colleagues discussed the department's new and improved Web page that boasted a more user-friendly design, and lamented the recent implementation of a policy limiting the use of the photocopier. When prompted, she provided her own course updates and nothing more, resisting the urge to scowl at her wristwatch as the minutes ticked past. She did not linger for the customary small talk afterward, but made a beeline for her Jeep, dialing her aunt's house as she drove away from campus.

"Hey, Mom," she said when Vivienne Maxwell answered. "Just wanted you to know that I'm on my way. I got out of my meeting later than expected."

"Don't tell me you're still planning to come over and babysit?" Vivienne sighed in exasperation. "You're just as bad as Vanessa. She bullied her administrator into changing her schedule, putting her on day shift from now on so that she could be here with me at night. Can you believe her?"

Imani grinned. "The nerve."

"Anyway, she's making popcorn and we're about to watch

Steel Magnolias. So don't you worry about me, baby. I'm fine. But you sound tired."

"It's been a long day," Imani admitted.

"Why don't you head home and treat yourself to a nice hot bubble bath? That always works for me."

"Sounds tempting, but I have to work on this essay. The rough draft is due on Friday, and I haven't devoted as much time to it as I should."

On the other end, there was a pregnant pause. "Would that have anything to do with the new man you're seeing?"

Imani's jaw dropped. "W-what do you mean? H-how do you—"

"Jackie called yesterday, told us what happened at the bridal shop."

Imani groaned, slapped a hand to her forehead. "I'm going to kill that woman," she grumbled. "I don't care if we're related. She's going down."

Vivienne chuckled. "When were you going to tell me that you and David had broken up?"

"I would have . . . eventually." Unconsciously, she tightened her fists around the steering wheel. "Are you disappointed? I know how much you liked David."

Again her mother hesitated before answering tactfully, "Let's just say I'm surprised. You and David have been together for so long. What happened?"

"Oh, Mom, it's so complicated. I don't even know where to begin."

"Sounds pretty serious, especially considering Saturday's episode. Jackie said Garrison Wade looked mighty determined. Of course, she thought it was incredibly romantic," Vivienne added with a smile. Then all too quickly her tone sobered. "So he's an FBI agent?"

Imani didn't have to guess what her mother was thinking. She said quietly, "Yes."

Both women fell silent for a moment. In Vivienne Maxwell's silence, Imani heard reservation, dread, the barest hint of disapproval. And as if she were in her mother's mind,

Imani relived the fateful night they were both awakened by the sound of the doorbell. She saw the two special agents standing in the foyer, men who had been guests in their home on numerous occasions, their faces grim masks as they delivered the news that had sent Vivienne crumpling to the floor like a paper doll, had torn an agonized scream of denial from Imani.

Vivienne's deep sigh filled the phone line. "They say that daughters always marry men who remind them of their fathers," she murmured in a resigned tone.

"No one's talking marriage," Imani quickly refuted. "Things aren't *that* serious between us." Even as the vehement assertion left her mouth, her heart tightened in contradiction.

Her mother didn't buy it, either. "You don't have to convince me of anything, Imani," she said gently. "All I care about is your happiness, you know that. When you're ready to tell me more about him, I'll be here. In the meantime, will you promise me one thing?"

"Anything."

"Be careful."

Imani tried to swallow past the constriction in her throat. "I will," she whispered. "Good night, Mom."

Slowly, mechanically, Imani returned the cell phone to her purse. It shouldn't have bothered her that her mother didn't approve of her relationship with Garrison. After all, she was a grown woman fully capable of making her own decisions, whether it involved her career or finances or love life. And as much as she admired and respected Vivienne Maxwell, she certainly didn't need her permission to date Garrison.

Deep down inside, however, Imani knew that the only reason she couldn't dismiss her mother's misgivings was because she shared them.

Imani heaved a ragged sigh as she pulled into her driveway. Getting involved with Garrison Wade had only complicated matters, making it nearly impossible for her to walk away from him with her heart intact. Because walk away she must. On that score she was convinced.

Preoccupied with these gloomy thoughts as she entered the house, it took her a moment to realize that something was terribly wrong. By the time it registered on her brain that the light in the upstairs hall was on when it wasn't supposed to be, the intruder was already advancing stealthily toward her, a shadowy figure cloaked entirely in black, the face obscured by a black ski mask. All the fears and suspicions of the past few weeks coalesced into sudden, choking certainty. Someone *had* followed her to the restaurant that night and planted the threatening note on her windshield. Someone *had* been lurking in the shadows outside her house, waiting for the opportunity to strike.

Hot fear lanced down her spine, filled her veins with ice. Galvanized into action, she tossed her briefcase toward her assailant and ran for the front door. Before she made it three steps, a hand shot forward with lethal speed and wrapped around her throat, cutting off the scream of terror that rose to her lips.

Gasping for air, she struggled to wrench herself free, clawing desperately at the iron hand choking her. But her faceless attacker was relentless, ruthlessly tightening his stranglehold on her windpipe. With no oxygen reaching her lungs, she knew it would only be a matter of minutes, seconds even, before she passed out. Never to regain consciousness.

She felt her vision dim as steely arms dragged her away from the door. Her assailant was exceptionally strong, his body trim and athletic, emanating the faintest odor of tangy sweat and something else. A vaguely familiar scent, the memory of a subtle fragrance that eluded her.

Throughout the struggle, he had remained deadly silent, not releasing even a breath to betray his identity.

Black dots danced before Imani's eyes, signaling that her time was almost up. Fighting instinctive panic, she gradually allowed her body to go limp. As she sagged to the floor, the viselike grip around her throat loosened slightly, enough to permit her a quick intake of breath. Marshaling what remained of her waning strength, she rammed her elbow backward, landing a sharp blow to her assailant's solar plexus. He reared backward, clutching his throat, and before he could recover, she swung her right leg up and kicked him in his groin.

As he doubled over with a hoarse grunt, Imani scrambled for the front door on her hands and knees, lungs burning from the sudden deluge of sweet, blessed air. In another moment the intruder was upon her again. But instead of punishing her for her little stunt, he shoved her savagely aside and flung the door open, sprinting outside and disappearing into the chilly night.

For a moment Imani remained on the floor, staring at the empty doorway in stunned disbelief, wondering if her attacker planned to return with accomplices. Not taking any chances, she sprang to her feet, slammed and bolted the door before collapsing against it in a trembling heap of relief that bordered on hysteria. Dizziness swept through her in radiating waves, and nausea churned viciously in her stomach.

When a muffled whining penetrated the fog of her brain, she stumbled drunkenly to the closed powder room door. Opening it, she gave a startled cry at the piteous sight of Shiloh sprawled across the floor with all four legs tied and a muzzle clamped over his face. Imani was on her knees in an instant, freeing the golden retriever of his restraints, stroking his fur, and whispering soothing words of comfort she was far from feeling.

Both started violently at the sudden pounding on the front door. Shiloh's body grew rigid before he bounded toward the door, barking furiously. Heart hammering wildly in her chest, Imani followed more slowly, fear scraping the raw edges of her nerve endings.

"Imani? Are you in there?" At the sound of Garrison's voice, she hastened to open the door, relief coursing through her.

Garrison took one look at her disheveled appearance and felt stark panic seize him. He didn't think, just grabbed her fiercely in his arms and held fast. "My God, baby," he uttered raggedly into her hair. "What happened?"

Swallowed in his embrace, Imani welcomed his strength and the protection he offered. Shiloh settled on his hind legs, eased by Garrison's presence. "Thank God you're here," she whispered brokenly. "I was so scared."

He drew back and cupped her face in his hands, sweeping a frantic gaze across her features. "Are you hurt?" he demanded.

"I'm okay," she answered shakily. "Someone broke into the house and attacked me when I got home. He's gone now, ran off a few minutes ago." She shuddered, still reverberating with shock.

"The police are on their way," Garrison said, kicking the door shut behind him and leading her gently toward the living room. He lowered himself to the sofa and brought her with him, afraid to release her. He scanned the living room, mentally noting the books torn from the shelves and strewn across the floor. It was the only disturbance to the room, which suggested that the intruder had been searching for something specific.

"How did you know to come here?" Imani asked him.

"Apparently one of your neighbors phoned to report a possible burglar leaving the premises. I rushed right over as soon as Detective Moses called me." He didn't add that he'd violated every possible speed limit in his blind desperation to get there, that his world had tilted on its axis when he received the call.

"Someone just tried to kill me," Imani murmured, amazed and horrified. Another wave of nausea swept through her. As Garrison watched in concern, she got to her feet unsteadily and made her way to the powder room, had barely closed the door before she lost her lunch.

Garrison followed her and pushed the door wide open, kneeling beside her in front of the toilet. When she had finished, he flushed the toilet and helped her to a sitting position on the floor. He soaked one end of a decorative hand towel under cold tap water and passed it to her.

Mumbling her thanks, she pressed the cold cloth to one cheek, then the other. She felt drained, depleted beyond repair. "So much for maintaining a sexy image with my lover," she joked lamely.

Garrison smiled only slightly, appreciating her feeble attempt at humor while something dark and primitive twisted inside him, snarling for release. That someone had tried to kill her tonight sickened and infuriated him. The sight of her propped weakly against the wall in a corner of the room was almost more than he could take. She looked small, incredibly vulnerable in her wrinkled silk blouse and ruined pantyhose. Rage simmered in his gut, settled over his vision in a lethal haze.

He stepped from the bathroom, began checking doors and windows for signs of forced entry. "Tell me what happened," he commanded as he returned from the kitchen. An examination of the back door had revealed a partially jimmied lock. "Start from the beginning."

Horrifying images danced behind her closed eyelids. Her throat felt raw, bruised. "W-when I got home about thirty minutes ago, I noticed that the hall light was on upstairs. And then the next thing I knew, I was being strangled."

"Did you get a good look at the person?"

She shook her head. "It was too dark with only the light from upstairs. And he was wearing all black and a ski mask."

Garrison's gaze sharpened on hers. "He?"

"I think so. I kicked him you-know-where," she confessed almost sheepishly.

"Did he say anything?"

"Nothing, not a word. He was so cold, so methodical." Another shiver rippled through her at the memory of how close she had come to dying.

The doorbell rang, followed by an insistent knocking. The police had arrived. Garrison lifted Imani gently to her feet and skimmed a knuckle tenderly across the smooth curve of her cheek. "Hey," he murmured. "You okay?"

His concern made her want to bawl her eyes out. She responded with a jerky nod. "Would you mind getting the door for me?" she asked. "I want to go change my clothes and brush my teeth before answering any questions."

He nodded, watching her head slowly upstairs before opening the door to Detectives Moses and Porter.

A moment later, Imani's startled cry sent all three men bounding up the staircase, guns drawn in readiness.

"It doesn't make any sense," muttered a dismayed Imani as she watched two police officers comb through her ransacked office, dusting for fingerprints they all knew weren't there. She shook her head at the chaotic scene, papers littering every surface of the floor, file cabinet drawers wrenched open and hanging at haphazard angles. Her computer hard drive looked as if a bat had been taken to it, the parts smashed into tiny pieces.

"What could someone be looking for in *my* office?" she speculated aloud. "I'm a college professor, not some top-secret government spy." Garrison, standing across the room with the evidence technician, glanced up at her comment, the corners of his mouth quirking ever so slightly.

"We've ruled out burglary," Detective Moses said. "Nothing was taken from any other room—money, jewelry, everything's intact. Whoever did this was only interested in finding something in here."

"The destruction of your computer suggests it may have been a file the perpetrator was looking for," Detective Porter added. "Do you have backup files?"

"Yes, thank God." Imani could feel the beginnings of a migraine behind her eyelids, adding to the sore discomfort of her throat. She had changed into jeans and a ribbed turtleneck, brushing her teeth and vigorously gargling Listerine to remove the sour taste of bile from her mouth. But nothing could obliterate the sense of violation, the chilling reminder that she had nearly met her end tonight.

"Would you mind letting us take a look through your files?" Porter asked. "We may come across something that will give us clues into this break-in."

Imani nodded. "I'll make you a copy. Just as soon as I get my hands on a functioning computer."

"And you're sure you can't identify this person?" Moses clarified, notepad in hand.

"Absolutely sure. As I said before, he was dressed completely in black and wore a ski mask. And the house was too dark for me to really see his eyes."

"You're positive it was a male?"

"Not one hundred percent, no. But I'm fairly certain. He was very strong—and agile," she added as an afterthought.

Moses raised an eyebrow. "Agile?"

She nodded. "Athletic, someone who was definitely in good shape. From what I could tell, he was about average height. Not tall like you and Gar—Agent Wade. A few inches taller than me, maybe five-ten." She paused, lips pursed thoughtfully. "About your height, Detective Porter."

Cole Porter glanced up quickly from making notations. He chortled at the observation. "Don't look at me," he joked. "I was at home settling in for Monday Night Football."

Imani managed a wan smile. "That's a good matchup tonight, Giants versus Eagles. Hopefully you won't miss too much of it. Are we almost finished, Detective Moses?"

"Just one more question." Moses tapped a pen against his notepad. "You report that the perpetrator took off when you fought back, and you didn't see him getting into a car. Did you happen to observe any unusual vehicles parked along the street as you drove into the subdivision this evening?"

"Not that I remember. But even if I had, I'm not sure I would have given it much thought. I just moved here less than two months ago. I'm still learning who my neighbors are, let alone which cars they own."

As Garrison started across the room toward them, another thought struck her. "The person was wearing cologne," she said.

"Cologne?" The two detectives exchanged nonplussed glances.

"Or some type of woodsy fragrance. It was very faint, but for some reason I recognized the scent."

"Do you think you'd be able to identify it if you smelled it again?" Moses asked.

"Possibly." Imani blew out a deep breath, pushed a stray curl off her forehead. Exhaustion was settling into her bones, making her crave a hot bath and the comfort of her bed. Once Garrison and the police left, she would take some aspirin and call it a night. But as an image of her unseen attacker raced across her mind, she shuddered. There was no way she could stay at that house tonight. What if the intruder returned to finish the job he'd started?

"We're done here," Moses told Garrison as he rejoined them. "We'll canvass the area one last time, see if any of the other neighbors saw anything. We already talked to the woman who called. And we've got everything we need to send to forensics, including the muzzle and rope that was used on the dog. Poor mutt."

"He's not a mutt," Imani protested, albeit tiredly.

"My apologies," Moses retorted over his shoulder, trailed by the two police officers and evidence technician.

"We'll catch whoever did this, Ms. Maxwell," Cole Porter assured her. He flicked a wary glance at Garrison before following the others from the room.

Garrison turned to Imani, tipped her chin upward so that he could peer into her eyes. "How are you holding up?" he asked quietly.

"Barely," she admitted with a brittle half smile. "I keep hoping this is all just a horrible nightmare that I'll wake up from any minute." She cast a despondent look around the office. "Needless to say, I'm not looking forward to cleaning up this mess."

"Don't worry about that," Garrison said, ushering her

gently but firmly from the room. "Come on, I'm taking you home with me."

"I was just going to stay at my aunt's house. My overnight bag's still in my trunk, in fact."

"Good. Let's go."

"To—"

"*My* apartment." And Imani knew from his tone and formidable expression that she had no choice in the matter.

"All right," she acquiesced. "But I'm not leaving Shiloh behind. Does your building allow pets?"

"They do now."

From the dim interior of his Taurus, Cole Porter watched with Aaron Moses as Garrison led Imani and her dog to his truck, parked in the driveway behind her Jeep. He opened the passenger door, helped both inside before rounding the fender to climb in behind the wheel.

Cole glanced at Moses seated beside him. "Think he's sleeping with her?"

Moses snorted. "Without a doubt. Wouldn't you?"

A vision of Imani Maxwell's soft, pretty lips flashed through Cole's mind. He grinned almost sheepishly. "Better believe I would." He watched Garrison's truck pull from the driveway, disappear down the street. "Guys like Wade always get the good ones."

"You don't know why?" Moses gave a derisive laugh and shook his head as if the answer should be obvious.

Cole frowned. "What do you think of him? Still dislike him?"

"Wade? He's all right," Moses said grudgingly.

Cole threw his partner a surprised look. "A few weeks ago you wanted nothing to do with him."

Moses scowled. "I never said that. Anyway, what are you supposed to be? The kid on the schoolyard who instigates fights? Come on," he said impatiently, "let's go knock on some doors so we can get home. I want to catch that game."

Cole nodded, reaching for the door handle. "Hey, what do you make of that whole cologne bit?"

Moses shrugged nonchalantly, stepping from the car. "If we ever catch the perp, we'll bring in the professor for a scratch-and-sniff test."

Cole laughed loudly, inwardly relieved that he had taken a shower before arriving there that evening.

Chapter 21

"Make yourselves at home." Garrison laid his keys on the console near the front door, then deposited a duffel bag containing Shiloh's supplies in the kitchen before carrying Imani's overnight bag to his bedroom. When he returned, shrugging out of his suit jacket, he found Imani and Shiloh rooted to the same spot, looking like Little Orphan Annie and her dog, Sandy.

Chuckling softly at the thought, Garrison walked over to them and relieved Imani of her briefcase, prying it from her stiff fingers and setting it down on the floor. His eyes searched hers, his heart constricting at the unmistakable fear and shock reflected there, residuals from tonight's ordeal. "Hey," he said softly. "It's going to be okay. You're safe now."

Imani's gaze drifted lower, fastening on the leather shoulder harness strapped like a belt around his upper torso. Her expression was a mixture of horror and fascination as she stared at the huge nine-millimeter Glock tucked into the holster. Growing up, she had seen her father's weapon on a regular basis, had even handled it once or twice under his watchful supervision. But not since his murder had she looked at a gun, except those on television shows and movies—and even those always served as jarring reminders of the night her father's life had ended violently. Seeing Garrison's gun now, especially given her traumatized state, was more unsettling than she could have imagined.

Reading her mind and seeing the bewildered alarm in her eyes, Garrison stepped backward, keeping his gaze trained on her as he unstrapped the harness with an economy of motion. He laid it atop his suit jacket draped across the back of the sofa, then removed the Glock and slipped it inside the console drawer. "Okay now?" he asked gently, as if she were a skittish mare ready to bolt.

His question seemed to pull her out of her trance. She blinked, averting her gaze and smoothing a hand over Shiloh's silken fur. She knew that the animal was as rattled as she was. God only knows what had been done to him before she found him locked in the bathroom. "Thank you for letting us stay here like this, Garrison," she mumbled.

"No thanks necessary. I could use the company."

This drew a dubious, albeit wobbly, grin from her. "As if *you* ever have to worry about being lonely, Garrison Wade."

Something soft and brooding flickered in his dark eyes. "You'd be surprised," he murmured. Before she could respond, he turned away and started for the kitchen. He filled Shiloh's water dish and set it on the floor, and after only a slight hesitation, Shiloh trotted over to quench his thirst.

"Good boy," Garrison said, giving the golden retriever an approving pat on the head. When he glanced up, he found Imani watching him with warm gratitude in her eyes.

"You're so kind to him," she said quietly. "Thank you."

Garrison lifted his shoulder in a dismissive shrug. "No big deal. I told you I wanted a dog when I was a kid. Are you hungry?"

"Not really."

"Eat anyway. I'll order a pizza. Got any preferences?"

She shook her head, her lids at half mast as she rubbed the back of her neck. "Whatever you choose is fine. All I want is a hot, steamy shower."

Banishing the sensual images her words evoked, Garrison cleared his throat guiltily. The woman had just endured a traumatic experience, and he couldn't even control his libido. "Help yourself. Guest towels are in the hall closet to your right."

Imani nodded her thanks and headed from the living room.

While she was gone, Garrison ordered the pizza and checked in with Eddie, who had attended that afternoon's strategy meeting in Garrison's stead. After Eddie provided an update, Garrison filled him in about the day's developments.

"How is she?" Eddie asked in concern.

"As well as can be expected," Garrison answered grimly. "She's pretty shaken up."

Eddie muttered an expletive under his breath. "What do you think the scumbag was after?"

"I have some theories I'm working on. It's obvious from the way her office was tossed that it wasn't a random B and E. Whoever it was came prepared, with a muzzle and restraints for the dog, which spells planning and premeditation." Garrison frowned. "And then there's the point of entry."

"Door or window?"

"Back door. The lock was tampered with, but not enough to do the trick. It's like someone tried to jimmy it, and when they weren't successful, they simply came through another entrance they already had access to. The front door."

"With a key," Eddie said flatly.

"Exactly. Imani told me that she had the back door lock changed shortly after moving into the house because it got stuck a lot. She never planned to change the locks on the front door. Anyway, I'm running a background check on Sylvia Jerome first thing in the morning."

"You think it could have been her?"

"It's possible, or someone she hired. Whoever it was didn't have the stomach to finish the job—if that was the plan."

Shiloh padded into the living room and settled on the floor at Garrison's feet. Absently, Garrison reached down and scratched behind his ears, smiled when the dog made a contented sound at the back of his throat.

"If the ex wants to get rid of Imani," Eddie ruminated, "why destroy the computer? What's the connection?"

"Your guess is as good as mine. Could be a red herring for all we know. Something to throw us off the scent." He heard the shower stop running and ended the call. A minute later, the doorbell signaled the arrival of the pizza.

Imani emerged from the bedroom as he was setting the table. She wore a simple cotton two-piece pajama set, the high-cut shorts emphasizing the sleek expanse of rich, brown thighs, the jaunty swell of her breasts outlined beneath the halter top.

Garrison swallowed hard, forced himself to look away from the tempting vision she made. "Feel any better?" he asked huskily.

"Much. Your shower head has great water pressure." She had washed her hair and was rubbing coconut-scented oil through the damp thickness. He had observed the ritual before, had marveled as her trained hair dried to the soft ebony curls that formed a shiny cloud atop her head.

"Pizza smells good," she said, approaching almost shyly. "What'd you get on it?"

"Sausage, pepperoni, green peppers, and mushrooms. That okay?"

"Perfect." She washed her hands at the kitchen sink and took the seat he gestured her into. When she glanced up at him, his gaze zeroed in on the darkening bruise around her slender throat. Anger rose swiftly inside him. His fist clenched reflexively at the need to strike out at whoever had done this to her.

Imani's hand lifted self-consciously to the bruised flesh. "It looks worse than it feels," she said, her tone low and strained.

Garrison wanted to kick himself. Why couldn't he have

just looked away? "You should probably take something anyway," he said in a roughened voice.

"I'll take aspirin later."

They ate mostly in silence for the next several minutes, reflections of that night's harrowing episode uppermost in their minds. After two slices of pizza, Imani pushed her plate away and fixed him with a steady look. "I don't want you handling me with kid gloves, Garrison. Treating me like some helpless damsel in distress."

"Imani, you've been through hell tonight," Garrison said, incredulous. "You don't have to put up a brave front for me."

"I'm not putting—" Her voice broke, and she clapped a trembling hand to her mouth. Tears shimmered in her dark eyes, but were held stubbornly in check.

On the edge of his seat, Garrison watched her, aching to wrap her in his arms, hold her and make the pain disappear. And not just tonight's wounds. Every time they broached the subject of her family, specifically her parents, she retreated post-haste. It didn't matter that they had made love countless times, had expressed their love for one another. When it came to divulging personal details about herself, Imani clammed up or became defensive. *Why did she keep shutting him out,* he wondered in frustration. Why couldn't she confide in him, share her past with him?

Perhaps for the same reason he hadn't shared with her. He was scared to death.

"Look, I don't want to upset you," he said quietly. He reached across the table, covered her hand with his. "I realize how difficult this ordeal has been for you. All I want to do is take care of you, keep an eye on you for a few days. Will you let me do that?"

She gazed at his hand upon hers before lifting her eyes slowly to his. Behind the veneer of strength, he saw a combination of trepidation and trust. "Please don't think I'm ungrateful," she whispered. "I appreciate everything you've done for me, Garrison. I really do."

"I know," he said softly.

"I'm scared," she admitted hoarsely. "I hate being scared. It pisses me off."

Garrison raised his hand and touched her cheek, stroking his fingertips down her jaw. "There's nothing wrong with being scared. Anyone would feel the same in your position."

Her smile was tremulous. "I'm afraid I'm not going to be much company tonight. Would you mind if I went to bed now?"

"Of course not. You can take my bed, I'll sleep on the sofa."

She rose from the table. "I really hate to put you out—"

"Imani."

The quiet authority in his voice halted her apology. She leaned down, pressing a kiss to his forehead that was so tender his heart clenched painfully. "Good night, Garrison. Thank you."

"Don't mention it," he said gruffly.

After she left, he cleared the table and loaded the dishwasher. It was only ten o'clock, and his nerves were too wired for sleep. He removed his shoes and shirt, then threw the shirt across the sofa before his body followed. Shiloh had claimed a corner of the living room and was fast asleep, snoring lightly into his paws. Grabbing the remote control, Garrison flipped blindly through channels before settling on Monday Night Football. Not even a slug fest between the NFC Division rivals could hold his attention. All he could think about was the woman in the next room, the unique paradox she presented. Fire and ice, soft or tough as nails, she was a woman full of contradictions.

A movement to his left caught his eye, and he glanced up to find her standing across the living room, watching him uncertainly. He sat up straighter.

"What's wrong?"

She shook her head slowly from side to side. "Nothing. I was just wondering . . . Would you mind staying with me until I fall asleep?"

Garrison was on his feet before she completed the request. He followed her into the darkened bedroom, climbed into the king-sized bed with her, and pulled the thick comforter over them. Imani snuggled against him, tucking her head beneath his chin and wrapping an arm around his chest.

Within minutes, she was fast asleep.

Imani slept fitfully that night, her dreams filled with haunting sounds and images. Deep male laughter, dark shadows behind trees, violent splashes of bright red. Blood running in great, crimson rivulets from a body lying prone on the ground. Her father's blood, seeping from a gaping bullet wound.

But, no, not her father. As she drew nearer, she saw another face, another pair of dark eyes staring sightlessly into hers.

Garrison.

She opened her mouth to scream, but no sound came forth. Only spasmodic convulsions and gasps, with hands like steel bands of fury clamped viciously around her throat, cutting off her air supply.

"Imani?" Garrison murmured soothingly, trying not to startle her. "Wake up, Imani."

She thrashed about desperately, still trapped in the horrific nightmare. "No!" she choked out, clawing frantically at her throat. "Please God, no!"

"Imani." This time his tone was firmer. He drew her quivering body into his arms and held her tightly against him in an effort to calm the raging storm. "Wake up, baby. It was just a bad dream."

Slowly her eyes cleared, focused on his bare chest. "Garrison?"

"I'm right here," he whispered, cupping her face in his hands, willing her to see him and not the specters in her nightmare. "You had a bad dream, but it's over now. You're safe."

Relief bloomed in eyes glistening with crystalline tears.

"It was so awful. I thought . . . I thought you were . . ." She gulped, then promptly dissolved into silent, racking sobs.

Garrison gathered her protectively against him, her anguish slicing through him like jagged shards of glass. "Don't think about it, baby," he whispered urgently into her hair. "It's over now. I'm right here, everything's going to be fine."

Imani buried her face in the crook of his neck and wept, succumbing to the sheer terror of the nightmare that had been all too real. Garrison held her tightly, and she clung to him, absorbing his strength, craving the warmth and protection he provided. He brushed his lips across her forehead, whispering endearments and tender reassurances. He kissed the side of her face, tasted the salt of tears on her cheek. She turned her mouth into his, and he kissed her with the kind of hunger born of desperation, aware of how perilously close he had come to losing her.

Imani opened her mouth beneath his and felt a wild rush as his tongue touched hers. She ached and trembled with the vibrancy of sweet, precious life. She never knew when they shed their clothes or Garrison sheathed himself with a condom. All she was aware of was him rising above her in the moonlit darkness, his warm, naked skin against hers and the achingly exquisite sensations of him moving deep inside her. She wrapped her legs around him, whimpered his name and clung to him as the delicious rocking motions swept through her like wildfire. Their lovemaking was different this night, subdued for the first time ever, but punctuated with an urgency, an unspoken intensity that was communicated through their locked gazes. The pressure between their joined bodies built as they climbed higher and higher, reaching toward release. Then their world shattered, a shuddering crescendo that drowned them in pure ecstasy, an endless rapture.

And Imani knew then, like never before, that she wanted to spend the rest of her life with this man.

She sighed languidly, satiated and utterly exhausted. "I love you, Garrison," she mumbled sleepily before drifting off.

Garrison smiled, lightly kissing her forehead. "Sweet dreams, baby."

With one arm, he curled her into his body, savoring her scent and the sleekness of her damp skin against his own, marveling at how perfectly she fit. Her heart, her soul, the very essence of her had wound itself around him and infiltrated his unsuspecting heart. Her happiness, her security, everything about her had become as vital to him as the very air he breathed. Whatever her demons were, he would break down her barriers, help her overcome them. She was the living embodiment of everything he'd envisioned his soul mate to be, and if it took him from now until eternity, he would convince her that they belonged together.

Empowered by the decision, shaken by the responsibility, Garrison at last fell asleep.

At six-thirty A.M. the phone rang, rousing Imani from the warm enclave of a deep, peaceful slumber. One arm snaked out from beneath the covers, groping blindly for the telephone on the nightstand. She uttered a low groan when she didn't immediately locate it, irritated with herself for keeping the darned thing so far out of reach. Her annoyance crept its way into her voice when she finally found the phone, mumbled groggily, "Hello?"

There was a heavy pause on the other end, and then a woman's surprised voice answered, "Yes, this is Rosemary Wade. I'm looking for my son, Garrison. Is he there?"

For a moment her words didn't register, and Imani frowned in confusion. Why on earth was Garrison's mother calling him at *her* . . . ? She opened her eyes suddenly, wide awake and alert.

And thoroughly embarrassed.

She turned her head to find Garrison lying in the massive bed beside her, one arm flung across her waist. Although his eyes were still closed, his lips curved into a slow, wicked grin that told her he was enjoying her predicament.

"Hello?" Rosemary Wade prompted on a note of rising indignation. "May I speak with Garrison please?"

"Um, sure. Yes, of course." With flaming cheeks, Imani passed Garrison the receiver, mouthing a sheepish apology.

He chuckled softly, accepting the phone from her. "Hey, Ma."

"Hey, yourself," his mother said dryly. "So that's why you haven't been returning any of my calls. I should have known it was a woman." She hesitated. "That isn't Desiree, is it?" It was more a statement than a question.

"No," Garrison answered. When Imani tried to ease slowly from the bed, his arm tightened around her waist, imprisoning her beside him. She scowled, poked her tongue out at him like a recalcitrant child. He grinned, winked playfully at her.

His mother continued, "I hope I didn't interrupt anything. I know it's early, but I figured you would already be up and about. This is pretty late for *you* to still be in bed." Realizing what she had just said, she added knowingly, "Of course, considering that you have company, I guess it's not too late after all."

Sensing his mother's disapproval, Garrison tried to change the subject. "How are you, Ma? Everything okay?"

"I'm fine, Damien's fine. I just thought I'd try and catch you before you left for the day, make sure you were all right. But I guess you're *more* than all right."

"Ma—"

"I know it's not my place to comment on your love life, Garrison. After all, you're thirty-two years old, a grown man perfectly capable of making your own decisions." Her tone softened, grew plaintive. "It's just that I worry about you sometimes, baby. I want to see you happy, settled down with a woman deserving of you."

"I know, Ma." Garrison stroked a hand down Imani's bare back as she lay in the curve of his arm. She was silently grateful that Rosemary Wade had not recognized her voice.

She wondered what the woman would think of her, sleeping with her son after knowing him less than three weeks. She doubted that Rosemary Wade, who by her own admission was from the old school, would approve.

"Anyway, I didn't call to give you a lecture. I wanted to find out how the case is going, see if you're making any progress. Oh, and that reminds me," she continued excitedly before Garrison could answer, "I met the nicest young woman last week. Last Monday, as a matter of fact. She gave your brother a ride home when his car broke down—the transmission's completely gone, by the way. I'm taking him car shopping this weekend. If you have some free time, maybe you could go with us. You know I don't know anything about cars, and you're the only one those shady salesmen don't try to take advantage of. Remember how easily you talked them down on the sticker price for my car? By the time you were finished with them, they were ready to just hand over every car on the lot."

Garrison smiled at the memory. "I'll be there."

"Thank you, baby. Anyway, I was telling you about that young lady. She's a professor at the University of Maryland College Park—isn't that the school the missing girl attended? Maybe she was one of the girl's professors. Anyway, she was delightful company, so smart and well-mannered. A pretty little chocolate thing, too—"

Garrison's hand stilled upon Imani's back. "What was her name?"

"Oh, it was a beautiful name, I'll never forget it. Imani. Imani Maxwell."

Imani watched, curious, as another slow grin spread across Garrison's face. "You're right, Ma," he murmured into the phone, "that *is* a beautiful name. Almost as beautiful as the woman herself. I assume," he added swiftly, smoothly.

"Mm-hmm. Well, I don't want to get you in trouble with your lady companion," Rosemary Wade said, the wistful note in her voice contradicting her words. "Maybe you can invite whoever she is over for dinner this weekend." The invitation was unenthusiastic, almost perfunctory. "I'm sure I would enjoy meeting her."

"Oh, I'm sure you would."

"Good. Well, let me run. I promised one of the patients at the nursing home that I'd be there for his dialysis treatment. For moral support, you know. Have a good day, baby, and I'll talk to you later."

"What's so funny?" Imani asked as Garrison passed her the phone to hang up.

His grin widened as he lifted his head from the pillow and propped it in his hand, facing her. The other hand traced the curve of her hip in a slow caress that sent frissons of heat rippling through her. "You've been a naughty girl, Imani Maxwell," he said huskily.

"I didn't mean to answer your phone," she said, still slightly mortified. "I was so disoriented when I first woke up. I honestly didn't remember where I was."

Garrison shook his head slowly, deliberately. "That isn't what I'm talking about. Why didn't you tell me you had met my mother?"

Imani's eyes widened in consternation. "Please tell me she didn't recognize my voice," she begged.

"She didn't. So when were you going to tell me?"

"I don't know," Imani hedged, biting her bottom lip. "It was completely by accident. Okay, I knew who your brother was when I offered him a ride," she amended, "but it wasn't like I was trying to get in good with your family behind your back or anything, like some *Fatal Attraction* stalker—"

She broke off self-consciously at Garrison's deep roar of laughter. He scooped her into his arms, settled her on top of him. His dark eyes danced with mirth and undisguised adulation as he gazed into her face. "God, where have you *been* all my life?" he murmured in wonderment.

Imani smiled shyly, even as her body reacted to the friction of naked skin against naked skin, the steel of Garrison's thighs against hers. "Why didn't you tell her I was here?"

"Because I want to enjoy the look on her face when she sees you this weekend."

"This weekend?"

"Yep." He smiled, his hand roaming down her back once again. "You've been invited to dinner."

"Are you serious?" Imani warmed with pleasure. "Does this mean I'll get to meet your father, too?"

He sobered, his body tensing beneath hers. He dropped his gaze. "My father left home when I was ten years old."

"I'm sorry," Imani said quietly. "I didn't realize. That must have been very difficult for all of you."

"We survived." Garrison hesitated, remembering the resolution he'd made to himself last night. If he ever hoped to break through Imani's barriers, he would have to be the first partaker. It was time for him to let down his own defenses.

"My father was diagnosed with severe manic depression when I was a child," he began slowly. "Before that, we never knew what was wrong with him. He used to leave home for extended periods of time. Suddenly, without warning. And then he would be back as if nothing ever happened, back to his normal, easygoing self. He didn't drink or smoke, was never abusive toward any of us." Garrison's dark eyes flickered with pain. "Sometimes I wondered if that would have been better. If he'd been this terrible father, it would have been easier to deal with his absences. If he were beating my mother, I would have hated him and wanted him gone."

Imani listened in silence, melting inside at heartrending images of the disillusioned boy Garrison must have been. She imagined him trying to be so brave for everyone. It was obvious from his phone conversation with his mother, and Imani's own chat with Damien Wade, that they depended upon Garrison, a trend that must have started years ago. She fell harder in love.

"The final straw was when he lost his job with the police department," Garrison continued in a low voice. "Shortly after that, he left home permanently."

"Have you ever seen him again?"

He hesitated, haunted by memories of giving his valedictorian speech at high school graduation, imagining he saw his father standing on the fringes of the audience, pride shining in his eyes. But when Garrison searched frantically for him after the ceremony, Roderick Wade was nowhere to be found. The same thing had happened when he graduated from Columbia and the FBI Academy, and after a while Garrison had convinced himself that his mind was playing tricks on him, that he was simply a victim of wishful thinking.

"No," he answered softly. "I never saw him again."

Imani bit her bottom lip as tears threatened. "Oh, Garrison."

"Baby, don't." He captured her hand, held it as his dark gaze entreated her. "Don't feel sorry for me. It was a long time ago, and I've moved on with my life. We all have." When her troubled expression remained, he spread her hand against his chest. "Feel that?"

She nodded. His heartbeat was strong and steady beneath her palm.

"Ever since you came into my life, Imani, my heart hasn't been the same," he said huskily. "It belongs to you now. Promise me you'll take good care of it."

"Oh, Garrison." This time the tears did fall. She bent her head, kissing him with all the tenderness she felt, whispering, "I promise."

They kissed deeply, warmly, before pulling apart. Garrison wiped the dampness from her face. "How are you feeling?" he asked quietly.

Her expression darkened as memories of the previous night resurfaced, as she was reminded that someone had broken into her home, ransacked her office, and tried to kill her. But daylight had diminished the terror and brought a touch of anger, and she said as much.

Garrison frowned. "I want you to call the school, tell them you're working from home today. You don't teach class on Tuesdays, anyway," he added when she opened her mouth to protest. "You can use my computer and work on your essay uninterrupted—whatever you need to do. You'll be safe here, where I can keep an eye on you."

She arched a sardonic eyebrow. "So you plan to sit around babysitting me all day?"

His lips curved in a wolfish grin. "Actually," he whispered as his hand gently cupped her bottom, pressing her against his hardened length, "babysitting wasn't quite what I had in mind." And before Imani could utter another word, he swung his legs over the side of the bed, swept her into his arms and carried her to the bathroom.

A few minutes later, steam clouded the glass-encased shower stall, enveloping the two lovers in a private, sensual world. Breathless moans and sighs pierced the vapors, punctuated by names shouted in ecstasy.

An hour later, after the most erotically stimulating shower she had ever experienced and a light breakfast consisting of a western omelette and toast, Imani sat curled up on the sofa with her research materials, Garrison's laptop propped on her legs. Completing her outline on Saturday had helped a great deal, and now her fingers flew nimbly across the keyboard as she filled in the missing information.

In the tiny second bedroom that doubled as a weight room and study, Garrison made phone calls while he accessed files from his computer, which was connected to the network at the office. Imani could hear the low murmur of his conversations through the walls, detected the terse agitation in the timbre of his voice. She knew he was anxious to solve the mystery of Althea's abduction, knew the prolonged nature of the investigation was taking a severe toll on his iron self-control and patience. Last night's incident hadn't helped matters any.

Imani frowned, pausing in her typing. There was something about the break-in that didn't sit right with her, apart from the obvious reasons. Questions swirled through her mind in rapid succession, demanding answers she simply didn't have. Why had someone ransacked her office and smashed her computer? What was the intruder searching for? What on her hard drive was so vital—or incriminating—that it warranted destruction? And why had her assailant taken off so quickly, without warning? Although she had disarmed him momentarily, she'd known she was outmatched, that unless she found a way to escape, it would only have been a matter of time before he killed her.

Unless that wasn't his original intention.

It was entirely possible that the intruder had not anticipated her arrival. Indeed, the more she thought about it, the more plausible it seemed that her assailant had been caught off guard by her sudden appearance, had attacked her in a fit of panic, and had beat a hasty retreat when she fought back, perhaps realizing that she couldn't identify him, anyway. Whoever it was had come prepared with a muzzle to silence Shiloh, which suggested that the individual had either been watching her movements or was personally acquainted with her and knew that she had a dog. Knew, also, that she wouldn't be home on Monday evening.

Going on this theory, Imani tried to recall everyone she had told about her faculty meeting. Her students, her mother, Garrison, Jada . . . Wait a minute. Had her office door been closed during her phone conversation with Jada? Could someone have been eavesdropping from the corridor? She had seen Malik and Sylvia Jerome outside *after* she hung up the phone. But what if one of them had already been to her office, was leaving the building when she happened to glance out the window?

Imani's frown deepened. Malik had been acting strange lately, downright evasive even. But she had no reason to suspect him of trying to harm her. And what would *he* have been looking for in her computer files? Her personal and financial records, research documents and articles, the course syllabus and related assignments . . . answers to the upcoming midterm exam.

Imani shook her head adamantly. Malik was a bright kid

who would never resort to cheating. Even if his recent absences *were* jeopardizing his grade, he certainly wouldn't go to such extreme lengths as burglary and property destruction. And the intruder had been much shorter than Malik, no doubt about that.

What about Sylvia Jerome? Julian Jerome's ex-wife who had shown up unexpectedly one afternoon to collect nothing more than junk mail. Sylvia Jerome, who had seemed more interested in Imani and her decorating skills than anything else. Even Julian had seemed baffled by the news of his estranged wife's visit. And what *had* she been doing on campus yesterday, asking for directions to Imani's office?

Imani rose from the sofa and padded to the second bedroom, knocking lightly on the closed door. "Garrison?"

After a moment he appeared, the cordless phone in his hand. "Everything okay?"

She nodded. "I apologize for disturbing you, but I've been doing some thinking. It may not be anything at all, but there's something about Sylvia Jerome that doesn't sit right with me." She proceeded to tell him about the woman's visit to the house two Fridays earlier.

Although Garrison's expression remained impassive, Imani sensed a barely perceptible sharpening of his instincts, an alertness that told her he would take all leads seriously, however remote.

"Do you think it could mean anything?" she asked.

"Possibly. Could be that she simply wanted to check you out, satisfy her curiosity about you."

Imani frowned, confused. "Why would she be curious about me?"

"You're renting her former house. Why wouldn't she be curious?" Garrison turned away as the fax machine began receiving a transmission.

Imani stepped further into the tiny room that was just as immaculate as the rest of the apartment, save for the reams of paper littering the desk. "There's something you're not telling me."

Before he could respond, his cell phone trilled. He snatched it up, then listened for a few moments before saying tersely, "I'll be right there. Wait for me." When he turned back around, his expression was ominous, forbidding.

Without realizing it, Imani took a step backward. "What is it?"

"I have to go. That was Detective Moses. They just picked up a suspect on a routine traffic stop, ran the tags, and discovered that the vehicle was stolen." He hesitated. "They also found a ski mask on the floor in the backseat."

"Does that mean . . . ?"

"Could be, we'll have to see." Garrison deliberately omitted the name of the arrested suspect. "Listen, I want you to stay here, Imani. There's a security guard posted at the main entrance downstairs, and I've instructed him to keep close watch on anyone entering or leaving the building—including you," he added sternly. "Don't go anywhere, you hear me?"

Imani didn't like the directive any more than she liked the lethal glint in Garrison's dark eyes, which struck her as hauntingly familiar. And then suddenly she remembered why.

Don't go, Irvin. Stay here with us, you don't have to go out there . . .

Imani forced a strangled half laugh. "Hey," she teased, following Garrison into the living room, "you're only going to *question* the suspect, right?"

Garrison slid his nine-millimeter into the holster and shrugged into his suit jacket. "Right." He crossed to her, cupped the nape of her neck so that she lifted her face to his. "I'm not trying to frighten you or anything," he said gently. "I just need to know that you're safe while I take care of some business. Do you promise me that you'll stay put until I get back?"

Imani hesitated, then nodded wordlessly.

"Good." He bent, touching his lips tenderly to hers. He tweaked her nose as he drew back, murmured huskily, "I want to take you out to dinner tonight, finally have a *real* date with you. Would you like that?"

"Very much." She walked him to the door, visualizing her mother doing the same thing on the night Irvin Maxwell was killed. She reached out, laying a hand upon Garrison's arm. He turned back, one heavy eyebrow lifted inquiringly. "Be careful."

He winked before slipping out the door, locking it behind him. Restless, Imani wandered over to the wall of windows and peered out at the gray downtown skyline, at the bustle of pedestrians hurrying to various destinations, hunched in warm overcoats against the brisk October wind. Shiloh stood silently beside her.

Without giving it a second thought, Imani marched to the phone and dialed Jada's number. "It's me," she said as soon as her cousin's groggy voice answered. "You're off today, aren't you?"

Jada yawned. "Uh-huh. Why, what's up?"

"I need a ride somewhere."

"What's wrong with your Jeep?"

"Nothing. It's a long story, I'll tell you when you get here."

"Where's here?" Jada asked, sounding suspicious.

"Garrison's apartment, a few blocks from yours." Imani provided the address. "Now hurry up!"

Chapter 22

Joaquin Torres had not inherited his sister's camera-ready looks. His face was more rounded, his complexion ruddy, where Elizabeth's was smooth and unblemished. His dark hair was thick and unruly, skimming the collar of his frayed sweater. At five-ten, with a trim, athletic build still outfitted in dark clothing, he matched the description of Imani's masked assailant well enough to satisfy Garrison's suspicions.

It took a supreme effort of will for Garrison not to lose his control upon seeing him. "Let me talk to him first," he said tersely to the men gathered outside the interrogation room at the Palmer Park police station.

"Do you think that's such a good idea?" Cole Porter countered skeptically. "You seem to have a personal conflict here if Torres is the one who assaulted Professor Maxwell."

Garrison barely spared him a glance, his tone coldly mocking as he said, "I think I can handle it, Detective. But thanks for your concern."

Porter looked askance at Aaron Moses, who simply shrugged his shoulders.

"Just don't do anything crazy, Wade," Chief Taggert

warned. "If this is our guy, we need to do everything by the book. And for God's sake, don't—"

But Garrison had already stepped inside the interrogation room, closing the door rudely in the chief's face. Taggert scowled, throwing a surly sidelong glance at Eddie. "Is he always this bullheaded?"

Eddie chuckled, watching his partner through the one-way mirror. "Worse."

"Mr. Torres," Garrison said, pulling up a chair at the table and straddling it nimbly, "you're a hard man to catch up with. We've been looking for you."

Joaquin Torres regarded him with dark, hostile eyes. "For what?"

"We'll get to that in a minute. Why don't you tell me where you were last night between the hours of six and eight P.M."

Joaquin's gaze shot to the window behind Garrison's back. "You think you're going to just walk in here and get me to confess to some crime while your friends watch from behind that mirror?" He sneered, jabbing his middle finger toward the window with sinister glee. "*That's* what I say to that, man! Screw all of you, you got nothing on me."

"No?" Abruptly Garrison stood, rounding the table to stand beside him. He leaned down, whispered coldly in Joaquin's ear, "You sure about that? Think hard for a minute."

Joaquin grew very still, keeping his gaze trained on the table. "I'm not some dumb kid off the street, Agent Wade," he said stonily. "Do you know who my father was?"

"I do. But Daddy Dearest ain't here anymore, is he?" Garrison taunted cruelly. "See, I've got you all figured out, Joaquin. You blew your inheritance on booze and life in the fast lane, and when your money ran out, you got desperate, started looking for a quick gig to bankroll your expensive tastes. That's why you're back in town, isn't it? Thought you'd hit your mama up for cash first, play on her sympathies a little bit. But when she refused to bail you out the way Papa used to, you got mad and went looking for baby sister to help you out. But you forgot that she won't be eligible to collect her inheritance until she's eighteen, so you're a few months too early. Ain't that right, Joaquin?"

Joaquin remained silent, a solitary muscle in his jaw working furiously. Garrison chuckled softly, menacingly, as he straightened. He sauntered across the room and propped a shoulder against the cinderblock wall, seeming to have all the time in the world. "Who did you finally hook up with, Joaquin? Who agreed to fund your habit in exchange for your services?"

"I don't know what you're talking about," Joaquin said fiercely. "Just because I took some guy's car—"

"And had in your possession a ski mask matching the description of one worn during a break-in last night."

"That doesn't prove anything!"

"Think it doesn't?"

"*I know* it doesn't." Suddenly Joaquin smiled, a slow, sadistic smile. "What're you gonna do, Agent Wade? Pin something on me just because someone messed with your girlfriend? Oh, I heard the detectives talking when they brought me in this morning. I know what this is all about."

"Do you?" Garrison came off the wall and approached the table, purposeful, predatory. Joaquin watched him warily as he deliberately removed his jacket and draped it across the chair. "Then I guess you also understand just how desperate I am to make someone pay." He rolled up his sleeves, retrieved his Glock from the holster and made a show of checking for bullets before clicking the magazine back into place.

"Hey, man, what're you doing?" Joaquin asked, licking his lips nervously as Garrison once again straddled the chair opposite him.

Garrison's expression was lethal. "You like breaking into people's houses, Joaquin?" he said, dangerously soft. "You like attacking defenseless women in their homes? That your MO?"

Joaquin smiled narrowly. "You can't prove a thing, and you know it."

"Tell you what." Garrison leaned forward, sliding the nine-millimeter toward the center of the table, an equal distance between them. "Let's play a little game of Russian roulette. With a twist."

Joaquin eyed the gun suspiciously. "What kind of twist?"

"Whoever gets the gun first can do whatever he wants with it."

Joaquin glanced toward the one-way mirror. "You're loco, man. There's no way they're gonna let me walk right outta here if I shoot you. Even if I blasted my way outta here like some Hollywood action hero, your feds would be on my tail in a heartbeat."

"That's just a chance you'll have to take," Garrison said softly. "At the very least, you can take me as a hostage. So how about it, Torres? How big and bad are you? Or were you just a little Daddy's boy? Soft and weak, always needing Papa to come to your rescue."

Anger flared in Joaquin's dark eyes.

"Is that why you got off on stalking and assaulting those innocent girls in high school? As a way of asserting your questionable manhood?"

"Shut up, man."

Beyond the glass window, the others watched the exchange in tense silence. Chief Taggert fidgeted restlessly. "I don't like this," he muttered uneasily.

"What's he doing in there?" Porter whispered harshly. "What kind of stunt is he trying to pull?"

Eddie crossed his arms and shook his head slowly. Even after six years, Garrison's recklessness never ceased to amaze him.

Moses said nothing, his fascinated gaze glued to the unfolding scene.

A sudden commotion to their left made all four men look up quickly, hands instinctively reaching for weapons. To

their surprise, Imani Maxwell burst into the outer room, fol-
lowed by a protesting desk sergeant. "I tried to detain her,
Chief, but she said she had to see you and just kept going.
Some idiot told her where the interrogation rooms were."

"You can't be in here, Ms. Maxwell," Chief Taggert blus-
tered loudly. "This is a secured area."

"Some security," Imani retorted. "I practically waltzed
right in."

Eddie stepped forward. "Imani," he said gently, "you really shouldn't be here."

"Where is he?" she demanded. "The guy you think broke
into my house last night. Where is . . ." Her words trailed off
as her gaze went to the window. The others watched as alarm
filled her expression, as Garrison's low voice drifted through
the speakers. "W-What is going on?"

"That's what *we're* trying to figure out," Porter muttered
under his breath.

Imani felt as if she were watching some horror film. She
could not believe what she was seeing. Garrison was baiting
a potentially violent criminal with his own gun, whispering
deadly taunts to him. Had he completely lost his mind?
What kind of sick game was he playing?

As she stood there staring in shock, Garrison reached
across the table, sliding the gun even closer to Joaquin
Torres. Imani surged forward with an instinctive cry of
protest. Eddie quickly restrained her, murmuring soothingly,
"It's okay. He knows what he's doing, don't worry."

Trembling with fear and outrage, Imani shook off Eddie's
hands and hurried from the room, tears blurring her vision.

When Eddie started after her, Moses said tersely, "Let her
go." He nodded toward the window where the tense standoff
between Garrison and Joaquin Torres continued. Even from
this distance, they could feel Joaquin's mounting fury as
Garrison's ruthless jabs landed like strategically launched
missiles, steadily eroding Torres's restraint.

"Jeez, this guy should be on a shrink's couch," Moses
muttered as tears welled in Joaquin's eyes when Garrison ac-

cused him of secretly wanting his own sister, acting out against other women to assuage his frustrated desires. "He's got serious issues."

"Who?" Taggert asked. "Wade or the kid?"

Moses snorted. "I meant Torres, but Wade could probably use some therapy, too."

With an outraged wail, Joaquin finally made a move—but it wasn't to reach for the gun. Burying his face in his hands, he wept uncontrollably, his sobs interspersed with savage profanities directed at Garrison and his whole lineage.

His expression grim, Garrison retrieved his Glock and sheathed it in the holster. Satisfied that Joaquin was sufficiently weakened, he stood once again and rounded the table, perching a hip against the edge near the boy. "There's still hope for you, Joaquin," he spoke softly. "You don't have to continue down this road you've started. You can get help before it's too late."

"Screw you," Joaquin mumbled angrily.

Garrison leaned close. "Suppose I told you that your accomplice is in the next room at this very moment, spilling his guts about how he hired you to break into that house last night, trying to cop a plea by ratting you out first."

Joaquin stiffened, lifting his head from the table and glaring at Garrison. "You're lying."

Garrison's smile was narrow, sharp. "Think so?" he countered calmly. "After I just gave you ample opportunity to blow my brains out? I'm disappointed, Joaquin. Haven't I just proven to you that I don't bluff?"

"If I tell you who it is," Joaquin said in halting, measured tones, "do I get some sort of deal?"

"Talk first, negotiate later." Garrison's icy tone brooked no argument.

Joaquin wavered, his gaze darting furtively toward the window. "M-my sister, she hooked me up with this dude at her school."

"I need a name."

"He's a professor. Jerome. Julian Jerome. She told me

he'd done her a favor, and now it was her turn to return it. He wanted me to break into his old house and look for some file this lady professor had, some research paper she was working on. He was going to copy it and say she had plagiarized his work. I-I couldn't find it, so I just smashed the whole hard drive like he told me to."

Garrison's gaze sharpened. "What kind of favor had he done for your sister?"

"I don't know. She wouldn't tell me."

"What do you know about the disappearance of Althea Pritchard?"

Joaquin frowned. "Nothing, man. I didn't have anything to do with it, I swear. My sister and this guy were really secretive, just told me to take care of things and I would get my money. He told me if the lady came home while I was still there, I should just give her a scare, nothing more. I didn't kill her, man," he added pleadingly. "I could have, but I didn't!"

"How very lucky for you," Garrison said, low and ominous. He stood and strode purposefully from the room.

"What about our deal?" Joaquin called after him.

"No comprendo."

The others met him as he stepped from the interrogation room, their expressions ranging from disbelief to grudging admiration. "Throw the book at him," Garrison barked to Chief Taggert, ticking off the list of offenses without breaking stride. "Grand larceny, identity theft, extortion, breaking and entering, assault and battery."

"Where are you going?" Taggert called after Garrison's retreating back, as Eddie and Detectives Moses and Porter fell in step behind him.

"To pick up Elizabeth Torres and Julian Jerome. We're gonna have a full house tonight."

Elizabeth had just reached her dormitory after class when the police cruisers screeched to a halt at the curb. She looked about wildly as uniformed officers spilled onto the sidewalk, descending rapidly upon her.

"W-what's going on?" she demanded, trying not to panic.

"Elizabeth Torres, you are under arrest for conspiracy to kidnap and as an accessory to a breaking and entering. You have the right to remain silent . . ." She nearly fainted as she was handcuffed and the Miranda warnings were recited to her. Her friends were openly gawking, some shaking their heads at her.

And then she saw Garrison Wade leaning indolently against his truck. He stepped forward as the officers ushered her toward a waiting cruiser.

"Agent Wade," she beseeched him, "you have to help—"

He shook his head slowly, deliberately. "I told you what would happen if you lied to me twice," he said, lethal promise in every inflection. As tears filled her eyes, he gave a subtle nod for the officers to take her away.

Their next stop was to Lefrak Hall, where they discovered that Julian Jerome had not shown up for class that morning. "He called in sick around seven A.M.," the flustered department secretary informed them.

Anticipating such a possibility, Garrison had sent Detectives Moses and Porter ahead to Julian Jerome's Annapolis apartment. Garrison's cell phone rang as he and Eddie left campus a few minutes later. "He's not here," Moses brusquely announced. "Neighbor says she saw him flying the coop early this morning, with a suitcase. We're putting out an APB."

Garrison hung up and relayed the news to his grim-faced partner. "Looks like we've got ourselves a fugitive," Garrison murmured, recognizing the familiar adrenaline surge that accompanied every manhunt.

"Something else you should know," Eddie said soberly. "Imani was at the police station earlier. She barged in on us while you were interrogating Torres."

"What?" Garrison didn't know which to react to first: the fact that Imani had disobeyed him and left the apartment, or

that she had somehow managed to circumvent security at the bustling police station.

"She was pretty upset over your little game of Russian roulette. Left in a hurry."

Garrison swore violently under his breath, tempted to go after her and explain himself. But it would have to wait.

Right now he had to catch a fugitive.

"Are you sure you're okay?"

Imani sat on the suede sofa in Jada's living room, staring blindly at the television with a forgotten cup of herbal tea in her hand. Other than to provide a brief explanation of what had happened to her last night, she hadn't spoken more than ten words since their departure from the police station that morning.

"I'm fine, Jada," she said quietly.

"You don't *look* fine," Jada countered, pacing the floor as was her custom whenever she was agitated. "God, I can't believe someone broke into your house and did that to you." She shuddered, still shaken by the news herself. "Are you going to tell Aunt Vivienne?"

"Absolutely not." Imani shook her head firmly. "I don't want to worry her."

"Imani, your mother deserves to know if your life is in danger."

"It's not. Not anymore." Her smile was mirthless, filled with bitter irony. "Garrison got his man."

Jada stopped pacing, her eyes narrowed suspiciously on her cousin's face. "Why doesn't that sound like a good thing?"

"It is. Hopefully they caught the person who broke into my house."

"*What* exactly happened at the police station this morning?"

"Nothing." Imani averted her gaze to avoid the shrewd speculation in Jada's dark eyes. She hadn't told her what she had witnessed that morning. She didn't want to hear that she'd overreacted to Garrison's unconventional interrogation tactics. She knew she hadn't.

"Imani—"

Imani was spared from further cross-examination when Jada's phone rang. Scowling, she went to answer it in the kitchen.

Imani picked up the remote control and was about to channel surf when a late-breaking news report interrupted a rerun of *The View.*

"In dramatic developments today in the case of missing student Althea Pritchard, police have arrested two people wanted in connection with the kidnapping of Prince George's County Executive Louis Pritchard's niece. In just a moment, we'll take you live to police headquarters in Palmer Park where we're awaiting a press conference from Chief of Police Wayne Taggert. But first we'd like to go to College Park, to the campus of the University of Maryland, where our beat reporter, Virginia Albert, is on standby. Virginia, what can you tell us about this rapidly developing situation?"

Imani sat straight up as the dark-haired reporter excitedly began her account. "It all started this morning with the arrest of twenty-one-year-old Joaquin Torres, who was taken into custody for driving a stolen vehicle. Torres was also questioned in connection with a break-in that occurred last night right here in College Park. During interrogation, Torres revealed to investigators that he had been hired—yes, *hired*— to break into the home of Imani Maxwell, a professor here at the University of Maryland who could not be reached for comment. Shortly afterward, police and FBI descended upon the campus to serve arrest warrants for two individuals implicated in the break-in and disappearance of Althea Pritchard. Because one of the suspects is a minor, police are not releasing her identity at this time. But, incredibly enough, the other suspect is a popular, well-respected professor at the University of Maryland, thirty-five-year-old Julian Jerome.

Because Jerome did not report to work this morning and was seen fleeing from his Annapolis home, police and FBI have issued an arrest warrant and an APB for his capture."

Imani almost fell off the sofa. *Julian?* Julian was behind last night's attack? And now he was on the run?

"Details are still forthcoming," Virginia Albert continued with almost salacious glee, "but I must say that this story is unfolding like something straight out of a Hollywood film. Joaquin Torres is the son of the late businessman and former Republican candidate for county executive Carlos Torres, whom viewers may recall was forced to withdraw from that race as a result of a fundraising scandal. Before you even ask, Sharon, I can tell you that there is already speculation about whether *that* has any connection to the disappearance of Althea Pritchard, the niece of Carlos Torres's political rival. Once we learn the identity of the third suspect, I'm sure we'll have a clearer picture. Back to you in the studio."

Jada emerged from the kitchen more agitated than before. "That was my station producer. Did you hear—"

"Every word," Imani muttered, still reverberating with shock. She lowered the volume as the news anchor droned on, recapping the sensational story. Questions raced through her mind at warp speed. Wasn't Elizabeth Torres the daughter of Carlos Torres? That made Joaquin Torres her brother. What was the other connection?

Jada had her own questions. "Julian Jerome? Isn't that the one whose house you're renting?"

"One and the same." Imani drew her legs up to her chin and passed a trembling hand over her face as she struggled to absorb the magnitude of everything she'd just heard. "I can't believe it. There must be some mistake. Why would Julian hire someone to break into the house? His flunky almost killed me, and for what?"

Jada sat down heavily beside her. "It gets worse. Greenberg told me that they're sending reporters over to the house to get your reaction—all the networks probably are. He asked me if I knew where you were."

Imani stared at her. "Did you tell him?"

"Of course not. Did I tell him that you were the first recipient of the kidnapper's notes? Why would I want to unleash those hounds on you?"

Imani's mouth twisted with irony. "Those 'hounds' happen to be your colleagues."

Jada shrugged dismissively. "Blood's thicker than water—and ratings." She drew a comforting arm around Imani's shoulders as they leaned back against the sofa, watching the exhaustive news coverage, knowing their families would be calling any minute. After a while, Imani rested her head on Jada's shoulder, fighting sheer exhaustion and despair. Would any of this bring them closer to finding Althea?

God, she hoped so.

By noon, news of Julian Jerome's possible connection to Althea Pritchard's abduction swept through the region like the biting October wind the forecasters had failed to predict. Thanks to the help of every television station, radio station, and major newspaper in the area, a single person couldn't be found who hadn't formed an opinion about what a sad state of affairs it was when college professors took to kidnapping those whose minds they were supposed to help shape. Reporters from everywhere camped out at the university to document scandalized reactions from Julian's colleagues and students, to be aired and replayed on evening broadcasts. Some resourceful reporter beat his peers to the chase when he delivered to his station manager news of Julian's past conduct that led to his resignation from Wesley College.

Maryland state troopers were dispatched to area airports and bus and train stations in search of the fugitive professor. The police released the description and license plate number for Julian's car and asked the public to come forward with any leads—and it worked.

Shortly before one o'clock Julian was arrested by police acting on a tip from a motorist who had seen Julian's car speeding down the highway, heading toward Ocean City. Within an hour, he was taken into custody at the Palmer Park police headquarters.

From the privacy of her aunt's house in Bowie, Maryland, Imani and her family members watched the dramatic events unfold on television. They had retreated to Vanessa Jamison's home to avoid the press lurking around the Maxwell residence in Upper Marlboro.

Were it not for the dire circumstances surrounding the day, it could have been a typical family gathering, with Jackie's four children chasing each other around, heedless to their mother's threats. Aunt Vanessa fussed with meal preparations in the kitchen, poking her head around the corner for regular updates. Even Vin had left work early to check up on his sister. Everyone was concerned about her, attributing her downcast mood to the surprising revelation that a trusted colleague had plotted to harm her.

Only Jada and Vivienne Maxwell took note of Imani's reaction when Garrison and Chief Taggert appeared before the media for a press briefing.

"That's him," Jackie blissfully announced to everyone. "That's the man who came into the bridal shop looking for Imani that day. See, Ma, didn't I tell you he's fine?"

"You didn't lie," Vanessa concurred, staring at a stern-faced Garrison as he fielded questions from reporters. The smile she sent Imani was knowing and intuitive. "It all makes sense now."

Vin's perplexed glance shuttled between his aunt and sister. "What was he doing looking for you there?"

"Long story," Imani mumbled. "Don't worry about it."

She purposefully avoided the speculative gazes of her mother and Jada, successfully dodging the bullet.

Three hours later, she answered the door and was stunned to find Garrison standing there. A traitorous surge of relief coursed through her.

"Garrison." She threw a quick glance over her shoulder. "What're you doing here? How'd you know where to find me?"

His mouth twitched humorlessly. "I knew where *not* to find you."

Not missing the mild censure in his tone, she crossed her arms defiantly. "You didn't really expect to keep me locked away in your apartment all day, did you?"

"Actually, I did. And I certainly didn't expect you to follow me to the police station like some Nancy Drew wannabe chasing a hot clue."

Temper flared in her chest. She opened her mouth with a stinging retort when her aunt called from the living room, "Who's at the door, Imani?"

"Just a salesperson, Aunt Vanessa. I'll get rid of him." Teeth clenched, Imani stepped onto the porch and pulled the door shut behind her, heedless to the frosty temperature. She was incensed enough to start a campfire.

Garrison frowned at her. "You need to put a coat on."

She ignored him. "First of all," she hissed, jabbing a finger into his chest, "how *dare* you come over here to berate me?"

"You shouldn't have been there," Garrison said tersely, shrugging out of his suit jacket and holding it out to her. "You had no business barging into that interrogation room like that."

She swatted the proffered jacket away, knocking it from his hand. "What's wrong? Don't want me to see how absolutely crazy you *really* are?"

The muscles in his jaw tightened. "You have no idea what you're talking about."

"No? So tell me, Garrison, is it regular protocol to interrogate dangerous suspects while offering them your gun to blow your brains out?"

Garrison's voice was low, forbidding. "Please don't question my methods."

"Your 'methods' could have gotten you killed!"

"They didn't."

"Not this time. But what about the next time? And the time after that? Do you ever stop to think about that when you're performing your little John Wayne stunts? What if Joaquin Torres had grabbed your gun first, Garrison? He could have—" Her voice broke, and she turned away as hot tears stung her eyes. When Garrison made a move toward her, she held up a hand. "Don't."

"Imani—"

"I can't do this. I thought I could, but I can't. I *won't*."

Garrison flinched. He said very quietly, "What are you saying?"

"I'm saying this can't work, Garrison. Us. You and me. I can't go through life wondering when you're going to walk out the door and do something stupid to get yourself killed. Isn't the job hazardous enough? Do you really *have* to go out of your way to create danger? What is it with you men, anyway? Some sort of testosterone overload?"

Garrison reached for her, pulling her against him. Her hands jerked up in protest, fury and grief suddenly warring for supremacy. She lashed out blindly, pummeling his chest with her fists as tears spilled down her face, as sobs were wrenched from her body. "I can't do this," she cried. "I can't!"

He wrapped her in his arms and whispered fiercely into her hair, "I'm not letting you walk out of my life."

"You don't understand—"

"Tell me." He drew back, took her face urgently in his hands. "Make me understand, Imani."

"It won't matter. *He* didn't listen, either."

Garrison grew very still. "Your father."

Without answering, Imani withdrew from his arms and walked to the balustrade that wound around the wide porch. She hugged herself to ward off a chill that had nothing to do with the cold.

After a minute, she began in a low voice, "They were conducting a sting operation for a reputed drug dealer who was also wanted in connection with several police shootings.

Daddy wasn't even supposed to be there that night, but he just had this gut feeling that something was going to go wrong. He had mentored Benjamin straight from the Academy, so he felt responsible for him. Ben was the special agent who had gone undercover for the investigation. He was just supposed to buy cocaine from the dealer, then Daddy and the others doing surveillance would move in for the arrest." She paused, drew air raggedly into her lungs. Silently, Garrison moved to stand beside her.

"See, although Daddy was a supervisory special agent and worked mostly from behind a desk, he was still in great shape, even better than some of the younger special agents. He used to tease them about that. I think he missed that aspect of being an agent. Kicking in doors, the thrill of the chase, the adrenaline rush. You will, too," she said with bitter certainty.

Garrison said nothing, her words ringing like an indictment he couldn't deny. When he made no attempt to, she shook her head ruefully. "Mom and Dad used to argue about his job, about the fact that he couldn't seem to leave those past responsibilities behind him. They had a terrible argument that night. Mom didn't want him to participate in the sting operation, begged him repeatedly not to go. But he wouldn't listen. I remember the way he kissed her at the door, the way he looked into my eyes like he knew it would be the last time." Her voice hitched, grew husky as she continued.

"It was Ben's first undercover assignment, and he must have gotten nervous. The dealer got suspicious, and before anyone could react, he pulled out his gun and shot Ben point-blank in the head." She squeezed her eyes shut as the memories flooded her. "Daddy was the first to give chase. He pursued the dealer down an alley, and they both shot and killed each other."

"Baby, I'm so sorry," Garrison told her quietly.

She lowered herself shakily onto the wrought-iron porch swing. "You don't know how long I've blamed myself, wondering if I might have been able to change his mind about going. Maybe work my Daddy's little girl magic on him, guilt trip him or something. *Anything.*"

"You know it wasn't your fault," Garrison said gently, joining her on the swing.

"You're right. If his own wife couldn't persuade him, what chance did I have?" She swiped impatiently at her tears. "For a while I struggled with anger—toward my father, the FBI, the police, even poor Benjamin for botching the assignment. I was mad at the world."

"That's understandable."

"It did me no good. And meanwhile, my mother wasted away right before my very eyes. She's never gotten over losing him, and I honestly don't think she ever will." When Imani raised her head, defiance glittered in her eyes. She said thickly, "I don't want to end up like her, Garrison. I love her and would give my life for her, but I don't want to *be* her."

Garrison's heart constricted at the raw emotion on her face. "Imani—"

"Can you promise me that I won't become a widow like her? Can you promise me that you won't get yourself murdered in the line of duty—or in the course of interrogating a suspect, for God's sake?"

Garrison braced his elbows on his thighs as he sat forward. He did not answer her.

"I mean, don't get me wrong. I understand that people from all walks of life are killed every day. Tragedy can happen to anyone. Look what almost happened to *me* yesterday." Imani shuddered, shook her head slowly before continuing. "But the reality is that people in law enforcement face greater risks, and you can't tell me any different. Do you know what my father said to me shortly before he died? He told me not to marry anyone whose job required the use of firearms. Even *he* knew."

Garrison blew out a deep breath. He rose, walked to the balustrade, and stood with his arms crossed, his back to her.

"I can't argue with anything you've said, Imani," he said with quiet gravity. "I understand the rationale behind your father's warning. I won't let my kid brother join the Bureau for the same reasons. As much as we all love the job, not very many of us encourage our loved ones to follow in our footsteps. But the truth is that I *do* enjoy my work, just as your father did. And I make no apologies for that."

Imani swallowed with difficulty. "I can respect that, Garrison. Just as I'm asking you to respect my feelings on the matter."

"I can't do that. To do so would be to cave in to fear of the unknown, and I refuse to live my life that way." He turned, his dark eyes burning with determination. "I also refuse to let you go. Not in this lifetime, not without a fight."

She shook her head helplessly. "Garrison—"

"I can't guarantee the future, Imani. None of us can. But I *can* guarantee that if you give me a chance, I will spend the rest of my days on earth, however long God gives me, proving to you that you made the right choice." He knelt before her on the ground, cupping her face in his hands. His gaze brimmed with fiery intensity, piercing her very soul. "I love you, baby," he said huskily. "I can't imagine spending the rest of my life without you. Please don't make me have to."

Imani stared at him as tears lodged in her throat. "What are you saying?" she whispered, heart pounding madly.

"I'm asking you to be my wife," he said. "Will you marry me?"

"Oh my God." Imani nearly swooned with shock and would have were he not holding her. "Garrison—"

He began kissing her passionately, whispering against her mouth, "Say yes. Say you'll be my wife."

"Garrison—"

"*Please,* Imani. Say yes."

"Yes," she breathed, kissing him with equal fervor, her tears mingling with the exquisite taste of him. "Yes, I'll marry you."

Garrison held her tightly like he would never release her.

And she no longer wanted him to. She had been holding on to her fears for so long, allowing them to cripple her emotionally and rob her of future happiness. No more.

After a long time they drew apart, gazing deeply into each other's eyes. "I never thought this crazy day could end so happily," Imani said contentedly.

Garrison smiled, tracing a finger along her delicate jawbone.

She turned into his hand, kissed the center of his palm. A flutter of movement from the window caught her eye, and she grinned sheepishly. "Don't look now," she said in a stage whisper, "but I think we have an audience."

A slow, knowing grin curved his mouth. "I guess it's time you introduced me to your family, then."

"With pleasure." She stood and took his hand, leading him into the house, where the occupants were scattering quickly from the window. Imani cleared her throat pointedly, and four pairs of eyes looked up with varying degrees of guilt—except Jada, who looked unapologetically euphoric.

"Everyone, I'd like you to meet Special Agent Garrison Wade," Imani said, meeting her mother's gaze meaningfully when she announced his title. Tears of joy, not regret, glistened in Vivienne Maxwell's eyes.

She was the first to step forward to greet Garrison. "I know that you're going to make my daughter happy," she said, smiling with genuine warmth. "Her father would be proud."

Deeply touched, Garrison said quietly, "Thank you, Mrs. Maxwell."

"Welcome to the family, Garrison," the others chorused, surrounding the couple with hugs and hearty congratulations.

Only Vin Maxwell stood apart, shaking his head from side to side. Finally he stepped forward and extended a handshake to Garrison. "I don't know how you stole her away from my man David," he said congenially, "but you did, and I respect that. Welcome to the family, brother."

Garrison grinned, and everyone laughed. Vanessa took Garrison's arm and began ushering him gently toward the dining room. "Come on in and have a seat, baby. You've had a dreadfully long day, and we were just about to have dinner. You like steak and potatoes?"

"Yes, ma'am."

Flanked by her mother and Jada, their arms around her waist, Imani followed. "Looks like we'll be having that double wedding after all," Jada teased. "Or a sequel wedding, at least."

Imani could only grin like a sap. In that moment, nothing could diminish her happiness.

Chapter 23

Although Garrison wanted nothing more than to whisk Imani away to a secluded paradise retreat, as he planned to do once they were married, he knew it would have to wait. The mystery of Althea Pritchard's disappearance loomed above his head like a ghostly apparition, demanding that he solve the puzzle before it was too late.

If it wasn't already.

Hoping for leniency, Elizabeth had confessed to her involvement in the break-in, but only on the condition that Garrison be the one to take her statement. "Julian helped me out by telling Dr. Yusef that he also suspected Professor Maxwell of favoritism when she chose Althea for the minority recruitment program. Without Julian's backing, Professor Maxwell wouldn't have been removed from the committee, and I never would have been selected as the student panelist."

"Prior to that, had you ever suggested to Julian Jerome that you wanted to make Althea Pritchard disappear so you wouldn't have to compete with her anymore?" Garrison demanded.

Elizabeth nodded tearfully. "I mentioned it jokingly once, but I never expected him to actually *do* anything. I'm just as shocked as everyone else, Agent Wade, I swear."

After hours of interrogation, Julian Jerome had maintained his innocence in all of the charges filed against him. With his high-priced attorney at his side, he admitted his affair with Cecilia Dufresne and Elizabeth Torres, and explained that he'd panicked and fled when Joaquin Torres threatened him with extortion in exchange for his silence. Prohibited from questioning Jerome due to his personal involvement with Imani, Garrison had been forced to watch from the other side of the window as police and federal investigators—including one of the Bureau's best hostage negotiators—took their turns at bat.

It was just as well, Garrison reflected grimly as he lay awake in bed late that night. He didn't entirely trust himself to be left alone in a room with Julian Jerome, not if he was responsible for trying to hurt Imani.

Garrison angled his head, gazing down at her as she slept soundly in his arms. He still couldn't believe that she was finally his, had made his dreams come true by agreeing to marry him. And as much as she tried to downplay it, he'd sensed her excitement that evening as her family began making plans for their pending nuptials. Once her cousin Jackie plopped down a leather-bound binder filled with sample wedding invitations, Garrison, Jackie's husband Omar, Vin Maxwell, and Jada's fiancé Marcus excused themselves from the table.

Garrison's mother was no better. She had called as they were arriving home to ask him about the news she'd heard on television, expressing concern for Imani Maxwell's safety. Smiling, Garrison had not only assured his mother that Imani was fine, but he'd told her everything, then held the phone away from his ear as Rosemary Wade squealed her unabashed delight over their engagement. She and Imani talked for over an hour after that. By the end of the conversation, his mother had arranged for the families to celebrate Thanksgiving together and had scheduled a date for all the women to go bridal gown shopping.

With an absent smile, Garrison shifted restlessly in the bed. Other than a soft whimper of protest, Imani remained fast asleep as he gently disentangled himself and crept stealthily from the bedroom.

Shiloh, snoozing in a corner of the kitchen, lifted his head when Garrison opened the freezer to grab a Popsicle. Seeing that there was to be no treat for him this time, he settled back on his paws and went back to sleep.

Garrison stood before the windows as his mind worked furiously, dissecting and discarding theories, sifting through scenarios like a deck of cards. Although the actions of Elizabeth and Joaquin Torres were nothing short of detestable, he had no reason to doubt their story implicating Julian Jerome. But even if Jerome *had* hired Joaquin Torres to raid Imani's office to steal her anthology essay, did that mean he was capable of kidnapping?

A search of Jerome's apartment had revealed a bulk supply of the same granite parchment paper used in the series of notes, but that wasn't necessarily incriminating evidence. Plenty of people bought and used that stock of paper. And even if tomorrow's lab results confirmed that hair strands found in Julian's car belonged to Althea Pritchard, he could still deny any connection to Althea. By his own admission, he'd given Elizabeth rides on several occasions, and since Elizabeth and Althea were roommates, it didn't take a genius to explain how strands of Althea's hair could be found on Elizabeth's clothing.

Garrison heaved a frustrated sigh. Without concrete evidence, the reality was that their case against Julian Jerome was largely circumstantial, boiling down to his word against that of Elizabeth and Joaquin Torres, both of whom had credibility issues. Any lawyer worth his salt would rip their testimonies to shreds.

Then there was Sylvia Jerome. She was the only child of

wealthy Washington, D.C. socialites who died earlier that year when their private jet crashed, leaving her the sole heiress to a small fortune and an eight-bedroom Potomac estate. She had defied her parents by marrying the biracial Julian Jerome. Son of an affluent white financier that abandoned him and his mother when he was born, Julian fell far short of their stringent qualifications for a son-in-law. No doubt Sylvia had been ostracized for her decision, her humiliation compounded by her husband's philandering. Had this driven her to commit an unspeakable crime? Other than a few minor traffic violations, her record was clean, which Garrison knew meant nothing. Some of the worst atrocities were often committed by people who appeared to be model citizens. And in his experience, he had seen far too many jilted lovers pushed over the edge, spurred into violent acts of retribution as a result of betrayal or rejection. They were called crimes of passion for a reason.

For that reason, Sylvia Jerome could not be dismissed as a potential suspect.

"Is this what I have to look forward to for the next fifty years?"

Garrison glanced over and saw Imani standing across the room watching him with her arms crossed. A slow, automatic smile curved his mouth. "What?"

"You sneaking out of bed in the middle of the night to brood under the moonlight." Smiling softly, she crossed the distance to him in her bare feet. She had lovely feet, Garrison thought idly. Slender, graceful, the toenails neat and polished a rich burgundy wine. He turned as she reached him, her dark eyes twinkling with mirth as she noted the Popsicle stick dangling from the corner of his mouth. "Oral fixation?"

He nodded, smiling as he removed the stick he'd chewed to death and tossed it in the trash. "Did I wake you?"

"Indirectly. I missed your warmth in the bed." She grinned sheepishly. "You've spoiled me already."

"Get used to it," he murmured, touching her face lightly.

But she could tell that he was still distracted. "Thinking about the case?"

He turned back toward the windows, raising his arms and bracing his palms against the cool glass. Tiny pinpoints of light winked from the downtown landscape stories below. "Yeah."

Imani studied their moonlit reflections in the glass. Garrison was bare chested and wore loose white cotton pajama bottoms, while she wore the other half, the shirt's hem hanging low on her bare thighs. "Want to talk about it?"

He shook his head, his expression grim. "I think we've both had our fill for one day."

"You're probably right." She glanced at his hardened profile. "But if you need to talk or bounce ideas off someone, I'm here. I'm also good at massages," she added almost shyly.

He chuckled. "I'll have to remember that, milady."

"Know what else I find relaxing?"

He glanced over his shoulder as Imani retrieved the lavender votive candles she'd brought from her house. She moved soundlessly through the living room, lighting the fragrant candles that cast long willowy shadows against the pristine walls. She took a spare quilt from the hall closet and spread it across the hardwood floor before popping Will Downing into the CD player. As she started back toward him, she resembled a mythical creature silhouetted against the flickering flames dancing throughout the room.

Anticipation tightened in his groin. "What're you doing?"

As always, Imani's heart rate kicked up a notch at the smoldering intensity in Garrison's dark eyes, the raw need in his voice. Forcing herself to ignore both, she smiled whimsically. "I'm helping you relax." She took his hands and drew him to the floor with her. "Let's pretend it's a warm summer night and we're lying on a hilltop gazing up at the stars. Didn't you ever do that when you were a kid?"

"Can't say that I did," he drawled, amused.

"Well, there's a first time for everything."

Something told Garrison he would be experiencing many delightful firsts with Imani Maxwell. He could hardly wait.

They stretched out beside each other on the comforter, listening in companionable silence to the romantic ballads of Will Downing. Garrison actually felt the tension begin to ebb from his body. "I think you're onto something here."

"Isn't this nice?" Imani murmured.

He slid her a sidelong glance. "Who'd you used to stargaze with? And I'm warning you right now that I'm the jealous type, so you'd better not tell me any stories about makeout sessions with the cute jock from school."

Imani laughed. "Nothing sordid like that. Actually, me, Jada, and Vin used to do this a lot when we were younger. Jackie thought she was too grown up." A poignant smile touched her lips as she recounted cherished summer vacations spent at her family's mountain cabin in West Virginia. The days had been long and idyllic, filled with swimming, hiking, and fishing on the lake. While the grownups napped, she and the others had gone on their own expeditions through the mountain trails, pretending to hunt for lost treasure.

Garrison watched her animated face, envying the carefree youth she had enjoyed. Although his mother had worked hard to provide for them and give them a stable upbringing, the stress of being a single parent had taken its toll on her. After dealing with a roomful of energetic middle schoolers all day, she was often too exhausted by the time she got home to do more than fix dinner and check their homework, which she never failed to do. Garrison attributed his academic excellence to his mother's tireless efforts, the way she had drilled into them the importance of education.

Noticing his remote expression, Imani reached over and touched his shoulder lightly. "I'm sorry. I didn't mean to ramble on like that."

"Don't apologize," Garrison said quietly. "I was enjoying it actually. I wish I had been there with you, although I probably would have just picked on you the whole time."

"Is that what you did to girls you secretly liked?"

"Of course."

They exchanged playful grins. Sobering, Imani sat up, ventured cautiously. "Remember what you told me about Desiree Williams being there for you during a difficult time in your life?"

Garrison hesitated before nodding slowly.

"I was wondering if you could tell me about that." Sensing his resistance, she plowed ahead, "I want to know everything about you, Garrison. I'll admit that what I saw at the police station yesterday morning threw me for a loop. You were so cold, so ruthless, saying all those cruel things and taunting him. I'll be honest, it sent chills down my spine."

The corner of Garrison's mouth curved ruefully. "Afraid you've agreed to marry some deranged schizophrenic?"

She sent him a stern look, crossing her arms. "I'm still waiting."

Garrison sighed, reminded himself of his pledge to be transparent with her. If they were to be married, there could be no secrets between them. No ghosts. "Four years ago," he began without inflection, "I was heading home from work when I stopped at a 7-Eleven. I walked right into a robbery in progress. The gunman told me to leave, I refused. And then the next thing I knew he had grabbed a little girl." Emotion crept into his voice, as inevitable as the familiar guilt. He clenched his jaw against it. "He had an accomplice waiting in the car who got out and just started shooting. It's a miracle that he missed me, since my back was facing the door. Everything happened so fast. But to make a long story short, by the time it was over, both the gunman and accomplice were dead." He hesitated. "And so was Kayla Dyson."

"Oh my God, Garrison," Imani breathed in horror.

"I thought I had shot her, too. I couldn't accept that I hadn't until ballistics confirmed that the bullet came from the accomplice's weapon, not mine. But it didn't matter. I felt as responsible for her death as if I had actually pulled the trigger that killed her."

"Why?"

"Because I should have just done what that bastard said, instead of provoking him. It's one of the first rules of hostage negotiation. If I had just walked out of that store and called for backup like I should have, Kayla might still be alive today." He passed a hand tiredly over his face, said in an embittered voice, "She'd be eight years old now, not buried six feet underground."

"Oh, Garrison." She reached over to comfort him, felt his muscles stiffen beneath her touch. His profile was stony, closed off to her.

"I run into her mother every now and then," he continued in a low voice. "She works downtown. Every time I see her, she thanks me for what I did, ending the life of her baby's killer. All I want to do is apologize, get down on my knees, and beg her forgiveness."

"It wasn't your fault, Garrison," Imani said softly. "You can't go through life blaming yourself for a situation that was beyond your control. Isn't that what you told me earlier about my father's death?"

Irony twisted his mouth. "Using my words against me already?"

"They were true. But I guess it's easier to dish it out than take it." She hesitated. "So what happened afterward? Did you have to undergo psychological debriefing or something?"

"They gave me a clean bill of health and sent me on my merry way," he said sardonically. He stared into the darkened night sky, distant and brooding. "And then I decided to change specialties."

"You can do that?" Imani asked in surprise.

"It's not easy, especially when you're leaving a high-security specialty. But I had help from a friend who pushed the transfer through for me."

And suddenly she understood the reason behind his decision to join the Maryland Joint Violent Crime Fugitive Task Force. Losing Kayla Dyson had changed his perspective on everything. Every abduction or murder case he solved was, in a sense, his attempt to avenge her death.

"What were you doing before your current task force?" she asked quietly.

He answered carefully, "Foreign counterintelligence."

Her eyes widened. "You were a *spy*?"

He grimaced. "I prefer not to use that term. Let's just say I monitored communications between Russian operatives and traveled on occasion."

"No wonder you gave me a funny look when I made that remark to Detective Moses yesterday about not being a government spy. You probably weren't even aware you'd done it." She grinned, tilting her head to one side as she considered him. "Garrison Wade, the spy who loved me."

A wry smile curved his sensuous lips. "How'd I know that was coming?"

"What made you decide to go into foreign counterintelligence?"

"This really fascinates you, doesn't it?"

She smiled, blinked innocence. "Everything about you fascinates me, Garrison."

He chuckled. "Clever. Very clever."

"So? How'd you get involved in the spy track?"

"It was during a visit to Russia, actually. With a friend from college. We were at a store, and an American tourist was asking for directions, but the guy behind the counter couldn't understand him. So I translated for them, and a special agent from the Bureau happened to be standing nearby. He overheard me and approached to ask if I'd ever considered working for the FBI. I agreed to have lunch with him the next day. After hearing about my educational background and asking me a ton of questions—and looking me over like I was champion thoroughbred material—he said he thought I'd make a good special agent candidate. So he strongly encouraged me to apply when I returned home, even made a point of following up with me a few weeks later. He wound up being my mentor, actually," he said, thinking of the many ways he would be forever indebted to Ross Cavanaugh.

"Were you even remotely interested when he first approached you?"

"Somewhat. I had grown up with the desire to follow my father into law enforcement, and got away from that when I went to law school. I still went ahead and took the bar exam, but by then I had already made up my mind about joining the Bureau."

"Did you pass?"

"The bar? Yeah." He chuckled ruefully. "Seems a waste, doesn't it? All that cramming for nothing."

"Not at all. If I ever need legal assistance, you can represent me."

Garrison sent her a half smile. "What about David?"

"I think David would sooner throw me in jail than help keep me out of it," she said, a touch guiltily. "I can't imagine what he's going to think when he hears about our engagement."

"Things happen, Imani," Garrison said gently.

"I know." She pushed out a deep breath. "Things were over between me and David long before you entered the picture. Of course," she added wryly, "falling in love with you didn't exactly help matters any."

His mouth twitched. "I believe in going after what I want."

"I'm glad you did," Imani said truthfully. They smiled at each other before she jumped up and padded to the kitchen. "Want anything?"

"No, thanks. I'm good." Garrison grinned lazily at her when she returned with a cherry Popsicle. "Ah, a convert."

She grinned. "I never said I don't like Popsicles. Just not as much as *you* obviously do." She unwrapped her snack, slid the frozen treat into her mouth. "So does the Bureau ever utilize your Russian language skills, now that you're a defunct spy?"

He smiled distractedly at the term. "Sometimes I translate documents and audio material for critical national security–related investigations. I have a special classified status." The sight of her mouth closing over the Popsicle was shockingly erotic, making his loins tighten in a rush. He watched in happy agony as she suckled, her tongue flicking out occasionally to catch melted juice from the corners of her lush lips.

"Truth or Dare."

"What?" It emerged as a rough sound of need.

"Let's play Truth or Dare. Since you like playing games so much," she added with a lingering hint of reproach. She hadn't completely forgiven him for that morning's stunt at the police station.

"I'll never live that down," he muttered.

"Not any time soon. Truth or Dare?"

He hesitated. "Truth."

"Are you shocked that we're engaged after knowing each other just three weeks?"

"Nope. I think when it's right, it's right. Truth or Dare?"

"Truth."

"Do you realize how crazy you're driving me with that Popsicle?"

Imani chuckled throatily. "I do now. Truth or Dare?"

"Dare."

"Umm . . ." Reading the unmistakable desire in his dark gaze, she faltered for ideas to challenge him with. "I dare you to sing a line from your favorite Commodores song."

Garrison inched closer, and his low baritone was dangerously seductive as he sang a few bars from "Three Times a Lady" into her ear.

Imani blushed like a schoolgirl. "That was nice," she breathed. "You should sing to me more often."

He grinned. "Your turn. Truth or Dare."

"Dare."

"I dare you," he said, his eyes glinting wickedly, "to let me lick Popsicle juice from your body."

She was already unbuttoning her pajama top as Garrison eased his body over hers. He took the Popsicle from her hand and let the remaining cherry-flavored juice trickle languorously over her breasts. She shivered convulsively, then moaned with pleasure as his warm tongue slid across her skin in a slow, tantalizing caress, tasting the sticky sweetness mingled with her own natural nectar.

He took his time exploring and cherishing her, teasing and pleasuring her until her head rocked back and forth on the quilt, breathless whimpers escaping from her lips. It staggered him, watching her responses. The graceful slope of her neck as she arched back with her eyes closed. Moonlight poured over her, so bright and full, cascading upon her glorious curves like an ethereal fantasy. Her moans and cries swarmed into his blood until it was all he could do to keep from devouring her.

Imani had stopped questioning how it was that he knew just where, just how to touch her. It was as if he'd always known, as if their bodies had been molded for each other from the beginning of time. She wanted to hold him forever, lose herself in him. Her back arched and she lifted her arms above her head, her fists gliding across the quilt. Garrison slipped on a condom, pushed her hands open, and entwined his fingers with hers as he buried himself deep inside her heat. Joining not just their bodies, but their hearts, their very souls.

They made love intensely, passionately, like there was no tomorrow. And when the end came for both of them in a shattering climax, Garrison pushed his face into hers. "I love you," he whispered urgently.

She gazed into his smoldering eyes. "I love you, too."

Chapter 24

"I don't know where to start, Professor Maxwell."

Imani had been pleasantly surprised that afternoon when Malik Toomer showed up for class. Afterward when he lingered to talk to her, she invited him upstairs to her office so that they could speak in private.

"Don't tell me anything you're not comfortable sharing," Imani said mildly. She didn't know what concerned her more: the tortured look in Malik's dark eyes, or the gauntness of his frame beneath the baggy sweatshirt and jeans he wore.

His hands twisted in his lap as he sat across the desk from her. "But I *want* to tell you, Professor Maxwell. I want you to understand what's been going on with me, why I haven't been coming to class."

"All right."

Eyes downcast, Malik confided in low, halting tones about his affair with Elizabeth Torres and her threats to blackmail him. Imani listened in impassive silence, showing no visible reaction to the news.

"That was when I *really* knew I had messed up," Malik said, his expression one of abject misery. "I've never cheated on Althea before, and the fact that it was with her best friend made it even worse. I'll never forgive myself."

" 'Never' is an awful long time," Imani said gently. "Are you sure you want to spend the rest of your life punishing yourself over a terrible mistake?"

Malik bobbed his head vigorously. "I betrayed Althea in the worst kind of way."

"Yes. You did. I won't dispute that. But it was a mistake, Malik. I'm sure you didn't intentionally set out to hurt Althea."

"I should have known better. I feel like I let everyone down. Including you, Professor Maxwell."

"Is that why you stopped coming to class?" Imani asked quietly. "Because you were too ashamed to face me?"

He swallowed hard before nodding mutely.

Imani leaned forward, her expression gentle. "Malik, I'm not here to judge you. My first priority at this university is to educate my students, to give them every opportunity to excel. But I can't help you if you won't let me."

"I know. That's why I decided to come to class today and just come clean about everything." He took a steadying breath and stared out the window at the late afternoon sun. "I can't put all the blame on Elizabeth. What she did was dead wrong, but I have to accept responsibility for my own actions. If they ever find Althea . . ." His voice faded as he struggled against the thought that Althea might be lost to them forever. Drawing more air into his lungs, he continued with quiet determination. "If I ever get the chance, I'm going to tell Althea the truth about everything. I think she deserves to hear it from me."

"I agree," Imani said softly.

Malik turned his head to meet her gaze. "Do you think she'll forgive me?"

Imani hesitated before answering truthfully. "It's going to be hard, but I believe in time she would. After the ordeal she's been through, Althea's going to need as much moral support and as many friends as possible."

Malik nodded slowly. "It's ironic. Before Elizabeth and I even slept together, Althea suspected that Elizabeth had a thing for me. One night, out of the clear blue, she asked me if I thought Elizabeth was hot. Like a dummy, I said yes. Big mistake. Althea got really mad, and the next thing I knew we were arguing. Just screaming at each other like we'd lost our minds. It was crazy." His mouth twisted in self-deprecation. "I can't believe I was so gullible when Elizabeth came to me that night. She was playing me the whole time, and I didn't even realize it."

"You're young, Malik—"

He shook his head vigorously. "Being young is no excuse for being stupid. I should have known better, especially since Althea and I had *just* argued about Elizabeth."

"Stop beating yourself up, Malik. What's done is done. All you can do now is move on and try to rectify your mistake. The first step is being honest with Althea. Focus on that, and leave the past in the past. Can you do that?"

"I'll try," Malik said quietly. Then, after a slight hesitation, "Do you think Professor Jerome kidnapped Althea?"

"I honestly don't know." Imani crossed her arms and leaned back in her chair. She knew she couldn't continue avoiding the question, especially since she had been linked to Julian Jerome as his possible next target. From the moment she arrived on campus that morning, she had sensed the speculation surrounding her. The way hushed conversations had skidded to an abrupt halt when she entered the main office, the sympathetic looks thrown her way when she happened to make eye contact. Although none of her colleagues had approached her to confirm the media reports, she knew it was only a matter of time before they would.

Her students, on the other hand, suffered no such inhibitions. She had barely walked through the classroom door before they bombarded her with questions. Did she think Professor Jerome was guilty of kidnapping Althea? Did she hate him for hiring someone to break into her house?

Imani had provided a neutral answer. "Until Professor Jerome is found guilty of these crimes beyond a reasonable doubt, we have to presume his innocence."

Their incensed grumblings had swept through the room. They, like many others at the university, were already convinced of Julian's guilt. They were also unanimous in their condemnation of Elizabeth Torres's conduct. Not only had she conspired against a beloved professor, she had also betrayed her best friend by scheming to take her place as a student panelist in the minority recruitment program—achieving this nefarious goal by sleeping with Julian Jerome. Like a fallen parishioner, Elizabeth had been excommunicated from the society of her peers.

And despite what Elizabeth had done to her, Imani couldn't help feeling sorry for the girl who now faced a prison sentence and an uncertain future. The senselessness of it all angered her.

"It would be crazy if it turned out that Professor Jerome took Althea," Malik continued with a snort. "I'd have guessed his wife before him."

Imani looked up in surprise. "Why's that?"

Malik shrugged. "The way she was always sneaking around on campus spying on him. Althea told me that Mrs. Jerome once followed her and Elizabeth all the way to their dorm, creeping along in her car like they couldn't see her. Althea suspected Elizabeth might have been sleeping with Professor Jerome, but she didn't want to ask her in case Elizabeth got mad."

Imani nodded slowly. "What were you and Sylvia Jerome talking about on Monday, when I looked out the window and saw you?"

"She was just asking me if I knew where your office was. And when I told her you were one of my professors, she started asking me questions about you." At Imani's raised eyebrow, he quickly elaborated. "You know, questions like whether the students liked you, whether you were a good instructor, stuff like that. She said you were renting out their old house and she was just curious about you, since she'd only met you once."

Imani pursed her lips thoughtfully. "I see."

Malik frowned. "Did I do something wrong by talking to her?"

"Not at all. I just wondered, that's all. Don't worry about it." Imani glanced distractedly at her watch and saw that it was after four o'clock. Garrison would be arriving at five-thirty to pick her up after adamantly refusing to let her drive herself to campus that morning. "Anyway, what are we going to do about your slipping grade in my class, Malik? The midterm is on Friday."

"I know." He sat up straighter in his chair, clearing his throat. "Yvette and Denise agreed to let me join their study group."

"Good." Imani nodded briskly. "Now what about your paper that was due on Monday? You know I've already had to take one letter grade off since it's late."

"I know." He grimaced. "It's finished, actually. I was going to print it out and bring it with me to class, but my printer broke. Honest to God, Professor Maxwell, it really did. None of my roommates could fix it, either."

"I'll give you the benefit of the doubt, Malik. Why don't you bring the disk to me and I'll print the paper out for you."

"Today?"

She nodded. "I'll wait here while you run back to your dorm and get the disk. I have some loose ends to tie up anyway."

Malik was already halfway to the door. "Thank you so much, Professor Maxwell. I owe you big time."

"You can repay me by not missing any more classes. Are we understood?"

"Yes, ma'am. I'll be right back, I promise."

* * *

Half an hour later, Imani glanced up from her paperwork to see Dr. Anthony Yusef standing in the doorway, handsome and debonair in a well-tailored black tuxedo, his wingtips polished to a glossy shine.

Imani laid down her pen and greeted him with a smile. "Good evening. What's the special occasion?"

Yusef stepped into the office, his hands shoved into his pants pockets. "Charity banquet in Washington, D.C. that I'm running late for. When are you heading home?"

"In a little bit. Just finishing up some paperwork. I'll have my rough draft to you by Friday, as promised."

"No problem." He jiggled his keys in his pocket, brownish-gray eyes fixed upon hers. "Listen, I want to apologize for my hasty decision to remove you from the program committee. I gave credence to Elizabeth Torres's claim when I should have given you the benefit of the doubt."

Imani hesitated, then nodded. "Apology accepted."

"If you're still interested, I'd like to reinstate your position as committee chair. Seems we have a vacancy anyway," he added with a sardonic twist of his lips.

Imani grimaced at the reference to Julian. "Of course I would love to be involved with the program once again, but not necessarily as chair—"

"I met with the committee today, and everyone would like to see you return as chairperson. Is that what you're concerned about? That some members may still harbor misgivings?"

"Well . . ."

"Rest assured that is not the case. We all feel that you're the most qualified for the job, and always have been." His voice softened to a plea. "So will you consider coming back?"

Again Imani paused. "Yes."

Yusef beamed. "Wonderful. Actually, I have the committee notes in my car. You can look them over this weekend and bring yourself up to speed."

"All right."

He flicked a hurried glance at the gold Rolex on his wrist. "I'm really running late. Would you mind following me out to the car to get the notes? I'm parked right out front."

"Sure." Imani rose from her chair and followed him from the room to the elevator. The offices they passed were dark; the faculty members had headed home earlier than usual. Outside nightfall had arrived, plummeting the world into shadowy darkness. Yusef led her to a midnight blue Cadillac that sat at the end of the first row, a lone sentinel in the near-empty parking lot.

Imani rubbed her arms against a sudden chill that whispered across her skin. It was colder outdoors than she had expected. She should have put her coat on first. Almost longingly, she threw a backward glance at the silent building before turning back around.

"When's the next committee meet—" The rest of her question was smothered in the damp cloth clamped viciously over her face.

Stricken, she had only a fleeting glimpse of the maniacal satisfaction in Anthony Yusef's eyes before blackness enveloped her, plunging her into unconsciousness.

Garrison wore a grim expression as he strode from Wayne Taggert's office followed by Eddie. Their case against Julian Jerome had suffered major setbacks that day. Not only had lab results concluded that the hair strands found in Jerome's car did not belong to Althea Pritchard, but more neighbors had come forward to substantiate his whereabouts on the night of her disappearance. Even after additional questioning, Jerome vehemently denied his involvement in the break-in and Althea's abduction. And as more details emerged about Joaquin Torres's past conduct, as the names of his defrauded victims multiplied, the more his credibility took a beating—which Jerome's attorney seized upon when his client was granted bail. In a statement to the media,

Julian Jerome's slick-tongued attorney painted a portrait of a sibling crime duo more cunning than Bonnie and Clyde, whose sole motivation for kidnapping Althea Pritchard was revenge. Elizabeth Torres was identified as a "willing pawn in her brother's game of greed and depravity, a Tonya Harding ruthlessly bent on removing any and all perceived rivals—be they friend or professor.

"County Executive Pritchard needs look no further for the perpetrators of this heinous crime against his niece," Julian's attorney cried theatrically into cameras as if delivering a closing argument. "The ones responsible for Althea Pritchard's disappearance are the very ones who stood to gain the most from their father's successful bid for the county's highest elected office. Two spoiled, self-indulgent, immoral individuals who had motive and opportunity to commit this atrocity. By his own admission, Joaquin Torres purchased a voice scrambler to make anonymous phone calls to people, calls in which he threatened them with extortion if they didn't heed his greedy demands. Are we to believe that such an individual would stop at extortion? That such abominable behavior would not escalate to violence? Ladies and gentlemen, my client is innocent of all wrongdoing, and we're going to prove it!"

Even the memory of that inflated speech made Garrison scowl again as he climbed into his truck. If this case went to trial, he was not looking forward to listening to Julian Jerome's attorney pontificate for hours on end. It would be nothing short of torture.

As if reading his mind, Eddie threw him a sympathetic look. "With any luck," he drawled, "Jerome will just cop a plea and spare us all."

Garrison snorted rudely. "Why should we be so lucky," he grumbled morosely as he steered out of the parking lot, "when nothing else about this case has gone our way?"

"So Sylvia Jerome's alibi checked out too, huh?"

"So it appears." As it turned out, Sylvia Jerome was at a support group meeting for spouses of cheaters on the night

Althea was abducted. The indignant women had quickly corroborated her story, incensed that the police could even suspect one of their members of kidnapping. Garrison had a feeling they would be less outraged at the idea of Sylvia Jerome dismembering her philandering ex-husband.

At any rate, she had been cleared of any involvement in the kidnapping and break-in. She'd admitted to following Imani around campus a few times, merely to satisfy her curiosity about whether Imani and Julian were having an affair. Her fears had been put to rest when she saw Garrison dropping Imani off at school that morning—she'd put two and two together.

Garrison merged onto the Beltway and joined the flow of evening traffic surging north. It had been a hellishly long day, leaving him mentally and physically drained. But all that would change once he was back in Imani's presence. She had that effect on him, the ability to both soothe and invigorate him. She was his wellspring of life.

"I know what that smile means." Eddie was watching him with an amused expression. "I take it that the lovely Professor Maxwell has forgiven you for yesterday's little stunt."

"Even better." Garrison couldn't keep the ridiculously happy grin from spreading across his face. "She has agreed to put up with me till death do us part."

Eddie's eyes widened in shock. "You popped the question?"

"And wouldn't take no for an answer."

Eddie laughed. "Well, whaddya know? Miracles *do* happen." He reached over, clapping Garrison heartily on the shoulder. "Congratulations, my friend."

"Thanks, man."

"I knew she was the one. Didn't I tell you she was special right from the start?" Eddie grinned unabashedly, pleased with himself. "Set a date yet?"

"First weekend in June. Gives her a little time after spring semester ends."

"When did you get the engagement ring?"

"Haven't yet. Going this weekend to pick one out while my mother keeps her preoccupied."

Eddie slanted him a knowing look. "Scared?"

"You know it. I want to get her something really special, not just flashy." He grinned sheepishly. "I don't have a clue what I'm doing. Thank God her cousin volunteered to go with me."

Eddie grinned. "Think she'll do the same for me when it's my turn?"

Garrison chuckled. "And deprive your sisters of the honor?" He slid his partner a meaningful sidelong glance. "So when will your turn be?"

"Soon enough," Eddie answered smoothly.

When they arrived on campus, he waited inside the truck while Garrison went to get Imani.

The building was virtually empty save for the janitor, who greeted Garrison loudly before returning to an off-key rendition of U2's "Beautiful Day," cranking from his Walkman stereo. Shaking his head in mild amusement, Garrison boarded the elevator to the second floor.

Imani was not in her office. Both the light and her computer were still on, the tropical fish screensaver drifting idly across the silent monitor. Her leather briefcase rested against the desk on the floor.

Even as cold unease slid down his spine, Garrison told himself not to overreact. Imani was more than likely in the ladies' room. He glanced at his watch. He was only ten minutes late. She'd probably wanted to use the bathroom before they hit the road since traffic was always so unpredictable, often lengthening the ride to Baltimore by twenty minutes or more.

But something about the stillness of the office didn't feel right. It didn't feel like a room that had only recently been vacated.

Frowning, Garrison walked over to the desk and pulled open the bottom right-hand drawer to confirm that Imani's suede purse was still there. It was.

His gaze landed on a floppy disk lying atop a pile of papers on the desk. He reached over to pick it up, scanning the attached note: *Professor Maxwell, You must have stepped out for a minute. Anyway, here's my paper as promised. Thanks again for printing it out for me. I'll see you in class on Friday. Malik.*

Garrison's frown deepened. Dropping the disk back onto the desk, he strode from the office and located the ladies' room down the hall. He knocked once before entering.

"Imani?" There was no answer. A quick sweep of the stalls confirmed that the room was empty.

The janitor was wheeling a large trash bin down the corridor, still singing loudly. Garrison approached from behind, tapping him on the shoulder to get his attention. The man looked up with a start before lifting one headphone away from his ear.

"Something wrong, man?"

"I'm looking for Professor Maxwell. Have you seen her?"

The janitor grinned slyly, rheumy blue eyes crinkling at the corners. "Foxy Maxwell? That's her office right up ahead."

"I know," Garrison said, striving for patience. "Have you seen her?"

"Sure, she left about forty minutes ago."

"Left?"

"Yeah. I saw her walking out with old what's-his-name."

Garrison's gaze sharpened. "Who?"

"Guy who heads the African-American Studies Department. Yusef. Dr. Yusef."

"You saw her *leaving* with him?"

"That's what it looked like. She never came back, and I've been downstairs cleaning the whole time." Puzzled, the janitor frowned at him. "Something the matter?"

Garrison shook his head distractedly as he turned away. "Thanks."

Eddie stepped off the elevator just then. "What's taking

so—" He took one look at Garrison's troubled expression and frowned. "What's up?"

"She's not here," Garrison said dully. He walked back to Imani's office, then cast another look around as if expecting the narrow room to reveal the mystery of her whereabouts. His heartbeat was a deafening roar in his ears. Even as he prayed that nothing had happened to her, he knew better.

Abruptly he turned and stalked from the room. Eddie fell in step beside him. "Did anyone see her leave?"

"Janitor says she left with a colleague about forty minutes ago. Dr. Anthony Yusef. I'm going to drive around campus."

They bounded down the stairwell and strode purposefully from the building. Suddenly their steps slowed as they neared the GMC in the near-empty parking lot.

There, tucked between the windshield wipers, was a granite-colored piece of paper.

They exchanged grim looks. And reached simultaneously for their weapons.

Scanning their darkened surroundings, Garrison approached the truck and carefully removed the note. It was typed in Cyrillic font. Russian.

His heart plummeted when he translated the contents: *Beware of a quiet dog and still water.*

He swore violently and slammed his fist against the roof of the truck.

"What does it say?" Eddie demanded over his shoulder. When Garrison relayed the message, he scowled. "What is that? Some kind of foreign riddle?"

"You shouldn't be afraid of people who make threats and shout in loud voices," Garrison explained in a low voice. "It's the people who are quiet and say little that should be feared."

"He's telling us that we underestimated him," Eddie surmised.

Garrison nodded grimly, scanning the area once again.

Other than a faint rustle of wind through tree branches, all was silent. "You couldn't have been inside the building more than ten minutes."

"Which means someone was waiting for me to get out before leaving this note. Yusef?"

"No," Garrison said with quiet certainty. "He's long gone. Probably paid a student to do it beforehand."

He unlocked the truck and climbed behind the wheel. Grabbing his cell phone, he dialed Detective Moses and told him what had happened. "Get a tag number and put out a bulletin," he instructed tersely. "And get over to that home address. Search the place, talk to neighbors, find me something."

He disconnected and punched numbers for the Baltimore field office. "I want a complete dossier on a Dr. Anthony Yusef who works at the University of Maryland College Park. I want *everything*," he added succinctly. "If this guy so much as took a leak in a public park, I want to know. I'll be there ASAP."

He hung up and shoved the cell phone back into his breast pocket. Anger and powerlessness drove twin fists into his stomach. God, if anything happened to Imani . . .

"He knows you speak Russian." Eddie watched him with a shrewd expression. "What do you think that means?"

Garrison stared sightlessly through the windshield. "Cavanaugh used to recite that Russian proverb to me all the time because it reminded him of me." His mouth twisted ruefully. "He said it was my strong silent nature that made me the perfect spy."

"Still Water. Your alias."

Garrison nodded. His partner was the only person outside of foreign counterintelligence who knew his former operative code name.

"You don't think it's just coincidence that Yusef used that same proverb to bait you?" Eddie asked.

"No such thing as coincidence." Garrison started the ignition and pulled off.

* * *

"Wake up, sleepyhead."

The voice was a soft whisper, a chilling taunt. Imani opened her eyes slowly, her lids feeling as heavy as sandbag weights. What she saw confused her already-muddled brain.

Candles.

Everywhere.

Candelabras with tapers whose flickering flames cast long, writhing shadows against the walls.

Where *was* she?

Her head throbbed unmercifully. Her mouth felt as if it were coated with rubber cement around a tongue that felt bloated and useless. Carefully, she looked down at herself. She was seated in a straight-backed chair. Her arms were tied to the arms of the chair, her ankles bound to the legs. And instead of the wool slacks and cowlneck sweater she had donned that morning, her body was now draped in a silky black material that poured past her knees. The corners of her mouth tugged downward into a bemused frown. Whose dress was she wearing?

"It fits you perfectly," he spoke in her ear again. "I knew it would. After all the time I've spent watching you, studying you, I ought to know your dress size." He chuckled softly, tracing his fingertips along the column of her throat. Icy chills broke out all over her body.

Groggily, she turned her head to get a better look at her captor. Candlelight flickered across his handsome features in a macabre dance, illuminating the sinister gleam in his eyes.

She opened her mouth, but no sound would come forth. She tried again. "Why . . . why are you doing this?" she managed, her voice little more than a brittle croak.

Anthony Yusef laughed, thoroughly amused. "Ah, the eternal question. *Why?* What causes the darkness in men's souls, enables them to take life with no more compunction than the basest of animals? What indeed?"

The dizziness swirled around her. Nausea crawled up the back of her throat, and she swallowed it back down as a horrifying realization descended upon her. "You . . ." She swallowed again with difficulty. *"You* t-took Althea?"

Again that mocking laughter. "Time enough for questions, Imani," he said, almost soothingly. "We have a little while to get to know one another better." He cocked his head to one side, a whimsical smile playing about the corners of his mouth. "Isn't it funny how you can work with someone for so long and not really know them, except what's presented to you? That must be how you're feeling now. I sympathize."

Chuckling, he stood and started away from her, a menacing figure slipping in and out of the murky gloom—or so it seemed to her distorted vision. Her head was spinning like a whirling dervish. Drugs. He had given her something, she was sure of it. But all she could remember was the chloroform-soaked cloth pressed to her face.

And then nothing but blackness.

The drug pulled at her now, dragging her toward unconsciousness. She willed herself to remain awake, knowing it was her only hope of survival. Somehow she had to find a way to escape from here. But where was *here?*

She tried to focus on her surroundings, but the candlelight plunged the room into deceptive shadows. She glanced down and saw that the floor beneath her stockinged feet was cement. A basement or cellar. Come to think of it, she did detect a certain damp staleness in the air, and a draft consistent with underground rooms.

Suddenly her tormentor was beside her again. "Everything's ready," he whispered, an eerie note of anticipation in his voice. "Shall we begin?"

Chapter 25

"Are you absolutely certain you won't try the venison? I killed it myself, specifically for this special occasion."

Imani jerked her head from side to side in silent refusal. She and her jailer were seated at a low table that he had wheeled into the dim space, whistling as cheerfully as if he were delivering room service. To her utter astonishment, the table was draped in linen and covered with silver serving dishes containing assorted foods. Steamed vegetables, herbed potatoes slathered in white gravy, crusty rolls, and the aroma of roasted meat combined to make Imani's queasy stomach roil. Her arms and legs were still bound to the chair because he wanted her to suffer the indignity of eating with no hands, lapping at her plate like an animal. Even if she'd had an appetite, she wouldn't have given him the satisfaction of humiliating her in such a manner.

Across the table, Anthony Yusef ate with unabashed relish, gliding forkfuls of bloody deer meat through gravy before shoveling each morsel into his mouth. He closed his eyes as he chewed, savoring every bite. From somewhere above, the haunting strains of classical music could be heard—Mozart's Concerto Number 21, Imani's mind registered dully. Were the situation not so dire, she would have found humor in her ability to identify the piece. Despite David's best efforts, she had never developed an avid appreciation for classical music.

The scene was horrifyingly surreal. She felt like she was auditioning for a role in *Silence of the Lambs,* in which Anthony Yusef would portray Hannibal Lecter. God, if only it were as simple as a movie audition!

"A shame that you have no appetite," Anthony Yusef murmured, regarding her with a predatory smile. "Especially considering that this will be your last meal."

Her heart plummeted. She stared across the table at him. "Why are you doing this?" she asked, striving to keep panic out of her voice. "What have I ever done to you?"

For the second time he ignored the question. Closing his eyes once again, he let his hand float through the air as if he were conducting an orchestra. "Do you like classical music, Imani? They say that this arrangement is arguably Mozart's most famous and revered piece, but I'm quite partial to Symphony Number 31 myself. It's a remarkable example of Mozart's sense of adventure and melody, wouldn't you agree?"

When she said nothing, he opened his eyes slowly and looked at her. "Of course, I've always had an affinity for the Russian composer Tchaikovsky. He was brilliant. Quite tortured too, did you know that? But then I suppose they all were, to some measure." He paused, tapping a long finger against his mouth. "I wonder if your FBI special agent likes Tchaikovsky. I understand that he's quite fluent in Russian, well-versed in Russian history and culture."

Imani's blood grew even colder, if that were possible. "How do you know that?"

He chuckled as he lifted his long-stemmed wineglass. "The same way I know about your father. I have friends in high places, people who obtain classified information for me—no questions asked. You see, being a diplomat's nephew has its advantages. That's how I know all about your father and the way he met his end so tragically, so pointlessly. Six years ago today, as a matter of fact. Just before eleven o'clock, am I correct?"

Anger and grief swirled in Imani's belly. "That's none of your business."

Laughing softly, Yusef sipped his wine and gave an appreciative sigh. "There's nothing on earth like a vintage cabernet sauvignon. Go on," he said, nodding at the wineglass beside her untouched plate of food, "have a taste." At her baleful look, he grinned. "I promise that it's not laced with cyanide, if that's what you're worried about. I have other plans for you, Imani."

"Such as?"

"In time, my dear. In time." He finished the last of his venison, dabbed at the corners of his mouth with a linen napkin. "I'm of the opinion that the best-tasting meat is the meat killed and prepared by one's own hand. I enjoy hunting, always have for as long as I can remember." His eyes gleamed in the candlelight as he added softly, "The thrill of the chase is almost as rewarding as the kill itself."

Imani forced herself not to shiver at the sadistic pleasure in his gaze. She would not give him the satisfaction of knowing how terrified she was. "What makes you think you're going to get away with this?"

"Prior experience." As her eyes widened in horror, he nodded with cruel satisfaction. "That's right, my beautiful companion. There were others before you, and long after your remains have fossilized beneath the ground, there will be more. Although I must say that this particular experience promises to be rather memorable. Quite special."

"Why?"

He ignored her question. "I was just a child when my parents were killed right before my very eyes. They were Sunday school ministers who had taken a vow of poverty, had devoted their lives to helping the poor and weak, the un-saved masses." His harsh crack of laughter reverberated menacingly around the room.

"They had dragged me along on one of their missionary expeditions to West Africa. Not all of the natives were happy to see them. On our way to one of the villages, we were taken hostage by a group of militia rebels. My parents tried to reason with them, appeal to their sense of humanity." His mouth curved cynically. "The rebels shot them at point-blank range. Blew holes in their faces so that they couldn't even have the final dignity of an open-casket funeral.

"Afterward, I was sent to live with a rich aunt and uncle in England. I attended the finest private schools, enjoyed privi-leges I had never dreamed of when my parents were alive. I sometimes wondered if their murders had not been a bless-ing in disguise. Don't look so shocked, Imani," he drawled, amused by her aghast expression. "Not all of us are suited to modest living. Some of us want more, deserve more. That was something your mother never understood."

Imani tensed at once, staring at him. "My . . . *mother*?"

He nodded slowly, enjoying her reaction. "You mean she never told you about me? No, I guess she wouldn't have. She forgot about me as soon as she met your father. But I never forgot about her," he said in a soft whisper. "And I never will."

Icy foreboding settled over Imani's heart. "You and my mother—?"

"I'll never forget my first kill," he continued as if she hadn't spoken. "He was a classmate in junior high school, a spoiled brat who made a sport of bullying me because I was the only black student. So after school one day, I baited him into fol-lowing me into the woods. He never knew what hit him. I buried his body deep in the ground where it would never be found. They stopped looking after several months, assumed he had been kidnapped by a stranger. I sent his mother a sympathy card on the one-year anniversary of his disappearance. A rather magnanimous gesture on my part, I would say."

Suppressing a horrified exclamation, Imani said quietly, "You need help."

Yusef stared beyond her, his eyes glazed over. "This may sound outrageous to you, but I think that something supernatural happened when I saw my parents killed, when I looked into the eyes of their murderer. It was as if our spirits met and became one. He could just as easily have turned that machine gun on me, but he didn't. I was never the same after that, and it had little to do with mourning the loss of my parents.

"Still, I blame the U.S. government for not seeking justice on their behalf, for not taking some sort of action against the Nigerian government or those militia rebels. My uncle was a diplomat, and he wrote endless letters to the president, to Congress, the Secretary of State, even the CIA and FBI. But I guess Uncle Sam had more pressing matters to worry about than two poor black missionaries traveling overseas with their child. We were nobodies in the grand scheme of things."

Imani lifted a defiant chin. "So you became a murderer because of what happened to your parents."

He threw back his head and roared with laughter. "Became a murderer. You make it sound like an occupation, Imani. It's nothing like that, I assure you. Killing is far more fulfilling than any career."

"What happened between you and my mother?"

Yusef folded his hands across his midsection. "I met Vivienne during her senior year at Spelman. I was in my first teaching position at Emory, and she often used our library for research. She was like no other woman I had ever encountered. So confident and self-assured, so vibrant and full of life. To use a trite phrase, she lit up a room whenever she entered. She was beautiful, brilliant, and knew what she wanted out of life. I fell in love with her very quickly. I didn't realize, at the time, that my feelings were so one-sided." His expression hardened, and Imani nearly recoiled from the sudden hatred that filled his eyes.

"We talked about our future together," he continued bitterly. "I couldn't imagine a future without Vivienne. After graduation, she was going to remain in Atlanta with me and get her master's degree from Emory. She only returned home to tie up some loose ends and spend time with her family. And then she met him. She didn't even have the decency to tell me in person. She called me on the phone, telling me it was over and apologizing profusely for any pain she had caused me."

He stood so abruptly that his chair tipped backward and crashed to the floor. Imani started violently and eyed him warily as he approached. His voice vibrated with controlled rage as he said, "I spent a lifetime trying vainly to replace her, looking for her in every woman I met. So many hapless women paid for your mother's betrayal, Imani. So many lost their lives senselessly."

Nausea and revulsion burned the back of Imani's throat. "You're insane," she charged, her voice a sharp, trembling whisper. "I can't believe I ever admired you, respected you."

His smile was narrow, cold. "Disillusionment is a part of life, my dear." He reached across the table, taking the knife he'd used from his plate. The steel blade glinted in the candlelight, the edges still stained from the bloody venison. He made an exaggerated show of examining it, turning his head this way and that, before kneeling and bringing the blade close to her face. Her breath hitched, and her heart drummed hard and fast in her ears.

"I wanted to kill her, but could never bring myself to do it," he continued in a soft whisper. "I still loved her, as pathetic as that sounds. I wanted to be near her, so when the University of Maryland came calling with their tenured faculty position years later, I knew it was a sign from above. And then fate intervened again, bringing *you* to the university—first as a student, then as a colleague."

Imani said nothing, afraid to speak, afraid to breathe, as the blade point traced down her chin and down the center of her throat to the vulnerable hollow at its base. He leaned close, and when he spoke his lips brushed her cheek. "I knew who you were the minute I laid eyes on you. You were even more beautiful than Vivienne, if such a thing could be possible. And you had the same vitality, the same natural brilliance and drive. It was like stepping back in time. You don't know how many times I came close to killing you. But some small, weak part of me wanted to keep you around just to look at you, pretend you were her."

The knife inched lower and came to rest at a spot just above her breasts. Imani swallowed back the urge to vomit, felt the cool tip of the blade bite into her skin. Every cell in her body was quivering uncontrollably. Her eyes filled, but she held back the tears, held back the hysteria, and clung to a shred of hope that she would somehow come out of this alive.

Yusef smiled, reading the fear in her eyes. "I wanted her to suffer the way she made me suffer all these years. You can imagine my insurmountable joy when I learned of your father's demise. Shot down in an alley like the common dog that he was. I thought his death would be enough for me, but I was wrong. After all, what hunter can take pleasure in a kill not his own?"

A tear escaped and rolled unchecked down Imani's cheek. "I hate you," she whispered fiercely, forgetting her terror as outrage settled like a scarlet haze over her vision. "I hope you rot in hell."

Yusef laughed scornfully. "Maybe one day, but not before I send you there first." He grabbed a fistful of her hair, forcing her head back. His face loomed above hers, his features taking on a sinister cast in the shadowy glow of candlelight. "You could have been my daughter," he sneered, low and soft. "Instead, you're nothing more than a cruel reminder of everything I had and lost."

"My mother never loved you," Imani hissed through the

painful throb in her head. Common sense warned her not to bait a violent criminal holding a knife to her throat. One flick of his wrist, and it would be over for her. And still she said, "She couldn't have made herself love a sadistic maniac like you any more than she could have stopped herself from loving my father. In your wildest dreams you could never be *half* the man that he was."

Yusef's eyes narrowed to ominous slits. "You're just as cheap as she was," he said contemptuously. "All these years I watched you in a relationship with the same man. And then you betrayed him with the first good-looking thing to come along. You love your FBI agent so much? Tell you what. I'll give you one final opportunity to talk to him, to tell him goodbye."

Her heart constricted. "And then what?"

The blade point pressed into her flesh, drawing a tiny bead of blood that trickled down her throat and disappeared down the scooped neckline of the gauzy dress. She forced back a violent shudder.

A small, feral smile lifted the corners of Yusef's mouth. "And then we can let the games begin."

"He is completely without remorse, devoid of conscience. He has rationalized his actions, has convinced himself that he is far superior to everyone else in that he has evaded capture for so long. He thrives on maintaining control, keeping his victims powerless and submissive. He will prey on his victim's weaknesses, be they physical or emotional."

Garrison paced the floor restlessly as Donovan MacArthur's clipped baritone droned on. The Bureau's leading profiler had been called in to assist with the investigation by providing his expert analysis of Anthony Yusef's frame of mind.

It was just after seven when they descended upon Yusef's Georgetown home armed with their search warrant. A search of the luxurious townhouse had yielded nothing incriminating.

Until they reached the tiny room in the lower level of the house that had been converted into a darkroom.

There they discovered the black and white photographs, recently developed and left hanging to dry. Photo after photo revealed Imani on various occasions: leaving home in the morning, walking briskly across campus, jogging down her street with Shiloh in tow, standing in the front yard at her parents' house. Each image documented the photographer's obsession with his subject, and intensified the tight knot of fear and outrage growing in Garrison's gut.

"The psycho was stalking her," Detective Porter muttered, studying the photographs with an expression of grim disgust. "Right under our noses all this time."

The contents of a locked drawer in a metal filing cabinet provided yet more disturbing photographs. This time of Althea Pritchard, blindfolded and lying prone on what appeared to be a cement floor. A dark smear at the corners of her mouth looked suspiciously like dried blood.

"Seems that our boy was starting a scrapbook," observed Detective Moses, frowning as he sifted through the photographs with latex-gloved hands. "Wonder what else we'll find in here."

He didn't have to wonder long.

At the bottom of the drawer was a photo album with frayed edges, the pages filled with additional photos more grisly than their predecessors. Four different young women, naked and gagged, their hands and feet bound with rope. Their slender throats were ruthlessly slashed.

"Christ," Moses muttered, mopping at his damp brow. "A serial killer. We've got ourselves a bona fide serial killer, fellas."

"Upstanding scholar by day," Eddie murmured, "murdering bastard by night. Do any of these vics look familiar to you?"

Moses shook his head grimly. After a closer examination of the photos, Porter concurred. "We'll have to go through our cold-case files. See if anything comes up." He glanced around the room. "Might be a good idea to get in touch with the authorities down in Atlanta, too."

Donovan MacArthur calmly compared the photographs. "It would seem that Yusef intended to add photos of his next victim when he returned home tonight. A pictorial timeline of his crimes, if you will."

"He's not going to get that chance," Garrison growled, pacing the floor like an enraged lion behind bars. "He's keeping them somewhere. Somewhere close enough to have access to in the evenings after work."

Porter looked skeptical. "You don't think he's already killed Pritchard? She's been missing almost a month now. Why keep her around?"

Without answering, Garrison took the photographs of Althea Pritchard from Detective Moses. "We need to check out any abandoned buildings and warehouses in the area. He's keeping them in some kind of basement or cellar."

"I'm on it," said Porter, heading from the room.

"And I'm checking into his personal files," said Special Agent Kirk Spencer. "See if he owns any other properties."

Garrison nodded tersely and started for the stairs. Eddie followed him as they weaved past evidence technicians methodically combing through Anthony Yusef's lavishly furnished home.

Outside, neighbors stood on sidewalks gawking at the spectacle of flashing police cruisers crowded in front of the town house, yellow tape cordoning off the property from curious passersby. They were undoubtedly wondering who would dare tarnish the serenity of their affluent community.

Eddie, craving a cigarette badly, eyed his partner, who he knew could probably use a good smoke right about now. "How're you holding up?"

Garrison stood on the bottom step, his hands jammed into his pants pockets as he stared blindly ahead. His chest heaved with the effort to regulate his breathing. "I should have insisted that she stay home another day," he said in a low voice.

The look Eddie sent him was part sympathetic, part sardonic. "You tried that experiment already, remember? Didn't work out too well, if memory serves me correctly. She flew the coop the minute you left her alone."

Garrison would have smiled if humor were even remotely possible at such a time. If fury and something akin to panic didn't have a stranglehold on his emotions. "She's the most stubborn woman I've ever met," he grumbled irately.

Eddie grinned. "Then she's perfect for you. Congratulations, you've finally met your match."

"So it would seem." With a deep groan, Garrison threw back his head. His hands balled to fists inside his pockets. "This is torture, man. Waiting around, not knowing where she is or what's being done to her."

"We're going to find her," Eddie vowed firmly. He frowned as Garrison started away abruptly. "Where're you going?"

"To look for her. I can't stand around all night cooling my heels while some lunatic does God knows what to her." On the way to his truck, the cell phone nestled inside his breast pocket trilled. He dug it out impatiently. "Wade."

For a moment all he heard was a thin, shaky breath that made the hair on the back of his neck rise. Then came the soft, tremulous voice. "Garrison?"

He stopped dead in his tracks. "Imani? Baby, are you all right? Where are you?"

"I-I don't know." There was a muffled sound in the background, and then Imani cried desperately, "I love you. Don't ever for—"

His heart jammed at the base of his throat as the rest of her declaration was choked off. He gripped the phone as hard as if it were his lifeline. "Imani!" he shouted. "Imani!"

The next voice he heard was not hers. Eerily soft, it skated like a razor along his raw nerve endings. "Special Agent Wade. I have been anxiously awaiting this moment.

You might say I'm a longtime admirer of yours, ever since you annihilated those dime-store thugs in Baltimore four years ago. The ones who turned out to be cop killers who'd been evading capture for weeks. Oh, it was a highly publicized news event, and you came out of it a hero, didn't you? Except to yourself. And except to poor little Kayla Dyson." His chuckle was low and sinister. "Did you think it was mere coincidence that I left Miss Pritchard's backpack for you at the 7-Eleven? I thought it was a rather nice touch myself. Thought it might bring back fond memories for you."

"What do you want with Imani?" Garrison bit off tersely.

"Ah, yes. The love of your life. I regret that I had to interrupt that touching moment between you two, but time is really of the essence. I have plans for your sweetheart, plans that must not be delayed much longer."

Garrison swallowed at the tightness in his throat. Out of the corner of his eye, he saw that Detectives Moses and Porter had joined Eddie on the front steps. All were watching him with wary concern.

"It's rather unfortunate that your colleagues won't be able to trace this phone call," Anthony Yusef continued triumphantly. "I have the privilege of being wealthy enough to purchase high-tech equipment that enables me to play these games with you law enforcement boys. Perhaps the FBI's next order of business should be to push for reforms barring average citizens' access to technology more sophisticated than its own. Perhaps you might lead the charge, Agent Wade. That is, if you're not too distraught over the untimely demise of your beloved fiancée."

Garrison clenched his jaw even as his heart screamed in protest. "I'm going to kill you," he said in a voice lethal with intent.

"You'll have to find me first."

"I will find you, you sick bastard. Make no mistake about that."

Yusef chuckled softly. "If nothing else, I know you'll

enjoy the thrill of the hunt. We're not so different after all,
Still Water."

The line went dead before Garrison could utter another
word. Livid with outrage, he swore violently and threw the
cell phone to the ground, taking no satisfaction when it
landed with a loud crack and splintered apart.

"Destroying government property isn't going to improve
matters any," Eddie murmured, starting forward. Neither
Moses nor Porter followed him, keeping a safe distance from
the volatility of Garrison's temper.

Kirk Spencer appeared in the open doorway, his forlorn
expression confirming that Anthony Yusef's call had not
been successfully traced.

Hands braced on his hips, Garrison paced a few feet before sheer despair finally overtook him. He dropped weakly
into a crouch and covered his face with his hands. His imag-
ination tortured him with images of what sadistic "plans"
Anthony Yusef had in store for Imani. Nothing Garrison had
ever learned about hostage negotiation strategies could have
prepared him for the absolute horror of this moment.

Nothing.

After what seemed an eternity, Eddie appeared silently
beside him. He laid a hand upon Garrison's shoulder. "Don't
do this to yourself," he spoke gently. "You're doing everything you can for her. You know that."

Garrison rose abruptly and, without a word, headed for
his truck across the street. Yanking open the door, he climbed
inside and was about to pull off when he saw Kirk Spencer's
madly waving arms. Frowning, Garrison rolled down the
window.

Spencer jogged over to the truck. "Chief Taggert just
called. Seems that Julian Jerome wants to cooperate after all.
He told the chief that he sold Anthony Yusef a piece of property two months ago. No paperwork involved, just a cash
transaction. Yusef said he would be needing the place for a
few upcoming projects, but didn't want to have to report the

sale on his income taxes or anything. Apparently he didn't want it traced."

And suddenly it dawned on Garrison. "The cabin in Frederick," he whispered half to himself. The same cabin that Julian Jerome had taken Cecilia Dufresne to on their illicit weekend trysts.

"That's right," Spencer confirmed. "It's in Frederick, Maryland. About forty-five miles from here. I have the address and directions—"

Before Spencer could complete the sentence, Garrison snatched the paper from his hand and sped off down the street without waiting for backup.

Chapter 26

"You see, my dear, I am a firm believer that the sins of the forefathers are visited upon the ensuing generations. Of course in your case," Yusef drawled as he steered Imani down a darkened corridor, "it would be your mother's sins that have returned to haunt you."

Imani craned her neck around to look at him. "Where are you taking me?"

"For a visit with an old friend." He stopped abruptly and opened a heavy door that creaked on its hinges. The interior was dimly lit with the same damp staleness clinging to the air. A shadowy figure lay huddled on the floor in a corner of the windowless room.

Imani's heart thudded with a combination of relief and horror. "*Althea?*"

The girl did not stir, and trembling with dread, Imani whirled around to face her captor. "What have you *done?*"

"I thought I might give you a few minutes to get reacquainted. Make the most of it." Before Imani could utter another word, Yusef shoved her roughly into the room and closed the door quickly behind him as she fell to the floor.

Imani crawled on her bound hands and knees to the figure

on the floor, heedless to the rope chafing her skin. Although her eyes confirmed that it was Althea Pritchard, her heart would not accept it. The girl looked like a skeleton. Her cheeks were alarmingly hollow, and her skin was deathly ashen. The soiled clothes on her body—the same jeans and sweatshirt she had been wearing the last time Imani saw her—hung dangerously loose on her gaunt frame.

"Althea," Imani spoke tenderly, coaxing the girl awake. "Althea, it's me, Professor Maxwell. Can you hear me?"

Althea moaned softly and stirred. Her shoulders were nothing more than skin and bones beneath Imani's tied hands. Imani shook her gently. "Althea, sweetheart. You have to wake up."

The girl's body stiffened suddenly. Slowly her eyes fluttered open and lifted to Imani's face. For a moment she looked confused. Then the brown eyes behind the limp curtain of tangled hair swelled with tears.

"P-professor Maxwell?" she croaked in disbelief.

Imani nodded, holding back her own tears. "It's me, Althea," she assured her, wishing she could wrap the frail girl in her arms. She settled for pulling Althea against her own body the best she could. "I'm so sorry that he did this to you, sweetheart. So terribly sorry."

Althea wept hysterically. "Oh my God! I never thought I would see you or anyone else again. I was so scared!"

"I know," Imani soothed. "You've been through sheer hell. But you're going to be okay now, I promise you that."

Althea drew back, staring wildly into Imani's face. "Where is he? Dr. Yusef? He said he was going to kill me, Professor Maxwell." As the terror resurfaced, she began babbling feverishly. "He took me at gunpoint and brought me here against my will. H-he kept me locked away in here, only gave me water and bread and candy bars. Oh my God, why? Why?"

"Shh." Imani stroked the girl's tearstained face with the back of her hand, hoping to calm her even as she tried to

banish her own horror. But now was not the time to succumb
to panic. Now was the time to formulate a plan. Their very
lives depended upon it.

"Listen to me, Althea," she began urgently. "Anthony
Yusef is a very sick, angry man. He plans to kill both of us,
and my guess is that he's going to do it shortly before eleven
o'clock. We don't have much time."

Althea frowned in confusion. "Why eleven o'clock?"

"It's a long, complicated story. Anyway, the point is that
we need to think of a way to escape from here before it's too
late."

"How? There are no windows, and he always keeps the
door locked." Fresh tears refilled her eyes as a note of hysteria crept into her voice once again. "My uncle," she cried.
"I'm never going to see my aunt and uncle again."

"Shh, don't say that. You're going to see them again, and
all of your friends." Rising to her feet with difficulty, Imani
shuffled around the narrow room, running her hands along
the cold concrete walls and hoping vainly for a hidden panel
that existed only in the movies. She peered down at the floor
as if, by sheer determination, she could conjure a trap door.
Althea watched her expectantly and with such hope that it
broke Imani's heart.

Finally abandoning the futile search, Imani returned to
the girl's side. "There's only one way out of this room," she
grimly confirmed, "and it's through that door. Did you happen to see any part of this place when he brought you here,
or were you blindfolded like I was?"

"I was drugged and blindfolded," Althea said. "But one
night he was in a weird mood when he came to check on me,
and he removed my blindfolds and gave me a quick tour upstairs. There were creepy African masks all over the walls.
Masks and animal heads mounted everywhere."

Imani nodded briskly. "The advantage is that there are
two of us. Somehow we've got to get these ropes loosened,
but not enough to make him suspicious. One of us will dis-

tract him long enough for the other to escape and get help. I know it's the oldest trick in the book and a long shot by far, but it's the only chance we've got."

Althea stared at her. "What if he comes back with a gun?" she whispered fearfully.

It was a very real possibility that Imani did not want to contemplate. She set her jaw determinedly. "Then we'll just have to improvise. Now let's work at these knots while there's still time."

After what seemed an eternity, they heard the menacing shuffle of Anthony Yusef's steps outside the door. He unlocked the door and entered quietly, deliberately, his eyes glittering with anticipation.

"It's show time, ladies," he jovially announced. "Have you made your peace with your Maker yet?"

Imani and Althea sat huddled in opposite corners of the tiny room. After slight deliberation, Yusef approached Imani first—as she had hoped he would. He leaned over her, filling her nostrils with the scent of his expensive cologne. The same woodsy fragrance worn by Joaquin Torres. No wonder the scent had struck her as familiar.

Yusef had changed from his tuxedo into tan corduroys and a checkered flannel shirt. He looked like a bona fide lumberjack.

"You can't imagine how many times I have dreamed about this moment," he said softly, almost seductively. "What will I look forward to after you're dead, sweet Imani? What indeed?"

"I'm sure you'll find something," Imani said coldly.

He threw back his head with uproarious laughter—and Imani seized her opportunity. Raising her legs swiftly, she leveled a sharp kick to his solar plexus, one of many defensive maneuvers her father had taught her as a teenager.

Yusef reeled backward, gasping violently for air as he groped at his throat.

"Run, Althea!" Imani shouted. "Run!"

With a muffled cry, the girl leaped up and raced from the room. When Yusef lunged to his feet and started after her, Imani kicked the backs of his knees, and the professor's legs buckled beneath him and sent him sprawling once again to the floor. Casting off her own restraints, Imani jumped up and ran for the door.

But she was not fast enough.

Yusef clamped a steely hand around her ankle and yanked her off her feet. Pain ricocheted through Imani's body as she hit the cement floor like a ton of bricks. Although she struggled valiantly, she was no match for the maniacal strength of her tormentor. He climbed on top of her, savagely pinning her beneath the weight of his body with no hope for escape.

"I should have known you would have a trick up your sleeve," he snarled into her face. "As deceptive as your unfaithful mother."

"Althea's going to get help," Imani proclaimed with more bravado than she felt. "She's going to call the police and you're not going to get away with this!"

He laughed, and sent icy chills skittering down her spine. "Ah, but I never planned to get away with it. Haven't you figured that out yet? We were going to re-enact the night your father was killed. You with your devoted prodigy, just as your father was with that rookie agent he had taken under his wing from the Academy. We were going to have ourselves a final rendezvous through the woods—you, me, and Althea Pritchard." He shook his head, trailed a finger lightly down the front of her chest. "But now that your precious little apprentice has flown the coop and left you to fend for yourself, we'll have to adjust the rules of the game." His smile narrowed, grew more sinister. "And I just may enjoy this version even better."

Garrison hoped to God he wasn't too late.

He had driven like a madman down the Beltway, swearing profusely as he encountered construction crews doing roadwork. Traffic had been snarled for several miles with the closure of two lanes, and Garrison had zoomed down the shoulder like his very life depended on it, leaving the cacophony of blaring horns in his dust.

He found the cabin at the end of a narrow winding road past rows of cornfields, obscured by a dark thistle of forest. He killed the headlights, eased the truck to the bottom of the property's entrance, and climbed out. Other than the brisk October wind that sighed through the trees, there was no sound as Garrison crept stealthily toward the edge of the land surrounding the old cabin. He had not taken time to formulate a plan of action. Even if he could have calmed down long enough to strategize anything, he knew that it would fly out the window the minute he saw that harm had come to Imani.

No amount of training or restraint would keep him from killing the bastard who hurt her.

Garrison crouched behind the rough trunk of an oak tree. He performed a quick reconnaissance of the property and, seeing nothing, started forward again, keeping to a low crouch behind the thick cover of trees, skillfully sidestepping hidden roots and fallen branches. When he heard a rustle of movement ahead, he slid his hand inside his open jacket and eased his nine-millimeter Glock out of the holster, never averting his sharp gaze.

Suddenly a thin slip of a figure burst from the shadows and came barreling down the winding driveway toward him. As she drew nearer, Garrison realized with some surprise that she was the missing girl he had been sent from Baltimore to find.

Althea Pritchard. Emaciated, shell-shocked, but very much alive.

Hoping not to alarm her, Garrison stepped carefully into her path. She looked up at once, her eyes wild with unmistakable terror, and opened her mouth to scream. Garrison anticipated her reaction and clamped a hand swiftly over her mouth, spinning her around gently but firmly in his arms.

"It's all right," he spoke low and urgently into her ear. "I'm not going to hurt you. My name is Special Agent Garrison Wade. I'm with the FBI."

She relaxed a fraction against him, and he continued soothingly, "You must be Althea. A lot of people are going to be very happy to see you returned home safe and sound. But you have to help me, Althea. If I remove my hand, do you promise not to scream?"

She hesitated, then bobbed her head vigorously. She turned as Garrison released her, words tumbling frantically from her mouth. "Professor Maxwell . . . She's still in there. He's going to kill her!"

"Where are they?" Garrison demanded, trying not to let the girl's last sentence register in his brain.

"In the cellar." Her voice broke. "He kept us in a room until he was ready for us. Professor Maxwell kicked him when he wasn't expecting it, and I escaped. You have to help her! Please don't let him kill her. *Please.*"

"Do me a favor, Althea. Wait in that truck down there for me." He pointed and guided her by the shoulders at the same time. "The door's open. Just get in and lock it and wait for me. There's a blanket on the backseat that should keep you warm. The police are on their way."

She nodded dutifully, sending him worried backward glances as she scampered away.

Heart pumping with adrenaline, Garrison sprinted in the direction Althea had just come from, leading with his gun.

Hold on, baby, he silently prayed. *Hold on for me. Hold on for us.*

Oh God, I don't want to die. Not like this. Not now.

The frantic words pulsed through Imani's mind as she plunged headlong into the woods behind the cabin. Terror clogged her throat and tore through her brain in bright, hot bursts. Armed with a rifle, Anthony Yusef had given her a running head start before he began his deadly pursuit, stalking her with a stealthy deliberation that was more frightening than if he had chased her at full speed.

Imani could feel him behind her, could sense his presence as ominous as the thick moon-silvered darkness shrouding the forest. He was the hunter, ruthless and unrelenting, and she the prey, tracked down like a defenseless animal. It was all a game to him. A sadistic game of life and death.

But she had no time to theorize what had truly driven Anthony Yusef to this point of insanity. The need for survival was the driving instinct that propelled her forward, even as the bony fingers of tree branches whipped at her face and snagged her hair, impeding her progress. Exposed roots clawed painfully at her stockinged feet and shredded her pantyhose, rendering useless even that thin layer of protection from the elements.

At least Althea had gotten away safely. That was her one consolation, and she clung to it fiercely.

Her foot slipped on the crude mountain trail and she went down hard, her breath leaving her in a *whoosh!* as her right knee twisted and cracked against the dome of a rock buried in the soft earth. Pain seared through her in radiating waves, and for a fleeting moment as she sat there, she seriously considered surrendering. Just giving up the chase, letting the inevitable take its course. Her family would recover in time. They had faced tragedy before and survived. And Garrison . . . Oh dear God, she did not want to think about Garrison. To think that she might never see him again, might never again experience the true happiness she had glimpsed with him, was too excruciating to contemplate.

From the deep cover of the woods behind her, the eerie sound of laughter floated through the darkness to taunt her, and her blood ran like ice in her veins.

Time was running out.

From somewhere deep within her she summoned the

strength she knew she possessed and pushed herself to her feet. Her knee protested with the sudden movement, suggesting that it might be twisted, but she did not have the luxury to rest. Just as she stood, the harsh crack of Yusef's rifle splintered the air, signaling that the game was drawing to its conclusion.

Choking back an instinctive scream, Imani lurched forward into the night. There was nothing ahead but more darkness, an endless expanse of it. She did not know where she was or how close the nearest road was. She could detect no clearing in the woods, no sign of any other human life.

The rifle fired again, and this time the bullet whizzed so close by Imani's head that she could almost taste its metallic scent. Desperately scanning her surroundings, she took cover behind the bulky trunk of a pine tree. Flattening herself against the rough bark, she remained perfectly still and strained to hear her tormentor's approaching footsteps above the deafening roar of her own heartbeat.

All that greeted her was the wind whistling through the trees, a hauntingly lonely sound.

And then he spoke. "You must understand, my dear, that I am a skilled hunter. I can smell your fear from miles away." He chuckled, the cruel sound growing closer. "It's like an aphrodisiac to me."

Imani remained silent, her chest heaving with the effort to control her tattered breathing. She could taste the coppery flavor of her own blood in her mouth, and she wondered idly how badly her face was cut. Right now that was the least of her concerns.

"Ah, so you want to play hide-and-seek," Yusef continued, clearly amused. "I'm afraid that won't be much fun, beautiful Imani. You see—" and she imagined him hitching his rifle to his shoulder again and aiming to shoot, "I already know where you are."

For an agonized moment Imani did not know whether to remain hidden or make a run for it. If Yusef really knew where she was, she would die a very violent death.

"Come out, come out, wherever you are," Yusef chanted in a singsong voice. This time there was no mistaking the deliberate approach of his footsteps. He was coming right toward her.

Imani heard a distinct click as he cocked the trigger. She squeezed her eyes shut and braced herself for whatever would come.

Her muscles tightened automatically at the next gunshot she heard.

It was followed by an ominous silence, and without thinking she peeked slowly around the tree trunk to see what had happened.

She was stunned by the sight that greeted her.

Anthony Yusef stood just a few feet away, with a bullet hole ripped cleanly through the center of his forehead. His eyes were wide with the shock of someone who had been unexpectedly betrayed. As Imani watched in horror, his body pitched forward to the ground and did not move again.

A few moments later the trees parted with a soft rustle and revealed Garrison standing there, still holding his nine-millimeter and wearing a dangerous expression.

Imani thought she would pass out from the sheer relief that swept through her. All she could manage was a muffled groan as tears spurted freely from her eyes.

After checking to confirm that Anthony Yusef was dead, Garrison rushed to Imani's side and gathered her into his arms with such force that she thought her ribs would crack.

"Oh God, baby, I almost lost you," he uttered raggedly. He buried his face in the crook of her neck, inhaled her scent as if to assure himself that she was still living and breathing.

Imani wrapped her arms around him and allowed herself to bask in his warmth and protection. She had been given another chance at life, and she would never again take it for granted.

Garrison drew back, cupping her face in his large hands and searching her face desperately. "Are you all right? Did that bastard hurt you?"

"I'm okay," Imani said, gratitude shining in her eyes. "You've taken care of him."

Garrison shuddered deeply and she folded him back into her arms. They knelt on the ground for several minutes longer, clinging to each other like they would never let go.

It was only when Eddie and the others arrived that they reluctantly drew apart. Garrison helped her gingerly to her feet, frowning at the flicker of pain that crossed her features.

"Althea has been taken to the nearest hospital," Eddie announced. "Her aunt and uncle have been notified, and they're going to meet us there." He turned a concerned expression on Imani. "Do you need to see a doctor as well?"

Imani shook her head. "I'm fine. I really just want to go home."

"Not before you get that knee checked out," Garrison commanded. And without another word, he lifted her effortlessly into his arms and strode back toward the cabin and the waiting police cruisers.

Chapter 27

Imani closed the door silently behind her and turned to find Malik Toomer standing there, an anxious expression on his face. He carried an elaborate floral arrangement in one arm and a large teddy bear in the other—items he had probably purchased from the hospital gift shop just minutes before.

"How is she?" he asked almost tentatively. "I got here as soon as basketball practice was over."

"She's doing much better. She's been given an IV for dehydration, and her blood pressure is finally stable. She just finished eating dinner, in fact, and her appetite seems just fine." Imani grimaced before adding wryly, "After what she's been through, I'm sure even hospital food tastes like gourmet cooking."

Malik mustered a halfhearted smile. She could tell that his concern extended far beyond Althea's appetite. "Is . . . is she alone?"

"Her aunt and uncle are with her. They haven't left her side since she was admitted, but I'm sure they would give you two some privacy." Imani reached out and touched Malik's arm. His guilty eyes met hers.

"You don't have to tell her everything at once," Imani gently advised. "Give her time to recover from all that's happened to her first."

Malik hesitated, then nodded. "You're right. She's been through enough already." He heaved a deep sigh. "I guess I'm being selfish for wanting to relieve my guilty conscience right away."

"Not selfish," Imani corrected. "Honest. And I commend you for that."

His expression brightened. "Thanks, Professor Maxwell. That means a lot to me." He peered at her face closely, noticing for the first time the darkening bruise on her cheek. "How are *you* feeling? You've been through a lot, too."

"Nothing time won't heal," Imani said blithely. Almost at once the words echoed back to her. *Nothing time won't heal.* The anniversary of her father's death had passed nearly forty-eight hours ago, and for the first time in six years, she did not feel the overwhelming despair that always lingered for weeks afterward. Perhaps because she had gone through a harrowing experience and lived to tell about it, and in the process had learned to appreciate life, learned to truly allow herself to live.

Time had healed her. And so had love.

At that moment she looked past Malik and saw Garrison standing at the other end of the brightly lit corridor. As always, her heartbeat kicked up several notches at the sight of him. He stood near the nurse's station, his tie askew, his white shirt slightly rumpled, his hands thrust into his pants pockets. He looked tough and more than a little tired.

And Imani thought he was the most beautiful thing she had ever seen in her life.

Their gazes met and held. Garrison's lips spread in that slow, lazy grin she had come to adore. Before she realized it, she began limping toward him, heedless to the sprained knee Aunt Vanessa had nursed and clucked over for the past two days. Beneath the charcoal cashmere slacks she wore, her right knee was heavily bandaged, but she didn't care.

With a slight frown, Garrison strode purposefully toward her, saving her the extra distance. Imani laughed as they halted in the middle of the corridor, meeting in a big hug like some scene out of a movie. Nurses and passing visitors smiled at them.

"What're you doing here?" Imani asked, smiling into his eyes. "I thought you'd be tied up in briefings and press hearings for the rest of the week."

"I had to see you," Garrison said softly. The intensity in his dark eyes made her breath quicken. "How are you?"

"I'm fine. Not that you and my family are listening," she added impertinently. "Aunt Vanessa, Jada, and Vin would barely let me out of the house this evening to visit Althea. My mother feels so guilty that it was her former lover who came after me that she may never let me out of her sight again. And your mother, God bless her, has become a permanent fixture at my parents' house. If she and my mother force one more morsel of food down my throat, I'm going on a hunger strike, I swear."

Garrison grinned. "Stop being an ingrate," he admonished lightly. "Everyone's just concerned about you. And you're supposed to be taking it easy on that leg, not doing marathons down hospital corridors."

"I got excited when I saw you," Imani admitted sheepishly. She nuzzled his throat with her nose, basking in his familiar sexy scent.

"Let's get out of here," Garrison whispered against her mouth.

Imani drew back to look up at him. "What about my brother? He's on his way here to pick me up."

"I already saw him in the parking garage and sent him home." Garrison swept her easily into his arms and headed for the bank of elevators before she could utter another protest—not that she would have.

They left the hospital through a rear exit to avoid the remnant of reporters still camped out at the hospital, clamoring to interview anyone even remotely connected to the sensational kidnapping case that had captured national headlines for the past month. Not only had a prominent university professor done the unthinkable, but a colleague, Julian Jerome, had conspired to discredit a rival professor. In exchange for a reduced prison sentence, Julian had finally confessed to his involvement in the break-in. But even with the plea bargain his attorney had negotiated, Julian Jerome had lost more than his job and freedom. He had lost his respectability and the friendship of a trusted friend. Imani's family had already arranged to move her belongings from the house she had rented from Julian, and the sooner she could put the memories of his betrayal behind her, the better.

Elizabeth Torres would spend her eighteenth birthday serving time in a juvenile correctional center, separated from her older brother by cinderblock walls.

"Althea doing better today?" Garrison asked as he steered the truck away from the hospital.

"Much. She really appreciated your visit yesterday." Imani slanted him a sideways grin. "She's planning to name her firstborn after you, by the way."

Garrison laughed softly. "I'm humbled."

"I figured you would be." She sobered a moment. "Althea's not the only one forever indebted to you. I don't know what would have happened if you hadn't arrived when you did, Garrison. You may not agree with the media hailing you a hero, but in the eyes of many people, you are. I owe you my life."

Garrison met her intent gaze. "And that's why I intend to make sure that you spend the rest of it with me," he said huskily.

She warmed with pleasure. "Nothing would make me happier."

"Good."

They exchanged warm smiles. After a moment Imani glanced out the window at nightfall, at the disappearing bright lights of downtown Silver Spring as Garrison maneuvered onto the Beltway. "Where are we going?"

"You'll see."

"So mysterious," Imani teased. "I'll have to remember that about you, my dashing former spy."

Garrison grinned, deftly switching lanes. "So have you decided where you're going to stay for the next eight months?" he asked casually.

"Yes." Imani watched him out of the corner of her eye. "Jada has offered to let me take over the lease on her apartment once she and Marcus get married next month."

"Oh?"

Imani reached across the console and touched Garrison's cheek, sensing his disappointment. "It's not that I don't want to move in with you, Garrison. Nothing could be further from the truth. It's just that I'm a bit old-fashioned when it comes to this issue. When we exchange our vows, I want the anticipation of knowing that we will be returning to your apartment for the first time to live together as man and wife." Her smile was rueful. "I guess that sounds silly, considering that I've already spent the night at your place."

Garrison captured her hand in his, held it affectionately. "It doesn't sound silly at all. I think it's sweet."

"I knew you would understand," she said with quiet appreciation. She turned in the scooped leather seat to better face him. "I got a call from Johns Hopkins University. About a tenured faculty position I interviewed for two months ago." She paused. "They offered me the job."

"Congratulations." Garrison sent her a warm smile. "Are you going to accept?"

Imani bit her bottom lip pensively. "That's just it. I haven't exactly decided. Two months ago, I thought I wanted tenure more than anything in the world."

"And now?"

"Well, so much has happened since then, and I guess some of my priorities have changed. Don't get me wrong, I still want to be tenured. But the bottom line is that I really enjoy being at the University of Maryland. And I suppose there's a sentimental part of me that wants to be there for students like Althea and Malik." She pushed out a deep sigh. "So do I wait around for a tenured faculty position to become available, or do I move on to greener pastures while I have the opportunity?"

"I guess that's a question only you can answer," Garrison told her quietly. "You have to decide what's best for you. Not just in terms of your career, but as far as what you're willing to sacrifice personally."

Imani nodded slowly in agreement. "If only I had a crystal ball."

Garrison glanced at her profile. "I think you'll do the right thing, whatever you decide that is."

He drove to the Baltimore Inner Harbor, and as they walked along the pier Imani was instantly flooded with memories of their first date, that first explosive kiss shared under the silvery moonlight. Much like that fateful night, several couples strolled leisurely along the waterfront, occasional laughter spilling from their hushed conversations. This time Imani did not envy their intimacy or their freedom to be together without fear or reservation.

She no longer had to.

She turned her head to find Garrison's dark gaze already fixed on her. "Thank you for bringing me here," she said sincerely.

Garrison glanced down at her leg. "Do you want me to carry you?"

She shook her head. "I'm enjoying the walk. Besides, the doctor said the exercise will help the knee heal faster—as long as I don't overdo it." She glanced up as they neared the dock where a tiny luxury liner bobbed gently on the surface of the murky water.

"I didn't know the Inner Harbor sponsored dinner cruises this late on weeknights," she remarked, glancing at her wristwatch. It was well after ten o'clock.

"They don't. Shall we?"

Before Imani knew what was happening, Garrison had helped her onto the lowered gangplank, where a rotund uniformed gentleman awaited them. Upon closer examination, Imani recognized the grinning bar owner from Mulligan's.

She smiled in surprise. "Cappy?"

"Evening, milady," he greeted her in that thick Irish brogue she remembered so well. "Welcome aboard the *Lady Abigail*, Baltimore's finest cruise ship—or so my dear Abby would have said so, God rest her precious soul. Tonight you will experience the best in fine dining with a full-service waitstaff available at your service throughout your overnight stay. I will be your captain this evening. Shall we board? It is getting rather brisk out here, I daresay."

Shocked, Imani whirled around to gape at Garrison. "When did you plan all of this? How . . . ?"

Garrison shook his head slowly. "That's for me to know," he murmured, grasping her elbow gently and winking at his old friend, "and you not to worry about."

Feeling incredibly feminine and cherished, Imani allowed herself to be escorted into an elegantly refurbished dining suite whose only centerpiece was a linen-covered candlelit table set for two. Strains of a seductive jazz melody drifted from hidden speakers.

Shortly after they were seated, a bottle of merlot was produced and uncorked by a white-jacketed waiter. The twinkling contents were poured into wineglasses with a skillful flourish.

Imani gazed across the table at Garrison, knew her eyes were glowing with all of the love she felt for him. "I think I'm going to cry," she mumbled.

His mouth twitched with humor. "Already? But you haven't even tasted the food yet."

She chuckled. "You know what I mean." She reached across the table and covered his hand with hers. "This is the most romantic thing anyone has ever done for me, Garrison."

"Then you were long overdue," he said in a low, velvety voice. He raised her hand to his lips and kissed each fingertip slowly, watching her sooty lashes flutter and enjoying it immensely. After a moment his expression grew reflective as he gazed at their joined hands.

"You keep thanking me for everything that I've done for you," he said with quiet gravity, "when all I'm doing is expressing my utmost appreciation for the way you've changed my life. I was completely desolate before I met you. Going through the motions of life, just trying to get from one day to the next." He lifted those penetrating eyes to her face and finished huskily, "So the way I see it, Imani, *you* saved *my* life."

This time she could not stem the tears. They spilled from her eyes and slid down her cheeks. Garrison stood and took her hand, lifting her out of her seat. Sitting back down in his chair, he settled her into his lap and brushed feather-light kisses across her forehead.

"I almost lost you," he murmured thickly. "I never want to know what that feels like again."

Imani raised her head to meet his tumultuous gaze. "I'm not going anywhere, baby," she whispered fervently.

"Promise?"

"Till death do us part," she vowed.

Garrison's smile was achingly tender. He reached inside his breast pocket and withdrew a small velvet box, removing a stunning diamond ring from the satin encasement. Imani gasped in shock. She couldn't help it. It was the most exquisite diamond ring she had ever seen.

Slowly, never taking his eyes from hers, he slid the ring onto her finger. It was a perfect fit. "I love you, Imani Maxwell."

Her eyes swam with more tears. "Oh, Garrison . . ."

"I can't wait to spend the rest of my life with you. Providing for you, protecting you, cherishing you, making love to you, watching our baby grow inside you."

"Sounds good to me," Imani concurred on a deep, luxuriant sigh. She curved her arms around his neck and leaned close, kissing him tenderly. As the kiss intensified, Garrison wrapped his arms possessively around her waist and pulled her closer.

Imani whispered throatily against his mouth, "Does this love boat have a bed somewhere?"

"You'd better believe it," Garrison growled, already lifting her into his arms and striding from the room. They passed their smiling host on the way out. Were Imani not already intoxicated from Garrison's kiss, she would have sworn there was a conspiratorial twinkle in the Irishman's eyes when he promised to keep dinner warm for them.

In the master suite below deck, she had only a delightful glimpse of gleaming mahogany walls and red rose petals strewn across white satin sheets before Garrison lowered her lovingly onto the king-sized bed. She shivered at the simmering heat in his dark eyes and reached up to touch his face in wonder.

"I didn't think it was possible to love someone as much as I love you," she whispered fiercely.

Garrison gazed down into her face, seeing all her hope, her vulnerability, her pure and unadulterated beauty. He wondered if it were possible for one man to be so ridiculously happy, and so blessed.

"Meeting you has taught me that any miracle is possible," he said softly. "Mine forever?"

Tears shimmered in her eyes. "Until forever."

Garrison bent his head and kissed her deeply, his kiss promising an eternity of love and so much more.

ABOUT THE AUTHOR

Maureen Smith is a freelance writer whose articles have appeared in various newspapers, magazines, and online publications. She has a B.A. in English from the University of Maryland, College Park. Her debut novel, *Ghosts of Fire*, won the 2002 *Romance in Color Magazine* Reviewers' Choice Awards for New Author of the Year and Romantic Suspense of the Year. Maureen was also nominated for the 2003 Emma Award for Best New Author.

Maureen lives in San Antonio, Texas, with her husband and two children.